Praise for

THE NERUDA CASE

"Roberto Ampuero's *The Neruda Case* is a sweeping mystery set against the backdrop of the Chilean coup. This unforgettable book is brilliantly imagined, and features the poet Pablo Neruda in a remarkably intimate role. Roberto Ampuero's writing is exhilarating; he is a delight to read."

—Isabel Allende, author of *Daughter of Fortune* and
The House of the Spirits

"Ampuero offers a provocative depiction of Neruda, a man reevaluating his marriages and love affairs and feeling fresh remorse for having forsaken a hydrocephalic daughter to concentrate on his poetry. . . . Vivid . . . Although *The Neruda Case* is a prequel for his international readers, here in the United States, it should be a prologue for more novels from this shrewd and serious-minded novelist."

—*The Washington Post*

"The twists and turns of the quest through Mexico City, Havana, East Berlin, and La Paz deftly weave the personal and the political in a doleful exploration of the ways in which romantic and revolutionary ideals inevitably founder. Neruda himself . . . is unforgettably conjured."

—*The New Yorker*

"Sings with poetic metaphor . . . The plot twists from Mexico City to East Germany, from lies to truth, from uneasy peace to political coup, from life to death. Read this one as much for the story as for the wonderful way Ampuero has with words."

—*Publishers Weekly* (starred review)

continued . . .

"If the title sounds like something out of detective fiction, it is—for Ampuero asks us to consider the hypothetical possibility that Pablo Neruda, terminally ill, hires someone to track down a former lover."
—*Kirkus Reviews*

"Not just for mystery fans, or readers of Latin American literature."
—*Library Journal*

"The summer's most evocative fiction."
—*T: The New York Times Style Magazine*

"A superb translation by Carolina De Robertis whips the first of Ampuero's novels to be published in English into a pulsing, panting work."
—*The Daily Beast*

"Ampuero, a University of Iowa professor, is highly regarded in South America, and U.S. readers looking for good literary detective fiction might find themselves falling in love with Cayetano Brulé."
—NPR

"An auspicious introduction . . . The book is often wryly funny, even in the face of tragedy and ineptitude. . . . Let's hope that more books in Ampuero's Brulé series find an English-speaking audience."
—*Minneapolis Star Tribune*

"Mix ever-tightening suspense, South American history, the fictional treatment of a major world poet, revolutionary turmoil, and a reluctant sleuth and you've got a novel that is hard to put down and easy to remember. . . . Ampuero's prose, as rendered in the translation of Carolina De Robertis, is brilliant. . . . To call his book a noir thriller does not begin to suggest the sophistication and richness of this gorgeously textured novel."
—Washington Independent Review of Books

The
NERUDA CASE

Roberto Ampuero

TRANSLATED BY CAROLINA DE ROBERTIS

Riverhead Books

New York

RIVERHEAD BOOKS
Published by the Penguin Group
Penguin Group (USA) Inc.
375 Hudson Street, New York, New York 10014, USA

USA | Canada | UK | Ireland | Australia | New Zealand | India | South Africa | China

Penguin Books Ltd., Registered Offices: 80 Strand, London WC2R 0RL, England
For more information about the Penguin Group, visit penguin.com.

First published as *El caso Neruda* by Grupo Editorial Norma in 2008.
This translation first published by Riverhead Books, 2012.
Copyright © 2012 by Roberto Ampuero
Translation © 2012 by Carolina De Robertis
The Library of Congress has catalogued the Riverhead hardcover edition as follows:

Ampuero, Roberto, date.
[Caso Neruda. English]
The Neruda case / Roberto Ampuero; translated by Carolina De Robertis.
p.   cm.
Summary: "Originally published in Spanish as El Caso Neruda by La otra
orilla/Grupo Norma, Barcelona, Spain"
ISBN 978-1-59448-743-9
1. Neruda, Pablo, 1904–1973—Fiction. 2. Allende Gossens, Salvador, 1908–1973—Fiction.
3. Chile—Politics and goverment—1970–1973—Fiction. I. De Robertis, Carolina, translator.
II. Title.
PQ8098.1.M68C3613   2012   2012001890
863'.62—dc23

First Riverhead hardcover edition: June 2012
First Riverhead trade paperback edition: June 2013
Riverhead trade paperback ISBN: 978-1-59463-147-4

PRINTED IN THE UNITED STATES OF AMERICA

10 9 8 7 6 5 4 3 2 1

Cover design by Tal Goretsky

Cover images: Book © Miklav / IStockphoto; Man © Sergio Larraine /
Magnum Photos; Sky and Ocean © Michael Bader / Westend61 / Corbis
Book design by Amanda Dewey

FOR MY PARENTS

For the sixty-five years of their great love story

I ask you: where is my child?

Pablo Neruda, "The Prodigal"
(from *The Captain's Verses*)

Contents

The
NERUDA CASE

JOSIE

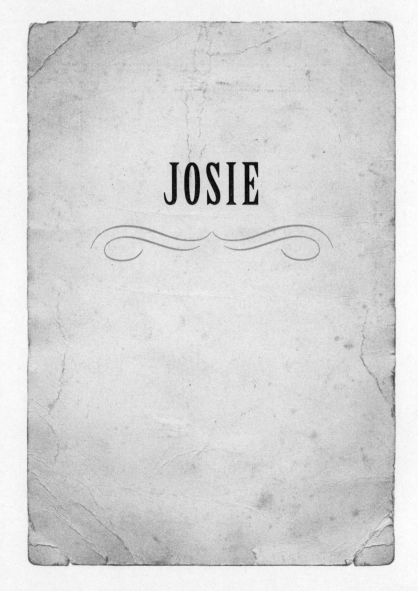

What could be bothering the partners of Almagro, Ruggiero & Associates, who had asked him to appear at their headquarters in such a hurry? Cayetano Brulé wondered one warm February morning as he left his office in the attic of the Turri Building, in the heart of Valparaíso's financial district, and took the elevator down to Prat Street. Ever since democracy was restored, AR&A had become the most influential consulting firm in the country, and it was rumored that no stipulation or public litigation of any importance could pass without its sanction. Its tentacles spanned from the presidential palace to the neo-Gothic headquarters of businessmen, and from Congress to the National Comptroller's Office, passing through ministries, political parties, embassies, and courts. Its attorneys could not only obtain laws and decrees, subsidies and pardons, exemptions, and amnesties, but also wash away disgrace and polish the prestige of public figures down on their luck. AR&A operated in corridors and behind the scenes, and though its top executives attended key receptions and dinners in the capital, its proprietors were essentially invisible, and rarely attended social gatherings or granted interviews to the press. But when they did decide to appear on the great stage of the nation's political and business affairs, they glowed in their Italian suits and silk ties, with their triumphant smiles and cosmopolitan manners, as they cryptically offered opinions on various matters, like the Oracle at Delphi. When Cayetano lifted his gaze along the buildings on Prat Street, the Turri clock marked eleven forty-five as its bells pealed mournfully and seagulls soared and cawed under the crystalline sky. He thought of *The Birds*, the Alfred Hitchcock movie he'd seen in a Sunday matinee at the Mauri Theater, before diving into the everyday din, whistling, keeping a steady pace.

At Plaza Aníbal Pinto, a rumbling in his gut made him stop at the Café del Poeta. It wouldn't matter if he spent a few minutes there. The big bosses at AR&A wouldn't be upset if he was late; on the contrary, in their nervous state they'd imagine other clients were in need of his services, he thought, as the aroma of roasted coffee slid through his Pancho Villa–style mustache. Many things delighted him about this place, aside from the coffee with a dash of milk and of course the sandwiches: the old polished floorboards, the display of porcelain English tea sets in the window, the oil paintings with port motifs, and the cozy light of the bronze lamps. He preferred the table by the entrance, from which he could contemplate the hundred-year-old palms in the plaza and the statue of Neptune seated amid the rocks and the multicolored fish of a fountain, as well as the cemetery at the top of Cárcel Hill, a capricious graveyard that, in every earthquake, spewed an avalanche of mausoleum bricks, wooden crosses, and ramshackle coffins full of cadavers down into the center of the city. From that table, he could also watch the imported trolleys, secondhand from Zurich, as they circulated from place to place with their original German signage, as if they were still running past the plain façades of silent Helvetian neighborhoods, and had never disembarked to find the potholes, stray dogs, papers, and street vendors of Valparaíso.

In any case, the illustrious Almagro and Ruggiero would have to be patient, Cayetano Brulé concluded as he adjusted the knot of his tie, which was bright purple with little green guanacos, and waited for the waitress, a pale goth girl with jet-black hair and black clothing who wore a Kanye West–style headset to communicate with the kitchen. He unfolded the local newspaper and read on the front page about the defeat of the long-suffering soccer team the Wanderers, the slashed throat of a model in the gardens of the Viña del Mar casino, and the alarming rise of unemployment in the region. This last piece of information didn't surprise him. The decline of Valparaíso was no secret. In the nineteenth century, it had been the most important and prosperous port on the Pacific; Enrico Caruso and Sarah Bernhardt acted in its theaters, Gath & Chaves and exclusive European boutiques opened along its streets, and a quarter of its population, being foreign, spoke no Spanish. But a ferocious earthquake on the night of August 16, 1906, devastated the city and buried more than three thousand of its inhabitants under the rubble of buildings, houses, and mansions, all in a matter of seconds. That same night, thousands of people abandoned the city for good, and those who remained, began, from that moment on, to live by evoking the splendor and glitter of the past, the beauty of the disappeared city, convinced that in some not-too-distant future a miracle would restore the march of progress. But just one day short of eight years later, that same progress dealt them another brutal blow: the opening of the Panama Canal, which was celebrated on August 15, 1914, and strangled Valparaíso. The bay became desolate overnight; the warehouses in the port went empty; the cranes stood still on the wharf; and the bars, shops, and restaurants closed their doors forever, casting employees, whores, and pimps into permanent unemployment.

Without any knowledge of this tragic history, of this unending decline (which seemed more like a deliberate divine punishment than the result of random fate), and captivated by the delirious architecture and topography of the city and the affable and taciturn nature of its inhabitants, Cayetano decided to settle in Valparaíso when he arrived in Chile, in 1971, on the arm of María Paz Ángela Undurraga Cox, his wife at the time. Those were the days of Salvador Allende and Unidad Popular, as well as of an unbridled social turmoil that would lead not to what the people dreamed of but rather to the dictatorship of Augusto Pinochet. How many years had passed since then, since the start of that period that so many preferred to forget? Thirty-odd years? In any case, the people of this port city, or *porteños*, ever dignified—and he now considered himself one of them—believed that good and bad luck crouched, waiting, around any corner or just beyond the curve of some stone staircase, and for that reason everything in the world was relative and fleeting. For *porteños*, accustomed to climbing and descending hills, existence was like their city: at times one soared joyfully, trusting the wave's crest, and at times one lay depressed and unmoving in the depths of a ravine. One could always rise or fall. Nothing was certain, nothing was forever. No circumstance was permanent. With existence came uncertainty, and only death had no room for change. For that reason—and because he was an incorrigible optimist as long as he didn't want for bread and coffee, as well as an occasional cold beer or glass of rum, and despite the fact that work opportunities were scarce for a private investigator in this city at the end of the earth, which had now become a respectable exporter of fruit, wine, and salmon, and where more and more families were acquiring second cars, vacationing in Havana and Miami, or getting into limitless debt—he didn't mind making the owners of AR&A wait.

Sixteen years earlier, in 1990, the Chilean people had regained democracy through peaceful protests, and now, in this supposedly gray and conservative country where, not too long before, divorce was illegal, the president was a divorced woman, a single mother, and a socialist, not to mention an atheist. President Bachelet was a clear sign that this stiletto of land, which extended from the Atacama Desert (the most arid and inhospitable one on the planet) to the South Pole, and which balanced between the fierce waves of the Pacific and the eternal snows of the Andes, always on the brink of collapsing with all its people and goods into the ocean's depths, was a unique place, inimitable and changing, that swung vertiginously from euphoria to depression, or from solidarity to individualism, like one of those complicated hieroglyphs from the archaeologist Heinrich Schliemann that no one could entirely decipher, and that one loved or hated, depending on the circumstances, changes in mood, or color of the season.

"Here no one dies forever," Cayetano mused as, from his table, he glimpsed the whitewashed niches, gleaming like the salt flats of Atacama, in the cemetery on Cárcel Hill. "At the first earthquake they'll return in a flash to the realm of the living."

"What can I get you, sir?" the goth asked him.

He requested a double espresso with a dash of milk and the sandwich menu, which he awaited anxiously, preening the ends of his mustache.

Now he recalled it with precision. He had landed in Valparaíso thirty-five years before, after disembarking from the LAN Boeing in Santiago with Ángela, a rather aristocratic Chilean with revolutionary convictions, who was studying at an exclusive women's college in the United States. One night, as they made love beneath the coconut palms on the still-warm sand of a beach in Cayo Hueso, she had persuaded him to join the movement for socialism as led by Salvador Allende in the Southern Cone. Both experiences—with Allende, and with love—had ended for good, in an abrupt and calamitous way, with Pinochet's coup on September 11, 1973. She sought refuge as an exile in Paris with the *charango* player of a folk band, while he ran aground like an old barge in Chile. He had to hide from the leftists, who spurned him as a Miami *gusano*, and the right-wingers, who spurned him as an infiltrating Castro supporter. During the dictatorship, he was forced to try his luck at various jobs: he sold books and insurance, promoted Avon beauty creams, and was an assistant for a judicial receiver, traversing the steepest and most dangerous hills of Valparaíso on foot, delivering notices to individuals such as petty thieves, black market merchants, or smugglers. The title of detective, bestowed by a shady distance-learning institute in Miami, would later save his life, as it would attract people who wished to task him with minor investigations—such as tracking a loose woman, the theft of a day's earnings from a soda fountain, or death threats from an aggressive neighbor—which allowed him not just to survive with a certain dignity but also to ply a trade that better fit the independent, fun-loving spirit of a dreamer like him.

"Here you go," the goth announced as she unfolded a menu containing full-color photos of the sandwiches and pastries served at the café.

The menu aimed not only to whet the customers' appetite but also to give a sense of culture, as it tried to describe the marvelous history of that city with seven lives, known as the "Jewel of the Pacific." Strictly speaking, the gem in question was quite worn down—it had not been founded by any official authority, civil or ecclesiastical, and now had half a million long-suffering inhabitants in its fifty teeming, anarchic hills. A horseshoe bay formed a dazzling amphitheater, and people risked their lives on shabby postwar trolleys and a handful of whining cable cars each time they rode to work or to homes with crumbling balconies and gardens that settled gracefully on peaks or clung precariously to hillsides. Declared a World Heritage Site by UNESCO in honor of its architecture and topography, Valparaíso now began, once again, to show signs of recovery, thanks to retired North Americans and Europeans who, dressed like adolescents and with pockets full of dollars and euros, disembarked en masse from cruise ships that arrived every day during the summer.

It wasn't a bad life in Valparaíso, he thought with satisfaction. He rented a yellow house, in the neo-Victorian style, on Gervasoni Avenue, on Concepción Hill, and from there he could gaze at the Pacific and, on warm and pristine summer mornings, even imagine he was in Havana, frolicking in the currents of the gulf, with the Malecón breeze at his back. In his work as a private investigator, he had the help of a man named Suzuki, a *porteño* of Japanese origin who spent his nights attending to the Kamikaze, a modest, tiny fried-food stall that he owned. It was in the port district, between the plazas Aduana and Matriz, on a narrow street lined with cobblestones and bars, which allowed him to stay abreast of the murmurs of whores and their pimps, who now again enjoyed, along with pickpockets and muggers, the generous fruits of tourism. Though already in his fifties, Cayetano still believed he might one day find the woman of his dreams and become the father of a little boy or girl (it didn't matter which, as long as the child was healthy) before going completely bald and becoming an arthritic, cantankerous retiree. And if in the beginning it had been hard for him to adapt to the severity of Chileans and the rigorous climate of its mountainous land, now the island of Cuba, its people, and its weather were more of a pale and distant evocation, because his new homeland, with all its light and shadows, had ended up conquering him, despite the fact that it was neither green nor an island, unless, perhaps, it was, just in a different way.

"Have you decided what to eat?" the goth asked as she served his coffee. She had translucent arms, riddled with thick blue veins.

"A Barros Luco with extra avocado," he said, and tried to imagine what it would be like to glide his fingertip along those blue lines until he reached her perfumed, hidden slopes.

And it was after he had sweetened his drink and tasted it that his gaze fell upon the back of the menu, with its photo of Pablo Neruda on a sofa in his Valparaíso home. He felt his heart freeze, sipping espresso slowly until the lenses of his glasses steamed up, and smiled faintly. It suddenly seemed that the palms, the crosses of the mausoleums on the summit, and even Neptune himself had begun to vibrate like mirages in the desert. His memory transported him to that winter morning in 1973 when he began his first investigation, which he never disclosed to anyone, as it was the most closely guarded secret of his life, the secret he'd still carry as they took him up the hill, feet first, to that cemetery where the dead, on warm summer nights, swung their hips joyfully to the rhythm of tangos, cumbias, and boleros, longing for the next earthquake to hurl them back down to the picturesque and winding streets of Valparaíso.

He closed his eyes and felt his surroundings begin to fade away: the growling of engines, the songs of blind men accompanied by accordions and player pianos, even the shouts of grocers selling herbs, avocados, and lottery tickets with guaranteed prizes, and suddenly there appeared before him, as if by some magic trick and with prodigious clarity, the coarse, rustic texture of the wooden door on Collado Way.

The door was made of knotted wood. It didn't open. He stroked the old bronze knocker, put his hands in the pockets of his fleece jacket, and told himself that all he could do now was wait. He exhaled wafts of white breath into the overcast winter morning and thought, amused, that it looked as if he were smoking, even though, in this city, there were no more matches or cigarettes.

He had just whiled away an hour at Alí Babá, a soda fountain around the corner, on Alemania Avenue, across from the Mauri Theater. There, he'd read Omar Saavedra Santis's column in *El Popular* and Enrique Lira Massi's in *Puro Chile* while Hadad the Turk made him coffee and a gyro and cursed the food shortages, the queues, and the disorder on the streets, terrified that political friction would tear the country apart and throw him in the garbage can. When Cayetano looked at his watch again, it was past ten o'clock. Perhaps he hasn't yet returned from the capital, he thought, glancing at the bay, half covered in mist.

He had met the man he was about to see a few days earlier, during a party serving *curanto a la olla*, a seafood specialty from the southern island of Chiloé, in the home of the mayor of Valparaíso. His wife had dragged him to the party so that he could rub elbows with politicians and progressive intellectuals from the region. According to Ángela, he should know Congressmen Guastavino and Andrade, the singers Payo Grondona and Gato Alquinta, the painter Carlos Hermosilla, and bohemian poets from the port, such as Sarita Vial or Ennio Moltedo, people who were innovative, creative, and committed to the process. Well connected as she was, Ángela refused to give up on her efforts to help him find work in those turbulent times, hard as it was for a Caribbean such as himself, who'd been in Chile for only two years. But beneath those almost maternal efforts, Cayetano sensed something else: the desire to attend to an unresolved issue so as to move on to other matters, which perhaps had been postponed only because of the problem at hand. Ángela's projects were concerned less with domestic and more with political life, and without a commitment or at least a public standing in the country he'd followed her to, he was a puzzle piece that didn't quite fit; and that's exactly how he felt, out of place and out of the game, at that party where no one would have invited him if it hadn't been for her and to which he, as he thought with growing crankiness, wouldn't have tried to be invited. He didn't feel like mingling with these VIPs, and was even more reticent to join the circle that had formed around the owner of the most illustrious name, the one most praised, the one surrounded by the most legends; Cayetano, vaguely disillusioned, preferred to withdraw to the library of that turn-of-the-century house, where the siding was renovated with sheets of yellow-painted iron, and which gleamed like a gold coin over the bay. The library—with its wooden floor, exposed-oak beams, and shelves full of elegant leather-bound books—offered the refuge of dimness and, as Cayetano had imagined, was deserted. He settled into a wing chair by the window that led out to the garden, where several guests smoked and talked with complete disregard for the cold, and as he inhaled the intense fragrance of the Pacific, he recalled another sea, and another Ángela.

He remained this way until he lost track of time. Apparently, no one missed him. But then, when the Chilean gathering seemed to be occurring in a very distant time and place, or perhaps during a nebulous dream, he heard steps behind him that snapped him out of his modest trance. Someone had entered: fortunately, this person had not turned on another light. The interloper, like himself, preferred the shadows; perhaps he also longed for solitude. He stayed still and avoided making any sound. Perhaps the other person had lost his way or, not seeing anyone, would leave him be. But the steps kept approaching, slowly, as though the feet doubted the very floor they walked on, until they finally stopped close to him.

"How's it going, sir?"

The new arrival's tone was so ironic yet amiable, as if they already knew each other and shared an inside joke, and his greeting so unusual, so personal and affable, that at first Cayetano was too surprised to respond. Since the silence made the isolated phrase seem even more unreal, he searched for a response.

"It's very nice here," he said. "If you're tired of all the excitement." Remembering the calm rhythm of the man's steps, he thought that he must be older. "It's perfect for gathering your strength." Why had he said that, as though inviting him to stay, when he wanted the stranger to leave? At least he didn't turn to look at him and kept his gaze on the horizon through the window. But the other man, whose presence he felt at his back, picked up the thread of conversation.

"It reminds me of Burma, during my youth," he said. Cayetano asked himself what this cold, southern country could have in common with that remote part of Asia that he imagined brimming with heat and rain forests. "The night of the soldier. A guy far out on the ocean and a wave—" He spoke as though lost in his own thoughts, but seemed to be describing himself. Where had he come from? The breeze flapped the curtains, and now Cayetano looked out at the waves. He guessed the other man was doing the same. "A man alone in front of the sea may as well be out at sea."

Cayetano needed to set a limit here. "Who are you talking about?"

"Aren't you a foreigner?" The man's use of the casual *tú* surprised him but didn't bother him; he wanted to be alone, and yet that voice managed to make him comfortable with its presence. "When you're far from your country, you have no home and lose your sense of direction. Back then, I also liked corners like this one."

"And you still like them." He sensed that now he was the one to surprise his interlocutor; the man laughed and moved even closer.

"You're right, I still like them." The atmosphere relaxed; nevertheless, as though to preserve some distance between them, they avoided looking at each other and kept gazing at the Pacific. "Now I have various refuges, friends everywhere, and nevertheless I still sometimes need corners like this one. You're Cuban, right?"

He thought the accent must have given him away. He offered a more precise description.

"I'm from Havana."

"Then you're Ángela Undurraga's husband." Cayetano suddenly felt naked; the stranger rushed to reassure him, as a friend might. "Don't be surprised, she's very well known here. Everybody knows she married a Cuban from Florida."

Who exactly was "everybody"? For the first time, he felt tempted to turn and look at the man. But he restrained himself: after the enthusiastic voyage in which he'd followed his wife's hips to the southern ends of the earth, and after two years of false steps, he had learned not to rush.

"The outskirts of Havana," he said cautiously.

The other man laughed.

"You have a beautiful wife. Intelligent, innovative. You should feel proud."

That wasn't the way he felt. And this was surely apparent. He took shelter in the distance, in the faraway waves that distracted their gazes, and faked it.

"Yes, people envy me. Very much. They must ask themselves what she couldn't find here that made her go for a man in the north."

This time the Chilean didn't laugh.

"Love troubles are the same in every climate," he declared brusquely, suddenly somber. An old sadness, dragged through more years than Cayetano could count, seemed quickly to enter the cultivated, amiable voice that had laughed and joked calmly just a moment before. Though he barely paused, when the man spoke again his voice sounded as if it carried a great weight. "Forgive my frankness, young man, but I know how much it hurts to wear these masks. From the moment I first saw you sitting there in front of the window, far from the garden, where you should be mingling on your wife's arm, I knew what was going on. I've seen too many people grow apart not to recognize the emptiness that results."

Cayetano himself was now that empty space. His silence was eloquent. His strange interlocutor seemed to have a great deal to say.

"At my age, one would think that I've already seen it all, that deceit wouldn't hurt anymore, that betrayal would come as no surprise . . . but no, on the contrary, all it takes is one push, some unexpected stumble on the path you take each day, and the equilibrium you thought you could count on falls apart. In addition, you lose your reflexes, and have less time." The voice grew low and impassioned at the mention of this threat; then it rose again. "What burns keeps on burning you, and you don't have anything that can quell it, or even help you to ignore it"— he hesitated—"nor strength with which to explore it." He searched for a different ending. "When you're young, despair comes easily, and you immediately think that if someone stands you up, that person will never come again. But this world keeps turning and turning . . ."

Despite the vagueness of this last allusion, Cayetano understood that the man was talking about himself. Nevertheless, he felt that the words he spoke somehow related to him, to Cayetano, as well. His intuition told him something.

"Are you a writer?" he asked.

"You've got the makings of a detective, young man," the stranger said, half joking. "When you get tired of your profession, you could always hang a sign on the door of some small, cluttered office and wait for someone to hire you for an investigation."

Cayetano couldn't have said whether the man behind him was making fun of him or revealing his destiny. Regardless, he went along with it.

"I'll remember that, Mr. . . ."

"Reyes. Ricardo Reyes." The man seemed to be smiling. "Cayetano, right? What sort of work do you do?"

"These days, whatever comes my way. I'm waiting for work, but after two years I'm starting to think that Ángela doesn't have such great contacts."

Now Reyes said nothing. He started to cough. Cayetano froze for a moment, embarrassed that he'd complained about his wife. Something in him reawakened a modicum of manners.

"Would you like me to close the windows?"

"Don't worry. The windows have nothing to do with this," Reyes replied. He cleared his throat, suppressing his cough. "So you're looking for work," he went on. At that moment a woman's high-heeled steps burst into the room.

"People are out there asking for you, and here you're hiding like an oyster." She was an energetic woman with light brown hair. "Let's go, because your eel soup is ready, and the mayor wants to say some words in your honor. Come on, come on."

The interruption made Cayetano finally turn around. In doing so, he realized that the man was not at his back but standing almost next to him. And, to his astonishment, he recognized him. During the party he hadn't dared to approach him, inhibited not only by the tight circle of admirers surrounding him but also by the authority he attributed to that thick-figured man, with his slow movements, and whose languid, saurian gaze had roved from the sea to him and then back to the sea during that conversation in which he, Cayetano, had not even deigned to look his way. And now the great poet and distinguished ambassador to France for Salvador Allende was moving away from him, tugged by that woman. He had never been alone with a Nobel laureate before. Emotion suddenly shook his body, and blood rushed to his head.

"What the boss says goes, and she's the boss," the poet said, and winked. There he went, with his poncho in the Chiloé Island style, the flat cap he always wore, and those cheeks speckled with large moles. "In any case, if you have any free time these days, come see me in my home, La Sebastiana. I have some old postcards from your city, young man. All you have to do is call me."

Cayetano wouldn't have dared make the call. But it was the poet who reached out first, who called his house and asked him to come for a visit. And that was why he found himself here, on Collado Way, and now someone was finally opening that door with its creaking, rusty hinges and its slats of knotted wood.

I t was the poet.

"Forgive me, I was reading and fell asleep. In addition, Sergio, my chauffeur, is off at the grocery store trying to scrounge something up, and it takes a lot for me to get down the stairs. You'll see that everything here is a bit complicated. Come, follow me, please."

They crossed the minuscule garden of the edifice beside the Mauri Theater. Through the bushes, Cayetano glimpsed the city and the squad of soldiers berthed on the breakwater, and, beyond that, the Andes. The poet began to climb a staircase, heavily, and Cayetano followed. On the second floor, they went down a hall and continued to ascend, this time on a curved and narrow staircase. Through a porthole, Cayetano could see luminous roofs and shaded passages, as if the house glided over Valparaíso.

The poet arrived on the third floor, out of breath. He wore the same cap as before and, on his shoulders, a poncho made of fine brown wool. What could he want? What did he need to talk about that would make him invite Cayetano to his home—

Cayetano, of all people, a sullen foreigner who had left him on his feet standing and behind him during the only conversation they had ever had, without the slightest consideration for his age, without even a flicker of the admiration or at least the respect that everyone else professed for him? The poet guided him to a living room with intensely blue walls and an enormous window that looked out over the entire city. He gestured for Cayetano to sit on a floral-print armchair that faced one made of black leather. The room was bright and ample, with a green carousel horse at the center, and next to it stood the dining room, bordered by the same great window. At the other end was a bar with bottles and glasses, a bell, and a bronze sign that read: DON PABLO EST ICI. Cayetano couldn't help comparing, once again, the hospitality he was receiving with his own social clumsiness, barely corrected during their brief contact over the phone the previous day.

"Thank you for coming," the poet said as he sat down on the leather armchair. Now he seemed to levitate over the belfries of the city. "I'm not going to beat around the bush, Cayetano. You must be asking yourself why I invited you here, and the answer is very simple—because I think you can help me. More than that, I believe you are the only person in the world who can help me."

Though he had decided to be friendlier during this visit, Cayetano kept his guard up.

"Please, Don Pablo, don't scare me with so much responsibility," he said. "How could someone like me help you?"

"Let me say that I know some things about you, but I know more about your wife. She's sympathetic to the Unidad Popular government, as I imagine you are as well. In these times, one cannot trust just anyone . . ."

Cayetano examined the poet's swollen hands, large nose, and haggard face. He had a robust complexion, but his shirt collar was too wide on him, as if he had suddenly grown thinner in the past few months. Then he remembered his sudden melancholy and his gloomy allusion to time running short. Only now, among his own things, in the clear light of day that shone in his home, he seemed decisive, enthusiastic. Although Cayetano didn't know where the conversation was headed.

"I'm Cuban, though by way of Florida," he said, trying to temper the poet's verve with a dose of humor. "I still don't understand . . ."

"It's precisely because you're Cuban that you can help me," Don Pablo cut in.

Cayetano adjusted his glasses and stroked his mustache nervously.

"Because I'm Cuban?"

"Let's take this one step at a time," the poet said, changing his tone. "I see that you haven't stopped looking around this room. First things first. This house is called La Sebastiana in honor of Sebastián Collado, the Spaniard I bought it from in 1959. For the terrace roof, he designed a great aviary and a landing strip for spaceships."

Now Cayetano feared his leg was being pulled.

"Are you being serious, Don Pablo?"

"Completely," he said, closing his large eyelids circumspectly. "One day, a cosmic Odysseus will make his landing here. Among my four houses, none of them floats like this one. The one in Santiago is hidden in the San Cristóbal mountainside, the one on Isla Negra is a beautiful barcarole ready to set sail, and Manquel, which was a brick and stone stable, and which I bought with the money from the Nobel, lives lost among the woods of Normandy. But La Sebastiana threads the air, earth, and sea together like a bracelet, Cayetano. That's why it's my favorite house. But it's not as a contractor but as a poet that I've called you."

Cayetano was amazed. What did he have to do with poetry? How could he possibly help a famous poet? A seagull soared outside the picture window.

"But it's nothing to get nervous about," Don Pablo added. "One is always less imposing in person than in the newspapers or on television. And also, the years—soon I'll be seventy— have begun to take their toll, though they still don't deprive me of the desire to write, and to love."

Cayetano wanted to cut to the chase.

"How can I help you, Don Pablo?"

The poet was silent, hands folded over his belly, bathed in the metallic, late-morning light that hardened the façades of houses and the contours of hills.

"I need to find someone," he said after contemplating for a few moments, gaze lowered. "And someone discreet needs to do the searching. It's a personal matter. I'll take care of all your expenses, and I'll pay you, obviously, whatever you ask," he specified, watching Cayetano with unease.

"You want me to find someone for you?"

"That's right."

"You want to hire me"—and here he remembered what the poet had said to him when they first met—"as a private detective?"

"Exactly."

"But I'm not a detective, Don Pablo. At least, not yet," he added with a faint smile. "Worse, I have no idea how a detective behaves."

The poet's hands picked up some books covered in red plastic from a nearby table.

"Have you ever read any Georges Simenon?" A foxlike look tautened his cheeks and creased his forehead. "He's a terrific Belgian writer of crime novels."

"No, never, Don Pablo." He felt embarrassed of his paltry literary knowledge, and apologized, as though that ignorance could offend his host. "I'm sorry. I've only read a few novels by Agatha Christie and Raymond Chandler, and, of course, some Sherlock Holmes . . ."

"In that case, it's time for you to read the Belgian," the poet continued forcefully. "Because if poetry transports us to the heavens, crime novels plunge you into life the way it really is; they dirty your hands and blacken your face the way coal stains engine stokers on trains in the south, where I was born. I'll lend you these volumes so you can learn something from Inspector Maigret. I don't recommend that you read Poe, who invented the crime story and was a great poet. Neither do I recommend Conan Doyle, Sherlock Holmes's literary father. You know why? Because their detectives are too eccentric and cerebral. They couldn't solve even the simplest case here, in our chaotic Latin America. In Valparaíso, the pickpockets would steal their wallets on the trolley, the kids from the hills would bombard them with stones, and the dogs would chase them down alleys with their fangs bared."

This sounded ridiculous. Detective by force, and on top of that, learning the job from crime novels? Anyone he tried to tell about this would immediately call it crazy. And not just call the poet crazy, but him as well.

"So take these books and read them," Don Pablo added

with complete authority, and placed them, not without some difficulty, in a woven bag.

One doesn't say no to a Nobel laureate, and much less to a seriously ill Nobel laureate, Cayetano thought, taking the bag. There were seven volumes, small, not heavy at all, wrapped in red and clear plastic, pleasing to the touch. If he learned something from them, this strange meeting would already be a different kettle of fish. The bag would at least come in handy for picking up his meat ration from the Committee for Supplies and Price, known as JAP, if the meat in fact arrived, since beef and chicken had been gone for several weeks, along with butter, oil, and sugar. And the prices on the black market bordered on abuse.

"Whom do I need to find?" he heard himself say, as though his voice already belonged to another man.

"I expected nothing less from you, Cayetano," the poet said, and let out a grateful sigh. He shuffled to the living room door in his slippers, to make sure no one was spying on them. "For that, please listen closely, and I'll try to explain the situation in a few words."

4

I need you to find one of your compatriots, an old friend I lost track of a long time ago," the poet said in his calm, nasal voice. His eyes gleamed with sudden, childlike hope.

"It's been a long time since I've set foot in Cuba," Cayetano replied. "I left the island when I was quite young."

"I'm not so naive as to suppose that you know all your fellow citizens, but the fact that you're Cuban can help you in your task. You'll see. I've thought about this for months, especially since my health began to suffer in Paris. I thought about turning to comrades at the Party, including a good friend at the embassy in Havana, but I decided against it because, in days like these, I wouldn't want anything to leak. Politics, you know . . ."

Cayetano Brulé looked at the poet. He didn't know what to say.

"You must be asking yourself why I'd trust a stranger," the poet continued, "and the answer is, simply, intuition. When I heard about you recently at a meeting with comrades in this house, I said to myself: He's the one I need. He doesn't know anyone in Chile, so he has no alternative but to be discreet. He's also Cuban, and can visit the island without awakening suspicions. And since he's unemployed, a job like this could come in handy."

"That's why you came to see me in the library the other Sunday, at the party, right?"

"*École!* Exactly! It was premeditated and calculated."

Cayetano smiled uncomfortably, his hands sweaty, while the poet kept his feet on the white leather footstool, sheathed in woolen socks. It would be difficult to help him, Cayetano thought, but if he didn't at least try, he'd let the poet down, and the man would never speak to him again. It wasn't good to lose a friendship—however nascent it might be—with a poet of such importance. In some ways, the poet, with his melancholy eyes and long sideburns, reminded Cayetano of his own father, a trumpet player in a tropical orchestra, a friend of bohemians who was affectionate with his family, who had died in the fifties after a concert on a snowy night in the Bronx, where he'd played for years with Xavier Cugat and even the one and only Beny Moré, the Barbarian of Rhythm, the one who sang "Today as Yesterday" and danced as if he'd been nursed with conga and bolero instead of milk. After his father's violent death one night on Canal Street, it had become financially impossible for Cayetano's mother to return to the island of Cuba, and she had to make ends meet as a seamstress in Union City.

"What's the Cuban's name, Don Pablo?"

"If you want to get into the details, you should promise me first that you'll do the work in utmost secrecy."

"You can trust me, Don Pablo. I'll be . . . I'll be your own private Maigret."

"That's the ticket, young man," the poet replied with enthusiasm. He turned toward the bar, with its pink walls and bronze bell, and asked, "How about a whiskey on the rocks? I mean a good one, at least eighteen years old. You should know that I'm the best bartender in Chile. Would you prefer a double or a triple?"

He went to the bar without waiting for a reply. Behind the bar, he picked up a glass, threw in a few ice cubes, and poured generously from a bottle of Chivas Regal. Cayetano thought that this might not be the best way to start his day, since he still had to pick up his canned Chinese pork at the JAP on San Juan de Dios Hill, but he admitted that it wasn't every day that a Nobel laureate prepared such a distinguished drink for a mere mortal and contracted him as a private investigator.

"I can't toast with you because of the treatment I'm receiving at Van Buren Hospital," the poet said, lingering over the whiskey's scent before handing it over. "Although at night, if I'm in the mood for it, I gulp down a glass or two of Oporto without letting my wife, Matilde, see. She'd raise hell if she caught me, but I know there's no better medicine than Oporto. A bit of whiskey can't hurt me, don't you think?"

With the ice cubes clinking in the glass, Cayetano asked himself how he could ever have been aloof with this man. "As long as you don't go overboard, Don Pablo, it can't do you any harm . . ."

"Don't worry, young man, at this age I'm no longer seduced by excess." He scrutinized Cayetano's face as he drank. Another gull passed the window with its wings extended and its legs tucked in, moving its head from side to side, cawing an alarm. It glided over nearby roofs and returned to the water, as though indicating the way.

Cayetano felt the first sip descend into his core like wildfire. He wasn't accustomed to drinking in the morning.

"How is it?" asked the poet.

"Superb, Don Pablo," was all he could say.

"I've got the touch. A poet who doesn't know his drinks or food is no poet."

Cayetano left the glass on the bar, under a bell that hung on a bronze arm.

"So? What's the name?"

"Chivas. Chivas Regal. Eighteen years."

"No, Don Pablo. What's the name of the Cuban I'm supposed to find?"

"Ángel. Dr. Ángel Bracamonte." He stroked the bronze bell.

"It doesn't sound familiar at all," Cayetano said, looking at the poet. He thought he saw a flinch of disappointment on his face.

But the poet kept on. "I met him in 1940, in Mexico City, when I was consul there. He was an oncologist. He studied the medicinal properties of some plants that the natives of Chiapas used to treat cancer. Bracamonte should be about my age, or maybe older. I lost track of him in 1943, after returning to Chile with Delia del Carril, my wife at the time. He might still live in Mexico."

So the rumors were true: The poet had cancer. At last he could see how the puzzle pieces fit together. Don Pablo, suffering from cancer, was sending him to find the Cuban oncologist for a cure, Cayetano thought as he polished off the whiskey to embolden himself. The disease explained the poet's exhaustion, his ragged breath, his protuberant ears, and ashen face. Perhaps, Cayetano imagined, he'd never return to his post as ambassador in Paris, and would die in his homeland, in Allende's revolutionary nation. He looked out the window in the direction of his own neighborhood, Marina Mercante; his house rose in full view on a hill riddled with yellow walls beneath a washed-out winter sky.

"Pardon me, Don Pablo, but don't you think an ad in the *Excelsior* would be enough to get Bracamonte on the phone the next day? You shouldn't gamble with your health."

"Who said this was a health issue?" Don Pablo asked, failing to mask the tension on his face.

"Well, since the man's a doctor . . ." It occurred to him that the poet might want to save face by hiding the motive of the search. He was young but not naive. There was no such thing as a naive person in Cuba. Idiots and opportunists, certainly, by the thousands, but not naive people. It was clear that the poet needed the oncologist and his plants to win the battle against cancer.

"I'm not looking for him because of my health. He's probably in Mexico. I need you to find him and inform me, but listen closely now," he said gravely, pointing at Cayetano with his index finger, "you can't mention a single word of this to anyone. Not to anyone! Not even to the man himself! When you find out where he is, you should tell only me. Then I'll tell you how to proceed. Understand?"

"Absolutely."

"You should know that it's not easy to trick a poet. Much less an ill poet."

"So should I begin my investigation at the Mexican embassy, Don Pablo?"

"Why go snooping around embassies like some librarian, Cayetano! What you should do is board a plane for Mexico City and start your investigation there. I need you to find Dr. Ángel Bracamonte as soon as possible!"

5

H e couldn't fly to Mexico immediately, because there were no available seats. He decided to kill time by leafing through Simenon's novels, which gripped him immediately, with characters who wandered the alleys, bistros, and markets of Paris. He also looked around for people who could tell him a little about the poet, something that went beyond what everybody knew about him, his travels and his loves. If he knew the man better, he'd feel more comfortable, as Neruda had begun to seem like a pretty mysterious guy, concealing facets of his life the way the thick spring fog hid some of Valparaíso's heights. He was cautious about investigating his client's life. Nobody could begin to suspect that he was on assignment. The flame of distrust that burned in his chest made him feel contemptible, but he needed to know the artist through others, using the same method employed by the diligent Maigret, who spied without qualms, but in great secrecy, even on his most trustworthy informants and closest colleagues.

Two days later, while eating a remarkable seafood dish at

Los Porteños in the Cardonal Market near the port, he received an encouraging tip from Pete Castillo, who happened to come into the restaurant for some clams in parsley sauce. A fisherman had just brought those "poor man's oysters" in a wicker basket. Their elongated shells gleamed like sand on the beach on a clear morning. Pete was a labor union leader who lived in a wooden stilt house in a ravine of Monjas Hill, near Cayetano's home. He had quit the university in his third year, after the triumph of Salvador Allende, to devote himself completely to local political activism, but he still devoured Latin American novels and was a great admirer of Julio Cortázar, Juan Carlos Onetti, and Ernesto Sábato, as well as Jorge Luis Borges, whom he considered a despicable reactionary who just happened to be graced with a magnificent pen.

"Neruda isn't among my saints," Pete said in a deep voice as he squeezed lemon with his coarse, dark hands, its juice sprinkling over an open clam, its pink tongue shrinking into the shell in pain. "His cantos to Stalin in *The Grapes and the Wind* and his rejection of the armed approach to building socialism in Chile make him suspect. That poet has gotten too bourgeois."

"Stop calling the kettle black and tell me, who can give me more information about him? I mean, about his personal life."

Pete thought for a moment. "Perhaps Commander Camilo Prendes could help you." He sucked the clam's tongue into his mouth, leaving the smooth shell impeccably clean, then washed the delicacy down with a gulp of house white wine. "The commander oversees a brigade of the most radical students from the School of Architecture at the University of Chile, and if memory serves, he has a cousin who's an expert in poetry, an encyclopedia on two marvelous legs, they say. She should know something about Neruda, and anyway it's never a waste of time to meet a woman like that."

"So where can I find this guy?"

"At the Hucke cookie factory."

"His job is to make cookies for afternoon tea? In times like these?" Cayetano fished a chunk of sea bass out of his soup. It was as white and smooth as the cheeks of princesses in stories by the Brothers Grimm.

"Don't make fun of the commander, Cayetano. Prendes means business. Hucke is in the hands of workers who are fighting for its expropriation, and he's leading the charge. He's succeeded in expropriating several factories and some country estates under one hundred twenty acres in size, despite the opposition of the government. Prendes participated in the Paris uprisings of 'sixty-eight, where he met Daniel Cohn-Bendit, and he also studied in Havana. He's a real threat to the reformists who infest the presidential palace, La Moneda. He's a little bourgeois, too, but he knows his stuff."

Cayetano headed over to Hucke that same night. With its illuminated windows and cacophonous machinery, the factory resembled an ocean liner navigating a dense, calm sea, or so it seemed to Cayetano as he approached it through the misty industrial zone. Flags of the Socialist Party hung from the walls, of MAPU and MIR, parties that described themselves as true revolutionaries and dismissed Allende as a mere reformer, as well as canvas signs demanding the expansion of the state's economic power and an end to capitalism. Despite the takeover, the factory continued to operate, although, according to Pete, the shortage of supplies was beginning to take its toll. Cayetano approached the large front door, where a few guards wearing helmets and armed with nightsticks smoked in silence.

"I'm here on behalf of Comrade Pete Castillo," he said, showing them the safe-conduct note Pete had scribbled on a paper napkin at the Los Porteños table. "I need to speak with Camilo Prendes."

One of the guards examined the document, jotted Cayetano's information down in a notebook, and after consulting with a superior by phone, allowed him to enter. He felt like something of an orphan as he crossed the empty patio of the factory and approached the office, where another guard handed him a long, flexible bamboo cane.

"Join the group over at the northern access door. Or do you prefer a nunchuck?"

"I've never held one."

"In that case, keep the cane. Carry it like a spear." He cast him an unfriendly glance. "And go to the left. They'll give you more instructions at the end of the hall."

At the end of the hall he encountered a few men with helmets and nunchucks, seated next to a large metal door. They told him that if he saw any suspicious movements, he should knock on the door with a hammer that lay on the floor.

"In case of emergency, everybody knows what to do. Don't worry about finding Commander Prendes. He visits all the sentry posts every night, and speaks with all the comrades. Good luck."

They left, taking their makeshift weapons with them, and Cayetano sat down on a stack of boxes and lit a Lucky Strike. Its aroma gave him solace in the midst of this uncertain night. He was lucky to have gotten these cigarettes from Sergio Puratic, a trader in the port neighborhood, since there weren't any left publicly and a carton cost an arm and a leg on the black market. He inhaled the smoke slowly, letting it warm his body, and he thought about the poet, the curious mission he'd been charged with, and the stories of Inspector Maigret. His life was taking on a surreal slant, yoked to a strange secret that separated him from others. Could he possibly be dreaming? Could this be a dream in which he was waiting, cane in hand, for a revolutionary in a country threatened by the phantom of civil war? Could he be dreaming that he lived in Valparaíso, while actually sleeping a thousand miles from there, in his old house in Hialeah, near Miami, or perhaps even in Havana itself? His fingers brushed against the Simenon volume he carried in his jacket. He had read a few of the novels in the last few days, not because he thought they could teach him how to be a detective, but because Simenon knew how to tell an entertaining story, and Inspector Maigret struck him as both honest and convincing. The book, with its transparent plastic cover folded neatly at the edges, was proof that he'd spoken with Neruda, and wasn't dreaming after all.

A vehicle approached the large metal door. Cayetano crushed the cigarette butt with his foot and hid behind a pillar. He didn't want to be seen from outside. It was said that members of the Nationalist Movement for Homeland and Liberty, or of the Rolando Matus Command, shot at the drop of a hat. He held his breath. The paved stones shone in the headlights of a vehicle that slowly approached. At last he saw it. It was a soldiers' jeep. Not long ago, the army had shot at workers at a factory they'd taken over, then refused to turn the murderers over to justice. The jeep turned the corner slowly, without its occupants seeing Cayetano.

"What are you reading?" asked a voice at his back.

When he turned, he saw a pale, bearded youth with long

hair. He wore a beret, a long jacket, and boots. Two individuals in olive-green jackets accompanied him but stood at a distance.

"Simenon." He showed the man the book cover.

"You like crime novels?"

"They're entertaining." He looked toward the street. No trace of the jeep.

"I read him for the first time in Paris, when I was studying there," the young man said as he sat down on the raised blade of a parked forklift. He was tall, thin, and good-looking, with an unmistakable resemblance to Che Guevara. He took out a case of Hiltons and offered Cayetano a cigarette. They smoked and listened to the clamor of the factory machines. "He's a prolific writer, and popular, a supporter of the French status quo. I'm Prendes, of course. You're Cayetano Brulé, and you're looking for me, or so my comrades say."

"That's right."

"And you like crime stories . . ."

"Though I prefer poetry."

"Oh, really? Like whose, for example?"

"Neruda's," he lied, to get to the point.

Prendes lowered his gaze and calmly stroked his beard. "Where are you from?"

"Cuba."

"Fidel is no fan of Neruda's."

Cayetano stroked his mustache and adjusted his glasses to buy some time. He recalled a venomous letter by Cuban writers criticizing Neruda for rejecting the armed approach to socialism, and for visiting American universities.

"There, they have Nicolás Guillén. *Sóngoro cosongo* and all that Afro-Cuban music," Prendes went on.

"You prefer Guillén?" Cayetano asked, feeling that he was treading in a field he was completely ignorant about.

"I prefer the way things are done over there: the workers' party, the revolutionary army, everybody eats the same thing, they go to the same schools and all have work, without bosses. That's how it should be here. But back to Neruda." He took a drag from his cigarette and let out a puff of smoke. "Do you like his love poems, or the political ones?"

"Love."

Prendes murmured, in a mocking tone, "'I can write the saddest lines tonight. / Write, for example: "The night is full of stars, trembling, blue, so far away." / The night wind spins in the sky, and sings . . .'"

A shot rang out like a cosmic lash, striking echoes in the distance, followed by several more shots.

"Mausers! They're from the Maipo Regiment," Prendes muttered, frowning. "They try to intimidate the people with their rusty World War Two guns . . ."

They stood still, breathing the pale night air, listening to dogs barking in the hills and the echoes rippling out across the bay. Suddenly the factory had gone quiet.

"It's the damn parts. I should go," Prendes said. He stood up. He threw his cigarette butt on the ground and crushed it with his boot. "If the Bulgarian comrades don't send us the replacement parts they promised, it'll be the end of those cookies."

"You know what they say. When there's no bread, cakes will do."

"Doesn't sound bad as a proverb, but the people prefer cookies," he said, massaging his hands.

"Pete Castillo told me you know someone who knows a

lot about Neruda," Cayetano said before Prendes could get away.

"He must mean my cousin. Her name is Laura." He smiled, lost in thought. For a moment, however brief, the question seemed to transport him from the troubles of the factory. "She studied in Moscow, at Patrice Lumumba University. She's been writing a dissertation on the poet for a long time, but right now she works in food distribution, at the Committee for Supplies and Price. Here, write down her number. . . ."

6

The night was as dark as the inside of a coffin. Down below, in front of the closed shops on Serrano Street, an empty Verde Mar bus passed slowly. Tropical rhythms rose from a bar called La Nave, and the squadron on the breakwater rocked in silent shadows. A pair of heels rang out in the darkness. Cayetano turned and glimpsed a woman in a long jacket and scarf near the Lord Thomas Cochrane Sea Museum, with her hands in her pockets, coming up the cobbled street.

The day before, he'd called the number Camilo Prendes had given him. Laura Aréstegui had been surprised that someone would be interested in her academic thesis in such turbulent times, when people talked no longer about verses but only about the seizure of power, the proletarian dictatorship, and the Chilean road to socialism, vertiginous days in which everybody quoted Lenin, Trotsky, Althusser, or Marta Harnecker's manuals on historical and dialectical materialism. They agreed to meet at the museum at eight o'clock in the evening, after a party meeting she needed to attend. It was now 8:20 p.m.

"Sorry to be late," Laura said. "There's always a comrade who comes up with something in the last minute."

She was attractive. She'd just transferred from the Communist Youth to the Party itself. She had a mole near her mouth, and deep-set eyes, like those of someone who slept very little because of insomnia or an excess of work or sex, Cayetano thought. He guessed, without knowing why, that Laura was experienced in the ways of love and that her eyes were the result of passion. They walked down the steps in front of Hotel Rudolf into the deserted grid of the city, and on to Plaza Aníbal Pinto for dinner at the traditional restaurant Cinzano.

"So a Cuban from Havana wants to know about Neruda," Laura remarked, amused, as they sat down at their table. A man with silver temples and an impeccable blue suit was singing tangos, accompanied by a gaunt, pale man on the bandoneón, a small kind of accordion, who looked as if he were being stalked by death. Two couples danced between the crowded tables.

"As I said before, I'm trying to write an article about Neruda's life in Mexico," Cayetano said. "Little is known about those years. I'm headed to Mexico City in a few days."

"Do you write for *Granma* or for *Bohemia*?" Laura asked. She had thin, arched eyebrows, like Romy Schneider. Only she was a Romy Schneider of the Southern Cone, Cayetano thought, enthused.

"First I write the articles, then I place them," he said, and immediately feared he'd failed to sound convincing.

They ordered a bottle of red wine, chicken soup, and, as an appetizer, *palta reina*, the avocados stuffed with tuna that had been ubiquitous in Chilean restaurants since the nation gained independence. Cinzano somehow had a guaranteed supply of food, but at prices that were going through the roof, Cayetano thought as he surreptitiously scanned the sad atmosphere of the place, feeling oppressed by a sense of the world coming to an end. The restaurant was one of the favored meeting places of the city's legendary bohemian revolutionary scene, which included poets and writers who self-published with blind faith and admirable perseverance; poorly paid though dignified and vehement professors of literature and history; bright university students of letters infatuated with extreme utopias; and local politicians who, at least on this night, seeing themselves reflected in the large mirror beyond the trays of clams and conger eels, managed to forget that the country had become the beleaguered *Titanic* of the Pacific.

All in all, it had been a productive day, Cayetano thought as Laura left for the bathroom. In the morning, after finishing another of Simenon's novels, which were happily short as well as highly entertaining, he had confirmed his flight and obtained a list of hotels in Mexico City with reasonable rates. Even though the poet had told him not to worry about cost, he didn't want to abuse his trust. Then, during lunch, Ángela had called to say she'd be extending her visit to Santiago, where she was applying for the position of inspector at a textile factory that had been taken over by workers. She hoped the distance might help them overcome the crisis in their relationship. If that's what she thinks, then that's on her, Cayetano said to himself skeptically as he put the matter aside. The most important thing he could do right now was learn more about the poet.

"Neruda lived in Mexico City from 1940 to 1943, as the Chilean consul," Laura explained a little while later, as they ate olives and drank red wine. "He was trying to escape his time as consul in Rangoon, Batavia, and Singapore—the worst years of his life. He didn't understand Asia, he didn't know anybody there. He had only brief affairs with lovers, many of them whores, and a woman who was half British and half Javanese by the name of Josie Bliss, who tried to stab him. Then he married a Dutchwoman and had a daughter with her, Malva Marina Trinidad."

"It seems you know all about Neruda's life and miracles."

"He arrived in Mexico on the arm of Delia del Carril, his second wife, a rich and cultured Argentinean who played a key role in his life," Laura went on, glad to be escaping, if even for a few hours, the great headache of Valparaíso's supply shortage. "In Europe, she'd introduced him to the intellectuals of the left, and convinced him to support the Republicans in the Spanish Civil War. She was the one who made him a communist. Without Delia, Neruda would have kept on writing hermetic poems like those in *Residence on Earth*, and he wouldn't have joined the left or become the poet we now know."

"She was older than him, right?"

"When they met, he was thirty, she was fifty."

"It was obvious that would last less time than a cake in front of a school—"

"You're thinking of writing about Neruda and you didn't know about that?" Laura exclaimed, suspicious. "He took advantage of her social contacts, her wealth, her ideology, and her need for company. Then he abandoned her in 1955 for Matilde Urrutia, his current wife, who at the time was a young cabaret singer with an amazing body, a woman who's an intellectual dwarf compared to Delia."

Several couples danced between the tables to the tango "Volver," and were reflected in Cinzano's beveled mirror, while others conversed passionately over their wineglasses, boiled blood sausage, and french fries, about the revolution and the counter-revolution, about Allende, Altamirano and Jarpa, the Communist Party, the Socialist Party and MIR, about the lessons of Sierra Maestra, the Vietnamese resistance and the October Revolution. Through the lace curtains at the window, Cayetano watched a military jeep drive down Esmeralda Street. He sipped his wine with his gaze lowered and a sense of helplessness creeping up his spine.

"That's my frank opinion of Neruda after prying into his life," Laura said.

"Let's just say he's not the saint you want to pray to." He recalled the poet at the top of the stairs, watching him in silence as he descended the steps of La Sebastiana with the envelope full of dollars in his hand.

"I have nothing against him as an artist. He deserved the Nobel. What I don't like is the representation of women in his poetry, nor do I like the way he treats us. It weighs on me, that whole issue of 'I like it when you're silent because it's as if you were absent.' Pure machismo. A guy's dream: for women to be docile, passive animals."

Cayetano stayed silent. Who was he to argue with Laura about poetry? He popped an olive into his mouth and said, "But listen, I'm looking for something different. In Mexico, I'm interested in the places he used to frequent, the friends he rubbed elbows with. Do you know any Mexicans over there who are well informed, and could help me?"

He knocked on the door of 237 Collado Way and waited with his hands in his jacket pockets. The cold snuck up the hills from the Pacific, which at that hour was submerged in a fog pierced by the siren of the Punta de Ángeles lighthouse, its moan like a dying bull. He walked back the way he'd come, while above him a goldfinch sang numbly on a balcony studded with potted carnations. At Alí Babá, the Turk Hadad prepared him coffee with a dash of milk and a gyro on hallulla bread, and Cayetano settled in, combing through the daily papers. A column by Mario Gómez López announced that the right was planning a coup d'état against Salvador Allende with the support of the United States embassy, but he warned that the attempted takeover would meet with stalwart resistance from the people. He read the column twice; he liked the way the reporter wrote. The radio played the song "Todos Juntos," by Los Jaivas, and at the grocery store across the street people waited in line for oil.

Maybe the poet was at Van Buren Hospital, he thought. He

needed to obtain final approval for his trip. He was haunted by the possibility that he might fail in his mission. The lessons from Maigret's novels were not enough to guarantee success. There the poet was guilty of naïveté. How was Cayetano supposed to find an old doctor, with the last name of Bracamonte, in a metropolis with millions of inhabitants that he had never visited before? He tried to bolster his own confidence. Perhaps with the help of the Mexican Medical Association and the guidance of Laura Aréstegui (who in the end hadn't known a soul in Mexico City) he could get his bearings in the capital. He would tell his wife he was off to fulfill a secret mission, which she would love, since she adored revolutionary political conspiracies. But the mission in Mexico was a secret between him and the Nobel laureate, something nobody else could ever know about, he thought, and then he whispered to himself, from memory, the verses that Neruda had written in honor of La Sebastiana:

I built the house.
First I made it out of air.
Then I raised the flag
and left it hanging
from the firmament, from the star, from
light and darkness.

"Talking to yourself?" Hadad stood beside him with a brimming cup of coffee. His black eyes glittered with sarcasm, and the naked bulb from the soda fountain shone on his bald Buddha head like a phantom reflection. "If you start raving about political parties in days like these, who knows how it'll end? Better you just sit back and enjoy my coffee: no one else makes one like it in Valparaíso."

Cayetano watched the strands of foam turn in the cup, lit a Lucky Strike, and let the liquid warm his insides. It tasted just passable, but it was better not to mention that to Hadad, who was intently chopping meat behind the bar with a big, sharp knife. Through the window, he saw some dogs sleeping curled up in the foyer of the Mauri, next to a sign for *Valparaíso, Mi Amor*. He thought that at times he himself had felt like a stray dog, lost in the south of the continent, without a woman, or, more accurately, with a woman he couldn't get along with, which was worse than having no woman at all. None of this would happen to Maigret—he and his wife enjoyed a honeymoon as perpetual as it was dispassionate; the wife cooked for him and seasoned his favorite dishes with angelic hands and didn't meddle in politics, and still less in feverish Caribbean guerrilla adventures. What was more, Maigret had his own apartment in Paris and dependable work at the police department, while he, Cayetano, rented a house at 6204 Alemania Avenue and was unemployed, and (too embarrassing to mention) he aspired to become a detective by reading novels. All because the poet, who placed far too much hope in the power of literature, believed that reading the crime genre could turn a young man like him into an actual private investigator.

"You read a couple of Georges Simenon novels, you enroll in some investigation course, and you're there!" the poet had said to him at the bar in La Sebastiana as he threw ice cubes into a whiskey glass.

Sipping his coffee, he recalled that, decades earlier, the poet had married a woman twenty years his senior, as Laura had described. Delia del Carril must have been an extraordinarily seductive woman back then, he thought, while Hadad served him a steaming, greasy platter of gyros. Was it possible that the poet had never asked himself what would occur in his bed when he turned fifty? Had he never imagined it or, intuiting it, had he opted to marry that woman out of sheer opportunism? What would it be like to go to bed with a fifty-year-old woman? How would her flesh feel and her mouth taste? An illustrious domino player at the Bar Inglés had once told him that though young women's firm flesh might seem more exciting at first glance, older and more experienced women outpaced them by far in the pleasure they could provide in bed. The devil knows more from being old than from being the devil, the domino player had affirmed, winking as he recommended that Cayetano seduce a fifty-year-old woman in Victoria Plaza. It was easier to seduce them on spring and summer mornings, because the heat, the blue sky, and the birdsong were on your side, he had said, eyeing his dominoes. One day, he'd go to Victoria Plaza to confirm the theory, Cayetano told himself, but not now, when he was attracted to young women with smooth faces, taut bellies, and firm calves. So the poet with the monotonous nasal voice, the thick body, and the melancholy gaze, whom he could almost consider a friend, had actually been a kind of gigolo in his youth? Had he conned a mature woman so that she'd open doors for him to the salons of European intellectuals, editors, and politicians? And had he then left her for a singer who was thirty years younger?

He sampled the gyro and nodded approvingly at Hadad, who waited behind the bar for his verdict, hands on his hips and an intimidating look on his face. If he wanted to work for the poet, it was imperative to know him intimately, he thought.

If he was to travel to Mexico on his orders, he should at least know with whom he was dealing. The fact that Neruda had received the Nobel Prize implied only that he was a phenomenal writer but not, necessarily, a good person. What would it be like to love a woman twenty years your senior? he asked himself again. Could there be desire between two people so distant in age? And what had become of Delia del Carril? According to Laura, she lived in the capital, old, poor, and alone, her family fortune squandered; she spent her time painting energetic, indomitable horses, and was still in love with Neruda.

At that moment he saw the man in question coming down Collado Way with his chauffeur. He walked slowly, slouched. Cayetano polished off his gyro in a hurry, finished his coffee, put a crumpled bill on the table, and left Alí Babá, releasing a small but satisfied burp.

P lease, have a seat!" The poet had settled into his favorite
armchair, which he had named La Nube, and was examining the pearly surface of a large conch with a magnifying glass
while his chauffeur, Sergio, arranged hawthorn logs under the
copper hood of the fireplace. "When do you go?"

"If you write a check for this amount to the money exchange
office, I can leave next week," Cayetano replied, handing him a
bill.

The poet gave the document a cursory glance and let it fall
on the top of the newspaper *El Siglo*, which lay on the floor
beside La Nube. He waited for his chauffeur to leave the room,
then said, "Better yet, you tell me how much you need and I'll
write you a check for the whole thing. I'm no good with numbers. Matilde is off in Isla Negra. I just got back from the doctor, and I'm exhausted. But I trust you won't let me down with
your business in Mexico, my friend."

"I'll find your doctor, Don Pablo, you'll see. Don't worry."

His first steps as an investigator had made him feel a bit more sure of himself.

"I trust you. You're a bright young guy, you've lived in three countries, and nobody will be surprised that you're looking for a fellow Cuban." He sighed and looked out at the cloudy Valparaíso sky. "I'm lucky to have met you."

Cayetano felt honored by the remark. And, confident in his new role, he proceeded with his questioning. "What's the story behind that shell?"

It was a good question. It drew a light smile out of Don Pablo.

"I bought it a half-century ago in Rangoon, Burma, where I held my first diplomatic post, thanks to some friends with contacts in the State Department." He turned his face upward, giving himself an air of importance. "Of course, it was only later that I figured out why nobody else wanted the job: it paid next to nothing. I ended up paying the bills by writing columns for Santiago newspapers. There wasn't much to do in Rangoon, so I wrote poems. Well, to be frank, my verses from that period were hermetic, indecipherable; to this day even I can't fully penetrate them. The academics of Europe and North America, on the other hand, enjoy them as though they were a naked woman on a bed, or a naked man, perhaps, because all things can be found on God's green earth, Cayetano."

He thought again of their first meeting, the day of the party by the shores of Playa Ancha, and thought that the poet, on occasion, could still be quite hermetic. But he kept his opinions to himself and stayed focused on the poet's reminiscence.

"I suppose the climate in Rangoon must be like Havana, no?"

"Rangoon is as humid, hot, and exotic as your city, Cayetano.

The air is so thick it won't fit in your mouth. The plants and trees are identical to those of your island, and the fruits are the same, too. At midday, you're forced to lie down in a hammock for siesta. I lived by the sea, between coconut palms, on a beach with sand as white and fine as flour . . . and now, my friend, there isn't even enough flour here to make *sopaipillas*. My house was modest, made of wood, with a pitched tin roof. I didn't manage to learn the language of the people, who were descended from typhoons. At night I'd drink at the bar of the Grand Hotel, on the river, where I'd go on the prowl for women."

"Beautiful?" he dared to say.

"Gorgeous." To judge from his smile, the poet hadn't forgotten them. "But I never knew what they were thinking. When they made love they were as silent as iguanas," he added, lowering his voice. "They had sturdy thighs, girlish waists, an ass that could fit in your palms, light and timid breasts, and there was something gymnastic about the way they did it within the confines of those mosquito nets. Cayetano, those women are nothing like ours."

The poet invited him to the top floor of the house to see his studio, up a few concrete stairs. It was a wood-paneled room with shelves full of books and a mirrored wardrobe. The city and bay struggled to slide in through the windows. Cayetano was intrigued by an old black Underwood typewriter on a worn desk between two windows.

"Do you write poems on that machine?"

"Are you crazy? Nobody writes decent poems on keys. Poetry is written by hand, with a pen, my friend. Verses descend from the brain like the tide on the Chiloé coast; they flow through the body to your hands and pour out on the page," he explained as Cayetano examined a door hidden behind a large sepia photograph of a slim man with a long white beard.

"What's behind that door?" he asked.

"A heliport designed by Sebastián Collado. This room was going to be a giant aviary, open to the city, but as you see, it's become my studio."

"Excuse me. Did you say heliport?" Cayetano repeated, astonished.

"Exactly." The poet calmly half closed his eyes.

A heliport. Sebastián was a great dreamer, a visionary. And now they'd moved from spaceships to heliports. Poets truly left no stone unturned. He was determined to keep up. "And the man in that photograph. Is he your father?"

"In a way," Don Pablo said, amused. "He was my poetic father. One of my greatest teachers. Look, I even have an outfit in his image." He opened the wardrobe by the door. "That's Walt Whitman, a marvelous poet from the United States."

"Is he alive?"

"Let's say that he continues to live. Great poets never die, Cayetano."

He took a hanger out of the wardrobe, from which hung a white beard, a cloak, and a wide-brimmed straw hat. He tied the beard around his neck with a cord and donned the hat and cloak. He took a pair of wire-rimmed glasses out of the cloak's pocket, along with a long, straight pipe.

"Do I look like him?"

Cayetano compared the portrait with Don Pablo. "I'd say it's he who looks like you."

"Well said, Cayetano. But without him, I wouldn't be who

I am," he said pensively as he searched the wardrobe again. "Put these clothes on."

"Me?"

"Who else?"

"But . . ."

"But what?"

Cayetano saw no choice but to bare his discomfort and prejudices. "Forgive me, but costumes and disguises make me think, with all due respect, of faggots, Don Pablo, to tell you the truth . . ."

"So what? It'll stay between us." He added, mischievously, "Walt Whitman was a faggot."

"You see? Better not to dress up. I'm happy simply to be myself."

"Nonsense! Life is nothing more than a parade of disguises, Cayetano. You yourself have, until now, disguised yourself as a Havanan, an emigrant, a North American soldier, and a husband, and now you're playing the part of private detective. One more disguise is neither here nor there, and in any case, the habit isn't what makes the monk. I love throwing costume parties for my friends. It's the best way of getting to know them. The costume they choose strips them completely, and they don't even know it. Come on, young man, don't be shy. Put it on."

He had no choice but to obey.

"It's a costume from the Caucasus. It fits you," the poet affirmed, stroking his false beard when Cayetano had finished dressing. "The cloak is called a *bashlik*, ideal for the winter, and the cap is made of *karakul* wool. I should tell you that the outfit costs a fortune. It was a gift from the Union of Soviet Writers, from Stalin's time. Better not to remember . . ."

"I look like a Cossack."

"And look at this." He reached back into the wardrobe and took out a lilac tie covered in small green guanacos. "Made on an indigenous loom. A gift from Delia, my second wife, but Matilde doesn't let me wear it. Women, you know, are like Christopher Columbus: they want your history to begin with their arrival. I'll give it to you because it brings good luck, and she could throw it in the garbage any day."

"Are you sure?" It had a coarse texture, though a nice feel. On the lilac background, the guanacos leapt joyfully, grazed placidly, or contemplated the horizon.

"It's always brought me good luck. It's almost forty years old. I was wearing it when I met some of the greatest European intellectuals when I lived in Madrid, in the Argüeyes neighborhood. I also wore it when I went underground in the fifties, when the Chilean government was searching for me to throw me into the concentration camp of Pisagua. I wanted to wear it to accept the Nobel Prize in Stockholm, but Matilde and Swedish protocols conspired to force me into a bow tie, like some waiter at a fine restaurant. All I needed was the tray. So ridiculous. But do you know what I did?"

"No, Don Pablo."

The poet closed the wardrobe door, and suddenly both of them—Walt Whitman and the man from the Caucasus—stood in front of their reflections in the mirror, motionless, surprised at themselves. Who was disguised as whom? Cayetano asked himself. Whitman as Neruda, or Neruda as Whitman? And who was he, Cayetano, in a life that, according to the poet, boiled down to a never-ending carnival?

"A detective who doesn't know how to disguise himself is like the poet who doesn't understand drink, food, or love," Whitman said, draping the tie around the Caucasian's neck.

"But you still haven't told me what you did with this tie in Stockholm."

"I folded it and kept it in the inside pocket of my suit jacket." Whitman adjusted the knot, smiling through his glasses. "So I still accepted the Nobel Prize with it. I'm giving it to you so it can protect you. It might not help you win the Nobel, but it might at least keep people from talking poorly about you as a detective. Let's go back downstairs."

In the living room, the logs crackled in the fireplace, while outside the thick fog dispersed, revealing a bit of clean sky.

"We were talking about the women of Rangoon," Cayetano reminded him, wondering whether he owed his sudden confidence to the disguise. The city's name struck him as voluptuous. He told himself that on some not-too-distant day he should leave the cold of Valparaíso for a visit to Rangoon, returning to the sticky intensity of the tropics.

"They're enigmatic," the poet said, settling into La Nube. The beard hung all the way down to his stomach. "And in matters of love, at the end of the day, frustrating. I never knew whether it was me giving them pleasure in bed, or whether they always enjoyed themselves that much. I could never tell whether I was expendable and everybody gave them the same pleasure, or whether I was the chosen one. Even today I ask myself whether women experience the same pleasure with different men," the poet added. He suddenly became taciturn.

Cayetano didn't want to lose the enjoyment they were sharing at that moment, so he went out on a limb. "Well, that depends on how you treat them, Don Pablo. My father used to say that they're like flutes. How they sound depends on how you stroke and care for them."

"The metaphor's a bit anemic, but your father may have been

right," the poet conceded benevolently. "In that case, it's not the same," he concluded.

"What do you mean, Don Pablo?"

"That if anyone can get the same notes out of a single woman, then the uniqueness and incomparable nature of each individual love is lost. Well, it's as I was saying," he added with a faint sparkle in his tired eyes. "In Rangoon, I ran into women of many different races and customs. Sometimes I'd invite three of them back to my place at the same time, and we'd go wild with ecstasy on those high, humid nights, bathed in sweat between the undulating walls of the mosquito net, and I wouldn't even know whose sex I drank from, whose mouth I kissed, or what folds I was exploring."

"But that's paradise, Don Pablo," Cayetano said, beside himself, and he placed the *karakul* cap on his knees. The tale had made him both hot and incredulous.

"It sounds exciting, but in truth it's not so much, in the end. I only entered their bodies, never their souls. Understand? I always succumbed like an exhausted castaway before the unconquerable walls of those graceful, mysterious women."

"I'd still like to have swum that far, Don Pablo."

"But in the end, none of that stays with you," he said with agitation. "There are people who would kill over love or jealousy, or out of spite or envy, but in the end no part of those passionate bodies remains, neither the echoes of their voices nor their images in mirrors, Cayetano."

He thought the poet was returning to the melancholy he'd exhibited the other day, and that, costumes aside, he had quite a bit of drama in him. As if, in addition to Whitman, he was playing the role of himself, as he'd said during their first meeting, in that dim room, when Don Pablo Neruda—whose real name was Neftalí Ricardo Reyes Basoalto—had displayed his passion and sadness with a sense of spectacle that made one wonder what lay behind it. He tried to imagine the poet as a young man. The copious dark brown hair falling over his forehead. His attractive gaze, fresh voice, and shapely chin. It was hard to accept that this old sallow-cheeked man had been that youth who used to hold orgies on the beach, on distant Oriental nights. Could the poet recall the roar of flesh gripped by the urge to touch and possess sweaty bodies, or were his memories of that time now calm and vague, devoid of passion? He picked up the conch that lay beside *El Siglo*, whose front page denounced the national transportation strike the right was devising to overthrow Allende. He considered that when the conch last slinked across Rangoon's ocean floor, the poet was a twenty-something, as he himself was now. An irrepressible chill ran down his spine as he imagined that, at this precise instant, over the sands of Valparaíso's ocean floor, there glided another conch that some young man would take into his hands half a century later, when he himself was in his seventies. With his fingertips, he felt the fine, dry-leaf texture of the conch, and a thought usually reserved for older people occurred to him, suddenly tormenting him, though he wasn't sure why: that life was fragile and fleeting.

"This conch is so slender, it feels like a paper kite," he said. "With a little southern wind, it could even fly over the roofs of Valparaíso, Don Pablo."

"What you say shows that you're turning into a poet," the Nobel laureate proclaimed, satisfied, stroking his long beard with a philosophical air. "Sometimes certain friends of mine begin to feel like poets, as if my poetry has become contagious. To become a poet, you should first read Walt Whitman, Cayetano. But what the hell am I saying? For what we're doing, you're better off sticking to Simenon, who has written a great deal."

"Hundreds of novels, according to the introduction in the first volume." Cayetano took off the cloak and carefully draped it over the back of the flower-print armchair.

"He wrote over three hundred of them. To tell you the truth, I have no idea when that guy finds the time to shit, piss, or have sex."

As the poet stood up and crossed the living room in his slippers, Cayetano wondered why the man trusted him, why he thought that he, Cayetano, would use the money, a small fortune now that the dollar was through the roof, in search of Bracamonte. The truth was that he could decide to forget about the doctor, the poet, and whatever else, and disappear in Mexico City. They'd never find him, not even with a fine-tooth comb.

"I already told you: simple poet's instinct," he intuited gravely, now behind the bar, still dressed up as Whitman. "Would you care for a Coquetelón?"

"A what?" the Cossack asked.

"A Coquetelón, a drink I invented years ago." He took out some bottles and a pair of glasses, and began to mix. "One part French Cognac, another part Angers Cointreau, and two parts orange juice. It's good enough to make you suck on your mustache, which, in your case, can be taken literally. Let's toast to our success, my Caribbean Maigret!"

Oh, Maligna. By now you've likely found the
   letter,
wept with rage,
and insulted my mother's memory
calling her a rotten dog and mother of dogs

> —from "The Widow's Tango"

W*here could she be, Josie Bliss, the furious one, the malignant
one, the Burmese panther who liberated me from the demure
and guilty sex I practiced as a student between the damp, icy sheets
of winter nights in Santiago, and who brought me to the feverish
physical combat of Rangoon? Never before had I held such a
lascivious, wise, and uninhibited woman in my arms. More than a
body, Josie Bliss was a lightning bolt, a goddess with blue hair and
long, fine limbs, with dark nipples and narrow hips, the owner of
penetrating and mysterious eyes. I met her after a deluge that
whipped through Rangoon one day and flooded the house I rented by
the sea, on a street called Probolingo. She was a beauty with drops of*

Asian blood evident in her face, a relatively pure Burmese woman, if there can be such a thing as pure Burmese in that nation of streets crammed with mestizos wrapped in captivating aromas and attire, and flanked with stalls of Indians as thin as needles exhibiting their combs, silks, and spices, geese awaiting sacrifice in bamboo cages, and prehistoric-seeming fish and their accompanying swirl of flies.

Water still dripped from the roof's gutters when Josie Bliss appeared at my house. She came on the recommendation of her brother, a young and inexperienced doctor who had not been able to pacify my stomach pains or ease the fever that had racked me since my arrival in Rangoon. She entered my room, as silent as a shadow, when I, in my mosquito net, had resigned myself to hearing nothing but the approaching footsteps of death.

"I'm here for whatever you desire," she said in languid English, with a girlish, caressing voice, and after resting her palm on my sweaty, burning forehead, she began to prepare a potion that saved my life.

During those first days, she dressed like an Englishwoman, but she soon abandoned the European style of dress for a sarong of diaphanous white silk that made her resemble a floating fairy. She was naked beneath it, as I discovered the day I took her to my bed. She laughed as though her mustard-colored body belonged to another woman and she were witnessing the act from a theater balcony. Josie Bliss gave me pleasures beyond the imagination for a melancholy young man from the rainy south, from the desolate streets of Santiago: she smiled as she offered me her sex, damp, aromatic, cracked open like a ripe fig; she swayed her breasts over my thirsty mouth like clusters of grapes. But she never let me kiss her, never allowed my lips to land on hers, or my tongue to rove between the rows of her teeth or explore the treasure trove of her mouth. I recall the night she told me I could use her body, enter its round, narrow boundaries as much *as I liked or let off steam between her lips if it pleased me, but that I should not try to kiss her on the mouth.*

Soon, Josie Bliss began to walk naked around the house. She brought me breakfast in bed that way, and ironed my shirts and ties, cleaned the floors, brought me a cup of tea at the end of my day. And she let me make love to her anywhere: while she prepared lunch by the stove, when she was picking my socks up from the floor, as she polished my white boots. She made me love her night and day, every day, every week. She was obsessed with one thing: keeping me satisfied and exhausted so it wouldn't occur to me to be unfaithful. She wanted me to quench myself between her thighs and her thighs only, never taking my thirst anywhere else. That's why she started to come to the consulate office unannounced to inspect my letters, destroy the ones that might contain amorous messages, smell my suits, and examine my back in search of scratches left there by another lover. At night, she stood at the window, motionless as a stone, watching for my return. She embraced me, full of impatience, stripped off my clothes, and then massaged me from head to toe with a milky, tepid, aromatic cream. After a while, she'd mount me to make sure that I hadn't been with someone else. But her mouth remained an impregnable fortress.

One night, I was woken by the creak of floorboards and saw her walking, circling the mosquito net. She was naked. Her body was coated in coconut oil, and her skin glowed like that of a Tantric god. She held a long, sharp dagger in her fist. I still recall the elusive shine of the blade, her agitated breath, the wild beating of my heart, the terror that numbed my limbs, my mouth as dry as if I were crossing the Atacama Desert.

"I know you're awake," she murmured as I pretended to sleep in my barricade of shadows. The steel blade shook in her hand. My body began to sweat with fear. Her eyes gleamed with jealousy and mad-

ness in the dark night of the room. "I'll kill you while you sleep. You'll never betray me if you're dead."

I fled the next day, in the early morning, to Ceylon, where I took a consul post secretly negotiated for me by a friend from the State Department. But the malignant woman lost no time in arriving there with the records and clothes I'd abandoned in my escape. She stalked outside of my house. Knife in hand, she harassed any woman who tried to approach my door. I had to flee again. Far away. To a place where she wouldn't ever be able to find me.

I still remember the last time I saw her. It was a suffocating morning at the port. The waters exhaled a vapor that smelled of logs and putrefied bodies, of gasoline and rotting food, cut through by the scent of spices. I was about to board the vessel that would save me from Josie Bliss when I realized with a shudder that she was waiting, purse in hand, in the middle of the gangway to the ship. I had no choice but to keep approaching in the queue of passengers, until the furious woman stood directly in my path. I stopped, sweating, terrified, having glimpsed the tip of a dagger shining eagerly at the edge of her purse. My heart leaped to my mouth, my surroundings became hazy and unsteady, and suddenly I saw Josie Bliss stabbing my chest with fury, each stab an ember biting at my flesh as blood poured out, dark and thick, staining my white shirt and suit and the old planks of the gangway, making me lose my balance and fall into the river. That vision took an eternity to dissipate, a product of my unfettered imagination and the water's pestilence, because in truth Josie Bliss had not made a single move. She simply stood in front of me, as if petrified, crying without words, reduced to a nuisance in the way of other passengers. As we met, she kissed my forehead, delicately, and then her kisses descended over my nose, chin, and chest, slipping down the length of my immaculate ironed suit, along my body, until she reached my freshly polished white boots. She remained there on *bended knee, prostrated before me, embracing my feet as if I were a god freshly arrived from heaven. Gulls cawed over us, flying in circles, and a ship's whistle rent the sky. When Josie Bliss lifted her beautiful face up from the ground, I saw something painful and indignant that I'll never forget: her cheeks, forehead, and nose were completely smeared with the polish of my boots. She cried in silence, distraught and tremulous, as pale as a sick ghost.*

"Don't go, please," she implored me, on her knees, on the swaying gangway.

"I'd stay for you," I remember telling her. The queue waited mutely behind me.

"Then why are you leaving, Pablo, if you'd stay for me?"

"I'd stay for you, Josie. But if I stay, I'll never become the poet I long to be one day," I replied, before moving her aside with a gentle yet decisive gesture, continuing up the gangway with my wooden suitcase onto the ship crowded with passengers and animals.

That was the last time I saw Josie Bliss.

10

That night, when Cayetano Brulé returned to his rented home in the Marina Mercante neighborhood, on San Juan de Dios Hill, he found his wife packing a suitcase in the bedroom.

"What's going on, Ángela?" he asked. "Weren't you going to stay in Santiago a few more days?"

It was almost ten o'clock, and mist had enfolded the city. After the conversation with the poet, Cayetano had confirmed his plane ticket and his hotel in Mexico City, and later, on a barstool at Antiguo Bar Inglés, armed with a pisco sour, he'd whiled away the time watching domino players assault the tables with their game pieces. Nevertheless, he did not expect to find his wife home, already repacking a suitcase no less.

"I'm leaving for Havana," she replied.

"Havana?"

"You heard me. For three months."

The news startled him and made him envious. He saw himself strolling through Old Havana, listening to the din of voices and music that erupted from tenement buildings until dawn, spying shaded interiors of houses through open windows while people lazed in doorways on warm nights, redolent of rum and sweat. He knew that his wife was politically radical, and that she supported Allende's government, but he would never have imagined that she could leave the country at such a decisive time, when the situation was "so complex," in the words of Commander Camilo Prendes. And she was leaving for three months. He felt disappointed, threatened, and betrayed, despite the fact that he himself was also preparing for a trip.

"Can you say what you're going to do there? Chile is falling apart, and you're wandering off to the Caribbean . . ."

Ángela leaned all her weight on the suitcase, which refused to close, and said, "It's a political mission."

"Political?"

"Right." She stared at him defiantly.

"What are you going to do?"

"I'm going to prepare for what's coming. I'm going to Punto Cero."

He sat down on the edge of the bed, tense and incredulous. Punto Cero was the military base where the Cuban government trained guerrilla fighters from all over the world. A shot rang out in the distance.

"Are you crazy? You're tired of inspecting factories, so now you're becoming a guerrilla?" he protested. "Are we that bad off? Do you really think the Chilean military is some kind of operetta, like Batista's? This isn't the kind of army you can beat with three hundred bearded guys with guns and rifles. It's irresponsible."

"Call it what you want, but that's where I'm going. This government is going to be overthrown if we don't defend it with weapons. The right is conspiring with Nixon and the military."

"What about that 'No to Civil War' slogan your party keeps proclaiming?"

"There won't be civil war if the enemy sees we're prepared to win it. That's precisely what the good old boys in the Party don't understand."

He had to admit that his wife wasn't the only one who thought this way. It was rumored that members of the Socialist Party, MAPU, MIR, and even the Christian Left and the Revolutionary Radical Youth, who had been moderate until recently, were now traveling to Havana for crash courses in military training. They were taught to shoot guns, leap over obstacles, climb ropes, make Molotov cocktails, and employ various tactics for attack and withdrawal, and then they took off from José Martí Airport on flights to Mexico City or Prague, taking long and winding routes back to their country. Punto Cero, at the outskirts of the capital, was one of the most prestigious and famous centers because its star instructor was the legendary Benigno, a commander who'd fought with Che Guevara in the mountains of Bolivia, and who had miraculously survived the siege carried out by Bolivian and American troops. And now it seemed that the communists, who until recently had faithfully defended the pacifist route to socialism that President Allende promoted, were also marching to Havana, only to return a few months later dressed in berets, olive-green jackets, and tall boots, with Caribbean accents, wild gesticulations, and cigars hanging from their mouths, as though they were the very commander in chief? As if all revolutionaries were required to become caricatures of Fidel Castro. These youths would return obsessed with iron and revolutionary theory, with the versatility of AK-47s, and the history of the Rebel Army, casting aside the Chilean political tradition and prepared to impose socialism with cries of "Homeland or death." And now his wife was involved with all this . . .

"I thought you'd talk to me before making such a significant decision," he said, smoothing his mustache. He didn't hide the tremor in his voice.

Ángela crossed the room with her hands on her hips and paused in front of the window. Behind her, the city seemed less solid and real to Cayetano.

"Our relationship can't be fixed," Ángela said coldly. "This separation will be good for us. Perhaps it would be best if you left Chile, where you've never made a place for yourself, and instead of returning to Miami, go back to your island to join the revolution. Here and in the United States you'll always be a foreigner. There's nothing worse than having no nation to call home."

"You know, this is too much. Now you not only don't know what's good for you, but you don't know what's good for me—or for the rest of the world," he replied, stung. He was irritated by his wife's impetuous vehemence, her tendency to make decisions hastily.

"It's better to have a mediocre time in your own country than a good time in a foreign one."

"Ángela, don't try to run my life, especially not now."

"At least I'm honest."

"You're accustomed to making decisions that affect the lives of others—in this case, mine."

"It's just not working between us, Cayetano. Don't kid yourself. What do you want me to say? Does my frankness bother you?"

"I thank you for it. And as far as it not working between us, there's no need for you to remind me. That's why I don't make a fuss when you leave the house for several days at a time. You live your life, I live mine."

"I'll have you know, darling, that I'm out there doing political work, not having love affairs. Let's be clear about that," she shouted, impassioned.

"I couldn't care less what you're doing, but don't even think of sending me off to Havana. If our marriage is completely broken, then I'll decide what I do and where the hell I go."

He had let himself be seduced by her words before. As a result he'd ended up in this very Valparaíso house. Before that, he was living tranquilly in Hialeah, which, if it wasn't Havana, at least had a climate and fauna similar to Cuba's that inspired in him a perpetual nostalgia for the island. It was strange. Cubans loved their island, but from a distance, while Chileans suffered in their own country but refused to leave it or change for anything in the world. And since he'd fallen in love with Ángela in the United States and become convinced it would be a good idea to participate in Allende's revolutionary process, he'd followed her to Chile, in March of 1971. At that time, the revolution was running smoothly, Chileans were full of hope, the world celebrated their government's efforts, while he himself enjoyed the enthusiasm that had swept the nation and heralded a new beginning. He wasn't acquainted with the socialism of the island, and in Florida he'd become accustomed to enjoying Cuban culture and character through newspapers and radio stations run by exiles, making up for his lack of actual Cuban experiences with the pranks that memory can play. He wasn't all that familiar with the tropical revolution that Ángela supported so enthusiastically from a distance, and now he was in a nation that wasn't his own, in which he'd arrived through a curious mix of love and politics. Chile was diametrically opposed to his native island, with winters that cracked the lips and presaged the end of the world; with its profoundly grave and solemn people, so far from the whimsical irreverence of the Caribbean; with an ethic of work and sacrifice unheard of on Cuba, the island of the never-ending party. In the Southern Cone, he concluded sadly, life was taken as seriously as in Frederick the Great's Prussia. No, he wouldn't take his wife's advice again. She might be very refined and delicate, conscious of the injustices and inequities of life, a graduate of La Maisonette and gringo colleges, an experienced skier and equestrian, the daughter of a family with land in Colchagua and company stocks, but he would not obey her. He was done with being a sheep, bowing down to a woman who lived off an allowance from her capitalist father but at the same time had no qualms about backing the expropriation of his properties. He'd never again take her advice; it had brought him only misfortune. From now on he'd do whatever called to him.

"You should go to Cuba, live there, soak up the revolution," Ángela insisted. The wooden floorboards creaked under her moccasins. Next to the still-open suitcase lay a bottle of Chanel No. 5, and a silk Hermès scarf poked out between the zippers.

"What you're saying shows how much you don't know me. What I long for most is independence, for God's sake, to be the way I was in Hialeah and Cayo Hueso. Here I can't even get a damn job."

"I've already told you, something could show up any moment—"

"That's ancient history. It's June of 1973 and I'm still waiting, driving the car your daddy gave you, in the house he pays for, with both of us putting food on the table from his wallet. That dependence is what killed our love."

"Killed, you said?"

"Yes, killed."

"So you're throwing away what we had."

"You threw it away already."

"I'm not going to argue with you over nonsense," she retorted as she tried yet again, and without success, to stuff the Hermès scarf into a corner of the suitcase. "I'm leaving for Cuba tonight, and that's it. Better that we talk about all this when I return. This is no time for petit bourgeois arguments, Cayetano. It's the moment of truth!"

$$\sim 11 \sim$$

He heard the breaking news flash at Alí Babá, on Radio Magallanes, and heard the musical gunshots in the background. The reporter spoke from the center of the capital, where the Tacna Regiment had risen up against Salvador Allende's government and was advancing toward the presidential palace, La Moneda. The attempted coup came live and direct over the radio, like in the American movies, turning the country into a passive spectator. Seated next to the window, as though refusing to admit the danger that was taking place outside, Cayetano drank his steaming cup of coffee and waited for the poet to walk down Collado Way toward his house, so that he could say good-bye.

"The rebel is a certain Colonel Souper," Hadad commented, drying his hands on his apron. "Now everything is really going to shit."

The reporters shouted over the fray to make themselves heard, describing the tank movement of that primary Chilean regiment as it moved into Santiago toward La Moneda. Another journalist called on the people to remain calm in their factories, rural towns, ports, offices, and universities. President Allende, another reporter said from a mobile post in Barrio Alto, had left his residence on Tomás Moro Street, and was advancing toward La Moneda as quickly as he could, with his bodyguards in a caravan of blue Fiat 125S. He planned to stop the coup.

"What about the military men on Allende's side?" Cayetano asked Hadad, who was gazing pensively through the window at the Mauri Theater, where stray dogs were resting. Collado lay before them, dirty and deserted. "Because if the president himself has to go out to face traitors in this country, then we really are screwed, my friend."

"It seems that not all the military squadrons are backing Souper," Hadad said.

Cayetano lit a cigarette. "Is that right? How do you know?"

Outside, life continued as though nothing had changed, he thought, worried, exhaling a voluminous column of smoke. That is to say, life continued mutely, without echoes or shrillness, without impassioned people coming out to protest what was happening in Santiago. A thick mist began to obscure the city, and to Cayetano it seemed a terrible omen. He felt a screw come loose in his soul. Where was his wife now? In some safe house in Santiago, prepared to take up arms for her government, or in the sticky heat of Havana already, in an olive-green uniform, crawling through mud with a Kalashnikov slung over her shoulder?

A communiqué from the party committee of Unidad Popular announced that the government would shortly give instructions for facing down the coup's perpetrators, and that for the moment Chileans should stay alert and ready for war in their schools and workplaces. According to the journalists, Allende was still heading downtown through morning traffic, on an interminable, winding journey, after which he would address the nation. What use was this call for calm to an unemployed foreigner like him? Cayetano wondered. Should he run off to the Hucke factory, where he'd stood guard a few nights earlier, and place himself at the disposal of Commander Camilo Prendes? Then what? Go out and face down armed soldiers, armored tanks, and the officials who'd been conspiring against democracy since Allende had arrived at La Moneda, if Ángela was to be believed? Face them with what? With the bamboo cane he'd been offered at Hucke, or with slingshots, stones, and nunchucks?

Two trucks passed down Alemania Avenue, carrying workers waving red and green flags, sympathizers with the popular government who seemed in a hurry to get somewhere. In Collado Way, however, the dogs were still curled up under the theater marquee, and there were no signs of the poet. Maybe he was still in the hospital? Would the doctors attend to him this week, or would the attempted coup distract them? He felt impotent. The situation scared him: a rebel colonel in the capital, Ángela about to leave for Cuba, their marriage on the rocks, the poet sick, and him charged with the mission of finding the only doctor who could save him. He feared that sedition was spreading through the country like the malignant cells in the poet's body.

He had no choice but to stay in Alí Babá, with the disheartening sense that he was a mere spectator. His wife was right. Being a foreigner was the worst. Better to suffer misfortune in your homeland than to have only a passable time overseas. He ordered another coffee from Hadad, and as the man filled the small coffeemaker with grounds and grumbled to himself behind the bar, a new radio dispatch began. This time, the reporter announced, in a hoarse, truculent voice like those sometimes heard on afternoon radio theater, that now General Carlos Prats, the army chief, was marching, pistol in hand, into the center of the capital to quash the rebellion. Whom would the rest of the armed forces support? the alarmed journalist asked himself amid shouts and blaring horns. Three coffees later, the tension waned. Souper surrendered, the radio now announced. Order and tranquillity were restored, the pro-government station celebrated Prats as a hero, and it was said that Allende was back in his office at La Moneda, in command of the nation from Arica to Magallanes, including the Easter Islands and Robinson Crusoe Island. The leftist parties immediately called a rally in front of the presidential palace for that afternoon, and "La Batea," the catchy song by the band Quilapayún, began to cheer up the day with its Caribbean rhythm. People walked on Alemania Avenue once more, cars and buses reappeared, Alí Babá filled up with happy patrons, and the city was bursting with life.

According to the people who sat at the soda fountain, drinking the smelly wine Hadad diluted with water every night, Allende had ordered the armed forces to crush the uprising and defend democracy. If they didn't, he'd made it clear from the radio in his Fiat 125, he'd do it himself with gun in hand and the backing of both his bodyguards and the people, and the men in uniforms would be responsible in the eyes of history for whatever happened. Faced with this threat, even the generals who had conspired against Allende stepped up to support him, and the loyal Prats was able to reach the street and, with his back covered, disarm the insubordinates. The story quickly spun into a legend: alone and with his gun at the ready, the general stopped the deafening advance of rebel tanks, while the people chanted his name from the sidewalks. Souper had stuck his head out of the top of his tank like a rat peering from its lair, and the crowd had frantically applauded the victory of democracy.

That night, all the plazas of Chile filled with rallies organized by the Single Center for Chilean Workers and Unidad Popular. In Santiago, thousands of citizens celebrated in front of La Moneda, where Salvador Allende stood on a balcony and thanked Prats, the armed forces, and the people themselves for their defense of the Constitution. In Valparaíso, Cayetano joined the festivities in the Plaza del Pueblo, where he danced cumbias and boleros with a young woman who had black curly hair, eyes the color of olives, and *café con leche* skin, and wore an amaranth-colored blouse, baring large, straight teeth when she smiled. He returned home at dawn, having drunk pisco sours with the girl at a restaurant called Jota Cruz, which was crammed with customers eating *chorrillana* over french fries, drinking beer and wine, and belting out "Bandera Rossa" and "La Internacional."

He was reading Maigret alone in his bedroom when the phone rang.

"Don't ask where I'm calling from," his wife said in a tone that sounded as if she were calling from another world. "This was only a practice coup, a test run. Now they know the people don't have weapons with which to defend themselves. They've got us now. Don't tell me you were one of those fools who went out to celebrate?"

~ *12* ~

The Mexico City sky was dense and gray, like the warships docked at the Valparaíso port, Cayetano Brulé thought. He rode in the backseat of a green taxi known as a "crocodile," which was taking him from the airport to his hotel in Zona Rosa. The Chrysler made its way slowly through traffic thick with buses, trucks, taxis, motorcycles, and the shouting street vendors flooding the city's central arteries, hawking needles, combs, drinks, and newspapers. New buildings of concrete and glass replaced mansions with pillars, balconies, and gardens, changing the character of the streets. Enormous billboards hid undeveloped areas studded with shabby hovels, while numerous Cadillacs with chrome accents and uniformed chauffeurs revealed the fortunes being made in Mexico. An enormous number of restaurants, with tables out on the sidewalk, for the benefit of the cheerful, boisterous crowds enjoying the benign climate of the capital, infected the city with an optimism born of the belief that the path of progress had been found. Cayetano sadly thought of the city of Santiago, which at this very moment was submerged in cold and darkness, the clamor of street chaos, and the threat of tear gas.

He still didn't understand the poet's need for discretion in searching for the man who could save his life. For a person who felt death close at hand, his reaction seemed inexplicable. Was it true that he was keeping his illness secret to keep from feeding the right's campaign against Allende? So many unanswered questions, he thought as he rolled down the window, inhaled the street's smell of gasoline and tar, and listened to the murmur of the motor and the entreaties of women running alongside the taxis, selling matches and candles. In all honesty, Neruda was an icon of the global left as an acclaimed poet, communist activist, and friend of Allende's. Was that why, despite the fact that Bracamonte was his last hope, he wouldn't look for him by crying out his name to the four winds?

Cayetano considered what he'd left behind: a sad, divided Chile, where food was scarce and uncertainty ruled; a Valparaíso lost every morning in a thick fog that erased outlines, softened echoes, and wrapped its inhabitants in sorrow. Though stifled, Colonel Souper's rebellion had had disastrous consequences for the government. A few days earlier, the wives of several generals had thrown corn at Prats at a public event and called him a faggot for failing to oppose communism. Discouraged by the campaign and the pressure, Prats had submitted his resignation to the president. Allende replaced him with a general who had little talent and poor oratory skills, a vulgar and affected man who, according to the constant commentaries of Bar Inglés's patrons, had at least one thing going for him: He respected the constitution to the letter. His name was Augusto Pinochet Ugarte.

What was the poet doing now? Cayetano Brulé wondered as he exited the taxi at the Savoy, in a beautiful neighborhood of two-story houses and tree-lined streets studded with restaurants, bars, cafés, bookstores, and galleries. At this very moment, he might be working on his memoirs or perhaps composing new poems, or running his hands across his collection of conches, immersed in his amphibian calm. After each session at Van Buren, he rested in bed for hours, quiet, without a spark in his eyes, dozing, trusting that the young Cuban would succeed in finding Bracamonte. Matilde probably came through periodically to tidy the books, costumes, furniture, and figurines brought all the way from France. The effort and detailed attention with which his wife organized these objects made the poet suspicious.

"I think that, more than organizing the things we've brought back to Chile, she's doing it for the museum they want to open after I die," he'd confided in the living room of La Sebastiana, just before Cayetano's departure.

"Your room, Mr. Brulé. Fourth floor," the receptionist told him as a bellhop took his suitcase.

The bed frame groaned pitifully when he sat down on it. He looked up Ángel Bracamonte in the phone book, and as he'd imagined, he found a long list of entries with that last name, but no Ángel. He wasn't daunted. He acted as though he were Maigret: The next day he'd visit the places where he could seek facts for his investigation: the Medical Association and the *Excelsior* newspaper.

It didn't take long to make both appointments by phone,

one with the public relations representative for the Medical Association, and the other with a manager at the paper. In both cases he introduced himself as a freelance journalist who wrote articles for the Chilean leftist magazine *Hoy*. And in both places they promised to welcome him with open arms. Salvador Allende and his government inspired sympathy in Mexico, where he was seen as a sign of hope on a continent riddled with corrupt politicians.

Then he called Laura Aréstegui in Valparaíso, promised to look for the books she'd requested, and assured her that Mexico City filled him with vitality and optimism.

"It won't be hard to reconstruct his time there," she said. She was in her office, trying to optimize the distribution of bread, meat, and oil in the port city's hills. This, when vegetables and eggs were also disappearing, not to mention chickens. "Neruda was friends there with the muralists David Alfaro Siqueiros and Diego Rivera, and in the 1940s he traveled to Cuba."

"To Cuba? Long before the revolution?"

"Even long before the *Granma*, the yacht Castro bought in Mexico to transport his tiny army to Cuba, set sail toward the island with its eighty-two voyagers, in 1956."

"In that case, my girl, the poet has always had a tremendous nose for politics."

"Don't kid yourself. There's a detail nobody wants to remember today."

"What do you mean?"

"In the forties, he admired Batista. In Havana he delivered an apologia in his honor, calling him the 'sublime son of Cuba.' At that time, Batista governed with the support of Cuban communists and the Soviet Union."

"Just a moment. Are we talking about Batista, Fulgencio Batista, the tyrant?" he asked, alarmed.

"One and the same. I guess that's why Fidel and Neruda can't stand each other. As the saying goes, they couldn't even swallow each other with codfish oil."

~ *13* ~

Cayetano ate coffee, tortillas, scrambled eggs, and beans for breakfast in his hotel room as he perused the newspaper. Later that morning, at around nine o'clock, he took a taxi to the Museum of Anthropology, following the express instructions of the poet, who had told him it was a must-see. The previous afternoon, the public relations representative at the Medical Association had confessed that she'd never heard of any Dr. Ángel Bracamonte, but that she was more than happy to assist Cayetano, and if he returned to her office the following afternoon, she would search the files for any more information. On his trip to Chapultepec Forest, he racked his brains but couldn't think of a single chapter in which Maigret visited a museum, not even the Louvre. It seemed that detectives did not usually interrupt their investigations to explore museums.

However, on arriving between those high walls, testimonies to pre-Columbian cultures, he found himself speechless, reduced to an uncomfortable insignificance, paralyzed in front of such marvels and shamed by his own triviality. The profusion of temples, sculptures, ceramics, and wrought gold and silver embarrassed him, not only for their richness, variety, and perfection, as well as the complexity of the societies they represented, but also because they showed him something that, as a Cuban, he'd never fully realized, because of the less developed cultures of his island's original peoples: The New World had existed millennia before the arrival of Christopher Columbus, and Tenochtitlán was a more advanced city when Cortés arrived than any European metropolis at the time. For the first time, he was clearly aware of the magnitude of disaster dealt to the indigenous people of the Americas by the invasion and domination of white men, whose blood, he could not deny as he glanced at himself in a windowpane, flowed copiously through his veins.

Suddenly, as he stared at two human hearts in the hands of a god carved into the center of a giant Aztec solar disk, he realized it was noon and he'd completely lost track of time. He rushed out to Reforma and flagged a cab to take him toward Zócalo. He struggled to catch his breath. He should try not to get worked up like this, he thought, alarmed by his shortness of breath; he should take Mexico City's elevation seriously, as it was more than two thousand meters. As he recovered his calm in the back of the taxi and tried to focus his thoughts, he had to admit that after this visit to the museum, he'd never again be the same Latin American as he'd been before. He could never forget the magnificence of this city's pre-Columbian era, or the oppressive, apocalyptic feeling that must have swept over the startled Aztecs when their emperor, Montezuma, first met that man with blond hair and white skin, Hernán Cortés, whom their ancestors had prophesied with precision. He, who felt proud of the legendary past of Havana and the vague origins of

Valparaíso, now understood that Mexicans, as a people, inhabited a realm unknown to him, rooted in millennial depths unimaginable to someone from an island that had barely five hundred years of recorded history. He lit a cigarette and watched the city and its inhabitants with new eyes, as though he could now see their ancestors as well walking through the translucent air of Tenochtitlán, traversing epochs, temples, and florid wars; he felt insignificant, and thought of calling the poet to tell him everything and ask how he was and how he had perceived Mexico when he had lived there. Had the poet had time to capture this sensibility, or had he spent his time consumed by his work at the consulate, poetic creation, love affairs, and remorse?

That very morning, as a breeze whispered in through the window, he had finished reading another detective novel, a very curious one. In the book, Maigret poured his memories out to Simenon. This original and engrossing approach, in which a fictional character addresses his flesh-and-blood author, had made him sympathize with Maigret, who resided in a Paris from the movies, where minor dangers lay in wait and colleagues were not always loyal. He also sympathized more now with Louise, his wife, who cooked his favorite dishes with care and devotion—scallops à la Florentine, duck in white wine sauce, and lamb shanks with lentils—while keeping his house clean and tidy. He was also entertained by the array of criminals that populated the book's pages, Simenon's gift for stirring one's sympathies for them, and the cozy bistros and bars where Maigret liked to drink Pernod and kill time, putting off his return home or the interrogation of a suspect as if for the express purpose of giving his literary father, Simenon, a chance to provide the novel with a few pages of reflection and psychological depth. Now, reading the Belgian and investigating in the real world, Cayetano felt he was grasping certain tricks used by crime novel writers to make their books more weighty and profound. Reading Simenon's novels, he had begun to envy Maigret's placid existence. Here was a guy who got up in the mornings without haste, and ate breakfast with his wife in an apartment with hardwood floors and old pictures on the walls, while outside the autumn rains, spurred by the wind, pattered against the windows. As if that weren't enough, the Eiffel Tower rose over many of the cobbled streets the detective roamed at a leisurely pace, its presence a pleasant and perpetual reminder of the city where he lived. He enjoyed reading such details, but he sensed that the lives of real investigators weren't as placid as Simenon portrayed them to be. That afternoon, after lunch and a small glass of tequila, he would start reading another of the Belgian's books. This time he'd approach it as a master class for a novice detective like himself. At least literature is good for something, he thought with pleasure, beyond mere entertainment.

Mónica Salvat was waiting for him in an office rented by the Medical Association on the fifth floor of a decrepit building. She was young, with black hair and eyes, and a melodious voice. She was just shy of beautiful. However, there was one thing she had plenty of that Ángela had lost a long time ago: tenderness. In Florida, he had first fallen in love with his wife's vivacious eyes, alternately languid and decisive; her voice, husky yet warm; her resplendent hair; but, above all, he'd been fascinated by her tenderness. It had erased any qualms he had about leaving the United States and heading to the southern end of the earth, guided by the sudden love she had inspired. When had Ángela lost her tenderness? What mistakes had he made that stripped it away from her? And through which crack in his soul had his passion for Ángela drained away?

"I've been examining the files, and I'm sorry to tell you that I haven't found a thing on Dr. Bracamonte," Mónica Salvat said, pulling him suddenly from his thoughts. "Would you like coffee?"

When she left the office to prepare it, he took advantage of the moment to examine the yellowing wallpaper, the dusty blinds, and the old Olivetti she wrote on. The office seemed sad and soulless, the dead space of a bureaucrat bored by her own existence. Down on Insurgentes, the traffic was slow and thick, and the signs on buses announced neighborhoods he knew nothing about. Mónica returned with a tray that held two cups and a tin sugar bowl, and he was cheered by the slight sway of her hips, which reminded him of Cuban women, and of course the aroma of the coffee, which he hoped would be superior to that unpalatable brew served by Chileans.

"The problem is that the files are completely disorganized," Mónica said as she held the tray toward him. "When you look for something, you never find it."

"In that case, what do you suggest?" He took a cup, added three spoonfuls of sugar, and stirred, looking skeptically at the reality of watered-down coffee. "I need to see Dr. Bracamonte. I came all the way to Mexico to speak with him."

"I don't know what to tell you." She sipped her coffee, which she took without sugar, another dismal omen. "But you're not Chilean, are you? You don't speak like a Chilean."

"I live in Chile, but I'm from Cuba."

They began to talk about how far Chile was from Cuba, and how different it was from Cuba and Mexico. They also spoke of Allende, the Unidad Popular, the Chilean revolution, and

Nixon's steely opposition to the South American nation. When she asked what would become of the so-called Chilean path to socialism, he was stumped. Would it turn into a Cuban-style socialist state, or would there be a different model? Cayetano said he didn't know, and that was true. Who did know? Not even Allende himself, he said. But it was nothing to get overly upset about; people behave as though they knew where life was headed, but in the end it was anyone's guess. Life wasn't only a parade of disguises, he added, plagiarizing the poet for a metaphor that clearly pleased Mónica, but also a lottery that dealt new tickets every morning. In reality, life was like Valparaíso. Sometimes you were up high, other times low, but in an instant everything could change. An unexpected staircase was enough to climb the heights, while a single trip over a stone could send you crashing downhill, just like the bones that had rolled from the graveyard to the docks. Nothing in our lives was forever, he said, nothing, except, of course, for death, he corrected himself, and then he tried the coffee, which was disastrous.

"I have to find Dr. Bracamonte. It's a matter of life and death," he insisted gravely, placing the cup back on the tray. "He researched cures for cancer in plants from Chiapas. Only you can help me."

"We should try another approach."

"What do you mean?"

"In addition to poring through files, it would be helpful to find a doctor who practiced in those days. Someone must remember Bracamonte. Over the next few days, I can make some calls."

"Over the next few days, you say? I don't have that kind of time, Mónica. That is to say, the ill person . . . you understand."

"I do," she said, and lowered her gaze. "Four years ago, that same illness took my mother. It dried her up until she was left with nothing but pain and bones. My mother was a saint, and, poor thing, what she suffered."

"I'm truly sorry, Mónica." He paused, stroked his mustache, and waited for the woman to regain her calm. "Could you help me as soon as possible?"

"Tomorrow you can look through the records yourself. My boss won't be here, so you can peruse them freely," she added softly, her eyes damp.

"And you'll ask around among retired doctors?"

"Don't worry about that."

"And you'll definitely let me into the records?"

Mónica let out a sigh, surprised at her own sudden willingness to comply with this stranger. "But don't get your hopes up," she added. "There's terrible chaos in there, and not all doctors register with the association. But, as my mother would say, may she rest in peace, there's no worse step than the one you don't take."

≈ 14 ≈

It didn't take him long to see how hard it would be to find anything on Bracamonte in that dim, windowless room, which stored not only dusty files but also teleprinter rolls, accounting books, and discarded furniture. The dry air irritated his throat and forced him to retreat from the battlefield and return to Mónica's office.

"If the doctor was around forty years old in the 1940s, then he should be about seventy today," she calculated. "Nobody lasts that long in our city. Did you find anything?"

"Nothing." He snorted in frustration and sat down across from the secretary. "Didn't you say you'd consult with some doctors he might have worked with?"

"I'LL DO IT THIS AFTERNOON, as soon as I finish some urgent business, Mr. Brulé. I'm being pressed by a lawyer called Hugo Bertolotto, who's determined to update even the General

Archive of Simancas. But to return to your matter, there's something that worries me."

"What?"

"If you're looking for a supposedly well-known doctor, and the name doesn't ring a bell to me or anyone else in this office, it can only mean . . ."

"That the doctor is dead?"

"Or that he simply never registered as a doctor with the association."

"Anything else?"

"That his research never succeeded, and that's why no one's heard of him."

"A charlatan?" he asked, discouraged. If that was true, the poet would have no cure and was wasting his time with this quasi–detective search.

"Maybe. Didn't you say he cured cancer?"

"So I've been told."

"Well, if he was a doctor and that was his work, it's strange that no one remembers him, don't you think?"

He imagined the poet seated in his armchair, La Nube, among books and newspapers, trying to compose his memoirs, placing his hopes in what he, Cayetano, was now doing in Mexico. The poet hated seeing himself as a fragile, sick old man, an impotent witness to how reactionaries cornered his friend Allende's government, and how illness invaded his body. First the French doctors' treatment had failed, then the Soviet specialists' attempt, and here, though he didn't know it yet, was the collapse of his final hope, which he'd placed in a Cuban doctor who had told Neruda decades before that he could conquer cancer with medicinal plants.

"Maybe Bracamonte left Mexico City a long time ago, and

that's why no one remembers him," he mumbled. "He could be in a Yucatecan town, or perhaps in the United States, like so many others."

"Let's not jump the gun here," Mónica said. "Are you sure he was Cuban?"

He left the office with the secretary's phone number in his pocket and an agreement to have dinner together the following night in a restaurant downtown. He liked the woman, her delicacy, which rose effortlessly from her gestures, from her gaze, and from within her. Being a detective wasn't so easy, after all, he thought. Maigret sometimes took days to fully launch his investigations. But he shouldn't place too much trust in the fictional detective. Even if he braved the underworld and greased his relationships with informants, Maigret could never accomplish anything in a region as chaotic, improvised, and unpredictable as Latin America. Just like the gentleman Dupin and Sherlock Holmes, Maigret could investigate his heart out in stable and organized nations like the United States and France, where a rational philosophy reigned over the people, rules and clear laws prevailed, logic shaped daily life, and solid, prestigious institutions and an efficient police force worked to ensure respect for the law. On the other hand, in Latin America—where improvisation, randomness, corruption, and venality were the order of the day—everything was possible. In a place where a communist nation coexisted with modern capitalist cities, feudally exploitative if not enslaving plantations, and jungles where history had frozen in the times of the cavemen, European detectives weren't worth a thing. It was that brutally simple. In those Amazonian, Andean, or Caribbean worlds, detectives such as Dupin, Holmes, or Poirot would find their dazzling deductive powers failing to clear matters up. The crux of the problem was that the North's logic simply didn't apply in Latin America. Nor would Miss Marple, Marlowe, or Sam Spade find any success.

Detectives are like wine, Cayetano thought, like wine, rum, tequila or beer, children of their own land and climate, and anyone who forgot this would inevitably fail. Could anyone imagine Philip Marlowe in front of the cathedral in Havana? The two o'clock sun would burn his skin, and he'd be stripped of his hat and raincoat without realizing it. Or Miss Marple, walking with the slow, distinguished pace of an elderly lady, through downtown Lima? She'd get drunk off the first ceviche she tried, and sinister cabdrivers would stray from their route to the airport to a hovel where delinquents crouched in wait. They wouldn't even find her well-crafted dentures. And how about the affected Hercule Poirot crossing Cardonal Market in Valparaíso with his tight rump and white-gloved hands? They'd steal his walking stick, his pocket watch with its gold chain, and even his bowler hat. People would mock them to their face, stray dogs would chase them with their fangs bared, and street kids would throw rocks at them without mercy. He now began to suspect that Simenon's novels, while pleasant and entertaining, could not make him a detective in the world south of the Rio Grande. The poet was wrong. A Maigret was incapable of taming the bursting, capacious reality of Latin America. It would be like telling Bienvenido Granda to sing Franz Schubert's *Lieder* in the bars of Managua or Tegucigalpa instead of boleros, or making Celia Cruz imitate María Callas at a jam session on Eighth Street. The tangled files of the Mexican Medical Association alone would pose an insurmountable, maddening challenge to the structured brains of Holmes, Maigret, and Marlowe, accustomed as they were to scrupulously perusing organized files in the silent amplitude of rooms in prestigious institutions, ensconced in stately buildings with parquet floors, chandeliers, and sumptuous drapes.

He took a crocodile taxi toward the *Excelsior*. At least he'd get to have dinner with Mónica Salvat. Hopefully, he'd find an experienced journalist and functional filing system at the newspaper, he thought as he passed Chapultepec Forest, nineteenth-century façades, and the scaffolding of buildings under construction. Mexico City teemed. It seemed to be dying and being born at the same time, as though it lamented the loss of tranquility and ancient edifices, and yet celebrated modernity, longed for it. Street vendors filled the central streets, where people in modern dress walked, as did women in indigenous clothing and men in jeans and hats, like extras from a Luis Aguilar film. From where he sat, behind the Chrysler's window, the city seemed to break apart into scenes both modern and traditional, as contradictory as disparate fragments. He speculated that Bracamonte could well be strolling with his miraculous concoctions through that motley Mexico City throng, although he could also be walking around Havana with his chest covered in revolutionary medals. Or perhaps he lived on a beach with turquoise water in Quintana Roo, in a cabin sheltered by the shade of many trees, like the cabin of which he and Ángela had dreamed when they were still in love. The truth was, Bracamonte could be wandering anywhere and at the same time nowhere. He might even be dead, he thought as the taxi turned around Zócalo, with its giant Mexican flag.

~ *15* ~

Á ngel Bracamonte, oncologist?" Luis Cervantes asked with a frown.

The reporter had thick ears and lips, and rosy cheeks and nose, like a rubber doll. That is, a sixty-year-old doll that typed in an office with stained walls, dirty windows, and faded curtains.

"In the forties. Mexico City. He was researching the medicinal properties of plants in Chiapas. He must have been well-known," Cayetano Brulé added, to jog his memory.

"Mexican?"

"A semi-Mexican Cuban."

Cervantes ran his hands over his typewriter. He looked uncertain. Despite his prodigious memory, he remembered no one with that name. Not all doctors were celebrities in Mexico, as they could be elsewhere, Cayetano thought. In Mexico there were even some who lived precariously close to impoverished Zócalo, especially those who, loyal to their Hippocratic oath,

devoted themselves to serving the poor in marginalized neighborhoods, ministering to patients who might never have felt the
cold pressure of a stethoscope on their chest.

"And you'll have to forgive me," Cervantes said, "but I doubt
this person was a doctor if he specialized in medicinal plants.
It sounds more like the work of shamans or witch doctors than
a gentleman who'd invested years at the university. Are you
sure he was a doctor?"

In fact, he had not considered this possibility. He had
turned certain things over many times in his mind, and considered the options, but had not imagined that the poet could have
mistaken an herbalist for a doctor thirty years ago. But why
not? When he couldn't even remember Ángel Bracamonte's
second last name. Of course, the poet was not a man concerned with practical details; he cared a great deal about poetic
details, but these were another matter altogether. Cayetano
supposed that the reporter had no intention of helping him. In
Mexico, Mónica had warned him, a yes often meant no, and a
no often meant "depends." Unlike the Medical Association secretary, the unobliging Cervantes seemed bothered by Cayetano's presence.

"To be perfectly frank," the journalist continued, "I've never
really liked Cubans, since one of them stole my girlfriend in
college."

"Then we're even. A Mexican took the love of my life in
Miami. That is, the woman I thought would be the love of my
life," Cayetano Brulé said, thinking fast, like Roy Rogers in the
comic books of his childhood. "But I don't resent Mexico for it.
Who knows, he may even have done me a favor."

The journalist gazed thoughtfully at the street, as though

watching his old girlfriend pass by the window. Cayetano wondered whether the man was right, and Ángel Bracamonte was no doctor, but rather someone who proclaimed his art to be a science, closer to the herbalists who hawked near the cathedral than to surgeons. Perhaps the illness was damaging the poet's memory. But it could also be a defense mechanism. If modern medicine could no longer save him, as the oncologists of Paris and Moscow had already made clear, then it was perfectly understandable that the poet would seek out a shaman in the hope of eluding death for a little while longer.

"Isn't there any way to find this guy?" he asked, picking up the thread of conversation. "I've been assigned to write about him for a Chilean newspaper."

"And those poor Chileans, with everything they're going through, have time to worry about some charlatan?"

"I ask you to consider one thing: Bracamonte's plants could save dying people in Chile."

"I'm sorry. Everything is possible, you never know," Cervantes acknowledged thoughtfully, as though Cayetano's words had moved him deeply. "I have an assistant who's quite bright and who may be able to help you. If we find anything, I'll let you know."

"I'd greatly appreciate your contacting me at my hotel, or through Mónica Salvat, of the Medical Association. Can I trust you?"

"Completely."

"Are you sure? Here people often say yes just to keep people calm."

"Where does that happen?"

"Here in Mexico, or so I've heard."

"Really. Well, that all depends, sir. In any case, you can count on me."

"I truly thank you. Many readers will feel their spirits lift when they find out Ángel Bracamonte is still alive."

"Don't worry, I'm on the case. But first, tell me this: How exactly did that compatriot of mine steal the love of your life?"

MARÍA ANTONIETA

16

What do you think about this?" asked Mónica Salvat.

In the din of Taquería El Encanto, in the Zona Rosa, they had just ordered Yucatecan *penachos* and three beverages each: tequila, sangria, and lemonade. A trio was playing a bolero for a table of outrageous, drunk North Americans in Hawaiian shirts who were roaring with laughter. Cayetano glanced at the newspaper clipping Mónica held. It was a typical photograph of diplomatic receptions, the kind that usually appeared in the social pages. In it, four men and three women smiled at the camera.

"Relatives of yours?" asked Cayetano. On the walk to the restaurant, Mónica had told him about her Russian immigrant mother, her Mexican father, and her upbringing in Coyoacán, near the house where Ramón Mercader had murdered Leon Trotsky with an ice pick.

"You see the man in the suit and bow tie?" she asked.

"Is that your father?"

"That's Ángel Bracamonte. At the home of the Cuban ambassador, October tenth, 1941."

Cayetano took a closer look at the clipping. He studied the features of the man at the center of the group, which dissolved into infinite dots as he raised the page toward his glasses. He made out a gaunt face, large and tired eyes, receding gray hair, and a thick mustache. This was the man the poet was looking for, he said to himself, trying to contain his excitement.

"Where did you find this?"

"Cervantes, the reporter, gave it to me. The text doesn't refer to Bracamonte as a doctor, and, what's worse, his name isn't in the association's register. Either he never joined, or he wasn't a doctor. But there you have it. He exists. He's not a phantom. Cervantes found this in the social pages of a magazine that came out around that time."

"Do I owe him anything?" he asked, without taking his eyes off Bracamonte's face.

"He'll be fine with a couple of books from the publisher Quimantú and a bottle of Chilean red wine."

"I'll send him all of that, don't worry. How did he find the photo?"

"Looking through the celebrations for the National Day of Cuba."

"And where is Bracamonte now?" He drained the glass of tequila, then drank the sangria so that the tequila wouldn't sting his insides. He felt like celebrating. This Mexican night was turning out to be perfect.

"We don't know. But at least you know the face of the man you're looking for." The trio was now singing "Nosotros." Mónica added, "And we know he may not have been a doctor."

Suddenly he was flooded with worry. If Bracamonte was

one of those charlatans who traveled around Latin America promising miracle cures, the poet would be devastated. A waiter refilled his tequila glass. "Do you know anything about the people around him?"

The women had Rita Hayworth hairstyles and gleamed in low-cut dresses. They seemed sure of themselves and their lives. The men were smiling, sporting dark suits, with a wineglass or Cuban cigar in hand. They were all older, except for the young woman next to Bracamonte.

"His daughter?" asked Cayetano.

"His wife. She must be about twenty years old there. She looks like his granddaughter. At this point she's probably in her fifties. Impossible to find her, since we don't know her maiden name. Your friend doesn't remember a Beatriz?"

"My friend knew the doctor, but I don't think he knew his wife."

Beatriz had light-colored hair, which she wore pulled back, and a melancholy gaze. She looked like a ballet dancer. She was by far the youngest and most beautiful member of the group, the least arrogant, and, judging by her jewelry, Cayetano thought, also the simplest.

"Did you take a good look at the caption?" asked Mónica.

"The gentlemen are identified by first and last name, the ladies only by first name. They're celebrating the National Day of Cuba."

"You missed that it also describes an upcoming dinner to benefit a foundation against cancer . . ."

"Then it must be him," Cayetano exclaimed, rereading the text. "This man has to be the Dr. Ángel Bracamonte I'm looking for! Mónica, you're a genius. Did you also find the phone number of the association?"

"I tried, but it no longer exists."

That news hit him like a bucket of ice-cold water. He returned to his tequila.

"Well, can't we find the other people in the photo?" he asked, with a resurgence of hope.

"They're dead. Except for the woman on the edge." Her finger landed on the photo. "She's the widow of Sebastián Alemán, the bald man on her right, a major stockholder in the biggest beer brewery in the country. She's still alive."

"So what are we waiting for to talk to her?"

"The hard part will be getting access. In this country, business tycoons are like Hollywood stars, Cayetano. They live behind huge walls, travel in cars with tinted windows, and are surrounded by bodyguards. But let's give it a try and see how it goes."

D on Pablo?"
   "Speaking."

"I'm calling you from Mexico City. Can you talk right
now?" Cayetano put Neruda's book down on the bed, an anthology of poems he'd borrowed from Laura Aréstegui. It lay
open to a page that began:

> *When you are old, my girl (as Ronsard has told you),*
> *you'll remember those verses I spoke.*
> *Your breasts will be sad from suckling your children,*
> *the final offspring of your empty life . . .*

"I'm in my chair, my Nube, young man. I just returned from my
treatments, wrung out like a rag. Your call woke me. Have you
found the man?"

"Almost, Don Pablo."

"What do you mean, 'almost'?"

"I mean, I don't know his whereabouts. But soon I'll be talking to someone who might know where he is."

"So you still don't know where he lives?"

"Nobody knows him. He isn't registered as a doctor. He may have gone abroad. Are you sure he was a doctor?"

Silence. A cough. Then the same tired voice.

"I thought he was. But now that I think about it, I don't know whether he was technically qualified in the eyes of the law. It's a good question, young man. . . ."

"Don't you think that, being Cuban, he might have gone to Havana, lured by the revolution?"

Another silence.

"We all feel drawn to the revolution at some point." He said this rather evasively. "But him . . . I don't know what to say. He also had a beautiful wife, much younger. You didn't happen to learn anything about her?"

"In a newspaper from the time when you were here, they appear together in a photo. Her name is Beatriz. You're right, an amazing woman, Don Pablo. What was her maiden name?"

"I don't remember. I met her as his wife. All I clearly remember is her face. She was from Germany. And incomparably beautiful. This is coming from someone who's always looked at women with great interest."

"And not only looked."

"And not only looked," the worn-out voice admitted, changing tone. "So as soon as you find the doctor, call me for your exact instructions. I repeat: don't even think of speaking to him before calling me. Don't go inside his house if we haven't talked. Promise me you'll do everything exactly as I say. That doctor is a capricious, reserved man. There's only one way to approach him, and I'll reveal it to you when the time comes."

He thought Don Pablo was being overly dramatic again, with all this mystery. He tried to calm him.

"Don't worry. I'll do as you say." Then he attempted to bring the poet back to reality. "How's your health?"

"Do you want the truth?"

He feigned composure. "Of course, Don Pablo."

Don Pablo was conclusive. "I can't be fixed."

"What?"

"Just that. The people around me, including my wife, want to make me believe I'll recover. They think I'm naive, that I don't know what's wrong with me. A look in the mirror each morning is enough to know the truth. Mirrors don't lie. Matilde says that it's a bone condition, but I know I'm screwed, Cayetano. There's no cure. Not for me, and not for Chile. Salvador suffers from a double cancer: one from reactionaries who won't let him build socialism democratically, and another from allies who want to impose socialism through armed force. His commitment to the people is to create socialism through peaceful means, but these people are going to screw him. It's sad to be an old man, and worse to be a sick old man in a sick country, Cayetano."

In the end, he thought, Don Pablo's dramatics were justified. His words were resonant with meaning, touching many layers at once. Those were his metaphors, the turns of phrase he said he'd learned from that bearded Whitman, or whatever the name was of that guy whose disguise he loved to wear. Cayetano had to respond with something, and he chose politics.

"Is there still a food shortage?"

"You think that sort of thing resolves itself from one day to the next?"

He felt clumsy and chastened.

"Of course not, Don Pablo."

"The lack of food and the black market are undermining the confidence of the middle class. You know that confidence can't last much longer. Nixon blocks us from selling copper abroad, and the right boycotts our economy from within. We're a silent Vietnam, Cayetano."

Perhaps it was the war reference that restored Cayetano's fighting spirit. He seized the opportunity. "We'll win this battle, Don Pablo. I'm going to find the doctor. Now you rest, and I'll have news for you soon. Have faith, Don Pablo, have faith."

$\operatorname{\underset{\sim}{\mathcal{18}}\underset{\sim}{}}$

"Á ngel Bracamonte died ages ago," said the elderly lady in the wheelchair.

Cayetano Brulé was crushed, since he'd hoped the distinguished millionaire would guide him to the Cuban who held the poet's cure. The years may have perforated Sarah Middleton's memory, but she had no doubt that Bracamonte had died a long time ago. Seated on an armchair, Cayetano thought the widow would soon only remain in photographs, oil painting portraits, the memories of children and grandchildren who visited her on Sundays after Mass, in that neocolonial Polanco mansion, with its thick walls, French tiles, and corridors flanked by wooden pillars. Nothing more.

"Are we talking about the same Ángel Bracamonte?" Cayetano insisted.

The elderly lady folded her hands in the lap of her black dress, looked at him with irritation, and asked, "Aren't we speaking about the man who worked with medicinal plants?"

"Exactly—the doctor."

"No, he was no doctor," she corrected him. Her dentures made a rattling sound, like bones shaken in a bag. "He worked with medicinal plants, but he wasn't a doctor."

"And he died in Mexico City?"

"I don't know where he died. It's all the same. You think it matters where a person dies? What matters is where you go after you die. He was a good person, in any case, that man. A biologist or something like that. He had a salary. At some point he devoted himself entirely to the struggle against cancer, and then he disappeared from the social circles of Mexico City," the woman said. At her side, a maid in cap and apron stood as impassive as a statue. "I think he died of the same disease he was researching."

"And you never met any of Bracamonte's relatives?"

"Listen, young man, strictly speaking, we were never friends. We saw each other at a reception here, a ceremony there. That was all. I don't even know where he came from." She gestured with her right hand, which bore a diamond-encrusted ring.

In that case, if Bracamonte was dead, he was at a dead end, Cayetano thought with dismay. He wondered how he would tell the poet. Immediately, by phone, or in person once he arrived in Valparaíso? His dark brown eyes roamed from Sarah's blue eyes to the Gobelin tapestries embroidered with fox hunt scenes that hung on either side of the fireplace, and then at the furniture, upholstered with leather in the *frailero* style, which shone in the light of the chandelier. What would be the least demoralizing way to break the news to the poet? If the everyday news in Chile depressed him, the fact that Bracamonte had died—and taken all the healing plants' secrets with him— would surely speed up his decline.

"And Beatriz, his wife? What do you remember about her?"

A surprising cough, as virulent as an electric shock, shook the woman's body. It was a hoarse cough, and sounded as hollow as a plaster statue. Her maid offered her a glass of water with a few drops of valerian.

"She was one of the most beautiful women in Mexico City," the old woman said, eyeing the glass distrustfully. Although she grumbled, she took the medicine. "And he was a handsome, intelligent guy, with personality. So attractive that, as a widower, despite his age, he married a woman young enough to be his daughter. But she vanished after he died. I have no idea where she is now."

He would return to Valparaíso with empty hands. The thought overwhelmed him. And the empty hands struck him as more than a mere metaphor. There was nothing left for him to do. The truth was the least that Neruda deserved. He couldn't join the adulating chorus that insisted he'd recover, that what he had wasn't so serious, but nor should he transmit the bad news by phone. If Ángel Bracamonte was dead and Beatriz had disappeared, then everything had gone to hell. What a mess! The mission was over, he should raise his anchor, return to Valparaíso, and tell Neruda he would never again see the doctor he needed.

"And what did Beatriz do?" he asked with a scrap of hope. The old woman blinked in her chair, perhaps sedated by the valerian. Was it possible that more than valerian went in Doña Sarah's glass? "That is, did she do anything in addition to being Ángel's wife?"

"It's just . . . so much time has passed." The bones in her hand made a macabre, creaking sound, like Caribbean keys.

"Now that you mention it, I believe I once heard that, as a widow, she taught at a high school for young ladies. She probably taught the codes of etiquette, that sort of thing."

"Do you remember the name of the place, Mrs. Middleton?"

"Four Roses. I remember because it sounds like a brand of whiskey. But that was a long time ago, it's been an eternity since Ángel's death. Now you tell me, Pancho Villa, why such a fuss over a couple nobody remembers anymore?"

19

B eatriz de Bracamonte, you say?"
    "That's right. She worked here in the 1940s."

"María, do you remember a teacher by the name Bracamonte?"

"What did you say her name was?"

"Beatriz de Bracamonte."

The old woman cleaning the windows of the Four Roses
Institute's secretarial office wrung gray water into a tin bucket,
then examined Cayetano Brulé at the table. Her eyes slid over
his strange purple tie with small green guanacos. She had never
seen such a striking piece of clothing, but that was life, and all
kinds of things could be found on God's green earth, she
thought. Nobody had ever asked about Beatriz Bracamonte.

"Maybe Mrs. Delmira could help him," she suggested.

"Well, please take this gentleman to Mrs. Delmira," the
secretary said before putting her glasses back on and returning
to the forms in her typewriter. "I'll call her and let her know."

The woman escorted Cayetano across a patio with a pool

and palm trees, lined with stone arches. She took him to a cool office with overflowing bookshelves and bars on the window. Mrs. Delmira, diminutive and fragile, was writing behind a wooden desk in a corner. She was probably around sixty years old. She smiled affably from behind wire-rimmed glasses, which gave her a distracted air.

"Did you know Beatriz de Bracamonte?" he asked her after they had exchanged greetings.

"Of course. Despite the years, it's not easy to forget a person like her."

He invited her to talk more at a nearby *taquería*. He needed something hot to drink after reading in the taxi, in the pages of the *Excelsior*, that things were getting worse in Chile. The truck drivers there, terrified that the revolution would expropriate their vehicles, had just agreed to launch a national strike of indefinite length, which would worsen the food shortage and lengthen the lines at grocery stores. The JAPs, neighborhood committees that strove to guarantee equitable distribution of supplies, were not reaching their goals, and the black market was thriving. It was hard to get gasoline, even for fire trucks and ambulances, and the price of kerosene, the fuel of the poor, was exploding through the roof. Yes, he needed a coffee: small, sweet, and strong, like they made it in Versailles or La Carreta, on Eighth Street in Miami.

"I've got thirty minutes for you," Mrs. Delmira warned him from her desk. She seemed convinced that teaching at the prestigious Four Roses of La Condesa, at her age, was a privilege that gave her special status.

They left the cracked walls of the building for the ceiling of clouds that hung over the city. They soon found a table on the street, in the shade of a jacaranda tree. The teacher ordered pork tacos with cheese and beans, as well as a coffee, since she had not eaten breakfast yet. Cayetano restrained himself to a coffee with milk, which he waited for impatiently while cars and pickup trucks drove by. This neighborhood had a village feel, he thought, something pleasant and tranquil, impervious to the immensity of Mexico City.

"Why are you looking for Beatriz?" asked Mrs. Delmira as the waiter placed a basket of corn tortillas and guacamole on the table.

"I'm actually looking for her husband." He tried a tortilla. It was as soft and supple as a nun's hand.

"He died a long time ago."

"Are you sure?"

"Completely. She worked here as a widow. Then she disappeared."

"What do you mean, 'disappeared'?" he asked, taking another tortilla, this time adding guacamole. The local cuisine was not bad at all, he thought. "Do you mean that she died?"

"She taught German and manners at the institute for a time, but when she became a widow, she left. He died in 1958 or 1959, and she left in 1960. They had a daughter."

"A daughter? What was her name?"

"Tina."

"Did she study at the institute?"

"No. I don't know where she went to school."

"Where do you think they went?"

"That's a mystery. Her colleagues are long retired. They were all older. Four Roses is known for hiring experienced people. Beatriz was the exception."

The waiter brought their food and drinks to the table, then left them in peace. The teacher dived into the tacos and began to devour them with relish. The street stretched before them with its closed doors and windows, as the sun warmed the pavement and their table.

"So you can't imagine where Beatriz might have gone?"

"That's something nobody knows. But if I were pressed, I'd say Havana."

"Why?"

"Perhaps because she met a Cuban," she said, smiling with her mouth full. Cayetano clung stoically to his coffee.

"You know this, or you're guessing?"

"I'm guessing."

He envisioned his native city, the way it looked from the sea, the buildings of the Malecón pushing into the blue sky, the stone fortresses guarding the bay as sunlight blazed against the tiles of colonial houses. He could taste the breeze that rustled the dresses of women with swaying hips and swirled in the afternoons with tropical opacity through the hallways. He imagined Beatriz making love behind the undulating lace curtains of a bedroom, attracted by a revolution freshly arrived from the Sierra Maestra. If Beatriz was in her forties in the 1960s, then she should be over fifty now, he calculated. But why was he so concerned with this woman, when it was Ángel whom he needed, and that man had already turned to dust?

The coffee tasted reasonably good, better than Hadad's, at least. He brushed his mustache, which made him feel at home in Mexico, but foreign in Chile. If in Mexico all men sported mustaches, in Chile all the revolutionaries grew beards, while the enemies of Allende's government had well-shaven cheeks and hair slicked back with gel.

"And that's all you know about Beatriz?"

"I've already told you. I think she went to Havana." She

pulled another piece off the pork taco. Those damn tacos certainly smelled good, Cayetano thought, but he stuck to his coffee.

"Did she ever talk to you about any Cuban men?" he asked.

"Never. But once I saw her having a meal at Café Tacuba with a Cuban, to whom she introduced me. One can imagine the rest. She was extremely beautiful."

"Is it true that Ángel was a doctor?"

"I believe so. He was convinced that the Indians had been treating cancer since before the Spaniards arrived, using medicinal plants that they kept secret. Beatriz mentioned it to me one day. She was worried."

"Worried?"

"She was afraid. She said the plants were dangerous, that just as they could save human lives, they could also end them."

"And how did Bracamonte die?"

"He was poisoned."

"By one of his concoctions?"

"That was never discovered. But his death was a sign that he'd made a deal with the devil, sir," Mrs. Delmira affirmed, crossing herself with her mouth full of meat.

20

He found the poet dozing in La Nube, wrapped in a blanket. A manuscript rested in his lap, and his feet were propped on the white leather footstool, which was stained with green ink. Hawthorn logs burned in the fireplace, and below, the city faded into morning mist. Sergio had told him that the poet had just arrived home from radiotherapy. Cayetano studied Neruda from the bar, his rhythmic breath, his hands folded over his abdomen, his cap tilted over his forehead.

"Did you find him?" the poet asked suddenly, opening his eyes.

"He's dead, Don Pablo."

"What?"

"Dr. Ángel Bracamonte is dead," Cayetano replied. He didn't want to become one more person feeding him daily white lies, as though the poet were a child, and death an inconceivable topic.

"Are you sure?" He threw the manuscript onto the day's

newspapers. He appeared to have received confirmation of his suspicions.

Cayetano slowly crossed the living room. "Completely."

With a deep sigh, the poet interlaced his hands again and stared in silence at the white ceiling. An Andean melody rose from the lower floors of La Sebastiana, sad, rather depressing, performed on *charango* and *trutruca* by a folk group that was currently popular. It was the theme music for the governmental television station.

"When did he die?" he asked, looking down.

"At least fifteen years ago."

The poet bit his lips and passed a nervous hand over his face. They remained silent, pensive, listening to the crackle of the fire and the caw of gulls as they glided around the house. As the birds flew toward the bay, they formed white crosses that slid against the vault of the sky. For a long time the poet watched them, as though they contained the answer to his search, and as though he smelled the intense perfume of distant eucalyptus.

"I feared as much," he said.

"I'm sorry, Don Pablo. I did everything I could. Would you like the details?"

"What did I hire you for, Cayetano, if not so you could find out and tell me everything?"

"It isn't much," he said, adjusting his glasses as he stood in the middle of the living room, which now seemed as large as an ocean. "Some remember him as a romantic. Others as a visionary unable to realize his dream. And there are those who believe he wasted his life's work by not leaving written evidence of his research."

"He didn't even leave disciples?"

"Not a single page of notes, Don Pablo."

The poet shook his head several times and muttered something unintelligible. Cayetano had the feeling that during his absence Neruda's cheeks had become bluer. He sat down on the floral-print armchair across from the poet, quietly, without making the floorboards creak.

"I did what I could, Don Pablo."

"Bracamonte may have been nothing more than an angel who sought to delay death. But it didn't work. Perhaps it's better this way," the poet murmured in resignation. "It would be terrible if we were immortal. There can't be anything more boring than eternity. Life would become a torment in later years." Beneath his philosophical tone lay certain rancor toward the reality of death. "Did you at least find his wife?"

"In a way."

Now he changed his position and attitude, as though trying to shed his sadness over the news.

"What the hell does 'in a way' mean?" he cried in irritation, imitating Cayetano's tone. "Now you're going to talk like the doctors and Matilde? You think I'm an idiot who'll buy anything you say? Did you see her or not?"

Cayetano suddenly felt a cold current seeping in through the window, and he wondered how it felt to the poet, whether the cold of death was different from the cold of winter.

"I couldn't find her," he explained. "Her name is Beatriz, but nobody knows her maiden name."

The poet looked at his hands. "I met her as Bracamonte's wife, and you know what an old man's memory is like? Pure fog."

Was Don Pablo hiding something? Cayetano wasn't getting

paid to play psychologist. He decided to press forward with his own information. "It seems she lives in Cuba . . ."

The poet frowned in surprise. "In Cuba? Since when?"

"Since around 1960. She left Mexico when she was already a widow, according to an acquaintance."

"She had children with the doctor, right?"

"A daughter. Tina."

The poet's large brown eyes grew more alert, as they always did when he was talking about women. Cayetano already knew this expression, with its fleeting, youthful glow. "A young woman, then. How old?"

"She was a teenager in the early sixties. So today she should be around thirty."

"Curious," he said, passing his hand over the moles on his cheek. "In 1960, I was also on the island. I spoke with Fidel. He didn't like that poem where I say that revolution is made not by leaders but by the people. Some writers and poets, recently converted communists, attacked me for it. They, who'd never once gotten their hands dirty for socialism, accused me, a life-long communist, of not being a true revolutionary. . . . In any case, young man, you can't give up the search for Beatriz Bracamonte."

Once again he sensed that Don Pablo was acting, as though he were hiding beneath another disguise, one that didn't hang in the top-floor closet but that he kept inside, under his skin. Could he be even more ill than Cayetano had believed, and hiding his despondency? He needed to tread lightly.

"Beatriz is probably in Cuba, Don Pablo. But I doubt she has the information you need. She taught German and manners at a girls' school in Mexico."

"Manners, now that I don't believe. Who cares about

manners these days? German, more likely. She had a lot of German in her. It's incredible that I can't remember all her last names, but she was definitely half German."

"But if she taught German . . ."

"What?"

"She probably knows very little about plants that cure cancer."

He had said the cursed word. But the poet was not afraid of words.

"What do you know? Women are the ones who taught me everything, starting with my grandmother Trinidad, who raised me after my biological mother died. Without her, I wouldn't be who I am, Cayetano," he affirmed with a sudden spark in his eyes. "If there's anyone who can help me now, young man, it's Beatriz, widow of Bracamonte. You have to find her, and now I'm going to tell you why."

21

They went for a walk on Alemania Avenue, despite the poet's exhaustion. He was the one who wanted to go out so they could breathe the clear, cold afternoon air and take in the bay as they talked. They walked past Alí Babá and the Mauri Theater, whose marquee read *"The 39 Steps,"* and passed Yerbas Buenas Hill with its Oriental banana trees, still without leaves, and Guillermo Rivera, with its grocers on three corners, and then they arrived at San Juan de Dios Hill, with its English architecture, where Cayetano lived. Echoes of cranes and metal rose from the port, as well as a briny aroma that comforted the poet.

"You have no choice but to travel to Cuba," he said as they sat down on stone steps that rose toward the houses. A few dogs dozed beside a kiosk selling bread and soda, where a sign announced that there was no butter left. Farther on, some children glided down the street on a *chancha,* a board with small steel wheels tacked on by hand, as the sun drew warm brilliance from the pavement.

"You want me to travel to Cuba?"

"Without anyone finding out why, mind you." The poet adjusted his cap, tipping it lightly over his eyebrows so that he wouldn't be recognized.

"But, in that case, you believe Beatriz Bracamonte can help you?"

"I am sure of it."

"Then I'm more confused than ever."

They watched the children hide their *chancha* under a car the moment a military jeep passed on Alemania Avenue.

"It's not for medicinal plants that I need you to find Beatriz," the poet said, studying the soldiers in the back of the vehicle, with their bayonets.

"No? Then for what?" So Don Pablo had been hiding something, after all. He didn't only toy with words according to his art, but also hid behind them as a way of toying with people. Laura Aréstegui was right. His budding detective's intuition had not misled him.

The poet gazed at the thick soles of his brown shoes and said nothing. Seated on a staircase, far from La Nube, which awaited him by the warmth of a lit fireplace, Neruda was now an anonymous, helpless person. A Plazuela Ecuador bus stopped in front of them, and out stepped a handsome woman, middle-aged and poised, along with her husband, who had a mustache and wore a suit and tie, and a gangly, long-haired young man wearing the amaranth-colored shirt of the Communist Youth.

"How are you, Don Roberto and Doña Angélica?" Cayetano called out.

They were neighbors of his, calm and amiable people. The man sympathized with Allende even though he worked at a traditional shipping business, Pacific Steam Navigation Company. Sometimes Angélica invited neighbors over for *piure* empanadas, made from that strange Chilean fish, that were good enough to make you suck on your mustache, or for a memorable *cochayuyo* salad, and on very rainy afternoons she fried up *sopaipilla* pastries and served them with Paita-style *chancaca* syrup, the best version of the dish Cayetano had ever tasted. In the spring, she cultivated roses from Wales and tulips from Amsterdam, which flourished as though her garden were in Europe, while her husband spent his free time carefully constructing marvelous replicas of English boats inside glass bottles.

"We're like the weather. How are you and the missus?" Don Roberto answered, smiling at the poet as well.

"I'm getting by, as always, and my wife is traveling."

"Well, if you like, stop by soon for a bite to eat. To take the edge off your solitude," Don Roberto said. Addressing the poet, he added, "By the way, my son is on a path similar to yours: he belongs to the same party and he wants to be a writer."

"What do you write, young man?" the poet asked. "Poems?"

The son blushed thoroughly at the question.

"Stories, Don Pablo," he said in a tremulous voice. "One day I'll write a novel."

"Just as well," the poet said, with mock solemnity. "In this country there are poets under every rock, growing like mushrooms. It's high time for some novelists. When you write your novel, include what I just told you. But don't forget. Do you promise?"

"I promise, Don Pablo."

The family kept walking up the steps of Marina Mercante as the bus disappeared up Alemania Avenue, spitting smoke from its exhaust pipe. Cayetano and the poet were alone again. They stayed silent awhile, watching El Poderoso, the legendary tugboat of Valparaíso, as it cleaved the waters of the bay.

"Now, listen closely, because what I have to say is extremely important," the poet continued, leaning his elbows on his knees. "You have to find Beatriz Bracamonte, any way you can. From this moment on, it's your main mission. What I need most at this stage of my life is that you find her and tell her—"

Don Pablo stopped short.

"Tell her what?"

The poet studied the shine of his shoes and scratched an eyebrow, doubtful, uneasy, looking at Cayetano sideways.

"You want me to tell her what, Don Pablo?"

"That I want to know . . . no, more accurately, I need to know . . ."

"Come on, Don Pablo. Today it seems like words have to be pulled from you like teeth."

The poet ended his sentence in a low voice, befitting a secret. "That I want to know whether the girl born in 1943 is my daughter."

Cayetano felt as if he were falling from a cloud. "What?"

"Just as you heard it," he said with determination. "And don't act scandalized. One day you'll have a similar experience yourself. I've already told you that life is a carnival, full of disguises and surprises."

Cayetano quickly put two and two together. Was he talking about Tina? If Tina was a teenager in 1960, the dates fit all too well. It must be her. He felt his way. "But didn't you tell me that Beatriz was married to Ángel Bracamonte, Don Pablo?"

"What, were you brought into the world by a stork from

Paris? Were you born this way or did you become dense here in Chile?"

He had caught the poet at fault. He lingered on the topic, not without cunning. "Let's see, let's see . . . so you're the father of the daughter of Ángel Bracamonte's wife?"

"That's what I suspect, and what you need to confirm," the poet answered, sulking.

"Well, that really takes the cake, Don Pablo."

The poet ignored him. He murmured something indistinguishable.

"'*Nel mezzo del cammin di nostra vita / mi ritrovai per una selva oscura* . . . Midway along the journey of our life / I woke to find myself in a dark wood. . . .'"

"What did you say?"

"It's Italian. The words of Dante Alighieri. When you're old, you'll understand me. What Dante wrote is inextricably related to all our lives. The problem is that we don't realize it until it's too late."

Again with the lessons. In this new occupation as detective, Don Pablo was turning bossy; Cayetano rebelled.

"So all that about looking for Ángel Bracamonte was just an excuse?"

"It was a way of getting close to her and also of testing you, my friend. Now I at least know that you're discreet, and that you have the right fingers for the piano of detective work."

He was still playing with metaphors, images, pretty words. Poets. Now Cayetano understood why people didn't trust them. He didn't back down. "Whatever you call it, you really took me for a ride. That much is clear, Don Pablo." Although he was still reproachful, he made his words gentler, almost conciliatory.

"Let's just say all that matters is for you to find Beatriz and ask her whether that girl, the one born in 1943 while she was married to Ángel, is his or mine."

End of conversation. The poet stood up and stared at the bay, which was at rest, so much so that it resembled a great plate of liquid mercury. Cayetano came to his side and cautiously resumed the conversation.

"So you had an affair with the doctor's wife?"

Don Pablo became approachable again. "Cayetano, in my life I have had many lovers. Without them I would not have written poetry. Or do you think poems come out of thin air?"

"From poetic inspiration, I thought."

"From life. They come from your life, Cayetano. From your longings and plans, your failures, insomnias, and frustrations, and they're created by a profound and hidden part of ourselves, a region of the soul whose location I have yet to find, and then, well, then, as I said to you the other day, they end up pouring onto the page."

"Or onto your leather footstool, which, I'm sorry to say, is quite stained with green ink, Don Pablo."

Cayetano rooted through his jacket for cigarettes, but couldn't find one. A Paul Anka song rose from the kiosk, its lyrics speaking of absence and distance and reminding him vaguely of the Havana of his childhood, at dusk. The woman at the kiosk had just hung out another cardboard sign, written by hand, announcing that she had also run out of cigarettes and firewood. The shortage, he thought, was another cancer.

"Everyone believes that I had only one child: poor Malva Marina," mumbled the poet. They began to descend the steps. In the distance, the children were still riding the *chancha*. "I awaited her with tender impatience, Cayetano, but when I saw that enormous head for the first time, attached to that tiny baby's body, I was terrified, I didn't want to believe it. I asked myself why the hell this had to happen to me of all people, when all I dreamed of was having a baby. She was a girl with light, sweet eyes, a snub nose, and a delicate smile. I tried to convince myself that time would adjust her proportions, and I refused to believe that I was fooling myself, but hydrocephalus has no cure, Cayetano. I left Malva Marina and her mother to end my own suffering, because if I stayed tormented like that, I would never be able to write the poems I wanted to write, and have now written. Do you understand?"

Cayetano didn't know what to say. It started to drizzle. The corrugated iron roofs lost their shine and muffled the echoes of the city. The dense Pacific rocked all the way to the horizon. What could he say? The disclosure discomfited him; he was saddened by the poet's pain and terrified of disappointing him. At the same time, he found his argument paltry and uncon- vincing, of having sacrificed wife and daughter in the name of work that he would have created anyway, that already flowed vigorously from his pen when the girl was born. But perhaps, in recent weeks, he'd been slowly conquered by the artist's dis- trustful spirit and his poorly concealed vulnerability. He told himself that he should be more tolerant, that maybe, as the poet claimed, he himself was still young and there were many things in life that he had yet to understand.

"I realize some things are inexplicable, such as my leaving those women," the poet continued. "I've fled many times in my life. In fact, I've been a constant fugitive of my circum- stances. I escaped from Josie Bliss, and then I left my little

Malva Marina and her mother in Nazi-occupied Holland. What's more, I used my diplomatic connections to keep them from evacuating to Chile with my compatriots."

At least he was learning how to handle the self-mythologizing the poet resorted to when confessing the unconfessable. Cayetano asked a single question. "Why?"

"Simply because I feared that, in Chile, they would make my life impossible . . ."

It was too much. He was pained by the surprising contempt he felt for this man whom he had, until now, admired more each day. Better to set up a boundary and keep the bitter portion from eating up the sweetness, from devouring the whole cake.

"Perhaps we should go back, Don Pablo," he suggested sadly.

"The casualties of our good fortune are a terrible thing, Cayetano. But the road to personal happiness is paved with the pain of others."

Cayetano thought that these mottoes brought solace to no one, but kept that opinion to himself. Had he let himself be taken in? Then he should grin and bear it. They made their way back, winding through the high parts of Valparaíso, past houses with sweeping views from their terraces and picture windows. The poet's house, a polychrome pyramid in the distance beside the Mauri Theater, stood out against the backdrop of the city. He was suddenly tempted to drop the case, along with his new line of work, but at the same time he realized that he couldn't. He was another man now: he was the detective to whom Pablo Neruda had given birth.

"So how did it end with Beatriz, Don Pablo?" he dared ask.

"I broke it off when I found out she was pregnant."

He understood that, in this new occupation, he had to be ready for anything. People would attack or defend themselves with anything. And he couldn't fear words, however difficult they might seem: paradoxically, it was difficulty that opened investigative roads.

"You abandoned her?" he asked, to clarify.

"I got scared. Haven't you ever been afraid in your life? I thought destiny was mocking me again, and had laid out a trap. It was a brief, passionate love. She was in her twenties, with a husband in his forties. We met in secret at a little hotel beside Café Tacuba, near Zócalo Plaza, and sometimes in her house, while Ángel was at work."

"You haven't spoken to her since?"

"I never wanted to see her again. I didn't believe her when she said I was the one who got her pregnant. I didn't want to be a father anymore. I was haunted by the grotesque nightmare of Malva Marina. I was happy then, with Delia del Carril, an older woman. She was rich and well connected, my fame was in full force, my poems were being read all over the world. What was I supposed to do with an unfaithful wife, carrying a potentially appalling baby in her womb, for whom I would be no good? That's why I left her."

"My God, Don Pablo . . ."

"Well? What do you want?"

"I don't know, I mean . . . something different . . ."

"It seems that one never matures, Cayetano. That in the face of life one is always a shitty youth. And when you do reach maturity, it's too late, because by that time you're at death's door. In my forties, I didn't care whether or not I was the father. My work as a poet demanded all my time and effort. I wasn't moved when I later found out Beatriz had given birth to a girl. I opted to eradicate that chapter of my life. Until now, Cayetano."

Now that the whole world recognized him as a sublime poet, that he was bathed in the light of admiration from every direction, the shadow of that old guilt had leaked in between the man and his fame, and could not be cleared away. Or could it? Cayetano felt compassion and responsibility: beyond the moral judgments that his first client—and creator—deserved was the fact that any hope of reparations depended on him. He had a mission to fulfill.

And a time frame, as Don Pablo's next words made clear.

"None of this mattered to me until now, that I smell death." His voice changed, sped up. "I already smelled it as a youth, you know. 'Death is in the bed frames: / in the slow mattresses, in the black blankets / she lives, spread out, and suddenly blows: / she blows a dark sound that swells sheets, / and there are beds sailing toward a port / where she awaits, clothed as an admiral.' Death clothed as an admiral, the one waiting for us all, yes, sure, I had smelled that one. But not my own, Cayetano! Not the real one, the one that counts! The naked one, who simply arrives without words and just adds up bodies—that one had yet to arrive." He stopped beside a public school. The loud clamor of children at recess carried over the walls. "I want to know whether that daughter is mine or Ángel's. Can I confess something else?" He paused and stared at Cayetano, serious, tense, a Neruda he did not know. "I need her to be my daughter!"

The sudden emphasis made Cayetano doubt the poet's lucidity.

"Are you sure?" he said, to test him.

"My women never gave me children. Not Josie Bliss, who was a tornado of jealousy, nor the Cyclops María Antonieta, who gave birth to a deformed being; nor did Delia del Carril, whose womb was dried up when I met her; nor Matilde, who had several miscarriages. I've had everything in life, Cayetano: friends, lovers, fame, money, prestige, they've even given me the Nobel Prize—but I never had a child. Beatriz is my last hope. It's a hope I buried long ago. I'd give all my poetry in exchange for that daughter." They resumed their walk through the drizzle as the children's voices flowed and ebbed behind them. "Immortality is bestowed by children, Cayetano, not by books; by blood, not ink; by skin, and not by printed pages. That's why you have to find out whether Beatriz's daughter is mine. My friend, you have to go to Cuba, find Beatriz, and bring me the truth before the old woman with the scythe gets the best of me."

22

María Antonieta Hagenaar Vogelzang entered my life at a British Country Club on the Island of Java, by a wide and sinuous river whose name I no longer recall. The breeze faltered that morning, soft clouds filled the sky, and the swamp scent of the river's currents pervaded the air. I saw her by chance as I walked past a tennis court, where María Antonieta was playing another woman on the lawn. The British colony had clubs, restaurants, shops, and offices, which only British people, diplomats, and a few chosen locals could patronize. I didn't usually frequent them because their colonial attitude disgusted me, but on that particular day, loneliness, or perhaps destiny, who knows, led my steps there.

María Antonieta captivated me immediately. She was taller than me, and had slow yet graceful movements, white skin, long limbs, and dark hair. Her figure reflected on the undulating surface of the river. Accustomed as I was to the slight bodies of Burmese women, I was seduced by her statuesque appearance, like a Greek caryatid at the door of a temple, and her Valkyrian vigor. I decided to wait for her to finish the game so that I could introduce myself.

Was I ever truly in love with her? I ask myself this now, seated in La Nube, breathing the sad sighs of this Valparaíso, which various earthquakes have conspired against, one after the other, as well as the opening of the Panama Canal and the centralism of Santiago. Of María Antonieta, I remember thick calves, upright breasts, and nipples as pink as certain beach pebbles. I recall her penetrating eyes, which over time lost their shine and depth, to be replaced by an air of resentful indifference. When we made love, her moans had a dark masculine resonance that disturbed me and stirred my own emigrant's loneliness. She was, I realize, noble, diligent, and honest, a true Dutch peasant, and she trusted me in a way she never should have.

In the mornings, her thighs gathered up the beams of sun that pierced the lace curtains of our bedroom. Then that light set fire to her sparse blond pubic hair and climbed toward her belly, where it submerged itself in the shade of her navel and slid to the heights of her breasts, from which my avid lips had drunk. I studied that dance of light in silence, spellbound. What a name she had! María Antonieta Hagenaar Vogelzang. Now that I slide it across my tongue, over and over, it tastes of the alfajor *cookies of La Ligua and of street names in Amsterdam. I regret that I didn't know how to appreciate her when we were a couple. Hagenaar. The third syllable, clear and sustained, like the murmur of a stream that splashes and flows over stones that blend into the shade of boldo plants, whose leaves provided an old natural medicine for anxiety. Vogelzang: a* v *that intones like the resolution of a full-bodied* f*, vehemently, and a* z *that demands a crackling snort, a dart grazing the ear. Vo-gel-zang. I think it means "birdsong" in Dutch. But I didn't want to hear the musicality of her name. My provincial ignorance, with its smell of a woolen poncho drenched by southern rains, made me change the name to something low and miserable: Maruca. How to compare* *that plain Maruca with the joyful fount of vowels that flows from the throat on saying María Antonieta Hagenaar Vogelzang?*

I met her in 1930, in Java. I abandoned her in Spain, in 1936. I left her for Delia del Carril, and never mentioned her again. Only two of my poems mention her, and only in passing. But when I abandoned her, I also abandoned our poor Malva Marina. That is what pushed her to pursue me with ferocity. Resentment is never extinguished, it grows over the years; time is its best fertilizer. In Chile she even became an ally of the tyrant of the moment, that despicable traitor Gabriel González Videla, in an attempt to destroy me. She could never stand for me to be happy with another woman.

I now recognize that, early on, things were good with her, that nothing about her bothered me. Not even the fact that she was taller than me or that we barely understood each other's English. She didn't speak Spanish, I didn't speak Dutch, and my knowledge of English was always lacking. I loved poetry and bohemian ways, while she embraced a practical and disciplined life. I liked to spend what I didn't have, while she preferred to save every last cent. We got married in Batavia, four months after we met. That day, without knowing it, I came between María Antonieta and the timid Dutch accountant who had been courting her for a long time, and who was also waiting for her by the tennis court. Why did I interrupt what was slated to become a marriage, and steal her from the road that fate had laid out? She could have been happy on the island; she could have loved her husband in Dutch; she could have visited Rotterdam every once in a while and admired the immaculate European cleanliness she so idolized. A consul without prospects or resources, who had come from a poor and melancholy country in the world's other south, should simply have returned alone to his slow Andean evenings. If, on that Sunday, I had continued home without stopping at that tennis court, another rooster, as they say, would have sung.

If memory serves, our relationship began to splinter, not long after the wedding, when Maruca contracted a strange illness that made her lose the first baby. Those were painful months. We lost the child, and the medical bills took all our savings. And Maruca's health did not improve. With the global crisis of 1929, the government had reduced my salary; in addition, it could not send me return tickets to Chile. A year into our marriage, Maruca no longer ignited any passion in me. To make love to her, I had to conjure up the soft skin, malevolent smile, and redolent cracked fruit of Josie Bliss.

We set sail from Batavia in 1932 in a boat bearing the beautiful name of a Dutch writer, Pieter Corneliszoon Hooft. Our final destiny met us in Valparaíso. In Chile, Maruca was modest, loyal, and self-sacrificing. She stayed at my side as we settled into a gloomy, windowless apartment in the center of Santiago, where my bohemian friends lingered until dawn, without her understanding the source of laughter or topics of conversation. Language kept us apart. I managed to once again escape my own nation and escape poverty as well, thanks to another position as consul, this time in Spain, where I met Delia. I am often tortured by a vision of a disconcerted and fearful María Antonieta in our last weeks in Madrid. I'm still haunted by the memory of her impotent despair on realizing that I was leaving her for another woman. Delia, cultured, refined, twenty years older than me, connected to the crème de la crème of European intellectuals, awaited me impatiently in a nearby city. I packed my suitcase, closed the door, and left, abandoning María Antonieta and our daughter. Why must happiness be built at the cost of others' misfortune? From this Valparaíso where I await my sunset, I want to beg your forgiveness, María Antonieta Hagenaar

Vogelzang. Forgive me, woman of noble soul, for having betrayed you and Malva Marina; forgive me for having taken advantage of your loyalty and naïveté, for having left you under such abominable circumstances, for having forgotten you as I ran, crazed, through the bombarded streets of the Spanish Republic, to be with Delia del Carril.

23

Stepping down from the Russian two-engine plane into the humid heat of José Martí Airport, Cayetano immediately recalled his deep connection to the island. The green alligator-shaped land seemed to recognize him and embrace him like an old friend. He had left Havana as a boy, and his remembrances were frequent, though tormented and diffuse. His memory retained the colors, noise, and aromas of the island; the scent of its fruit; the sensuality of its women; the exaggerated gestures of its men; and the caress of saline breezes on its streets. The scorching air, the perfume of flowers whose names had been lost to memory, the bright glare of the asphalt, the coolness promised by its doors: all of these reconciled him at once with his own Cuban soul. The island had inoculated him with its light and rhythm, its fierce enthusiasm for life, all the things that yoked him to it forever, making him a perpetual hostage to nostalgia.

He showed his passport to the officials in green uniforms,

who still vaguely resembled the bearded revolutionaries of Sierra Maestra, then took an Anchares cab—a 1951 Chrysler with shining chrome and muted speed—and got a room at a dilapidated hotel in El Vedado. El Presidente had simple architecture and looked out over the mansion that housed the Ministry of Foreign Relations, as well as a sports complex and the tower of La Casa de las Américas. He went out to explore his surroundings, guided by the mix of helplessness and euphoria he felt upon recognizing buildings and corners in their current state. Havana was falling to pieces and in desperate need of paint yet was still beautiful, exuding a pleasant rural calm. He got in line at a café called El Carmelo, and when he found a seat, he asked for a cup of coffee, a *guanábana* juice, and a *medianoche* sandwich. In Valparaíso, he thought, no one knew that black, syrupy coffee, or the lovely thickness of *guanábana* juice, or the delicate consistency of that legendary sandwich.

He needed to organize his next steps or else he'd lose his way, and not even Simenon's little novels would help him recover it. The poet's unexpected disclosures and the subsequent change in his mission disconcerted him. Was he fully aware of the responsibility in his hands? It was no longer a question of finding a doctor who could postpone death but of finding the woman who held the secret information Neruda needed in order to die in peace.

He devoured the *medianoche* sandwich, ordered another coffee, and left El Carmelo after generously tipping the waiter and assuring him he'd return soon. He flagged another Anchares, this time driven by a Spaniard with white hair and an aquiline, Marlon Brando nose, and requested a ride down the Malecón and through Old Havana. He burned to see the city pass before his eyes. Was Beatriz Bracamonte on the island now? Was it sensible to trust the speculations of a Mexican schoolteacher enough to come to Cuba? As he reflected on these questions, he looked out on peeling buildings, water running on the street, lines in front of grocery stores with empty windows, and shirtless boys playing ball, but he thought that the rhythmic waves battering the Malecón and the light on colonial buildings retained the same hair-raising beauty he recalled from his childhood. Downtown, he saw colossal signs praising Fidel and the Revolution, giant portraits of Che Guevara and Camilo Cienfuegos, and billboards that called on the Third World to fight imperialism. That's how this Cuba lives, he thought: bursting with patriotic and revolutionary harangues, with calls to fulfill missions and make sacrifices, with promises of paradise around the corner. Would he have stayed on the island if his father, a trumpeter who played with Beny Moré, had not taken him to the United States in the 1950s? he asked himself as a breeze entered through the Chrysler's open windows, cooling his face and combing his mustache. Would he have put up with Fidel's socialism with the same stoicism with which he now faced Allende's revolution? Or would he have emigrated to Miami, like the thousands of fellow Cubans who, on Eighth Street, re-created a vibrant and nostalgic Little Havana? There was no use in asking such questions. It was like Maigret asking himself what he would have done if Simenon had made him a lawyer instead of a detective. What was certain was that he now lived far away, and could travel the world, come and go from the island, and toy with questions such as this one. The bottom line was that he was a very lucky guy, with fate on his side, as the poet had said. And his good fortune consisted precisely of this, of having options, however much they hounded him.

He asked the driver to take him back to El Carmelo, where he felt at ease in the cool, air-conditioned room. The waiter prepared a table for him across from the Amadeo Roldán Theater and the shriveled garden of a mansion that now housed the Committees for the Defense of the Revolution. He lit a Lanceros cigar he'd bought at the airport, inhaled with relish, and estimated that the poet should arrive soon, the one who, according to Neruda, could help him find Beatriz. He was blacklisted for having written a collection of poems that criticized the Revolution. Although his name had also appeared in the letter Cuban artists had written against Neruda eight years earlier, the Nobel laureate knew from a trusted source that this blacklisted writer had not actually signed it.

"You can trust him," he told Cayetano as he wrote a letter on the Underwood in his studio at La Sebastiana. "He was the one who told me that Fidel couldn't stand my poetry. Tell him you're looking for a woman, but don't tell him the reason. Avoid Chileans, because over there there are only two kinds: the ones who are with the secret service, and the ones who wish they were. Imagine what would happen if they found out what I was looking for."

As he drank his coffee, Cayetano thought that few would believe he was here to invite poets to Neruda's seventieth birthday, which would be celebrated in the National Stadium in Santiago de Chile. Although the Chilean state department had backed him before the Cuban embassy, the latter office had dragged its heels in granting his visa, which, in essence, constituted a warning. He lit a cigarette, opened a Maigret novel, and started to read with gusto in that old café.

"Cayetano Brulé?" someone at his side asked after a while.

He was a young man, with thick-framed glasses like his

own, and a healthy mop of dark, curly hair. He resembled Roy Orbison, down to the sarcastic expression. His pants and short-sleeved shirt were tight, as were those of almost all the men in Havana.

"One and the same."

"I'm Heberto." He sat down. Outside, in the building's shade, the line of people waiting for a table was getting longer. "I was told that you wanted to see me."

"Coffee?" Cayetano asked, smoothing his mustache. From the radio, the voice of Farah María warmed the room. A waitress passed with a tray of Hatuey beers, singing along with the mulatta.

"I'll have a coffee, and one of those Lanceros you're smoking. They tell me you're Cuban."

"From Havana. The La Víbora section, to be more precise."

"From La Víbora, but with a foreign passport. Enviable," Heberto noted sardonically. "Like Bertolt Brecht, who applauded the communism of the German Democratic Republic but had an Austrian passport and a Swiss bank account. So you're a friend of Neruda's?"

"A friend, yes, but without a bank account in Switzerland or anywhere else."

When the waiter returned, the poet placed his order, imitating Neruda's nasal voice, and after exhaling a dramatic puff of cigar smoke, he began to recite in the Nobel laureate's droning tone:

> "*I love the love of sailors*
> *who kiss and go.*
> *They leave a promise.*
> *They never return.*"

Stunned, Cayetano listened to the perfect imitation of a man who, at this very moment, awaited news beside a cold cobalt ocean at the end of the world.

"So you're looking for young poets to invite to Chile. Tell me, what does 'young' mean to Neruda? Do I count as young?" Heberto said, going back to his own Cuban lilt.

"The young are those who aren't old. Do you feel old?"

"I feel emphatically young, but he might think my poetry is old. It doesn't matter. If you could convince Neruda that I'm young and if he were to invite me, and if the government were to let me off the island . . . well, better not to count on me. He'll have to celebrate seventy without me."

"But with an invitation from Neruda, I imagine the government would let you travel."

"That tells me how long you've been traveling without a Cuban passport, my friend. It wouldn't matter, they still wouldn't let me leave. The man"—he made as if to stroke a nonexistent beard—"doesn't like me. What else are you looking for around here? They tell me you've got some other little affairs to attend to."

The waiter placed the order on the table and left, muttering insults at the crowded Leyland buses passing by. Now Los Van Van were singing furiously, to the rhythm of drums and congas, while outside the queue baked under the tropical sun.

"I need to find a Mexican woman, Beatriz, widow of a Dr. Bracamonte," said Cayetano. "I don't know her maiden name, but I do know she arrived here thirteen years ago from Mexico. She's somewhere in her fifties now. She has a daughter who's around thirty years old."

"A poet?"

"Could be."

"I don't know anyone by that name. And I'm not going to ask what you need her for. Around here, it's better to know less each day. In addition, since my fall from grace, I'm forbidden to speak with foreigners. I have some friends who used to be connected with diplomatic circles, but these days they're all blacklisted. Maybe one of them can find this Mexican woman."

"That would be a great help. It's nothing political."

"Don't even tell me what it's about. It's enough to know the poet sent you. We have almost the same enemies. Beatriz Bracamonte, you say? The truth is, the name doesn't ring a bell at all. Is it possible that our Nobel laureate is looking on the wrong island?"

～ 24 ～

Beside the shelves of damp books in Heberto's apartment, they started drinking the remarkably good Havana Club rum Cayetano had bought in Miramar at a *diplotienda*, a shop only foreigners could enter. After a bit, a few more people arrived: the novelist Miguel Busquet, accompanied by a bus driver from route 132, and Sammy Byre, a small, sickly Jamaican with dark skin and frizzy white hair who made his living cleaning homes and standing in lines at corner grocery stores for women who had been distinguished ladies before the Revolution. A while later, the novelist Pablo Armando Bermúdez came knocking at the door.

The rum, accompanied by Manchego cheese and chorizo from the *diplotienda*, made everyone euphoric. Heberto recited verses inspired by a poem of Bertolt Brecht's, and Miguel put on a Bola de Nieve LP, flooding the little room with the black musician's piano and falsetto. Around seven in the evening, as the heat retreated and offered a cooler truce, they finished the second bottle amid shouts and laughter. On opening the third bottle, the group was ready to assist Cayetano in whatever he needed.

"But only those who didn't sign the letter may attend Neruda's birthday," he clarified, recalling that, in this matter, the poet had been inflexible. The assistants suddenly went silent, as all of them, with the exception of the good man Sammy, who was not an intellectual, had endorsed the letter, whether with their own hand or through the government.

"Don't get any false hopes, Cayetano," Heberto warned him, a glass of rum in his right hand. "No one from this island will be able to go, because in the eyes of El Caballo Neruda is not a saint. We may as well focus on finding that Mexican widow you were talking about."

He suggested that they go to the exclusive El Laguito area, inhabited by Revolution leaders, diplomats, and personalities of an international show business scene as conspicuous as it was secret. The people living comfortably in those confines included, so it was rumored, though nobody knew for sure, the daughter of the interior minister of Portugal's dictatorship, who had settled in Cuba in the 1960s, who was in love with Che; the pair of Bolivian military men who had recovered the campaign diary and the hands of the Argentinean guerrilla fighter; tycoons escaping the U.S. tax system; some hijacker of a North American airplane; and the widow of Colonel Caamaño, the leader of the failed Dominican revolution. It was possible that this widow might know Beatriz, Heberto said. Miguel, who, between sips, was enthusiastically describing to the bus driver a chapter of the novel he was writing, something about an early-twentieth-century Spanish immigrant, crossed the room and dialed a number on the phone. After hanging up, he told the group that his sources, who were generally very well informed on what took place on this island, did not know of a single widow of a Cuban doctor who had come from Mexico and now lived in Havana, however famous the husband may have been.

"Are you sure she's Mexican?" Sammy Byre asked, passing the tray of chorizo and cheese around the room with an experienced hand. Before the Revolution, he had worked as a golf caddy and waiter in Havana's exclusive clubs, which had now been turned into recreation centers for workers.

"And isn't it possible that this Cayetano is going to end up screwing us all with this mission of his? I'm dying to go to Neruda's birthday, but this guy is a Cuban from abroad, something we can't just ignore," Miguel warned.

"Well, as far as I'm concerned, with or without Cayetano, they'd never let me go to that birthday," Heberto said. "I've already had enough trouble with Chileans. We may as well talk to Caamaño's widow. It can't be a crime to ask around a little about a Mexican woman who came to the island a few years ago."

"We should think this out logically," Sammy said. He was wearing a New York Yankees cap. "I propose that first we look to the places where foreigners go."

"Oh, really?" Miguel exclaimed. "Are you going to go ask around at *diplotiendas* and embassies? Don't make me laugh. They don't even let Cubans set foot in places like that."

"Remember, I'm Jamaican."

"But the way you look, I wouldn't even let you enter the corner grocery store," the bus driver said. He was a broad-shouldered, light-skinned black man with magnificent hands and long nails. He smiled, his mouth full of chorizo. "Could it be that Beatriz is Cuban?"

"Well, in that case, there's no point in even looking. A Cuban woman, married to a Cuban doctor—there are thousands of those. That's why we revolutionized our health system, so we could have doctors doing everything, even driving tractors," Pablo Armando said, cutting open another black fig.

"But not many of them have lived in Mexico," Cayetano pointed out.

Miguel drained his glass. "They have to be shitheads, in any case, to have come back."

"The Cuban man was the doctor, not his wife," Cayetano clarified. "He was a specialist in jungle plants."

"So what are we talking about here, gentlemen? A physician or a witch doctor?" asked Miguel, who was always interested in the ethnological side of things, so he could gather material for his books.

"Beatriz arrived in Havana in 1960," Cayetano said, after gulping down another slice of sausage. Beyond the balustrade, the treetops formed a dense green ocean that covered the street below.

"I know what to do," Sammy insisted. He had large, deep ears. He had just married a twenty-year-old Havanan who dreamed of escaping the island under the protection of her husband's Jamaican passport. "If you need to find out something about a foreigner and you can't turn to State Security or embassies or *diplotiendas*, the most practical solution is the nightclubs. The dancers and musicians know all the foreigners, especially the men."

"Now we're really putting the cart before the horse!" Pablo Armando said, with elegant diction, as he ate and drank pensively, reluctant to trust a Cuban who could be an agent of the CIA or of the Cuban secret service.

"As if we didn't have enough to deal with, with the horse we already have . . ." Heberto let out a puff of smoke out the window that dissipated over the dense green ocean.

"Don't joke around. This is exactly why what happened to you happened," warned Pablo Armando. His hair was unkempt, and he clung to a dog-eared copy of Bulgakov's *The Master and Margarita* that someone had just lent him.

The group continued with its discussion of how to find the Mexican woman. Cayetano went to the phone and called the number Ángela had given him in case of emergency. A man's voice answered in a mysterious tone, and took his number down to call back at a later time. He hung up, despondent. That he and Ángela now needed an intermediary in order to see each other only underlined that their separation was complete. For a long time he didn't listen to the group's digressions, nor did he feel the humid, suffocating heat that hung in the room, redolent of rum.

All of a sudden the front door of the apartment opened, breaking his reverie. It was Belkis, Heberto's wife, a poet and painter who worked at the National Union of Writers and Artists of Cuba, also known as UNEAC. She stood, astonished at the fauna congregated in her home. She hated it when Heberto drank, as she feared that the regime would use the smallest misstep as a reason to do away with him in a car accident, now that he enjoyed vast international support. Miguel stood and crossed the living room, weaving past the other men's legs, to kiss Belkis on the cheeks.

"You look better than ever, my dear girl!" he said with a slanted smile, which revealed his small teeth. "Your most recent pieces in *La Gaceta de Cuba* are essential to any anthology of our poetry. Allow me to introduce you to the best-looking bus driver in the Caribbean . . ."

Jerónimo shook the artist's hand without a word, as if his body—equal parts Charles Atlas and Cassius Clay, and sporting an African lion's tooth on a gold chain, silver bangles, and a sleeveless shirt—were enough of a greeting. Belkis excused herself and went straight to the bedroom.

"I think it's time for us to go," said Pablo Armando, rising warily to his feet. He smoothed his hair and put the book he'd borrowed in the pocket of his guayabera.

"And for me to go back to Bruno," added Heberto, who was in the midst of translating *Naked Among Wolves*, by Bruno Apitz. He knew that, once again, under the instructions of the Commander himself, his name would not be credited in the publication.

The visitors rushed to drain their glasses and wolf down the last slices of chorizo.

"The Commander has arrived and sent us packing," Sammy said, with a mischievous smile, gathering the glasses and plates scattered on the table and floor.

"Let's go, then," Cayetano said. He headed toward the door, made dizzy by all the glasses of rum he'd drunk that evening.

"And don't worry," Heberto said to him. "I'll see to a meeting with the Dominican's widow. She's well connected around here, and can help us find the woman you're looking for. I'll call you at Hotel El Presidente as soon as I have news."

~ 25 ~

The colonel's widow was an impressive Mediterranean beauty, with long jet-black hair, pale skin, full lips, and dark eyes that sparked like lightning. When she received them at her mansion in El Laguito, she was wearing a black dress and a discreet gem necklace at her throat. Heberto, Sammy, and Cayetano crossed the marble floor and entered a bright, ample room with leather armchairs and mahogany furniture, where they all sat down. Beyond the picture window, a large green lawn surrounded a tiled pool, complete with diving board.

"You look wonderful, Heberto!" the woman exclaimed as they stirred their coffee. Cayetano felt transported to a distant country where Havana's poverty and shortages did not exist. "Any news?"

"None. They're still processing my travel visa."

"What a shame, young man. I'm very sorry."

Cayetano touched the upper pocket of his guayabera, relieved his passport was still there. He imagined that Sammy Byre, sitting beside him, must be feeling the same thing.

"About the Mexican lady your friend is looking for, I don't know anything," the widow added, glancing at Cayetano. "Let me tell you, we know a lot of people in Havana, but no one recalls a Beatriz Bracamonte. I wouldn't lose hope, though, because many foreigners change their name around here, for security reasons."

When Heberto, Sammy, and Cayetano walked back out to the avenue lined with palms and the flamboyant trees with their red flowers, they were crushed by a sun that beamed onto the city with full force. They were crestfallen. Not for a moment had they expected to meet with such indifference. The widow probably didn't want to get involved in a search spearheaded by a Cuban who lived abroad, or so it seemed to Heberto. They walked in silence, sweating buckets, hoping for a taxi to pass. After a while, they managed to flag down a Russian truck that was transporting bricks for the renovation of a home in Miramar, the residence of a party leader. Cayetano offered the driver five dollars in exchange for a ride. They had to travel in the back of the Zil, where the sun burned brutally, and they got off at Coney Island to catch a bus to El Vedado.

As they waited under the shade of some flamboyant trees, Sammy said to Cayetano, "Look, I don't like to get involved with what doesn't concern me. Right now I should be waiting in line at the butcher shop, since today's chicken day. But I'm telling you that you're never going to find anyone this way. People change their names around here, as the widow said. And many people prefer not to get involved with foreigners. At this point, you're a foreigner on your own island."

"So what do you propose?" Cayetano wiped the sweat from his forehead with a handkerchief, distressed that this Jamaican would consider him a foreigner in his own country.

"What I said the other day."

"Forgive me, but it's hot as shit and I've even forgotten my own name."

"The nightclubs. They know more there about foreigners than the secret service. There's not a single foreigner here that doesn't party. That's how it was before the Revolution, that's how it is under it, and that's how it'll be until Judgment Day. This will always be the island of parties long into the night. The rest is just poetry, with no offense to Heberto."

"I think your tactic would work for a man, Sammy. But we're looking for a woman."

"It doesn't matter. You'd just have to go to La Zorra and Cuervo, to La Rampa, or to El Gato Tuerto or Manila. Or maybe to the clubs at certain hotels, like the Riviera, the Havana Libre, or the Capri. But I would start at the Tropicana."

"The Tropicana? Why?"

"Because if memory serves," Sammy Byre explained, gesturing with hands as long and thin as claws, "Heberto's wife mentioned some time ago that the state security representative at the National Union of Writers and Artists has a single weakness: his passion for the Tropicana."

"I don't know where you're going with this," Heberto said testily, adjusting his glasses.

"If we can get a couple of tickets to Tropicana for that gentleman, then maybe he could tell us about the Mexican woman."

"Not a bad idea," Heberto muttered, gazing at the cluster of people sweltering at the bus stop. A few sat waiting at the side of the road, others on fallen tree trunks, and one young man in a high school uniform had climbed into a tree, like a monkey. "But how do you plan to get there and ask about Beatriz without raising suspicion? Cayetano officially came to the island to extend an invitation to Cuban poets, not to look for a Mexican woman."

"The devil knows more because he's old than because he's the devil," Sammy said, and at that moment a Leyland crammed with passengers passed the waiting cluster and stopped two hundred meters down the street.

A raucous mob rushed toward the bus, hurling insults at the driver and his mother. Elders, pregnant women, and children fell by the wayside, as well as a man whose large girth was inexplicable in a nation where food was so scarce, assisted (the man, not the nation) by an elegant old-fashioned lady carrying a purse and fan. The only people to reach the bus were two tall, strong guys who looked like athletes, a few high school students, and Heberto, Sammy, and finally Cayetano, panting heavily. The Leyland spit out pestilent black smoke through its exhaust pipe and began to move, tilted by the weight of its passengers. Cayetano saw, to his surprise, that the driver was none other than Miguel's friend, the ethnographic novelist, Jerónimo. He presided over an enormous black steering wheel and a rearview mirror decorated with Che and Fidel stickers and necklaces of plastic red beads.

"We're not playing around here, gentlemen," Jerónimo said, and sped up on Quinta Avenue as though he were in the Indy 500. The bus roared forward, bucked with each change in speed, and jostled the passengers as it overtook other vehicles. This was more than a bus: it was a cocktail shaker, Cayetano thought, thirsty, squeezed between students. The inside of the bus smelled of burned tires and armpits rubbed with Russian talcum powder. Jerónimo shifted gears with an offhand sadism, enjoying the cruel lurch of passengers through the rearview mirror. He leaned to one side as he drove, with his legs wide open, as though his balls could barely fit between them. Along the way, people announced their stops by shouting and slamming the tin roof. After passing through Quinta Tunnel, the bus left the trio near the Riviera, which gleamed like a golden lion's tooth beside the sun-drenched Malecón. At the hotel's marquee, they approached an Anchares whose bumper was tied on with rope.

"So who can help us at the Tropicana?" Cayetano asked as the car started moving with a melancholy creaking of gears.

"A young, talented clarinetist who was recently blacklisted as a *gusano*. Give me a few days to find him," Sammy Byre said, and then he took delight in the saline air that slipped in through the Chrysler's windows, which had no glass.

≈ 26 ≈

Three days later they arrived at the Tropicana for the daily rehearsal, as the afternoon sun tore at the stones and, on the stage, a tall thin fellow with long hair and a mustache drew a joyful Mozart melody from his clarinet. They had just finished their lunch at a FrutiCuba location in Marianao, where they'd enjoyed a tray of mango, guava, banana, and pineapple before taking an Anchares to the nightclub. They spent a good while listening to the clarinetist's music in the Salon Under the Stars, which by day resembled a simple open-air restaurant, but that by night, according to Sammy Byre, took on a surreal atmosphere with its music, its graceful dancers in glittering outfits, and the dizzying play of spotlights.

"That's my friend," Sammy said, pointing at the musician on the stage. "Paquito D'Rivera."

They had to wait for the rehearsal to end to get a word with him. They were plagued by thirst and heat, as the bar was always closed at this hour. Nevertheless, the wait was worthwhile, as they enjoyed the music and the Lanceros de Cohiba cigars supplied by Cayetano. Soon the dancers took the stage, shaking their hips, accompanied by a few slim, agile performers in ruffles and wide belts, bearing thick makeup and smiles. The show became deafening when the Irakere band electrified the afternoon with their wind instruments and drums. Cayetano thought of the poet, with his notion of life as a parade of disguises, and it occurred to him that Neruda was right, that life was actually the way he'd envisioned. After those women danced, with their narrow waists, firm thighs, and sharp, provocative scent, Paquito played another solo on the clarinet. He sat on a stool at the center of the stage, marked time with his foot, and poured out a medley of nostalgic Cuban songs, eyes closed, like a magician extracting silk scarves from a great hat with moves learned by heart. Paquito had narrowly escaped ruin, Sammy told them; he had managed to cling to a job and an instrument despite the inquisition unleashed by Luis Pavón, the minister of culture who condemned anyone who criticized the government. Saumell, the director of Irakere, had saved Paquito from ending up in one of those remote town bands after losing his place in the Tropical Orchestra of Havana when he was labeled a *gusano*. Saumell had called him in those days, and said, "My friend, come play with us. I don't give a damn about this *gusano* business."

"Could you do it?" Sammy asked Paquito, after explaining why he needed eight tickets to the Tropicana. The clarinetist, still stroking his instrument, said they could count on him as long as this was for a good cause and not on behalf of some commie.

"A good cause? There's no better cause on this whole island than Cayetano Brulé," Sammy assured him, taking off his baseball cap and baring the white hair on his small head.

"In that case, don't give it another thought," Paquito D'Rivera replied. "You'll have a table right in front of the stage, but, please, don't get me involved in any problems. I've already got enough of those. And now stick around, I've just ordered mojitos to my tab. You've got to enjoy these boleros we've arranged for Saumell's orchestra."

~ 27 ~

Late that humid night, Cayetano Brulé and Heberto Padilla walked down dark streets scented with jasmine and flooded with the sounds of people chatting on their stoops, until they reached the door of the National Union of Writers and Artists of Cuba, or UNEAC, armed with the promise that Paquito D'Rivera would obtain a table at the Tropicana for the head of security. The success of their mission depended on this, Cayetano thought as he watched Heberto wipe sweat from his forehead with a handkerchief.

The winds seemed to be blowing in their favor that night, as he'd received a message from Ángela, which he carried in his pocket: she would meet him the next day at seven in the evening, in Miramar, at the plaza in front of the Belgian embassy. The prospect of seeing her again renewed his hopes of finding some sort of reconciliation here in Cuba, far from the political turmoil of Chile. The streets of El Vedado smelled of young men decked out for the night. A cardboard sign at the union's iron gate announced a reading by Ernesto Cardenal, the bearded poet from Solentiname who always appeared in a white tunic.

When they tried to enter the front garden, a man with a gaunt face, glasses, and a well-groomed beard like Don Quixote's blocked their way.

"Your card," he said to Heberto, standing in front of the doorman's stall. He held a copy of *Casa de las Américas* magazine in his hand.

Heberto gave him identification.

"I mean your UNEAC card, not your regular ID."

"I'm a poet."

"Your UNEAC card."

Heberto dug nervously through the pockets of his pants and shirt. "I think it's just been stolen."

"Well, if you don't have it, you can't come in. UNEAC is only for writers and artists."

"I've already told you I'm a poet."

"That's what you say, just as I could say I'm Mikhail Bulgakov, who, of course, I have no desire to be. Only your UNEAC card proves you are a poet, novelist, or artist. If you don't have one, you aren't one. It's that simple."

"I had it," Heberto mumbled, glancing at Cayetano. "I had it and I lost it."

"Did you lose it or did they confiscate it?" Quixote asked him with a withering look.

"I think it got lost, comrade."

The doorman became as silent as a bishop. His gaze was malevolent; his jaw trembled with impatience.

"And you?" he asked Cayetano. "Another undocumented poet?"

"I'm a tourist. And it seems that I won't be able to enter, either."

"That's an entirely different story, my friend. Our revolutionary government goes to great lengths to welcome tourist comrades who break from the confines of imperialism. You may even be able to enter UNEAC. Where are you from?"

"Chile."

"In that case, right this way. And tell the writers and poets inside about Allende and the Chilean people's struggles to build a socialist state. The youth here have such a good time of it that they even idealize the brutalities of capitalism."

"Don't worry. I certainly will. And can this Cuban poet come with me, since we're together?"

"Let's say I accept that he's Cuban and that he's with you, but the part about being a poet is still unproven. Whom do you want to see?"

"Remigio," replied Heberto. Belkis had told them that this was the man who oversaw security for UNEAC, and that his office was next to that of Nicolás Guillén, the permanent president of the institution. Among other duties, Remigio examined the reasons foreigners gave for inviting Cuban writers and poets to appear abroad. He scoured these cases in search of attempts at escape or treason.

"So you're here to see Comrade Remigio?" the doorman asked, now affable.

Between the bars, the UNEAC mansion brimmed with lights and gave the neighborhood an air of unreality.

"Exactly. We came to visit Comrade Remigio," Heberto said, emboldened. "Can we pass?"

"That's all you needed."

"So is Remigio a poet or a novelist?" Cayetano asked Heberto as they walked through the vast garden to the white mansion that housed Cuba's official intellectuals.

As soon as Remigio saw Cayetano and Heberto entering his office, he invited them out for a walk on El Vedado. Cayetano was reluctant to leave the cool office, with its stately lamps and closed shutters—he would have preferred to stay and catch his breath, but in the end they went down to the first floor and walked down a cool hallway lined with beveled mirrors. In the event room, a few women spoke loudly to each other as they set up seats and a microphone for Cardenal's reading. They went out onto the street, ignoring Don Quixote, who was engrossed in his magazine, red pen in hand.

"Did you get it for me?" Remigio asked as they walked toward Línea, passing signs extolling the Committees for the Defense of the Revolution and calling on citizens to report for duty as night guards.

"Don't you worry. A table for six, this coming Saturday. It's right in front of the steps where the dancers take the stage," Heberto said. "Just call Paquito at the Tropicana on Friday night, and leave him a message."

Remigio breathed a sigh of relief. They continued on shaded streets, weaving past people taking refuge from the heat in doorways, where they chatted or played dominoes. "We'd better take our coffee in Línea," he said. "The walls have ears around here."

He was a slender man, with nervous gestures and a baritone voice. He wore sunglasses, a Rolex that seemed fake, and a Lacoste-style shirt. He smelled of Old Spice. He walked with an energetic pace, his face severe, as though burdened by the larger problems of humanity.

An enormous crowd had formed in front of the café. Remigio waved his state security badge and opened the way for the three of them just before a 132 line Leyland with rattling pistons stopped in front of the place, crammed with people. The engine emitted hot steam that stank of burned oil and petroleum. The driver, who sported a comb in his Angela Davis Afro, disembarked with a decisive air, trailed by a mob of caffeine addicts.

"Well, I obtained some of what you asked me for," Remigio said. In his student days, he'd succeeded in having one of his stories featured among the finalists of the March Thirteenth Literary Contest at the University. Perhaps that was why he now held the reins at UNEAC. "It's not much, but it might give you something."

They drank their coffee, leaning on the bar, in the midst of the noise and shoves of people struggling for their turn.

"Well? What do you know about Beatriz?" Heberto asked.

Remigio rubbed the face of his watch, worried about one of its hands, which had come loose. "First: that woman isn't Cuban."

"We already know she's Mexican," Heberto said in irritation.

"And that she was married to a Cuban doctor by the name of Bracamonte, and that she lived in Mexico in the forties."

"It turns out she isn't Mexican, either."

"What?" Cayetano put down the little cup of coffee, the best he'd had in years. "Not Mexican? What the hell is she, then?"

"Before I answer, I want you, Heberto, to clarify one thing, because at this point I'm not playing around: are you sure about the table in the Salon Under the Stars this Saturday? There are several of us who want to go hear Irakere."

"I'm sure, my friend. So what nationality is she?"

"German."

"German?" Cayetano repeated, incredulous. The Leyland had resumed its route, snorting like a bull in heat, leaving behind the passengers who were still waiting for their taste of coffee. Outside, as the three of them walked back toward Paseo, they were assailed by a sea breeze that rose from the Malecón, its scent blended with the odor of asphalt from the street.

"German," Remigio said again.

"And she's in Cuba?"

"Beatriz, widow of Bracamonte, whose maiden name is Beatriz Lederer, spent only two years here with her daughter."

"What was her daughter's name?"

"Tina Bracamonte."

"And what did Beatriz do here?"

"She worked as a translator in a department of the East German embassy, here in El Vedado, near the Hotel Nacional. And Tina studied at a school in Marianao. They left the island eleven years ago."

"In 1962? Where did they go?"

"To Berlin, my friend. To the German Democratic Republic. To live behind the anti-fascist wall, as they call it."

"What for?"

"How do I know!"

"Then what?"

"Then nothing, man. One morning in 1962, at the José Martí Airport, by the steps to an Aeroflot plane, the footprints of Beatriz Lederer and Tina Bracamonte disappeared forever from the island of Cuba. Now, what's that Paquito's number?"

∽ 29 ∽

The night was as fragile as a Swarovski statuette when Cayetano saw his wife below the hibiscus trees of Zapata Plaza, in Miramar. Along Quinta Avenue a Zil of the Youth Workers' Brigade passed, heading east, laden with singing troops, as well as a Leyland packed with passengers down to its stairwells. His wife—whom he still considered as such, since they were, after all, still legally married—had just disembarked from a blue Lada, which was waiting for her nearby, its lights off. She was wearing the olive-green uniform of the Armed Revolutionary Forces, or FAR, which disturbed him.

"What are you doing in Cuba?" she asked after kissing his cheek.

"I'm on a mission. What's with the uniform?"

"I'm doing what I told you about before. I'm a woman who lives by her word."

Cayetano gazed at the thick trunks of the hibiscus trees, which resembled twisted anacondas, then returned his attention to Ángela. With her hair pulled back under her soldier's hat, her uniform fitted to her curves, her face tanned by days spent out in the sun, she looked more beautiful than ever.

"You look great," he managed, and stroked his mustache, feeling insecure.

"And you're on a mission? Here?"

"As you see."

"It makes you seem more mature. How long will you be on the island?"

"Two or three more days," he replied, giving himself an air of importance and aloofness. In reality he would have liked to propose that they give it another shot, that as soon as she finished her training at Punto Cero, they should try to get back together in Valparaíso. If there was still love between them, they should give it another chance. Things could change when they returned to Chile; one day the country would regain its stability, and he also held out hope that the poet might recover his health and help him find work among his legion of contacts. Perhaps it was just a matter of trying, he thought, of giving it one more chance. But he said nothing, and only her voice was heard.

"I'm going to stay here a few months. The situation in Chile is getting worse. We're approaching the hour of truth—or, as they say here, the hour of the mamey fruit, that Caribbean mango."

"So what are your plans?"

"If you're on a mission, then you know they can't be discussed."

He had to admit she was right. They sat down on a marble bench, still warm from the sun, and looked at each other in silence. He was captivated by Ángela's fine features and full, delicate lips. The night was turning into jet-black linen, warm, fragrant, and impenetrable.

"I've been thinking about you," Ángela said, looking at her hands, the nails now chipped and dirty.

"Really? In what way?"

"I've been thinking about how I still don't understand why you don't return here for good."

"So we can be close?"

"I don't want to hurt you, Cayetano, but I honestly feel that what we had can't be salvaged. You should go back to your own life. There's nothing like the land where you were born."

"Is there someone else?" He felt as though he'd plagiarized the question right out of the soap opera *An Italian Girl Comes to Get Married.*

"No, nothing like that. You think I'm in any mood to start another relationship? The best thing for you would be to go home to your roots. This is where you're from, not Miami or Valparaíso."

Exiles should never return to their homeland, he thought. Nostalgia laid traps and played tricks. Nobody was built for the strain of return. Disappointment was always waiting on the arrivals platform. People were made to remain in the place where they were born; that was the only way of living without nostalgia. And one should never return, one should always leave for good. Nostalgia fed the illusion that returns were possible, that lost paradise itself could be regained.

"Your dream is a mirage," he said in a firm, steady voice, as if he were sitting on another bench, spying on the scene from a distance. "If the war you're preparing for does arrive, you have no chance of winning it. The Chilean army is nothing like that of Fulgencio Batista. Who's making young idealists like you martyr themselves in the name of a cause that, however just, is impossible to attain?"

"Don't talk that way, out of respect for this uniform if nothing else, Cayetano. There's no other way to defend Allende. If we don't take up arms, the right will stage a coup. And if they did that, more people would die than in a battle of equals."

"Don't you realize that you're dealing with a professional army?"

"What do you want me to do?" she said in a raised, angry voice, and she stood up and tore off her hat. Her hair spilled copiously over her shoulders, and her cheekbones became more prominent under her tanned skin. "Renounce my role as a revolutionary, in the tradition of Manuel Rodríguez and Che, so I can go back to Valparaíso with you to wait for the army to rebel? Or to put down my weapons and take up yarn and knitting needles so I can make you a scarf while the enemy prepares for a coup?"

"I just don't want you to risk your life."

"I'd rather die on my feet than live on my knees! And that's not just a slogan!"

He was about to tell her to calm down a little when the Lada at the edge of the park turned on and flashed its lights a couple of times.

"I should go," murmured Ángela.

Cayetano stood up, feeling like a man sentenced to death who no longer sees the point in begging for his life or one more minute of time. He approached her and held her tightly to his chest.

"I had to say it, Ángela." As he kissed her cheeks, he recognized the Coco Chanel she always wore. She was the same bourgeois girl as always.

"I won't forget you so easily," she assured him. "I was happy with you. Do you remember the cabin we used to dream about building on some Caribbean beach?"

"And the three children we were going to have, who wouldn't go to school, but would be free to roam instead?"

She kissed his lips and hurried off through the park, hat in hand, her hair loose around her shoulders like a shawl. Cayetano followed her with his gaze until she disappeared into the car. The Lada drove off down Quinta Avenue, toward Havana, and then he was alone, listening to the muffled, anonymous whispers of the night and the rapid drumming of his heart. He thought it had begun to rain, but then realized there were no drops on the lenses of his glasses; the tears in his eyes had blurred Miramar's hibiscus trees.

$\backsim$ *30* $\backsim$

"I t all happened just as I've told you, Don Pablo. What should
I do now?"

Static crackled on the phone line, like a shortwave radio station. Cayetano had the distinct impression that his call to Chile
was being tapped, that his words were being listened to by the
CIA or Cuban state security in a dismal room somewhere on
the planet. He had no choice but to speak in ambiguous terms.
It had served him well to read Simenon's crime novels, after all,
those calm, delectable stories about Peter the Lett, Maigret's
first case, or Maigret's memoirs, which were truly entertaining,
and which transformed their author—a man addicted to the
pipe, sex, and writing—into a simple fictional character.

"Well, follow her tracks," he heard the poet say with enthusiasm. Cayetano pictured him with his feet on the leather stool,
with its green ink stains.

At the outset of the conversation, Neruda had suggested
that he was feeling more energetic and hopeful, as though he
were making a recovery, and that for that reason he was diving

into verses in the afternoons and dictating his memoirs to Matilde at night. Cayetano imagined that the memoirs were incomplete, that they would later be filtered through his wife, though he also suspected that the poet said this only to throw off his enemies. His heavy breathing made Cayetano doubt his claims of getting better. He had just arrived home from the hospital and had probably already settled into La Nube, wrapped in his woolen poncho, looking out over the bay as it split into a play of light and shadow under the metallic Valparaíso sky.

"Do you still believe the same thing, Don Pablo?"

"Of course I do. The same as I described it that day on Alemania Avenue, when we sat on the steps. I just need you to confirm my suspicions."

Fragile as a bird but stubborn as a mule. That was the poet.

He pressed further. "Don't you think you're better off just deciding that it's as you imagine, and letting things be?"

"You don't know what you're saying, young man. I can't just leave things as they are. The fact that you'd even say that makes me think you don't understand me, that we've wasted all this time."

"I don't know, Don Pablo. Sometimes hope is better than disappointment. That's what I say."

But Neruda said the opposite. Despite the doubts his words described, his voice was firm, convinced, emphatic. "The young are nourished by hopes, the old by certainties, Cayetano. Suspicion has a corrosive effect, and speeds up death. I'd give anything, including my *Canto General* or my *Residence on Earth*, to know the truth. Believe me, I'd give them up gladly, right this moment, to find out."

At that point Cayetano took a chance. "What about love?"

"What?" The voice sounded disconcerted.

Through the window, Cayetano studied the Hotel Habana Libre as it hovered, clear and light, over the city, under soft clouds that glided toward Miramar. The whir of the air-conditioning muted the echoes of El Vedado. He knew that he had hit the nail on the head. "Love, Don Pablo, I'm asking you whether you still believe in love."

"Don't be naive, young man. That's a lifelong thing." He felt that the poet was putting him in his place. "Which is good news for you, incidentally, since you're just starting out. Look at me, I'm almost seventy and I'm still strong. The Greeks were wrong to think that old people were more fit to govern because they had lost their physical appetites. At my age, I have more heat and urges than ever, since I know the reapers are following me everywhere, eager and impatient."

Two packed buses drove by at a feverish pace, passing a knot of people waiting at the stop. Beyond them, others baked in the sun while standing in line at Vita Nova Pizzeria. Steam rose from the tar on the street, making the neighborhood oscillate like a mirage.

"Once the spurs of desire leave me, I won't be able to write," the poet continued. "Desire feeds my poetry, young man. Don't forget, it's that simple." He took a surprising turn. "Any news from Ángela?" They barely brought her up since that night, by that window facing Valparaíso and the sea beyond, when they had shared what he now knew was their mutual anguish.

"It's over, Don Pablo. 'We, the ones we were, are no longer the same.' Your own words."

"I remember them, and I also remember why I wrote them.

But once I was older and wiser, I also wrote, 'together we face the tears!' Don't forget that. Life is long, even though there's little left for me."

He didn't know whether he should feel comforted or saddened. He asked, "So what do we do now?"

"Do about what?"

"Don't forget that I'm in Havana, Don Pablo. What should I do now that the trail has gone cold?"

"Keep following it. Wait there until I get you a visa for the German Democratic Republic."

"I go to Germany from here?"

"To East Germany. Call me as soon as you land. I'll give you the name of someone who can help us. I trust you'll find the person we're looking for there. But, Cayetano, don't forget the most important thing of all: discretion."

DELIA

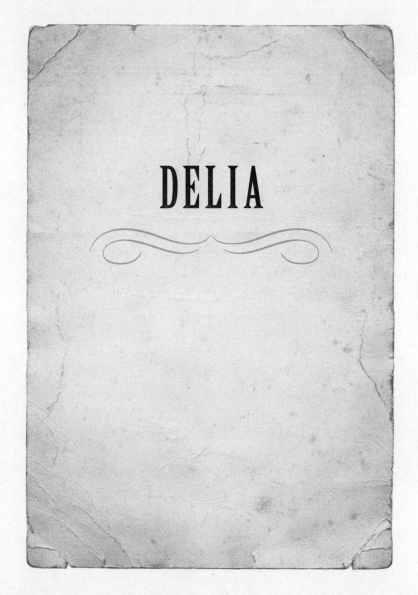

$$\sim 31 \sim$$

B efore touching down on Schönefeld's landing strip, the
Aeroflot Ilyushin II-62 circled over the divided city, tur-
bines whirring. From a sky streaked with clouds, Cayetano
glimpsed the line—sometimes straight, sometimes sinuous, but
always wide and clear—of the Wall, with its mined areas,
observation towers, and wire fencing. As the plane turned, it
glided through the air from east to west and back to east, ignoring the border between the two sides of greater Berlin, gliding
from one world to another with the still indolence of a pelican.

At first, Schönefeld seemed like any other airport in the
West: cold, modern, functional. It did, however, lack the colors,
scents, and sheen of capitalism. People were wearing clothes
that had gone out of fashion, in muted colors, as though life had
frozen in the 1950s. Perhaps that was why Cayetano sensed a
tranquillity he associated with places far removed from the fre-
netic pace of major Western cities, an atmosphere that reminded
him of Sunday siestas in Havana and the Valparaíso hills.

"Cayetano Brulé?" asked a voice from behind.

He turned and saw a man with unkempt hair, a thick mustache, and small dark eyes. He looked a bit like Charlie Chaplin, with the same pale, melancholy, mischievous face; the same high eyebrows; the same sad, ingenuous expression; and gleaming eyes.

"I'm Eladio Chacón." They shook hands. "I'm the director of labor affairs at our embassy. I handle relations with the main office for the Free German Trade Union Federation, the FDGB. A few days ago, the state department notified me of your visit so that I could be of assistance. Welcome to the land of Karl Marx and Rosa Luxemburg!"

"I'm most thankful, Chacón."

"You can call me Merluza, if you like. That's how I'm known to comrades in the Party. You can also call me Carlitos Chaplin; personally, I think I resemble the comedian more than the *merluza* fish. But you know how Chileans are, handing out nicknames right and left. So. I know that you're Cuban and you're looking for a Mexican woman of German origin who emigrated to East Berlin some time ago."

"Ten or twelve years ago, to be more exact."

In the parking lot, Merluza placed the luggage in the trunk of his Wartburg. The car clattered like a scooter as they drove down cobblestone streets, and Cayetano wondered whether everyone had a double hidden somewhere in the world. Proof abounded: the blacklisted poet in Havana looked just like Roy Orbison, and the Chilean diplomat was identical to Charlie Chaplin. Somewhere, there must be someone who strongly resembled Neruda, Ángela, and Cayetano himself. At some point he should articulate it to the poet. He was sure of at least one thing: he was Cayetano Brulé, and not a double of himself.

In the distance, beneath the incandescent sun, he glimpsed the Television Tower, as well as the skyscraper that housed the Stadt Berlin Hotel. The Wartburg dived into downtown, weaving between cars of unfamiliar makes, such as Volga, Škoda, and Trabant, as well as Ikarus buses and Czech trams. They turned onto a crowded commercial street. Pankower Allee, Merluza explained. As soon as he laid eyes on it, Cayetano realized that East Germany was not at all like Cuba. Here, the store windows were packed with wares, there were no lines outside grocery stores or restaurants, and the people enjoyed a well-being unimaginable on the island. Merluza told him he'd be staying at the Stadt Berlin, near Alexanderplatz, but that first they'd go to lunch at Ratskeller, a restaurant with seven hundred years of history.

"They make the most incredible ham," Merluza went on. "Though there are also some *Klösse*, from Thuringia, that are good enough to raise the dead. And what can I say about the baked carp and boiled potatoes? Do you prefer Bulgarian wine or Czech beer? We diplomats don't need to wait for a table there. We rise over the mortals, and that's how it is."

Fifteen minutes later, seated at the restaurant in the basement of Red City Hall, they ordered oxtail consommé, ham with boiled potatoes, and Czech pilsner. The poet's East Berlin contact was clearly offering Cayetano a very special reception. Merluza was a member of MAPU, a tiny petit bourgeois group, as the communists put it, that history would record as a cell capable of dividing and dividing until it disappeared altogether. Merluza had been sent to East Berlin because, in Chile, he'd dared to call for the expropriation of not only North American investments, but also the English, even at risk of stripping

Queen Isabel herself, which had sparked an uproar in the government, loath as it was to make enemies in Europe. There, in the German Democratic Republic—in East Germany—the first nation by and for workers and peasants to grace German soil, as the banners proclaimed—Merluza was tasked with absorbing true socialism and the day-to-day operations of the FDGB, as presided over by the hard-drinking Harry Tisch, instead of stirring up the henhouse with his utopias in Chile.

"Well, nobody here knows this Beatriz," Merluza said after draining his first pilsner and letting out a discreet burp.

"Why didn't you tell me before?" Cayetano asked, stroking his cold glass.

"What?"

"That no one knows anything about the woman."

"Calm down. The situation isn't hopeless, either."

"How can it not be? If I'd known that nobody here knows her, I could have saved myself the trip. I was doing just fine in Havana."

"I'll bet you were. Lovely ladies over there, right?"

"They're unsurpassable. But if Beatriz is a complete stranger here, unknown to anyone, I may as well go back to Schönefeld as soon as I've digested the ham you promised."

"Listen to me. I don't know a thing about your Beatriz, but I found a Spanish translator who can help you."

"I don't need a translator. I understand a little German. I lived in West Germany for years."

"Calm down." He grasped Cayetano's wrist. "According to a Chilean woman, in the JHSWP—"

"The what?"

"JHSWP, the Jugendhochschule Wilhelm Pieck, a school

of the FDJ, on the outskirts of Berlin, on the shore of Lake Bogensee."

"The FD what?"

"FDJ, the Freie Deutsche Jugend, East Germany's youth association," Merluza explained impatiently. "Under socialism, we speak in acronyms, Mr. Brulé."

"Fine. So what happens there?" The oxtails had an acidic taste, forcing him to wash down the first spoonful with a gulp of beer.

"Well, in the sixties, there was a woman worked there who had arrived from Mexico. It could be a coincidence, or she just may be the person you're looking for. Her age is the same, as are the period of time and her nation of origin. We learned about her through a retired Chilean translator."

"Can I speak with this translator?"

"Forget about meeting her. She lives in Bucharest now. She married one of Ceauşescu's government officials. And all she knew was that a woman from Mexico had translated there. What's important now is that you check out the Wilhelm Pieck School."

"So what are we waiting for?"

"We need a permit to enter there. It's a place where they indoctrinate revolutionaries from all over the world."

The hams landed on the table. They were the most extraordinary Cayetano had ever seen. The pigs in East Germany's cooperative farms must be as big as cows, and live like princes, or like princes sentenced to death, he thought with an appetite so enormous it nearly verged on the demonic. It was strange that Chilean food had so little in common with food in Cuba, and so much more in common with that of Germany.

"They're expecting us the day after tomorrow, at ten o'clock sharp," Merluza added, examining the dish. "But please, Cayetano, explain this to me, because these days I just don't understand what goes through our Chilean leaders' heads. Why is that woman so important right now, when Chile is in such a mess?"

~ 32 ~

I was attracted to Delia del Carril from the moment I first saw her.
It was in a pub called Correos, in Madrid, in 1934. I was dazzled
by her self-assurance, her elegance, and the circle of intellectuals with
whom she rubbed elbows. I was thirty years old, and she was fifty. I
had just arrived in Spain as a diplomatic consul, accompanied by
María Antonieta and poor Malva Marina. The Civil War there
was brewing.

Delia gave meaning to my life, made me a communist, dissemi-
nated my poetry, and refined my tastes and manners. Back then I
was unkempt and poorly dressed, my fingers always stained with
ink, my pockets stuffed with scribbled paper instead of money. She
turned me into the poet I am today. That afternoon, when we first
met, I placed my hand on her shoulder, delicately, and from then on
we were never apart. Not ever. Well, that is, until I met Matilde
twenty years later and left one woman for another.

Delia was absentminded, sensitive, and forgetful, a curious mix
of artist and pragmatist, and a disastrous housewife. She couldn't
even fry an egg, mash potatoes, or organize a dinner for friends, yet

at the same time she was an outstanding, tireless worker, well versed in the ways of the world, and skilled at forming friendships. That's how she got the nickname La Hormiga, the Ant. She succumbed like a marionette without strings the day that, in our house in Los Guindos, Santiago, she found a letter from Matilde in my jacket pocket, confessing that she was carrying my child.

"But it's you I love, Hormiga," I mumbled. The letter trembled in her hand, and her face was distorted by shock and suffering. "That was just a passing passion. You have always been and always will be my only queen."

"Without love, our relationship means nothing," Delia answered coldly. "We're not some bourgeois marriage, tied by social conventions, Pablo, but a communist couple bound by nothing but love. If that love has died, we should end it."

She demanded that I leave the house at once. When I did, Santiago was blurred by rain, the thrushes were silent, and the distant peaks of the Andes were enfolded by snow. I moved into La Chascona, a house at the base of Santa Lucía Hill, the house I'd secretly bought for Matilde years before. She was waiting for me there. I switched houses and women like a rider who changes horses in the middle of a race. I haven't seen Delia since; she's never spoken out against me and, according to some trustworthy friends, she still loves me. She's in her nineties now, surrounded by the same walls and furniture that witnessed our breakup. She's received some recognition as a painter and engraver, and as far as I know, she's never had another partner. By now, some comrade has probably told her that I'm sick. When I die, her hope of our reuniting will die with me.

In Madrid, she introduced me to Louis Aragon and Elsa Triolet, Paul Éluard, and Pablo Picasso. She was the one who published Canto General *secretly in Chile, and fought to end the exile imposed on me by that tyrant, González Videla. Delia was Argentinean, divorced, the daughter of a fallen aristocratic family, and she had arrived in Europe to study under the painter Fernand Léger, which was how she came to frequent the Continent's communist intellectual circles. When we were first living together, she persuaded me not to keep writing hermetic poems like* Residence on Earth, *and to instead write about love and the political causes that shake the world. Without her, I would not have been a communist, nor would my verses ever have reached millions of readers.*

But the truth is the truth: despite the fact that I was married to María Antonieta and responsible for Malva Marina, Delia surreptitiously slid into my life, and seduced me. I admit that it wasn't hard for me to leave my wife and daughter to move into la Casa de las Flores, my lover's house in the Hilarión Eslava section, near the Ciudad Universitaria district of Madrid. In that house, we enjoyed salons with García Lorca, Bergamín, Altolaguirre, Acario Cotapos, and Miguel Hernández. We drank red wine and anisette from Chichón, and then we'd go to the Correos pub, or a nightclub called Satán, which was run by Mario Carreño at 60 Atocha Street, where half-naked women performed "the dance of cocaine" to the rhythm of the Lecuona Orchestra. We drank Montserrat champagne, La Guita sherry, and Sorracina cider, and we'd come home late, quite drunk. I separated from María Antonieta and Malva Marina in 1936, and washed my hands of them in 1943, when they were living in Nazi-occupied Holland.

Delia helped me give refuge in Chile to thousands of Republican Spaniards fleeing the Civil War. We saved them from thick-walled prisons by sending them to Valparaíso on a ship called Winnipeg. *They made Chile their second homeland, and made their mark on our culture. How could I be so altruistic for the anonymous masses, yet at the same time be so cruel and heartless toward a person I'd loved and another person who carried my blood in her veins? It was Delia who bought, with her own money, the land where we built the house in Isla Negra, which despite its name is neither black nor an island, and which I love and many consider to be my favorite house. Dramas, terrible dramas, surround my homes: the ones in the Orient were devastated by typhoons; the one in Las Flores by pro-Franco gunfire; the one in Los Guindos witnessed the epilogue of our love; the house in Isla Negra was purchased by the woman who shaped me and whom I left for a much younger woman; the home in Santiago, in the Bellavista neighborhood, was acquired so that I could hide that very same younger lover. Only La Sebastiana, this opus of air that levitates over Valparaíso, with its aviary and landing strip, was conceived without stains.*

I wish I could have had a daughter with Delia, a healthy and joyful girl who could have helped me forget the melancholy smile that would glimmer on Malva Marina's monstrous face. But Delia was already barren when I met her, and could not give me what I longed for. Perhaps I'm confused by my own memories. The fact is, I couldn't have borne another disaster, another Malva Marina. Which is exactly why I escaped from Beatriz when, years later, at Xochimilco Lagoon, she told me she was bearing my child. I refused to believe it. I lacked the courage to cast aside my literary career with Delia and face the uncertainty of new fatherhood. And much less could I risk a change of such proportions in July 1943, when I had just symbolically married Delia in Tetecala, in the state of Morelos. She was fifty-nine at the time, and I was thirty-nine. She was beautiful and still desirable, no matter what my enemies might whisper to the contrary. The Tetecala night brimmed with mosquitoes. Under the full moon, I gave her a silver necklace made by the indigenous people of Oaxaca, and promised her that we'd be together until death did us part.

"Are you sure I'm the father?" I asked Beatriz in Xochimilco. We

were gliding through canals, holding hands in a canoe adorned with flowers. The lead-colored water smelled like deep roots, and the moon's patina lit the fireflies.

Beatriz glared at me. "Who else would it be?"

"It could be your husband," I said quietly, letting go of her hand.

She said nothing. Behind us, the boatman kept rowing through the water with long strokes.

"I don't have the balls to be a father," I confessed in a whisper. "You know about the monster that was born to me in Spain. That could happen again. If it's mine, I'd like you to have an abortion. All I can father is deformed beings—and my poems."

Beatriz leaped out of the canoe and waded through the dark water to a nearby field. Then her silhouette disappeared among the bushes and tree trunks. I never saw her again. Years later, I found out she'd given birth to a different child, a boy, or perhaps a girl, I didn't even want to know. I supposed at that point that it must have been the offspring of the good Dr. Bracamonte, since they were still married . . .

"We have a meeting with Comrade Valentina Altmann," Merluza informed the *Volkspolizist*, who had emerged from a wooden sentry box hidden among birches, to meet them on the asphalt path. "We're from the Chilean embassy."

The JHSWP School was in northeastern Berlin, on the shore of a small lake called Bogensee, surrounded by forests. Across from the Wandlitz, another nearby lake, stood a gated neighborhood, home to leaders of the United Socialist Party of Germany, or USPG, headed up by Erich Honecker.

The crossing gate rose slowly, and Merluza drove down a winding gravel path that ran through the shadows of trees.

"This was Goebbels's summer refuge," Merluza said. Through the greenery, they glimpsed a stone mansion with a wooden roof. "After the war, it was transferred into the hands of the Soviets, who gave it to the East German government. First it was a center for denazification. For thirty years now, it's belonged to the FDJ, the nation's youth association."

Cayetano looked at the building with a sense of loneliness

and despair. He couldn't understand why Beatriz had abandoned the vitality of Mexico City and the luminous exoticism of Havana to settle in such a remote, anonymous place.

"Now it's a monastery for teaching Marxist Leninism," Merluza went on. "They say the Stasi recruits foreigners here. Classes start in September and end in June. In the summer, the only people here are teachers and translators, who live at the school or in Bernau, a nearby city."

"And the Mexican woman we're talking about?"

"Don't be so impatient. The comrades here should know."

He parked the Wartburg beside a rusty Volga, and walked to a plaza surrounded by robust, gray three-story buildings of Stalinist design. Valentina was waiting at the front steps. She was a slim woman with sharp features and blue eyes. Merluza introduced them, and they entered the building together. They crossed a spacious lobby and entered a large, desolate restaurant with imposing bronze lamps.

"I'll wait for you outside," Merluza said, and left discreetly.

"Ask me anything you like," Valentina said as she ordered tea for both of them. "If there's information I can't provide, there are experienced people in the administrative office who know the school's history inside out."

After explaining that she knew he was an emissary of an Unidad Popular leader, Valentina declared, out of the blue, that she recalled no one at the school by the name of Beatriz Lederer. She warned him that his investigation would be complicated by the fact that the school used pseudonyms, and prohibited taking photographs. When Cayetano showed her the photograph of Beatriz, the translator assured him that she'd never seen the woman. The tea was Russian, and a slice of lemon perched on the lip of every cup. They drank in silence. Cayetano feared the terms of "reasons of state" could be blocking his efforts. If that was the case, not even Neruda could push the investigation forward unless he disclosed his real purpose.

He felt depressed, not only by the bitter tea that smacked of lemonade, but also because he recalled Maigret and envied the faith that man had in his own talent, experience, and skill. Reality, he thought, was much harder on people than any fictional world ever was on its characters. The fates that reigned over the universe were crueler than the flesh-and-blood writers who composed novels. It was easier to be an excellent detective in a crime novel than a mediocre detective in implacable reality. He'd have to discuss this one day with the poet, over drinks, while relaxing in that comfortable floral-print armchair, beholding the gorgeous view out of La Sebastiana's windows.

"How long have you worked here?" he asked Valentina, who was squeezing her lemon slice into the tea.

She had arrived at the school four years earlier, in 1969, and liked the grounds and the foreign students, though not her colleagues, whom she found dull and lacking in passion. A drop of lemon juice struck her chest and rolled down the triangle of skin revealed by the collar of her blouse. Cayetano pictured small and upright breasts, tanned from sunny afternoons that she surely spent naked by Lake Bogensee. He wondered what it would be like to spread that acidic teardrop over her breasts with his fingertip, and pictured Valentina translating paragraphs of *The Communist Manifesto*, by Marx and Engels, and Lenin's *The State and Revolution* in classrooms packed with revolutionaries from Africa, Asia, and Latin America, who after a few months would be staring at her with eyes full of desire. He saw young men determined to share ideals and study political theories, just like his wife at Punto Cero. He saw the

JHSWP full of youths anxious to learn the secrets they needed to topple the bourgeoisie and create socialist societies in Third World nations. He saw them studying revolutionary texts by morning, singing battle hymns and organizing forums in the afternoons, and forging secret alliances over long nights of beer and dialogue, during which they fell in love with German girls and fornicated with them in the forest. He saw many of them dying in combat, or being tortured or killed by the police back in their own countries. And as for him, Cayetano, to what was he devoted? What utopias drove him? His wife was right to criticize his skepticism, his refusal to embrace any cause, his tendency to watch things from a distance.

"If you arrived here in 1969, you obviously couldn't have met the person I'm looking for," he grumbled, returning from his musings in a bad mood.

"That's right," Valentina admitted as she wiped the drop from her chest with the edge of a napkin.

"In that case, why don't you take me to meet your colleagues who have been here longer?"

As they crossed the plaza, on their way to the administrative office, they ran into a young woman with a pale face and light-colored hair, dressed in a long smock that drew attention to her hips. Her name was Margaretchen Siebold, and she hugged a stack of thick-covered books to her chest with a certain theatricality. She asked them what they were doing, and Cayetano explained.

"I don't remember anyone by that name. But I'll walk with you. I also need to speak with Käthe."

The office was on the top floor of a building on a hill overlooking the edifices clustered around the plaza. It housed the library, the auditorium, classrooms, and the school's administrative office. Valentina walked through a door and left Cayetano with Margaretchen in the hall.

"Historischer und Dialektischer Materialismus, Grundlagen der Kapitalistichen Wirtschaft, Geschichte der KpdSU," Cayetano read aloud from the spines of the books the young woman carried. "Is that what you teach here?"

"I don't teach. I translate for Latin Americans. You have to keep up with your subject matter."

"So that's why you speak perfect Spanish."

"If you say so."

"It's a shame that nobody remembers your colleague anymore. We spend our lives thinking we're essential, and then, when we die, we're lucky if our own children bring us flowers on the Day of the Dead. Then nobody remembers us anymore. And to think how urgently I need to find Beatriz!" He shook his head, a burdened man.

"They won't tell you anything here," the translator whispered. "They never disclose information about their employees. Nobody has a name or face here. Didn't you know?"

"I knew, but they're going to help me because I'm backed by the Chilean embassy. That makes for a convincing argument."

"Really?"

"Of course. I have a good godfather. And relations between Allende and Honecker are optimal," Cayetano answered, put out by the woman's dubious tone.

"Your chances will only improve with the Stasi's support," she said.

"I'm not playing around. The Chilean who sent me has a great deal of influence."

"Don't be naive." She adjusted her hair around her shoulders. "Here no one will tell you anything. Much less about Beatriz."

"So you know her?"

"Who is this influential Chilean who wants to see her?"

He would not tell her. She could be a Stasi agent, he thought, charged with finding out the reason for his visit. Through the window, he gazed at a bronze, life-size statue that gleamed in the central plaza. It showed a row of children holding hands and leaping happily on the lawn.

"I understand your distrust," she said. The hall stretched out before them, polished, empty, with gray doors on one side and clean windows on the other. "If you'd like to keep talking, you can find me tomorrow, at eight o'clock, in the Zum Weissen Hirsch. Come see me if they don't give you anything."

She walked away the moment Valentina opened the door, accompanied by an old woman with pink skin and blue eyes who resembled a Lladró porcelain statue.

"Come on in, Cayetano," Valentina said. "My comrade Käthe here will fill you in on everything you need to know."

～ 34 ～

The Zum Weissen Hirsch was on Eberswalder Strasse 37, in Bernau, near a highway lined with apple trees that led to the industrial city of Eberswalde. Its old walls were covered in vines, which occasionally thinned to reveal bricks poking out from the worn stucco like rotted teeth. When Cayetano walked in, he was met with smoke and the thick stench of beer. He walked through the dimness, through which the husky, unmistakable voice of Karat sidled, singing "Schwanenkönig." It took him a moment to find Margaretchen, who was smoking at a table by the window, with a pilsner and a small glass of *Doppelkorn* in front of her.

"I warned you. They never reveal anything about their people," she said. Cayetano was struck once again by her pale face, the dark circles around her eyes, and the metallic brilliance of her gaze.

"You were right." Cayetano settled in across from Margaretchen. "Neither Valentina nor Käthe knew a thing about Beatriz."

The radio now played a ballad crooned by Karel Gott, the golden voice of Prague, reminiscent of Elvis Presley and Lucho Gatica. In a corner, behind an umbrella stand, an older couple dined; just past them, some long-haired customers in flowered shirts sat at a table, and beyond that the tables were packed with boisterous customers. Cayetano and Margaretchen ordered onion and Klösse soup with potatoes, and a bottle of Stierblut, a Bulgarian wine that, according to the translator, wasn't half bad.

"So you know Beatriz?" Cayetano pressed.

"I knew a woman at the school who was called Beatriz." She ran her fingers through her hair. "She may be the woman you're looking for. She came from Mexico, and her last name was Schall. Beatriz Schall."

"Schall? Are you sure?"

"Absolutely."

"But people use false names at the JHSWP."

"The foreign students do. But the staff and the German students use their real names. My name is real."

Cayetano took the photograph of Beatriz out of the pocket of his guayabera, the one from the Mexican newspaper, and held it in the lamplight. Margaretchen examined it closely.

"She looks a lot like her," she said, lowering her eyelids sensually, mysteriously.

"Is it her or not?"

"Beatriz Schall was more heavyset. And she was a resolute woman."

"But she was only twenty in the photograph. People change over time. When did you say you knew her?"

"In her last year at the JHSWP. She was leaving, I was just arriving. I couldn't say that in front of Valentina. She's an apparatchik of fear. Don't trust her."

Cayetano stroked the tip of his mustache and gazed at the older couple, who were paying their check and preparing to leave. "Forgive my asking," he said as the old man helped his wife into her raincoat. "How old are you?"

"Twenty-seven," she said as she drained her glass of schnapps.

"If Valentina, who's been there for seven years, never met Beatriz, then you would much less have had the chance— unless you started working at sixteen."

"The thing is, I met Beatriz as a student at Wilhelm Pieck," she said. She gestured to the waiter for another glass. "I met her in 1963, ten years ago."

"If we're talking about the same woman, she would have been forty then."

"That's exactly how old she seemed."

He was disconcerted by the change in Beatriz's last name. From Lederer in Havana to Schall in East Berlin. What was her real name in Mexico City? Fichte, had the poet said? In the files at the Four Roses Institute she was known as "de Bracamonte." He put the photograph away and lit a Cuban Populares, which emitted a penetrating odor of dry grass. He inhaled the smoke, worried.

"Tell me, what did she look like?"

"She had light hair and green eyes. White skin. A German woman with Slavic features."

"And what did she do at the school?" He let smoke out through his nose, feeling like a humble dragon in the great Prussian grasslands.

"She translated for the courses on Marxism and Leninism for Latin Americans. Just like I do now. It's enjoyable work, and well compensated. You get to meet people from different countries."

"Did you ever know of her having a lover?"

"If she did, it was outside the school. She rented an apartment in front of the Verdugo tower, near the city's medieval wall. I also recall that Beatriz had a daughter. Tina was her name, I think."

"How old was Tina?" The facts were coming together, he thought, perking up.

"Around twenty. I saw her two or three times, at school functions. For the first of May and the seventh of October, when we celebrate the founding of East Germany."

Cayetano myopically took in the dirty afternoon glare that leaked in through the windows. Things seemed to be falling into place: Beatriz was of German origin, which was why she had taught German at the institute in Mexico City, and why she'd come to East Germany. But was this Beatriz Schall the same Beatriz Lederer from Cuba and the same Beatriz from Mexico whom he was looking for? Assuming it was the same person, why had she left Mexico City, and later left revolutionary Cuba, to hole up in some isolated ideological school in East Berlin? If she'd arrived in East Germany soon after the Wall was built, she had to be a woman of leftist convictions. Why did she change her name? Who was she hiding from? He wondered whether she might have been involved in the death of her husband, an older man. Had she inherited money from him?

The barman placed the bottle of Stierblut on the table, opened it with a brusque gesture, filled the glasses to their brims without giving his customers a chance to taste the wine, and slipped back into the shadows of Zum Weissen Hirsch.

"Why do you trust me?" he asked the woman as he crushed his cigarette butt in the ashtray. A tune by the Puhdys now sang of the yearning to live as long as trees, which made him think of Neruda. "I'm a foreigner, the JHSWP trains revolutionaries, and you're giving me information about one of its former employees. I believe that could be called a form of treason."

Margaretchen sipped her Stierblut slowly, as if searching for her answer in the red wine, then said, "I trust you, quite simply, because I like you."

"That's a rather naive answer for someone who works with undercover agents."

"You're the one who's mistrustful."

"And you could be a Stasi agent . . ."

"In that case, to the health of the Mata Hari of Bernau," she said mockingly, with a gleam in her eyes. She took another drink. "The Bulgarians have pretty good wine," she said, gazing at him steadily.

Now Demis Roussos was singing "Forever and Ever," suffusing the place with Mediterranean melancholy. Cayetano began to feel suspicious of Margaretchen's ingenuousness. Was it all an act? Was this beautiful woman a Stasi agent or not? At the very least, she worked at a key political institution. He thought that he could be bungling everything even by speaking with her. He saw the poet in his armchair in Valparaíso, trusting Cayetano to devote twenty-four hours a day to the mission with which he'd been entrusted. And here he was, flirting, in the remote town of Bernau, with a German woman who could easily be an East German informant. He thought of Ángela, who at that moment could be crawling through swamps, climbing rope ladders, or taking apart AK-47s in the Cuban mountains, wearing an olive-green uniform covered in dirt and sweat.

"Why are you doing all of this, Margaretchen?" he pressed. "You don't know who you're getting involved with. This could bring you trouble. You could face punishment at the school."

"Do you know why I went to Wilhelm Pieck yesterday?" She quickly drained her glass.

"I imagine it was to speak with Käthe and pick up textbooks from the library."

"To clear out my office," she said slowly. She paused, holding his gaze. "It was my last day."

"What?"

"They fired me," she said, and bit her lip. The waiter poured another *Doppelkorn* in her glass. "My career is over."

"But why?"

"Political conduct inappropriate for work," she said, imitating an official tone. "They found out that, years ago, I'd had a Western lover. Someone told on me. But let's forget about that now. You only wanted to know why I'm helping you, right?"

"Maybe this isn't the best time to talk about that."

"On the contrary. It comforts me to change the subject. My colleagues have already started to avoid me. I'm going to have to leave my apartment and move back in with my mother in Magdeburg. In any case," she said, wiping two crumbs from the tablecloth with her knife, "I'm helping you because I think you must have a good reason to search for Beatriz. I admired her very much. In those days, I believed in all of this. She was a true revolutionary, someone who had done things in the Third World, one of those crucial people Brecht talks about. Not like us, here, who are like extras in a film, just numbers or statistics, people condemned to imagine the world from behind the Wall."

"So you were friends?"

"I would have loved that, but she was much older than me. One day she left the school, and we never saw each other again."

"What explanation did they give you?"

Margaretchen snorted. "None. She simply disappeared. Nobody even saw her pack her bags. One morning her office was empty, and nothing was heard from her again. And at that school, there are things one just doesn't ask, Herr Brulé. That was in 1964."

"And the daughter?"

"She was studying theater, or something like that, but in Leipzig. I never heard anything more about either of them."

Now he'd really hit bottom, he thought, suddenly disheartened. Not even the staff at Wilhelm Pieck knew of Beatriz's whereabouts. And he was getting involved with a controversial person, who probably wanted to help him out of sheer revenge. He thought of Maigret. In a similar case, the inspector would calmly consider various hypotheses while thoroughly enjoying an eggplant dish and a tray of *moules* at a bistro in the Gare du Nord. But he wasn't in a Simenon novel: he was in a run-down *Gaststätte* in Bernau, East Germany, one and a half kilometers from a Soviet garrison, with no experience as a detective beyond what he'd gleaned from novels. Maigret lived and worked in the center of the world; Cayetano was on its margins. And there lay the difference between a fictional detective, born from the pen of a popular First World writer, and a flesh-and-blood detective, an investigative proletarian, an exile surviving the rigors of the Third World. He glanced at the Russian Poljot watch he'd received from Paquito D'Rivera in exchange for a

Panamanian guayabera shirt, and which luckily still worked. It was past eleven o'clock at night.

"The last S-Bahn train leaves at eleven forty-seven," Margaretchen remarked laconically. "After that, you won't be able to return to Berlin until four forty-seven in the morning."

They gazed at each other through the cigarette smoke. From the radio, a slow voice described record carbon production in Leipzig and the strengthening of unbreakable ties between the German Democratic Republic and the Soviet Union. What would it be like, he wondered, to live with someone who knew the train schedules by heart? Would life with such a person be easier, or more complicated? The Germans lived by their watches, Cubans didn't need them, and Chileans, though they wore them, didn't seem to believe in them very much. It was obviously too late to arrive at the station on time.

"I'll take a taxi to Berlin," he said, wiping his mustache with a napkin.

"This isn't East Berlin, Herr Brulé. There are no taxis or buses at this hour."

"Then I'll find a nearby hotel."

"You're clearly unfamiliar with true socialism," replied Margaretchen. "The hotels here require reservations months in advance. You can stay at my apartment if you like. There's only one room, but I'm sure we can work something out. Would you prefer to walk all the way to Alexanderplatz, or just spend the night with me?"

35

In Margaretchen's apartment, time seemed to have stopped in the 1950s. It was on the fifth floor of a building on Strasse der Befreiung, and was limited to a studio living-dining room, which Margaretchen turned into a bedroom at night by turning down the sofa. A bookshelf held works by Marx, Engels, and Lenin, a small black-and-white television, and a radio-cassette player. A teddy bear rested on the sofa bed, wearing a golden crown. The kitchenette and bathroom with shower were on one end; on the other, a window and door led out to the balcony.

"This place is like you," Cayetano said as he removed his shoes. Margaretchen had placed hers behind the door.

"Like me?" she said, her eyes drowsy from the alcohol.

"Well, it's warm. Genuine."

She smiled, flattered, and Cayetano thought that sometimes affectionate words were enough to seduce a woman. Beyond the balcony, he glimpsed the lights of the Soviet regiment that, according to Margaretchen, stood ready to face down Western troops should they attack East Berlin. It occurred to Cayetano that if World War III should break out at that moment, they would be vulnerable not only to NATO missiles aimed at East Berlin, but also to Warsaw Pact missiles failing to reach West Berlin. Sleeping here, he thought, was like sleeping under a coconut tree: sooner or later a falling coconut was bound to crack your skull.

"Open the white wine that's in the fridge," ordered Margaretchen. "I'll take care of the rest."

She transformed the sofa into a double bed, then made it up with goose-feather pillows and sheets embroidered by her mother. She took two clean towels out of the closet. Her movements were routine and precise, as though sharing her bed with a stranger were something normal in her life. Cayetano took the wine bottle out to the balcony and breathed in the warm night brimming with stars and tart scents.

"Poland is that way," Margaretchen said, gesturing with her chin as she brought two wineglasses to the balcony. "And just a little farther, the land of Lenin."

Was her ironic tone meant to provoke him? Cayetano wondered. They toasted and stared out at the landscape in silence. In just a few moments he would share Margaretchen's bed. The thought dampened his desire, as he belonged to the Latin American school of love, which preferred amorous encounters with tentative beginnings and gradual consummation, wrapped in romanticism, and always initiated by the man. This female emancipation, born of true socialism, made him feel uncomfortable and inhibited. The wine was Romanian, and sweet, the kind that breaks your head open, he thought with concern. A train moved through the night, a faraway row of lights, and he thought he saw a dead kangaroo beside the highway to Eberswalde, which could only be an unsettling sign.

When he got back to Valparaíso, he'd have to see his friend John Stamler, the ophthalmologist. He obviously needed a stronger prescription.

"That's the express to Moscow," Margaretchen explained. "Every night it travels from Ostbahnhof to Warsaw, and then it crosses the steppes. It comes from Oostende, a city I can't visit while I'm young, because they don't let you leave East Germany until you retire."

The illuminated serpent rattled into the distance. Now the building stood silent and alone before the apple trees of Eberswalder Strasse, dappled by streetlights. Not even the remains of Bernau's kangaroo could be seen.

"Here's to you finding Beatriz." Margaretchen smiled and raised her glass.

They looked at each other in the semidarkness. The lace curtains filtered the living room light. Cayetano took the young woman by the waist and gently led her inside. He placed his wineglass on the windowsill, and they embraced.

She whispered into his ear, "Let's shower first."

Cayetano felt awkward. He didn't like to plan amorous acts as though they were visits to the doctor. When passion flared, one should throw on more coal, not put up obstacles or make demands. But there was little he could do. Margaretchen began to undress in front of him, letting her clothes fall to the floor like cut flowers. She had a long, fine neck, small breasts with pink nipples, and firm thighs. She entered the bathroom, imprinting Cayetano's retinas with the impeccable full moon of her behind.

~ 36 ~

She woke him the next morning with a bowl full of coffee and toast with marmalade. She wore a cotton bathrobe, and her hair was disheveled from sleep. Cayetano sat up, inhaling the aroma of coffee mixed with the tart scent of the Brandenburg countryside that sidled in from the open balcony, along with Soviet hymns.

"I only offer this service to my lovers on their first day," Margaretchen said with a teasing smile. On the wooden tray stood two glasses of Rotkäppchen, the famous East German sparkling wine. "And only if they've passed the test in bed. After that, we share the chores. That's how we women are in this country: equal pay for equal work. Take note."

"So how did I do?"

"Not bad, after such a long trip," she said, winking and sipping her Rotkäppchen.

Cayetano put on a blue silk robe that Margaretchen seemed

to keep on hand for casual lovers, and they went to finish their breakfast on the balcony. Beyond the military barracks, the highway glittered, the plains turned into cornfields, and the morning swelled with birdsong. Not a bad place to live, Cayetano thought as he cleaned his glasses and Margaretchen opened the *Neues Deutschland* paper on the table. He wondered what it would be like to move in here, behind the Wall, his back turned to the West, ready to start a new life yet again, this time with a young woman like Margaretchen. But he pushed those thoughts away. He should focus on his mission. At that very moment, the poet or Merluza could be trying to call him at the Stadt Berlin Hotel. What should he do now that Beatriz's footprints had become so complicated?

"You're the only person who can help me find Beatriz Schall," he said to Margaretchen. The Rotkäppchen reminded him of Valdivieso, a Chilean champagne. "You have to help me."

"First tell me why you're looking for her."

If he told her his reasons, he'd be betraying the poet, because, he thought, Margaretchen was probably a Stasi agent. He was suspicious of the fact that she, an employee of the JHSWP, would get involved with a foreigner like him. Valentina, on the other hand, had been distant. It also seemed too coincidental that Margaretchen had appeared right when he was asking about Beatriz in Bogensee. Perhaps the Stasi had been monitoring his phone calls and now wanted more details on his investigation. Or else Remigio, a member of state security at UNEAC, had alerted his bosses in Havana, and they in turn had contacted their colleagues in East Berlin. He also couldn't dismiss the possibility that Merluza had informed the Germans. Didn't the poet say that in Cuba many Chileans cooperated with the secret police as a matter of principle? Why would it be any different here in East Germany?

"I'm looking for Beatriz because of a love affair," he said, and it was not a lie, though it also wasn't the whole truth. A detective should learn to gain the trust of his informants, as he'd learned from Maigret novels.

"It sounds romantic, but I don't believe you," Margaretchen answered. She straddled him, opened the robe, and explored between Cayetano's thighs with her hand while her damp lips slid along his neck. "Beatriz involved in a love affair?"

"Why not?"

"Because she was incapable of loving someone. She was too pragmatic."

Cayetano sensed the warm caress of morning sun on his forehead as a soporific languor took over his body. He closed his eyes. Margaretchen's legs were soft and firm. He inhaled her wine-scented breath.

"She's a hard woman to locate," she whispered in his ear.

"Where did she go when she left the school?"

"She's too influential for you to reach her."

"At least tell me who can help me."

Margaretchen began to gently rock her hips. Over her shoulder, Cayetano glimpsed a group of cyclists pedaling beneath the apple trees of Eberswalder Allee. The air still brimmed with birdsong and the Soviet chorus.

"You won't be able to find her. She's part of a powerful institution," she said, her hips still moving.

"Who does she work for?"

"I can't tell you. It would be the end of me."

"Then who can help us?"

"Maybe no one, except her daughter."

"But we don't even know where she is."

"You're determined, but not sly enough, stupid," she murmured.

"What do you mean?"

"That, at some point, the daughter must have graduated from the high school in Bernau."

37

Margaretchen was radiant when she returned from the secondary school, in her wide green dress with white polka dots, which made her look like a student. Cayetano was waiting for her in Mitropa Restaurant, in the S-Bahn station, leafing through a magazine and nursing a bottle of Dresden Pilsner. The principal had found a Tina Schall in the school's files who had taught theater there on Saturday afternoons during the sixties, despite the fact that her weekdays were devoted to studying theater at the Karl-Marx-Universität, in Leipzig. The school in Bernau had accepted transfer units for her middle school education, which had taken place in Mexico. But then they had lost touch.

"You're a doll! That Tina is, without a single doubt, the daughter of Beatriz," Cayetano exclaimed, kissing her on the mouth. "What would you care for?"

"A schnapps would be lovely."

He immediately returned to the table with a glass of *Dop-*

pelkorn for her. A fan blended the scent of barley into the heat sliding in through the open door.

"I have to find Tina and speak to her," he said, knocking back his beer.

"In that case, you'll have to travel to Leipzig." Margaretchen shook her head, her expression sour after sipping the schnapps. "I have a friend there who's a dramaturge and may be able to advise us."

The next day, sporting the tie with small green guanacos that the poet had given him, Cayetano boarded the D-Zug headed south with Margaretchen. Five hours later they took a room at the central Hesperia Hotel. When they went out to stretch their legs on the cobbled city streets lined with peeling façades, they walked past wooden trams that screeched as they turned, through the penetrating smell of coal.

They dined at Auerbachs Keller, located in the vault of a central building, where they were to meet with Karl von Westphalen, Margaretchen's friend, who ran the workers' theater at Halle-Neustadt. He arrived as they were finishing a trout cooked in white wine. He was tall, with black eyes and thick eyebrows, and wore his hair in a ponytail. From the way they looked at each other, Cayetano gathered they'd been lovers. Karl vaguely remembered having had a student named Tina in a diction class in the theater department of Karl-Marx-Universität, in the city.

"That must have been in 1963, but I don't remember her face very well. Only that she spoke German with an accent."

"The woman I'm looking for lived in Latin America before moving here."

"That could be her. She spoke very good German," Westphalen emphasized, stroking his hair.

Drunken students at a nearby table were making a racket. Cayetano was intrigued that Beatriz would go by Lederer in Cuba, and by Schall in the German Democratic Republic. Was Schall a nom de guerre at the school on the lake? He should establish Beatriz's true identity for the investigation to move ahead. Now he envied Maigret, who always had access to official files, could count on the government's support, and received condensed information from registries that could confirm people's identity. There was no challenge, he thought, in investigating that way.

"The young woman I'm speaking of would be about thirty today," Von Westphalen said over the students' revelry. There was one guy among them who was slim, with a pale face and a harsh voice, dressed in black clothes that made him resemble a magician. Every once in a while, the magician pretended to fill jars at a stream of beer that poured from the wall, or at least to Cayetano seemed to pour from the wall, as in that scene from *Faust*. Cayetano didn't take the situation too seriously, as he'd drunk more than his share that night, too. He preferred to ask Karl about the usual path taken by theater graduates in East Germany.

"The best ones find work in Berlin or Weimar," Von Westphalen explained. "Others go to Rostock or Dresden, or they stay here in Leipzig. And the ones who don't have connections end up in some provincial theater, as happened to this humble servant."

"Do you think anyone at the theater department might know something about this former student?"

Von Westphalen replied that he knew a journalist from Berlin who worked for *Die Weltbühne*, an old cultural magazine, and kept abreast of the theater world. Perhaps he was the person to talk to. He wasn't a certain informant, as the journalist Hannes Würtz occasionally went through hard times, but he'd give him a call the following day. If he should learn anything, he'd leave them a message at the Hesperia. Then he ordered more beer and schnapps.

After barhopping in downtown Leipzig and stopping by a students' party in a building on Strasse des 18 Oktober, Cayetano and Margaretchen said good-bye to Von Westphalen and returned to their hotel room, staggering, arms around each other.

"What are you thinking about?" Margaretchen asked through the open door of the bathroom, where she was removing her makeup in front of the mirror.

Cayetano placed his glasses on the nightstand and said melancholically, "I'd love to show you Valparaíso. It's just like life: sometimes you're high up, sometimes down low, but there are always stairs and passages through which you can rise or descend or break your neck. And there, though you may not believe it, the dead come to life. Would you come?"

"You still don't understand this world, Cayetano. I can't leave here until I turn sixty. You'd have to wait a long time."

He said nothing, irritated by his own clumsiness. Light from the green Hesperia sign pulsed on the ceiling. He suddenly thought of Ángela under the hibiscus trees of Miramar Park, her hurried steps back to the Lada waiting for her in the distance, the loneliness that had overcome him. He also recalled the morning they first met, on Ocean Drive in Miami Beach, where retirees killed time in doorways, waiting for death. He saw her again in her olive-green uniform, dissolving into the soft shadows of Havana. He couldn't deny that he desperately longed for a companion he could fall asleep with every night and share breakfast with the following day, looking out over the sea in Valparaíso. At that moment, the phone rang.

"Cayetano, is that you?" Karl von Westphalen asked through the phone line. "My friend says the person you're looking for works in the Berliner Ensemble."

38

Her name was Tina Feuerbach. Or at least that was the name she used at the Berliner Ensemble, a theater founded in 1949 by Bertolt Brecht. This time the name change didn't surprise him, since many artists go by pseudonyms. Wasn't Pablo Neruda called Neftalí Ricardo Reyes Basoalto? And wasn't Gabriela Mistral really Lucíla Godoy Alcayaga? Von Westphalen's voice filled him with hope: Tina Feuerbach was Tina Lederer, the daughter of Beatriz Schall, born in Mexico in the forties! He wondered whether she was the poet's daughter. How could he find out for sure? And would she have any idea that her father might not be a Cuban-Mexican doctor, but a Chilean poet? Where was her mother now, the woman whom Neruda had loved when she was young, and the only person in the world who knew the secret truth the poet was so desperate to learn?

The next morning, they went to a tourist office and obtained a copy of the Berliner Ensemble's current schedule. It informed them that Tina Feuerbach was currently playing Virginia, the astronomer's daughter, in *Life of Galileo*, a piece written by Brecht during the Nazi era. Cayetano invited Margaretchen to have a drink at a café called Kaffeebaum, where they sat at an outdoor table under the white morning sun. He felt hopeful. If Margaretchen could recognize Tina as Virginia, he would devise a way to approach the actress and then reach her mother.

They returned to Berlin on the afternoon's first express train and made their way toward the Berliner Ensemble, where they bought the last two seats available for the weekend show. They were relegated to the last row, but could still count themselves lucky, as *Life of Galileo* was always a box-office hit in the German Democratic Republic, the vendor assured them. Even more so now that Wolfgang Heinz was playing Galileo, and no less than under the direction of Fritz Bennewitz. The poet was right, Cayetano thought. As they'd strolled through Valparaíso, he'd said that only under socialism would art and literature acquire real importance; it was the only context in which people paid devoted attention to writers and artists, which was why governments kept a close watch on intellectuals. Under capitalism, on the other hand, artists could say anything they wanted, because very few people listened.

In the few days before the show, Cayetano and Margaretchen made mad passionate love in his small room at the Stadt Berlin Hotel, while a cold, persistent rain fell heavily over the city, soaking its roofs and trams and cobbled streets with sadness. When the rain gave way to streaks of clear blue cracking open the dirty sky, they went for walks, hand in hand or with their arms around each other, trying to forget that their romance was condemned to die as soon as he passed through the Wall into the West. During those days, they ate at the Ganymedes, an exclusive restaurant near Friedrichstrasse

Station, and at Café Flair, on Schönhauser Allee. They went up to the revolving platform at the top of the Television Tower, from which they glimpsed the edges of the divided city, and they visited the Brecht Museum in the writer's former home.

"Anyone could be a communist, living like this," Margaretchen protested in Brecht's spacious apartment, as they gazed out a window at a cemetery housing the remains of famous figures from German history. "He supported the PSUA regime, but lived like the bourgeoisie, published in the West, and could travel freely wherever he wanted."

"My dear, let's say he was a believer, but not completely," Cayetano said, remembering the poet's three houses in Chile and the fourth one he'd just acquired in Normandy, as well as the flush bank account financing this very international investigation.

"He was just like Galileo. He knew how to live alongside the powers that be, how to shut up when it was in his own interests, and how to reap the advantages offered to him by the regime. That's why he wrote that play. Galileo was his hero. Brecht lost his courage, just like Galileo, as soon as they showed him the instruments of torture."

"Well, wouldn't you do the same?" Cayetano pressed.

"Who's got the makings of a martyr? Cursed is the nation in need of heroes. That's what Brecht said. And he was right. The powers that be reserve the title of hero for their cannon fodder," she said sadly.

The gravel crunched beneath their feet as they walked between the cemetery's trees. They had already passed the tombs of Hegel and Fichte, and now paused in front of the obelisk and self-portrait that Karl Friedrich Schinkel had sculpted for his own tomb. A cluster of sparrows flew away in fear. Down the path, large stones bore the names of Brecht and his wife, Helene Weigel. Drops still fell from the foliage, drawing the scent of fresh roots from the earth. They returned to the Stadt Berlin and made love in front of the window, looking out at the Wall and beyond it, past the border of death, at the streets of West Berlin, unreachable for Margaretchen.

The night of the event, they bought roses at a kiosk on Friedrichstrasse and took them along to the Berliner Ensemble, depositing them at coat check. Cayetano hoped to approach the actress when she emerged from backstage. They watched the play with utmost attention. On the stage, Virginia treated her father, an old and half-blind Galileo, with veneration, while he scribbled on papers, flattered the bourgeoisie, and vacillated before the priests of the Inquisition. Cayetano studied the actress's light brown hair, brown eyes, prominent cheekbones, and thick body, wondering whether he was looking at the poet's daughter. In her makeup, Tina Feuerbach could pass as Latin American, which increased the possibility that she might be his child. But Cayetano had to admit that her appearance meant nothing, because both the poet and Dr. Bracamonte were Latin American. The actress could be descended from either of them.

To his surprise, as he strove to find some resemblance between Tina and the poet, any remote trace in her face or body that could link them irrefutably, he discovered, to his discomfort, that as the narrative progressed, another character in the play seemed to reflect his own self: Andrea, Galileo's bold young disciple. The play seemed to force a mirror before his eyes. He couldn't deny it. That Italian orphan had devoted himself to science, and to emulating his teacher, with the same passion that he, Cayetano, the detective created by Neruda, now poured into his work, and he had to admit that this filled him with pride and unexpected fresh energy. Galileo, Brecht, and Neruda had more in common than their flights from threatened pain: all three of them were capable of transforming people around them, of making them see the world in a new way, of transmitting their teachings so naturally that they almost failed to realize they were doing so. He himself was not the same after meeting the poet. The final scene of the play—in which Andrea, after breaking with Galileo when the latter recanted his own theories, reconciled with his teacher and received his scientific legacy—moved him profoundly. Would he, Cayetano, be capable of fulfilling the mission the poet had bestowed on him? Could that young woman, pretending onstage to pray to the heavens for her father's faith, become the loyal daughter Don Pablo longed for?

When the curtain fell and the audience erupted in applause, Cayetano and Margaretchen immediately retrieved the bouquet and went outside, to the actors' exit. It was raining, so they sought refuge under an awning, near a knot of fans hoping for autographs, mostly long-haired, rebellious-looking youths who talked amid cigarette smoke as they waited for the actors to come out. Margaretchen was upset. She couldn't confirm that Virginia was Beatriz's daughter, whom she'd seen only from far away, ten years ago, at school celebrations by the lake. The makeup, the lights, and their distance from the stage, together with the intervening years, all conspired to muddy any chances of certain recognition. An hour later, when they wondered whether Tina had snuck out through some other door, they saw her emerge under the awning. They ran toward her, along with her other admirers.

"Tina, these flowers are for you!" Cayetano shouted at the

actress, in Spanish, as he extended the bouquet amid curious gazes.

Tina was wearing a jacket, black pants, and sunglasses. A bag was slung over her shoulder. Without the stage makeup, she looked older than Virginia, and more Latin, though with undeniably German features as well, Cayetano thought.

"*Für mich?*" she asked, surprised.

Her fans extended theater programs for her to sign.

"For your formidable performance, Frau Schall. Fantastic!" Cayetano went on, again in Spanish.

"Feuerbach. Not Schall," she corrected him as she took the flowers, gave autographs, and resumed her departure. On the street, a black vehicle with curtained windows idled in wait.

"We'd like to interview you for a Chilean magazine," Margaretchen added, trying to get closer to Tina. "Whenever and wherever is convenient to you."

"All the world's success to the Chilean people in building socialism!" the actress replied, this time in Spanish, without slowing her gait through the mob of fans toward the car.

"Here's my information." Cayetano gave her a piece of paper right as someone shouted that the director of the play was emerging from backstage. The fans ran en masse toward the door, leaving Cayetano and Margaretchen alone with Tina Feuerbach.

"Don't worry. I'll call you," she promised, putting the paper in her bag without slowing down.

"You don't happen to know a Beatriz Bracamonte?" Cayetano asked.

"Beatriz Bracamonte?"

"Yes, from Mexico City."

"No, I don't know anyone by that name. Is she a Mexican actress?"

"She lived in Mexico and Cuba."

"I'm sorry, but someone is waiting for me." She gestured toward the car. The driver had pulled up to the back door. "Good night."

"Before you go," shouted Cayetano, "where did you learn Spanish?"

"In school, when I was a girl."

"They teach such good Spanish at Bernau?"

"Good night," she said again, putting an end to the conversation.

The driver opened the back door, and Tina slid into the spacious interior. At that moment Cayetano glimpsed a dark-haired man in suit and tie, sitting in the back. The car drove rapidly down Friedrichstrasse, which was dark and deserted at that hour, and disappeared in the direction of the S-Bahn, followed by two Volga cars.

"Do you know what kind of cars those were?" Margaretchen asked him a while later as they walked along Unter den Linden in the light Berlin rain.

"Government cars, evidently," said Cayetano. He paused under a lime tree to light a cigarette. Light from an emaciated streetlamp reflected weakly on the wet pavement.

"Those are Stasi cars, Cayetano. The curtained one was a Volvo, reserved only for the highest leaders. Tina Feuerbach has some sort of tie with a very powerful person. This whole situation is giving me chills."

Cayetano calmly exhaled a tuft of smoke, put his arm around Margaretchen, and told her not to worry, that they should stroll in peace and then go dine and drink at the Stadt

Berlin because they'd taken an important step that night. He leaned his head against hers, and they walked that way for a time, in silence, gazing at the Television Tower that stood svelte and luminous at the end of Unter den Linden, just as the Eiffel Tower reigned over Parisian rooftops in Simenon's novels. Feeling amorous, he pulled Margaretchen toward him and kissed her on the mouth, thinking that Maigret could never understand the desires and agonies of a Latin American lost in Eastern Europe during the Cold War. At that moment, he saw a car and realized they were being followed.

39

He demanded that Margaretchen return to her apartment. Her fears had come true. The secret police was spying on them, and she couldn't afford to be seen involved with a foreigner. Margaretchen gripped his arm and refused to leave him there, on Unter den Linden, which stretched out long and solitary between the sparkling façades of historical buildings. In the distance, beyond the Staatsoper and Humboldt University, they made out the red sign of a bar, flickering ceaselessly like a winking eye.

"I won't leave you. Especially not now," Margaretchen said.

"Listen to me," Cayetano insisted. "Go." The drizzle covered the Volga's roof like gleaming velvet. "It wouldn't do any good for them to arrest us both. Go, and I'll come see you tomorrow. They can't do anything to me. I'm a foreigner. If you stay, you'll make trouble for yourself."

"I don't care. I've already been fired."

"Go, Margaretchen. Leave now and they won't be able to

follow you. I can leave East Germany, but you can't. Go away right now. Please listen."

"I won't leave you alone now." She pressed his arm tightly.

"I'm begging you, don't be stubborn. If you care about us, you have to leave. Right now."

She kissed him furtively on the mouth and retraced her steps down Unter den Linden in a manner that made it difficult for the Volga to follow. The car idled. Its occupants clearly didn't know whom to keep pursuing. A few moments later, the car kept on slowly, following Cayetano, and he breathed a sigh of relief. If Margaretchen could reach the metro or the S-Bahn, they'd lose her tracks. He kept walking, the Volga at his side. Across from Marx-Engels Platz, the interior of the Palast der Republik shone like a lamp shop with all its wares turned on, and the sphere at the top of the tall concrete Television Tower revolved like a flying saucer over Berlin. An airplane preparing to land at Tempelhof stabbed the clouds with its lights.

Suddenly two men got out of the Volga. The slam of car doors echoed through the silent night. They approached him without making a sound. A chill ran through Cayetano's body. He felt utterly alone.

"Good evening," said the burlier of the two. They both wore raincoats and black, wide-brimmed hats, and looked like ravens. Cayetano thought of Humphrey Bogart films he'd seen. But he knew that this was not a film, nor was it a Mafia novel, but something real that was happening to him in the misty rain of Unter den Linden. This was real life in the harsh world of East Berlin during the Cold War, not a scene shot in front of some cardboard Hollywood façade. He returned their greeting with gritted teeth, still walking, imitating a cornered Bogart to retain some dignity. He couldn't remember a single chapter in which Maigret was cornered by the police.

One of the men flanked him on the left, the other on the right. They walked for a while, keeping pace with him, without saying a word. The Volga followed them without making a sound.

"How can I help you?" he asked when it became clear that he couldn't shake them. Fictional detectives easily became heroes, but those of flesh and blood never transcended their status as investigative proletarians. Perhaps he was something like Galileo Galilei, he thought, a Galileo of the detective world, unwilling to be burned at the stake. Yet again he tried to recall a remotely similar situation in Simenon's novels, to help him figure out what to do, but his efforts were in vain. Which proved that things happened differently in fiction, according to a different set of rules, at the hands of that god who was never indifferent to his characters' fates: the writer. At last he knew why authors went to such lengths to protect their protagonists, especially if they were protagonists of a series. Because they wanted advance royalties for their future novels, writers became magnanimous gods and, twisting the hand of reality, threw lifesavers to their characters at the last minute, lifesavers that, strictly speaking, did not exist in real life, but that the reader was willing to accept as authentic. However, he was not a fictional character—though at that moment he wished he were—but a humble investigator working for a dying poet who was far away and unable to help. At least he, Cayetano Brulé, was made of flesh and blood and did not live in a novel, but in reality, an implacable reality that had no gods or, if they did exist, gods that were indifferent and impervious to human fates.

"Get in the car," he heard them order, pulling him out of his own thoughts.

"Police?" he asked with a serenity he did not feel. Freezing rain trickled into the collar of his shirt.

"Get in, I said!"

The pressure against his shoulders as they pushed him left no room for discussion and no possibility of escape.

He sat in the backseat of the Volga, between the monstrously large men. Two more men sat in the front, short-haired, in suits and ties. The one in the passenger seat spoke a coded message into a microphone as the Volga sped past the Palast der Republik.

"Can you tell me where we're going?" Cayetano asked.

The car veered off onto gloomy, deserted streets. It was quiet except for the dull murmur of the tires over damp cobbles and the deep voice dictating codes into the radio. They would interrogate him at a Stasi station and he'd be unable to lie. How would he explain his reasons for looking for Beatriz, widow of Bracamonte, without betraying the poet? How would he explain his visit to the school on the lake? Perhaps the famous Merluza could extract him from this mess, he thought as the car drove the length of the Wall. He regretted having gotten Margaretchen involved in this affair. He now saw how irresponsible it had been to request her help. The speedometer read one hundred kilometers per hour. He wondered what nerve of the German Democratic Republic he'd hit by approaching the Berliner Ensemble actress, to make the police come after him.

The car drove down a birch-lined street and reached a dark, empty parking lot surrounded by trees. The headlights swept over a sign that read "Treptower Park." The Volga pulled up. In the distance, Cayetano saw a concrete mass of indeterminate shape pushing up through the treetops.

"Get out."

They walked between the tree trunks, avoiding puddles and fallen branches, until they reached a terrace made of immense rectangles of concrete. The tall mass stood in the back. It was a statue, he realized, made of granite blocks, of a cloaked soldier carrying a child and a gun. His head was tilted downward to convey grief. It was the most monumental statue he'd ever seen in his life.

"Follow me," the man ordered. They climbed stone steps until they reached the boots of the colossus.

A silhouette emerged slowly from the darkness. Its unbuttoned raincoat waved in the breeze. It didn't take him long to recognize the man: that same night he'd been in the backseat of the Volvo that had driven Tina Feuerbach away from the Berliner Ensemble.

∼ *40* ∼

The man in the raincoat had a wide jaw, an aquiline nose, a penetrating gaze, and high, angular cheekbones. The face, Cayetano thought, of a Slavic aristocrat, sculpted from the same granite as the monument. Under the light rain, Treptower Park began to smell of damp earth.

"Why were you looking for Beatriz, widow of Bracamonte?" the man asked in English, with a strong German accent.

"Who are you?" Cayetano answered, sensing that, under these circumstances, his words were purely rhetorical.

The man calmly put his hands in his raincoat pockets and tilted his head with a tense yet curious expression. The roar of a lion rang out through the East Berlin sky. Cayetano wondered if he was going insane. In Bernau, he'd seen a kangaroo. Now he was hearing a lion. At least the roar was not a bad metaphor for his situation.

"I know quite a bit about you, and your travels through the German Democratic Republic, Mr. Brulé. But don't be afraid: you'll be able to leave the country just as you came. First, explain to me, in a convincing manner, why you are looking for that woman."

"Are you part of the Stasi?"

The man cleared his throat, ran his index finger under his shirt collar in irritation, and repeated, "Why are you looking for that woman?"

"First I need to know whom I'm speaking with. I'm a tourist. I don't deserve this kind of treatment."

"I just asked you a question."

"And you had to kidnap me to ask it."

"You can leave this very moment if you wish. My weapon is not an impediment, but persuasion," the man said in a more conciliatory tone. He had small teeth and thick, large lips, which made him look a bit like a startled child.

"You're sure that I can leave?"

"Absolutely."

"I'm not a fool, Mr. . . . what may I call you?"

The man took a step back and a ray of light sharpened the pallor of his face.

"You can call me Markus."

"I'm no fool, Markus. You could let me leave now and then detain me at the border when it's time for me to go. I'd rather clear things up here and now. I have nothing to hide, I'm not a spy. I come from the country of Salvador Allende and Pablo Neruda."

"That much I know. But you still haven't told me why you're looking for that woman."

He began to walk slowly, and Cayetano followed. The bodyguards did the same, keeping a distance. The granite colossus stood tall against black clouds, as though ready for battle. If he knew so much already, Cayetano thought, it could be only from Merluza, or Valentina, or Käthe, or maybe Margaretchen. The truth was, things were starting to get complicated.

"I'm traveling with the support of the Chilean embassy," he explained. "A Chilean leader charged me with the search for Beatriz. For personal reasons, no state secrets. There's no reason for the Stasi to interfere."

Markus kept walking in silence. Then he asked, turning to Cayetano, "Do you know about this?" He drew an envelope from his raincoat and took out a set of black-and-white photographs. He handed them to Cayetano, who studied them under the flashlight Markus lit for him. "Do you recognize anyone?"

In some of the photographs, he appeared with Margaretchen in Berlin, Leipzig, and Bernau, and in others, taken at the same locations, there were two men who looked like tourists. One of them was carrying a camera with a zoom lens, and the other had a sports bag slung over his shoulder. But something about their faces, a certain tension, suggested that they weren't on vacation, or, if they were, they certainly weren't managing to enjoy it.

"Do you know them?"

"First time I've seen them."

The roar sounded again. A nearby zoo, or perhaps a circus, thought Cayetano.

"They're Chileans. Army officers," Markus explained in a serious voice. "They're following you around Europe, and you should at least have some idea why."

"I don't know them," he reiterated, surprised. "And I have nothing to do with politics." He recalled the military jeeps patrolling Valparaíso, the rumors of a coup, the attempted bomb attacks, his wife's warnings. The hard truth was that no one living in Chile these days could be free from politics. "Are they still following me?"

"They're staying one floor below you, with military passports from the United States, but they're Chilean. Why are they following you? Just because you're looking for a woman? Are they following you, or providing you with logistical support? Who sent you here to search for that woman? You can't leave this country before clearing these matters up for me, Mr. Brulé."

"I've already told you. I don't know those men."

"But do you at least know what their presence means?"

"I've never seen them before."

"In that case, I'm going to propose an arrangement, but you'll have to honor it to the letter," Markus said serenely, more at ease. He turned up the collar of his raincoat, turned off his flashlight, and passed the photographs to one of his bodyguards. "You tell me what you're looking for in the German Democratic Republic, and I'll guarantee your exit through Friedrichstrasse."

— *41* —

S o you're searching for a cure for the Nobel laureate," Markus said gravely, hands in his pockets. They still walked through Treptower Park, enfolded in drizzle and shadows. A breeze drew murmurs from the foliage, and the divided city was a hoarse and distant pulse in the night, a mere opalescent gleam in the roof of clouds.

"That's what I'm here to do."

Now Cayetano felt miserable. As soon as Markus had shown him the instruments of torture, he'd betrayed the poet. He was just like Galileo and Margaretchen. Although he'd altered the story somewhat and hidden the real reason why the poet wanted to find Beatriz, Markus already sensed the presence of another secret. He wouldn't swallow the lie he'd been given for very long.

"But I still don't understand why you need the actress from the Berliner Ensemble," Markus said impassively.

"Simply because I loved her performance in *Life of Galileo*. Anyone who visits Berlin has to see the Berliner Ensemble."

"But you bought the bouquet two hours before you saw Feuerbach perform. Did you know beforehand that you would love it so much?"

He couldn't trick the man. Markus knew too much about him. Now he was pushing for a confession, a strange confession, a superfluous one, since it seemed Markus already knew the truth.

"Might I know what your relationship is to the actress?" he said as they began to scale the steps back to the monument.

"I'm the one asking questions here," Markus said firmly.

When they reached the platform, they paused to look at the terrace, which housed tombs for Soviet soldiers who had fallen in the battle for Berlin.

"The postwar era cannot be understood without remembering these heroes," Markus asserted. "I grew up in the Soviet Union. My parents took refuge there in 1934 because they were Jewish and communists, enemies of Hitler. Those who rest here morally justify who I am today and what I do, Mr. Brulé." He studied Cayetano's face, then added, "You still owe me an answer."

"In that case, I'll be frank, Markus. Tina Feuerbach is the daughter of Beatriz, widow of Bracamonte."

"That's what you suppose."

"You know it's true. You know very well who they are."

"I still don't understand you, Mr. Brulé. First you tell me that you're looking for a doctor who lived in Mexico, then that you're looking for his widow, and in the end you associate that woman, whom I don't know, with an actress in our Berliner Ensemble. At this rate, you won't get very far in your investigation, and the poet will die without the help he needs."

"Don't try to confuse me. You can help me find the

widow, because you know her daughter. She knows where her mother is."

The man in the raincoat shook his head and looked at his shoes, which were speckled with dirt.

"The fact that you're being followed by spies from the Chilean military, which is plotting a coup against Salvador Allende, at the very least means you're in a predicament."

"Do you think they can?"

"Neutralize you?"

"No. Succeed in a coup."

"You want to know too much. But no one can force the hand of history. Events occur when they have to, not decades before, and not after. Chile will return to its path, the same one as always, and pay a high price for it. But let's leave speculation to historical philosophers. Right now, you're in trouble with the military."

"I'm not losing sleep over them. They have no power. But if you'd lend me a hand with them, I'd be grateful. Perhaps you could stop them from following my trail."

"We'll see," Markus said pensively.

"I'd be very grateful, though my task is still to find the actress's mother."

"You are exasperating me, Mr. Brulé. How do you need me to say it? Tina's mother died years ago. She was German, a decorated member of the resistance against the Nazis. She never lived in Mexico. She was a citizen of East Germany. I doubt she ever left the republic."

If Tina's mother was dead, then his investigation was a sinking ship, Cayetano thought bitterly. He stroked his mustache, which was damp from the cold drizzle. At some point in the journey, he'd lost his way, like one of those mountaineers who vanished in the Andean winter, only to reappear with the spring thaws as a rigorously preserved cadaver. Perhaps the poet's old lover still lived in Mexico. He decided to make another concession, and said, "If circumstances are as you say, and those officers are following me, I'll promise you one thing in exchange for a single guarantee from you."

"What does Mr. Brulé wish to promise me in Treptower Park?"

"That I'll go, and leave your actress from the Berliner Ensemble in peace forever."

"In exchange for what?"

"For a guarantee that I'll be able to leave the German Democratic Republic, but that you'll give me a few more days' stay . . ."

"To spend them with the young woman from Bernau?" he asked sardonically. "Don't tell me you're the kind of man who falls in love so fast."

"I want to say good-bye to her," Cayetano replied seriously.

Markus turned on his heels and stood gazing out over the first timid glow of dawn, which tinged the horizon between the birches. His cheeks dimpled when he turned back to Cayetano with a smile.

∽ *42* ∾

H e had thirty-six hours left in East Germany, he thought
the next day at noon as he waited for Margaretchen at the
Mokkabar in Alexanderplatz, perusing a *Neues Deutschland* that
bore disheartening news from Chile regarding shortages and
the truck drivers' strike against Allende. At midnight, when it
was early evening in South America, he'd called the poet to
tell him the investigation was progressing, though he didn't
say he may have found his daughter in East Berlin. He was
extremely cautious about what he said, as he now suspected,
or, more accurately, knew without a doubt, that his conversations were being spied on. He didn't even dare mention the
spies in the photographs Markus had shown him, or his guess
that they foreshadowed an imminent counterrevolution as
bloody as Jakarta's.

Margaretchen arrived at the café, tense and exhausted.
She hadn't been able to sleep for fear the Stasi would break
down her door and arrest her. As he finished his tea, Cayetano
gave her a summary of what had happened the night before. It

clearly scared her. They took a taxi to Leipziger Strasse, near the building where Tina Feuerbach lived. He'd gotten the address by phone that morning from a secretary at the Berliner Ensemble. He'd pretended to be a Mexican diplomat who needed to deliver flowers to the actress, and this was enough to get the address. Leipziger Strasse was the most exclusive commercial avenue in Eastern Europe. Mere meters from the Wall, it boasted tall buildings full of shops, cafés, and luxurious restaurants named after the capital cities of socialist states.

"Are you sure this is the right address?" Margaretchen asked.

"Absolutely sure," Cayetano replied as they passed a store window displaying Thuringian vases and Bohemian glassware.

They entered the building. The doorman wasn't at his counter. Instead, he was in a small adjacent room, dozing in front of a chattering television. The room smelled of coffee, and the desk was cluttered with magazines and a bottle of *Doppelkorn*. He was an old man, with white hair and a beard. The PSUA symbol was attached to his lapel.

"We're looking for Miss Feuerbach," said Margaretchen.

The old man sat up, unsure whether he should be annoyed by the strangers' interruption or glad that his boss hadn't caught him watching television from the West. He cleared his throat and said, "She lives in 1507, *gnädige Frau*. But she's never here at this hour. How can I help you?"

"We have an official gift for her in the car," Cayetano said.

"What institution sent you?"

"The Cuban embassy. The gift must be kept extremely safe for her. When will she be back?"

"You never know. But my office, the office of Kurt Plenzdorf, your humble servant"—he gave a slight nod—"is as secure as the vault of a bank. So no need to worry. Nothing's ever gotten lost here. The Cuban embassy, you say?"

"That's right. The island of rum and music, my friend."

"There are so many Cuban bands playing rumbas on TV, and many Cuban workers in state factories, but it's been years since I've even smelled the label of a Cuban rum here in this country," the doorman complained, gesturing with his hand. Cayetano noticed he was missing his right pinky finger.

"Well, if you're patient, Kurt, I'll bring you a bottle right now. No, not one, but two. One white rum and one amber. Havana Club, the best of the best. And listen to this: the bottles will be signed by none other than Mauro Triana, ambassador extraordinaire, plenipotentiary for Cuba in the German Democratic Republic, direct descendant of the first European to see the land of the Americas."

"With two bottles of rum, a box of chocolates, and a crystal vase, our problems will be solved," Cayetano said to Margaretchen as they stood in line at the Intershop of the Stadt Berlin Hotel.

The shop, which sold goods only in Western currency, smelled of perfumes and detergents, and was filled with people who admired the wares, timidly asked about prices, and then bought nothing more than a paltry chocolate bar, a pair of stockings, or a packet of vacuum-packed Melitta coffee.

"I don't really understand, but whatever you say," murmured Margaretchen.

"The bottles are for Kurt, the chocolates are for his wife, and the vase is for Tina Feuerbach. And ask them to wrap each item as a separate gift, except for the rum, which I want in a bag."

"How can you think of approaching Tina again? Wasn't it enough to get picked up by the Stasi?"

"I just need to go inside her apartment . . ."

"Have you gone crazy? The *Genosse* doorman would never allow it."

"Just help me with this and follow my lead. You'll see how I get in."

~ *43* ~

When they returned, the doorman was dozing again in front of an episode of the American sitcom *Mister Ed*. The horse was plaintively telling his owner how he longed for a girlfriend. Cayetano sympathized with Mister Ed. He seemed like a noble and decent horse, more sensible than a lot of people he knew, a wise and privileged witness to a United States that was steadily disappearing. On the doorman's desk, the *Neues Deutschland* was lying open to the sports section. He woke up and smiled when he saw Cayetano remove the bottles from the bag.

"These are from Cuba, Grandpa. This bottle is yours, carte blanche," Cayetano said. "And I also have this gift for your wife."

Kurt rushed to close the door of his office, invited them to sit, opened the bottle, and poured the rum generously and diligently into glasses marked with the insignia of the Dynamo Football Club. His cheeks reddened as he savored the distilled liquor and launched into a description of his responsibilities in the building.

"Minor things. A blown fuse, a leaky valve, a stuck window." He took another sip, then procured a Hungarian salami from the key closet, cut a few pieces, and placed them on the *Neues Deutschland*. "It's ideal work for a retired lathe operator. And everyone here is very nice to me."

"This is the gift from the minister of culture, for Tina Feuerbach." Cayetano placed the largest package on the table. "Where can I put it?"

"Right here is fine. What is it?"

"We ourselves don't know. A present from very high up, if you understand me," Cayetano said in a dramatically solemn voice, pretending to stroke his nonexistent beard. "But you have to place it somewhere very safe because it's expensive, fine, and fragile."

"Nothing's ever gotten lost here."

"It's not a matter of getting lost," Cayetano said as he filled Kurt's glass again, "but of breaking. It would be an irreparable loss, not only because of its cost and quality, but also because it's an official package from far away. I'm sure you understand what I'm saying. There could be consequences, for us, and even for you . . ."

"Kurt Plenzdorf knows exactly what to do."

"What will you do, Grandpa?"

"I'll go put it in the apartment right now. That way you can go in peace and I can have a calm conscience. I don't want any problems with the commander."

"Wouldn't you prefer for me to carry the package?"

Kurt's eyes scrutinized his mustachioed guest as Mister Ed went on lamenting the monotony of his lonely stable life. Someone emerged from the elevator, walked past the door with clacking heels, and continued out to Leipziger Strasse.

"Could it be that you don't trust me?" Kurt protested, wiping his mouth with the back of his hand.

"Not at all. But perhaps you've had a little too much to drink."

Kurt guffawed and drained another glass in defiance. "This is nothing for Kurt Plenzdorf, former lathe operator at Wehrmacht, the Nationale Volksarmee, and the factory owned by the people of Narva," he muttered, shielding a burp. "You two stay here and don't worry. I'll leave this in Frau Feuerbach's apartment and come right back. But only on one condition," he added with a mischievous look.

"Tell me, Grandpa."

"That you leave me the other bottle."

"Kein Problem, Herr Plenzdorf."

Kurt opened the closet and grabbed one of the keys that hung inside. He hugged the package, pretended to fall for a moment, and headed to the elevator.

"Didn't I tell you? That *Genosse* Plenzdorf is a Prussian from head to toe," said Margaretchen. "He'll never let you enter the apartment."

"That remains to be seen," Cayetano said, refilling Kurt's glass.

∽ *44* ∽

When Kurt returned and hung the key back on its hook, Cayetano gave him the bottle of amber rum, which the groundskeeper jubilantly hid in the water tank of the toilet in his small bathroom. While he was inside, Cayetano pocketed the key and then announced that he was going out to reserve a table at a restaurant on Leipziger Allee.

Instead of going out, he took the elevator to the fifteenth floor.

The door of 1507 ceded with a creak, its hinges thirsty for oil. This Plenzdorf didn't fully attend to all his duties, he thought. He found himself in a large dining area, as clean and tidy as a showroom, with a window that framed the buildings of West Berlin. He explored the apartment. On a desk in the study he saw an Olivetti typewriter, a biography of Helene Weigel, and the *Tagebücher* of Bertolt Brecht. In one of the bedrooms, a photo of Tina Feuerbach displayed caught his attention. She was in a bathing suit, thin and young and smiling. The waves swayed gently behind her. In the kitchen he found an electric bill in the actress's name. Proof that Feuerbach was her real name! He felt satisfied. When he'd begun the investigation, he had no idea how to proceed, but now he believed that investigation was like life: it presented problems while at the same time offering tools for resolving them. But was Tina Feuerbach the daughter of Beatriz, the widow of Bracamonte? And was the poet her father? He shivered at the thought of Neruda immersed in the cold and instability of Valparaíso, dictating his memoirs to Matilde in La Sebastiana, composing poems, waiting impatiently for news from overseas.

In the drawer of a nightstand in a small second bedroom, he found pills, condoms, and a novel by Harry Thürk. Whose room was this? Did it belong to a son or daughter, or a lover of Tina's? It didn't matter. He should return to the first floor soon; every moment he spent inspecting the premises was like playing with fire. As he crossed the living room one more time, he saw the animal on the shelf, placed discreetly behind a glass door. It was a miniature llama, no taller than a bottle of beer, made with authentic hide and draped in a colorful blanket embroidered with the word "Bolivia." Behind the llama stood a photograph.

He opened the glass door and picked up the photo. A couple smiled at the camera, their arms around each other: the man had gray around his temples and the woman had light hair and eyes. They were posing beside a bronze plaque that read "Club Social." On the back of the photograph, someone had written, *Santa Cruz, Bolivia, March 1967*. At that moment, he heard someone turn a key in the front door. He put the photo in his pocket, grabbed a beer stein, and quickly hid behind the door to the studio. From that vantage point, through the crack, he'd be able to make out who was coming in.

It was a man. He was wearing a dark suit, and he was burly, with short hair and a flat nose that gave him the air of a boxer. Was he Tina's partner, or a Stasi agent on his trail? Or could he be from the Chilean army? A chill ran up his spine as he realized that if this guy came into the studio, he would inevitably discover him on the way out. He watched the man close the apartment door and pause in the hall, where he looked at himself in the mirror for a few seconds. Cayetano pressed the beer stein between his hands as the man approached the studio, adjusting the knot of his tie.

Cayetano knocked him down with one fierce blow, summoning the unflinching power of a Teófilo Stevenson. The man fell flat on his face on the carpet. Blood trickled from the nape of his neck. Cayetano feared he'd sent him on to the next world.

He wiped his fingerprints from the beer stein with his handkerchief, as criminals did in Maigret novels, and left the apartment. He rushed down the stairs. His heart pumped furiously and blood filled his head, disconcerting him and muddying his thoughts. He stopped on a landing to catch his breath. The smell of fried garlic and garbage in the stairwell made him nauseous.

Then, all of a sudden, he was plunged into total darkness. They've caught me! he thought. But he stayed put, crouching, pricking his ears and holding his breath. He heard no steps. He waited without moving or making a sound. He broke into a cold sweat; his legs shook. But he heard nothing. Nobody seemed to be following him. It must have been an automatic switch, he thought as he groped the wall for a button. He found one, pressed it, and sighed with relief when the stairwell flooded with light. He lit a cigarette to calm himself. He couldn't return to Kurt's room in such a state. That would make him suspicious.

He continued down the stairs, then, suddenly, the image in the photograph he'd picked up in the apartment passed before his eyes like a slow-motion movie scene, and he realized who the woman in the picture was. He took it out of his pocket, hand trembling, and stopped to examine it again. He couldn't believe it. It was as if a veil had suddenly fallen from his eyes. That woman was Beatriz, the widow of Bracamonte!

~ 45 ~

It was the winter's fault, for colluding against Wehrmacht with the Bolsheviks. At Stalingrad, I lost my little finger and two toes from my right foot. It was a miracle I didn't freeze to death," the doorman said to Margaretchen as Cayetano returned to the room. "Did you get a table?"

"Yes, very close by, Grandpa, at the Sofia. I hope Bulgarian food is at least as good as Cuban. How's that rum treating you?"

The television was now running an ad for the latest Audi model. Plenzdorf glanced at the bottle, nodded, and poured himself another drink. Then he said, "They made us rebuild Siberian towns and then denazified us." He poured a glass for Cayetano. Only one piece of the Hungarian salami remained. "At the prison camp, I studied historical materialism and dialectics, and became a Stalinist. And in October of 1949, just before the *tovarich* founded East Germany, they transported me with thousands of ex-soldiers on a cargo train to Frankfurt. We arrived in Berlin singing 'The Internationale.' Ten years before that, we'd left here intoning the 'Horst-Wessel-Lied.' That's history for you—the rest is all hot air," he muttered, glass in hand.

Cayetano drank the rum in one fast shot to calm his nerves. "It's time for us to go, Margaretchen," he said.

Kurt invited them to stay for some *Bockwürste* with mustard in his office, which he could prepare in a matter of minutes. It would be cheaper than taking their apéritif in a restaurant on Leipziger Allee.

"Please don't worry," said Cayetano. "The embassy is footing the bill for lunch."

"Well, then. I'd like to be a diplomat myself," Kurt huffed, eyes full of envy.

"Didn't you need to go to the bathroom?" Cayetano asked Margaretchen.

"Oh, in that case, allow me to go in first and make sure everything's in order, *gnädige Frau*. You know how messy we men can be," Kurt said, tottering into the bathroom.

As he wiped the sink with a sponge and moved cardboard boxes off the toilet, Margaretchen waited behind him. Cayetano used the moment when both their backs were turned to him to return the key to its hook in the closet.

Before they left, at the insistence of the *Genosse* lathe operator, they drank a toast of amber rum in honor of "Papaíto Stalin," whom Plenzdorf still admired, and then Cayetano and Margaretchen left for Leipziger Allee, where they caught a bus for Alexanderplatz. It occurred to Cayetano that what he'd just done was a far cry from anything in Simenon's novels, though he'd seen this kind of trick pulled off in the movies *Goldfinger* and *The 39 Steps*. The poet wasn't much of a film buff, he realized. He'd never heard him make any movie references.

"I found what I needed," Cayetano told her, clinging to

the handrail of the Ikarus. "Kurt helped me despite himself. Chances are he'll never know what happened."

"But Tina will suspect something when she receives a present from a stranger," Margaretchen pointed out.

"She'll think it's from some anonymous admirer. And in any case, she'll be more surprised by something else . . ."

They exited at Alexanderplatz and walked around the plaza, which at that hour was packed with Polish and Soviet tourists.

"Listen to me, Margaretchen," Cayetano said, pausing beside the World Clock. "We should part ways right now, for your own safety. I'd like nothing more than for you to come back to Chile with me. But we have to say good-bye."

Her eyes immediately grew damp, and he could imagine her thoughts precisely: such was love for her with men from the West. They crossed the Wall into East Berlin, took a girl out to eat and dance at places reserved for Westerners, slept with them, and then disappeared behind the Wall, never to return.

"You're leaving?" she asked, wiping her tears with her fingers.

"I have no choice."

"When?"

"Right now."

Margaretchen embraced him and hid her face in his chest. They stood that way for a long time, not saying anything, unable to find any words of comfort. Cayetano thought that life truly was as the poet described it: a parade of disguises and surprises, a play without a preestablished script. Around them, the city continued to vibrate, indifferent.

"At least let me accompany you to Friedrichstrasse," she said, disheveled, her eyes red from alcohol and emotion.

"You can't come with me." He kissed her forehead. Time

was not on his side. The man in the apartment would wake up and alert the Stasi, who in turn would waste no time in alerting the border guards. The border would close on him like a submarine hatch. Nobody would be able to help him. Not even the poet. Maigret had never faced such an urgent situation, he thought.

He kissed her firmly, inhaled her breath scented with rum and youth, and tasted the faint sourness of that skin whose warm and pleasant touch he would sorely miss. He held her tightly, recalling the balcony of her apartment, with its view of the Brandenburg countryside. In other circumstances, he thought, he could have had a chance at happiness with this young woman.

"If you return, you know I'll be waiting," she said as she let go of his hand.

"Good luck, Margaretchen," he mumbled before diving into the crowds of Alexanderplatz. He didn't dare turn around for one last look.

MATILDE

～ 46 ～

Once he'd safely crossed the Wall, Cayetano took the subway to the Tempelhof Airport, his mouth bitter and dry, his exhaustion steadily becoming intolerable as the empty, clattering train sought refuge from the tunnels' darkness in brightly lit stations. As the train sped through the bowels of Berlin, Cayetano glimpsed his reflection in the window. He saw himself, but something else far more important: his own eyes, behind their glasses, fixing their gaze on him.

Had he killed the flat-nosed man in the dark suit? he wondered as he tried to break the stare of his own eyes. There they were. They examined him severely, fiercely. He turned his gaze to the reflection of his hands, resting on his knees. Had he done it? Had he actually murdered someone? He, the son of a melancholy Cuban musician, whose fine, large hands knew only how to caress his brass instrument, his wife, and his little son, Cayetano? Did this make him a criminal? The train pulled into a new station. He had always believed that murderers chose to become what they were, that their souls had rotted early in life, that their destinies were forged with every step they took. Now, however, he realized that destiny could play tricks on you, that it could wait around any corner, in the middle of the night, ready to expose you to an enemy, put a weapon in your hand, and give you a reason to kill. Because Cayetano could have chosen not to strike the man. He hadn't been entirely sure the man was following him, or that he would definitely have discovered Cayetano behind the door. He hid his hands in his pant pockets as the train picked up speed again. Destiny—at least his own, he thought—was a train that ran madly on its rails, destroying everything in its path and rattling its passengers before reaching a moment of peace.

He was a different man, now. He was no longer that person whose clean hands had shyly knocked on the wooden door of the poet's house in Valparaíso. No, his hands were no longer the ones that had gently traced the curve of his wife's throat; or the ones that had reached for his glasses, buttoned his shirt, and tied his shoes in the morning; or the ones that on sleepless nights, full of anxiety, had pulled the covers over his own face in the vague hope that the sun would soon rise and bring clear light. He would never be the same again. He was not a violent man. He didn't believe in violence. In fact, he feared it. All he could do was imagine that the flat-nosed man, who surely had a wife and children, had only lain unconscious for a while and then risen with nothing more than a terrible headache. Oh, our Father, Cayetano whispered as the train approached the station, make that man rise to his feet again.

At Tempelhof, he took the first available flight to Frankfurt am Main, and checked into a hotel normally reserved for romantic trysts near the central station, on Kaiserstrasse, where prostitutes in miniskirts and low-cut blouses waited on corners. Pimps smoked and watched from the shadows, while drug addicts, pale as death, with bloodshot eyes, rummaged through trash cans. Despite all that, Cayetano felt safe now. He figured that once Markus discovered the dirty trick he'd played, he would free the Chilean army officers to go after him. He'd have to be careful. At night, after enjoying lamb and beer from Munich at a Kurdish restaurant, he called Merluza, the diplomat.

"Thank you for everything. I'm going back to Santiago," he informed Merluza. He could hear that, at his apartment in Pankow, Merluza had the television turned on to the news show *Aktuelle Kamera*, which described the record-breaking production of state businesses and farming cooperatives in the German Democratic Republic. At that breakneck pace, socialism would annihilate the West before the end of the millennium, Cayetano thought sarcastically.

"Don't worry about it," Merluza replied. "It was a pleasure. Where are you?"

"In the West." He preferred to keep the details vague. "About to board a plane."

"Did Comrade Valentina help you?"

"Everything turned out swimmingly."

"Well, as you know, if you need any more help, I'm here. And send my expressions of solidarity to Unidad Popular. Tell them I'm part of the struggle here in these trenches. The fascists will not win."

"They won't, Merluza," Cayetano said without conviction.

"Before you go," Merluza added, "did you hear the truck drivers in Chile are starting their national strike and saying they'll keep it up until the current government falls? Hunger and chaos await us, Cayetano."

He kept his own commentary to himself and hung up. He immediately asked the operator to put him in touch with the poet, in Valparaíso. He was in luck. He didn't have to wait very long.

"I'm speaking to you from Frankfurt am Main, Don Pablo. How are you?" He imagined him wrapped in his poncho, weathering his autumnal days, waiting for this call.

"Better, now that I hear your voice. I'm going over my memoirs, and Matilde is downstairs, making me a chicken casserole. One of those healthy ones, with lots of oregano. Afterward I'll drink my secret Oporto, you know how it is. What news have you got for me?"

His nasal voice sounded exhausted, his breathing somewhat ragged. But he also sounded distant, as though he knew someone else was listening and had to pretend the news in question pertained to some everyday matter, a foreign first edition, perhaps, or one of those rare objects he collected.

"I found the current whereabouts of the Mexican woman."

"That's great news," he said in the same tone. "Have you spoken with her?"

"Not yet, Don Pablo, but at least I know where she is. That's why I'm coming back to Valparaíso. We need to talk."

"Did you or didn't you find her?" At least now he was conveying impatience.

"I've located her. I know where she lives."

"Where?"

"In a nearby country, Don Pablo."

"In another country?" He sounded irritated. "What's she doing there? Is she with her daughter?"

"I don't know, Don Pablo. My plane for Chile leaves tomorrow. We'll talk more when I'm back. I want you to decide whether or not you want me to continue this search. It's up to you. I'll come see you as soon as I arrive. In the meantime, Don Pablo, please prepare me a Coquetelón. And make it a double."

47

N ow that the crab of this disease bores silently through my insides with such painstaking devotion, my old nightmares have returned to haunt me. They appear between sleep and waking, between the metallic echoes of these interminable, leaden winter afternoons in Valparaíso. I cross thresholds and more thresholds, but I always end up in a dark room. No matter where I roam, I always end up in that cool, dim dream space, where I sense that the woman and daughter I abandoned are crouched in wait. Their eyes study me with the same inclemency with which the crab digs corridors through my body.

At times, I glimpse María Antonieta and Malva Marina, my deformed little daughter, bathed in a vortex of light. They let out wrenching screams as they try to climb the Dutch dikes, hand in hand. When they're about to reach the safety of the dam's top platform, they slip and roll down the concrete ramp, covered with sand and algae. They're being hunted by a pack of soldiers in Nazi helmets and uniforms, and their faces are grotesque, like those painted by George Grosz. Malva Marina screams, "Papaíto, don't leave me,

Papaíto," while I, with resolve, but my soul torn in shreds, board a boat and row away as fast as I can to save my own life, listening to the girl's sobs until they are finally swallowed by the wind.

In that darkness, I also see Prudencio Aguilar, my old Caribbean friend who was killed by a spear in the Colombian tropics. After death, he's continued to age, and still bleeds from the same wound that took him from the world. I can tell he's waiting for me in all the rooms I enter, hoping the next one will be different. And just as I once lost Delia on a train in Italy because she exited at the wrong stop, absentminded as she always was, I then dream I've lost Matilde on the Paris metro, where we've agreed to meet at an uncertain time and at an unnamed station. And I also see the day when Matilde and I, strolling by the Charles River in north Boston, came upon a couple on a bench, and they were us, only thirty years older. From the path, without taking my gaze from the water, I gather the courage to ask them how they've spent their lives. As we approach them, we see something horrific: they are skeletons, perfect and complete, with hands entwined and macabre smiles sculpted to their skulls.

Existence is nothing more than a damn succession of disguises and good-byes, a journey brimming with traps and disappointments that impels you to make mistakes and then boasts an elephant's memory, not forgiving a single slip. I've said it so many times to that hardworking young man called Cayetano. Matilde entered my life in Mexico, when I was married to Delia and sick with phlebitis. She was a young Chilean woman, succulent and desirable, devoted to popular music and to the Party. She offered to take care of me. My naive wife accepted the offer, another ambush of life. What happened next was what tends to happen when a man and a woman find themselves alone beside a bed. Although Matilde likes to propagate the version in which we met long before, in 1946, in Forestal Park in Santiago, I don't remember that. That's a tall tale. A ruse of hers *to give our love a dignified prehistory. The truth is that this love grew from a betrayal of Delia, from the contemptible way we took advantage of the time and trust she'd given us, busy as she was with the work I'd assigned to her, disseminating my poems and striving to undo my exile.*

Matilde put my home life in order, since Delia had neglected it in her hard work with my translations, tours, and editors. At that stage, I needed a housewife, not an intellectual. The truth is that Matilde cooks the way she reads. She neither makes elaborate dishes nor reads sophisticated books, but she has good instincts, which means her literary tastes are closer to those of my readers than to those of so many bitter critics.

She did away with my friends' longtime habit of coming by my house whenever they felt like it, and created rules and protocols: without invitation there was no access to La Chascona, Isla Negra, or La Sebastiana. And, most important, when I met her, she resuscitated my lethargic desire. I'm grateful that she was already an experienced lover. Her artistic tours throughout Latin America had also served as torrid lessons in love. By the time Matilde arrived at my sickbed in Mexico City, on tiptoe, smiling in her makeup, with her tight blouse and fiery gaze, I was tied to Delia only by a sense of friendship and compassion. The night that I escaped with Matilde to the Island of Capri and left Delia preparing my return to Chile and the clandestine publication of Canto General, *the die had been cast: Matilde was forty-one, Delia sixty-eight.*

I ask the victims of my happiness for forgiveness. I ask it of Josie Bliss and María Antonieta, of Delia and Beatriz, and also of Matilde: all the women who were shipwrecked in an ocean of hopes nourished by my verses. They didn't know that words cobbled together by a poet are simulacra, artifices, not the actual truth. When was my behavior most despicable? When I left María Antonieta and

Malva Marina in Holland? Or when I anonymously published The Captain's Verses, *inspired by Matilde, even though I was still married to Delia? It was an homage to my lover, to her tenderness and intoxicating body, and a cruel slap in the face of loyal Delia. All of Chile guessed those poems were mine and that they couldn't have been inspired by an old woman. When I returned to the country, Delia suspected it as well.*

Matilde miscarried three babies that we conceived together. Now, with the bay stretching out before me, mute, gray, and still as one of those melancholy Carlitos Hermosilla engravings, I try to imagine what my life would be like today if those children had been born. It's too late to think about these things now, late and futile. One day I asked her if we could stop trying, and said that we should forget about children, that our love could endure without them. Instead of children, we'd have friends; instead of procreating, we'd travel all over the world; instead of telling fairy tales, we'd read Baudelaire, Whitman, and Dostoevsky; and instead of buying toys, we'd collect the most exotic objects imaginable—telescopes, bottles, shells, starfish, pottery, metal irons, and the figureheads of prows.

"Let's forget about children, Matilde," I proposed. "I can only be father to my poems, my true progeny."

48

"Alicia? She said her name was Alicia?" exclaimed Laura Aréstegui. They were in the Vienés, a traditional café in Valparaíso that hadn't lost its old-time splendor and that, despite the shortages that racked the country, still served fresh coffee and first-class pastries.

"That's right," answered Cayetano as he lit a cigarette. "She said her name was Alicia, and that the poet was in Santiago, correcting the galleys of a new book."

"That's Alicia Urrutia, no doubt about it."

"Who is Alicia Urrutia?"

"A niece of Matilde's. A young woman with big boobs and a pretty face. They say she's the poet's lover."

Cayetano put down his coffee in astonishment and looked out the window at Esmeralda Street, where Patria y Libertad nationalists were marching in their black pants and white shirts, armed with clubs and helmets. They waved Chilean flags, as well as white ones with a large black geometric spider at the center that resembled the Nazi swastika. Shouting anti-Allende slogans, they demanded the country be saved from communism. From the sidewalk, some onlookers applauded enthusiastically, while others watched in silence.

"That girl is the poet's lover," Laura insisted.

Could the poet really have a new lover? At his age, sick as he was? He wasn't some puritan who needed to police Pablo's fly, but still, this news hit him like a deluge of water that burst the pitcher of his patience. And why the devil was he scheming to send a detective all over the world to heal past wounds if he was also in the thick of a new affair? The nation suffocated in a climate of hatred and political division, about to capsize into civil war—and here the poet kept stoking the flames of his personal conflagration. If Matilde found out, she'd cut his balls off. Yes, with cancer and all, she would still cut them off and throw them in the fireplace at La Sebastiana, to heat the house in that implacable and interminable winter, because, Cayetano thought, she was a woman to be reckoned with. He loosened the knot of his tie, the one with the small guanacos, and sipped his coffee in disappointment.

"You're going to tell me that the poet has a lover, at his age and in his condition?" he asked Laura, not hiding his surprise.

"Why not? Let's face it, men can get it up even after they're dead."

"It's just hard for me to imagine . . ."

"It's because of Alicia Urrutia that Neruda ended up at the Paris embassy," Laura Aréstegui added.

"Now I really don't understand." He tore off another piece of his pastry. Vanilla cream clung to his mustache; he wiped it with a paper napkin. "Please explain how the poet went to Paris because of Alicia."

"A few years ago, Matilde took Alicia, her niece, to live with them as an employee."

"That much I know."

"Well, Matilde was out a lot, doing work for her husband, while Alicia attended to him at home. And the situation, a pair of impressive boobs, fear of aging, well, in the end, you know . . ."

"I know what?"

"Please, Cayetano. Don't try that with me."

"So how did Matilde find out?"

"*In flagrante.* One day she pretended to be traveling to the capital, but turned back and came home. She surprised them in bed. She immediately told him they had to leave Chile to get away from her niece."

"The same thing happened to her that she'd done to Delia del Carril in the forties, in Mexico City."

"And what Delia did to María Antonieta, in Madrid. We women are our own worst enemies," added Laura. The Vienés had filled with people fleeing the tumult outside.

"So that's why they became ambassadors to Paris?"

"The poet had no choice but to give in. He begged Allende to assign him to Paris. Who could do the job better than him? And so they went."

"But now he's back, though officially he's still the ambassador to France. He's back, sick as a dog, with Alicia Urrutia by his side."

"And I'll bet that if Matilde isn't careful, he'll end up marrying the niece. Are you going to include this aspect of his life in your article?"

Cayetano wondered whether he should continue the farce of preparing a piece on the poet for a Cuban magazine. Lies always have the shortest legs, as the saying went. The protest outside was growing: the new arrivals brought helmets, nunchucks, canes, and red and black flags bearing the image of Che Guevara. The chorus of slogans shook Esmeralda Street, nunchucks whirled furiously, makeshift spears jabbed at the sky, and stones flashed on swinging bolas. Cayetano thought of June's failed coup, when he'd been a simple spectator of events from Alí Babá. He felt that things were repeating themselves with astounding precision: he, Cayetano, sat at a table before a large window, while history flowed vertiginously outside; here he sat, doing nothing, passive and helpless, simply watching events as they occurred, without the strength or conviction to stand, run out to the street, and speak or act.

"I'm not going to write a single line about the poet's love life," he replied, keeping up the farce. "That's something private, and nobody's concern."

"I'm disappointed in you."

"Why?" Outside, a fight was breaking out between MIR and the nationalists. More people sought refuge from flying fists in the café. Vaccarezza, the owner, ordered the door to be closed and the metal curtains drawn just as riot police began to chase down the revolutionaries. "Why do I disappoint you, Laura?"

"Because his love life exactly reflects his whole being, and best reveals what he thinks of women." The lamps of Café Vienés lit up, radiating opalescent light as the metal curtains lowered and turned the place into a capsule. "He escaped from Josie Bliss; he abandoned María Antonieta and his daughter; he threw Delia away like a rag. Now that the years have caught up to Matilde and she's not the woman she used to be, he's sleeping with her niece. What do you think of the poet now? What do you call these dirty tricks? Sonnets, eclogues, free verse? If you don't describe it, who will?"

"You yourself, sweetheart. Aren't you writing your thesis for Patrice Lumumba University?"

"Don't be ridiculous, Cayetano. You know that if I include that in my graduate work, they'll deny me a degree. When have you ever seen the church defrock its own saints?"

≈ 49 ≈

From the soda fountain at Alí Babá, Cayetano saw the poet turn onto Collado Way. He walked slowly, slightly stooped, in a poncho and cap, assisted by his chauffeur. Cayetano polished off his coffee, put some coins on the table, and left the restaurant with the sense that Neruda's health was deteriorating at the same pace as the health of the nation.

As soon as Sergio opened the garden door, he informed Cayetano that the poet was resting in his bed, which was now down in the living room because he lacked the strength to go up to the second floor. Cayetano ran up the front steps and found the poet lying beside the window, his legs covered with a blanket. The green carousel horse, which had struck him so vividly on his first visit, no longer galloped through the living room.

"Where is she?" the poet asked after he sat up against the pillows and, in a gesture that both surprised and moved Cayetano, embraced him in silence, half closing his large saurian eyelids.

"I suspect she's in Bolivia, Don Pablo," Cayetano answered.

"In Bolivia? What's she doing there, young man?"

Cayetano told him what he'd managed to find out, though for the moment he omitted Tina from the story. He didn't want to raise excessive hopes.

"So you're sure this is the same Beatriz I knew in Mexico City in 1941?" he asked after listening without interruption.

"As sure as two plus two is four, Don Pablo."

"It's just that I don't understand what role the apartment on Leipziger Strasse has in all this. If Beatriz currently lives in Bolivia, why would her photograph appear in East Berlin? Show me the photo right now."

Cayetano took an envelope from his jacket and pulled out the photograph. "Do you recognize anyone here?"

The poet picked up the picture and examined it with his magnifying glass.

"This woman is Beatriz," he exclaimed, voice shaking, eyes wide. "That's how she was. It's her! And here is Ángel, a good man, unfortunate victim of our passion. In that era, Beatriz and I were lovers, Cayetano. So it's probable that after this reception, we saw each other in secret, and I kissed her lips, pressed her girlish form against me, and made love to her."

He was moved by his own past. Cayetano tried to bring him back to reality. "You two had just met then, Don Pablo."

In vain.

"October of 1941. The photo doesn't do justice to her beauty, but it's enough for me to recognize her. I am the cause of that joy, Cayetano. Do you know what that means? Here she is La Gioconda, and only you and I know why she's smiling. In that moment we shared a reckless and clandestine passion, and didn't know that only two years later we'd part forever, and that less than three years later a girl would be born . . ." He looked at his detective with damp eyes. "Our girl, Cayetano."

He sat down at the edge of the bed, oppressed by the realization that the poet, despite his lectures on the hopes of youth and the certainties of age, actually lived on conjectures, on a romantic and idealized vision of his own past. In the distance, the Pacific rose toward the city, whipped by the wind, and to the north the coastal hills loomed and blended into the snowy peaks of the Andes.

"I can tell you've become a true detective, young man," the poet said in satisfaction. "You see that crime novels aren't only here for entertainment."

"Could be, Don Pablo. But if you'll forgive my saying so, I don't think Maigret is always a very useful guide for me."

"Of course not. I told you that long ago. He's a Parisian, Cayetano, like Monsieur Dupin, not a born and bred Latin American like you. You're different, authentic, ours, a detective with the flavor of empanadas and red wine, as Salvador would say, or of tacos and tequila, or congrí and rum. But . . ."

"But what?"

"Why do you think Beatriz is in Bolivia?"

"Because of this other photograph, Don Pablo."

The poet picked up the picture and stared at it anxiously. His breath quickened. He used the magnifying glass.

"It's her! Years later, but that's her! No doubt about it," he murmured, trying to contain his excitement. "This woman is Beatriz Bracamonte, my sweet Mexican love. Those are her eyes, that's her face, her high, pale forehead, the soft undulation of her lips, only years later . . ."

"The mid-sixties, Don Pablo."

"Here she's less than fifty, then, young man. Still a girl."

Best to get right to the facts, Cayetano thought. "This was taken in front of a social club in Santa Cruz, in the tropical region of Bolivia, Don Pablo."

"And him? Who is he? Her husband?"

"I don't know yet."

"It must be her current husband. A woman that beautiful can't stay single for very long." Don Pablo's retrospective pride was palpable. "The suitors must have had to stand in line. Where did you get this?"

"It was in an apartment on Leipziger Strasse, Don Pablo."

"Say *departamento*, Cayetano, not *apartamento*. Learn to speak like a Chilean. Whose apartment was it?"

"An actress in the Berliner Ensemble, who I'm guessing received correspondence from Beatriz."

"An actress." He seemed to sink into his thoughts and then return, quick as lightning. "Young or old?"

Cayetano thought the poet was about to get burned, as he might meet with nothing but disappointment. He responded with resignation. "About thirty."

"What's her name?"

"Tina Feuerbach."

The poet stood up and walked toward the lit fireplace, dragging his slippers, hands behind his back, deep in thought. Behind him, the bay spread out like a sheet of frosted glass beneath the crepuscular sun.

"What's this actress like?"

"I don't think she's your daughter, Don Pablo."

"I'm not saying she is. What's Tina Feuerbach like? I ask you. Does she look like me?"

No, the sweet Virginia of the Berliner Ensemble stage did not look like this anxious animal.

"I'm not so sure she looked like you," Cayetano retorted defiantly.

"You saw her, right? Does she look like me or not?" he repeated, waving his arms, his voice impatient.

"She looks more German."

"Beatriz is half German. Can't you see it in the photos? That's why, even though Tina looks German, she could still be my child," the poet declared as he rummaged through the bottles on the bar with trembling hands. He placed ice cubes in two glasses and filled them with Chivas Regal.

"Is it really a good idea for you to drink, Don Pablo?"

"Don't pester me, you're not a doctor," Neruda warned as he brought over the two glasses, lit with the sunset's amber glow. "This is too important a day not to celebrate." He gave Cayetano a glass and sat back down on the bed. He drank and grimaced with his eyes closed. "Does she look like me or not?"

At the sight of him so worked up, Cayetano let down his guard. He vacillated. He sipped the whiskey. "Could be, Don Pablo."

He immediately regretted having said it. He was acting just like Matilde and the others. That wasn't what he'd been hired to do.

"What do you mean, 'could be'?"

"It's just that I'm not sure." This was true, but not as true as his fear of being mistaken. Which was why he didn't dare follow his intuition, which agreed with the poet's hopes, but preferred to stay objective and uphold a caustic ambiguity.

"Why didn't you bring me a photo of her, then? Isn't she an actress?"

He tried to buy time. "That's just it, Don Pablo. In *Life of Galileo*, she plays the part of Virginia, the astronomer's daughter. That is to say, she's in disguise, and wearing a lot of makeup. And in the signs in the foyer, she doesn't look like herself, but like the daughter of Galileo. See what I mean?"

"It doesn't matter," the poet answered brusquely. "You'd better tell me straight out: does she look like me or not?" He stood up with surprising vitality.

Don Pablo wanted to force an affirmative answer, as if Cayetano's doubts were the only barrier between him and his daughter. But his insistence was leading to the opposite reaction.

"She's a German woman with some Latin American features, Don Pablo, but . . ."

"But what?"

"Ángel Bracamonte was also Latin American."

The poet put his glass down on an end table, beside a manuscript, sat down on the bed, and hung his head, as though wounded. "You're right," he admitted sadly. He sighed and slouched, palms on his knees. "I forgot about Ángel yet again." He was silent for a few moments and didn't even look up to ask the next question, as if to recuse himself from taking any more initiative. "What do we do now?"

⁓ *50* ⁓

And then something marvelous literally came from the sky and broke the spell of their disenchantment. The beat of helicopter blades approached La Sebastiana. A twisting wind swept papers in Collado Way and frightened the dogs at the Mauri Theater. The living room began to vibrate as though gripped by an earthquake. The poet and Cayetano stared at each other in surprise before hurrying to the window. Then they saw it. It was high up, and resembled a giant dragonfly with its enormous head of shining glass and its reddish tail. It flew raucously around La Sebastiana, emitting furious flashes under the morning sun, thundering through the sky like a tin drum, alarming all the neighbors on Florida Hill.

"Sebastián Collado Mauri must be turning with joy in his grave," the poet exclaimed, raising his arms toward the sky. "At last his dream comes true! They're aiming for his UFO landing strip!"

The helicopter flew over La Sebastiana at a low altitude, studying its roof. Dogs barked furiously, children ran up the slanted streets, women stopped hanging clothes on lines in the wind, and even the people lined up in front of grocery stores forgot the exhausting wait and the shortages and turned their astonished gazes toward the sky, at something they'd never seen up close and had never dreamed would be so striking. Now the helicopter grazed corrugated iron roofs and flagpoles, so close to light cables and the tops of banana trees that it was possible to glimpse the two people traveling inside.

"It's landing on Modesto's roof!" the poet shouted euphorically when the chauffeur entered the living room. Modesto Collado was the original owner of the house. "Let's go up—nobody's ever used that landing strip before!"

They ascended the spiral staircase, full of excitement, the poet out of breath, moving his legs with great effort, cursing the pain in his knees; Cayetano followed him, with Sergio bringing up the rear, impatient, intrigued, and silent, spying on events with the all-seeing eyes of the house. When they arrived in the wooden studio, they feared the gusts from helicopter blades would tear it off the building. The poet rushed to open the door adorned with a picture of Whitman, and all three of them stepped onto the roof, where the wind vigorously shook their hair and clothes. In one fell swoop it snatched the poet's cap from his head and pulled it into the air, where it danced in circles, greeting the hills of Valparaíso. The scene reminded Cayetano of Cuban hurricanes, though the terrified driver, who had never seen such a thing, tried to hide behind the door and avoid walking farther onto the terrace.

"It's Salvador!" the poet shouted suddenly into the roar of rotors and fierce air.

"Who?"

"The president!" the poet shouted again, joyfully, gesturing toward the helicopter.

At that instant Cayetano recognized the figure next to the uniformed pilot. It was Allende, waving in his glass bubble, wearing sunglasses, in a striped jacket and tie, his hair combed back. It was him. There was no doubt about it.

"I should leave, Don Pablo!" Cayetano managed to exclaim.

"Don't be an idiot. Stay, I'll introduce you."

"He's here to see you, not me!" Cayetano answered at the top of his lungs.

The helicopter's black wheels were touching down on the cracked roof, and Valparaíso seemed to regain its color and stillness in the midst of the gale.

"Okay, quit clowning around and run to the wardrobe, where you'll find a waiter's costume," the poet ordered. "Put it on and go down to the bar and mix us a drink. You can't miss this. He likes whiskey on the rocks, no water, and make one for me, too, to keep him company. Look for the eighteen-year-old Chivas, and some ice cubes. The one that's eighteen years old. Don't get confused."

His naked sorrow for his lost daughter seemed to have vanished. Cayetano decided to play his game. He returned to the studio, where he found the costume and put it on as, through the window, he watched the president disembark, approach the poet with erect, decisive strides, and embrace him. Cayetano studied himself in the bathroom mirror and had to admit that he looked like a real waiter. With his mustache and glasses, he came off as the kind of waiter who presided over linen table-cloths and real crystal. He found the whiskey bottle just as the poet and the president were descending the spiral staircase.

They sat down in front of the picture window, the poet in his Nube, the president in the floral-print armchair, and started talking about the trip, how green and beautiful the central zone looked from the air, the turbulence of the wind through twisted streets, the city's infinite stairs and hills. They conversed as though no misfortunes plagued them.

"Well, here you have me, Pablo," the president said after a while, glancing sidelong at Neruda's bed in the dining room. "You wanted to read me your latest collection of poems. I understand it's quite political. So I was on my way from the south and told Captain Vergara to fly to your house. When Mohammed doesn't come to the mountain, the mountain comes to Mohammed."

The poet thanked him solemnly for the visit, and said the manuscript was about to be delivered to the publisher Quimantú. He wanted the leader to be the first to experience it.

"Well, that's why I came," said Allende. "And how's your health? Remember, you can't lie to a doctor. Much less a doctor-president."

"I'm in a bad way, Salvador, but I'm getting by. You know what's happening, let's not fool ourselves. But you didn't come here to listen to my complaints, you came to hear my newest poems. Whiskey?"

Cayetano hurried over with the full glasses. His hand was shaking as he extended the tray toward the head of state, who met him with a warm gaze and a relaxed hello. His hand still shook as he offered the second glass to the poet, who winked conspiratorially, enthused by his protégé's skill in playing the role of waiter. Neruda was right, Cayetano thought; life was a parade of disguises.

"Could you pass me the manuscript that's on my bed, please?" the poet asked him.

He picked it up quickly and glanced at the cover. The title was typed, and read "Incitement to Nixoncide and Praise for the Chilean Revolution." He gave it to the poet and returned to the bar. Neruda swilled a sip of whiskey through his mouth in preparation, then began to read the verses, which were hand-written in green ink. Although he pretended to be busy washing glasses, wiping down the bar, and pouring water from the faucet, Cayetano spied every moment of that unusual recital. Neruda read the verses in an exhausted and monotonous voice, in a nasal tone that lengthened his vowels and turned his reading into a kind of despaired lament, an orphan's song, while the president listened with his gaze fixed on the bay, legs crossed, chin resting on one fist. He remained immobile for a good while, then uncrossed his legs, scratched his temple, and elegantly pulled on the sleeves of his jacket, keeping his full attention on the poet, who kept reciting, sometimes reading, sometimes speaking from memory, occasionally refreshing his mouth with whiskey. Cayetano thought he must be dreaming. Now not only was he working as a private investigator for the world's most important living poet, but he was also the sole witness to an encounter that in the future would surely be considered historic. Was he dreaming? What was certain was that both men were here, a few paces from him, the poet and the revolutionary president, making history. Was it really happening, or was it possible that he was imagining the scene back in his old Florida life and that none of this was real, not Allende or Neruda or La Sebastiana or his own prolonged stay in Valparaíso?

"What an incredible political epic poem, Pablo," the president exclaimed from his armchair, still motionless, though deeply moved, when the poet had finished. "Never before has anyone written something so true about a revolution and its enemies. It has resounding strength and beauty. It should be known all over the world. An accurate artistic report of the brutal aggression aimed at us by the empire."

"Thank you, Mr. President," the poet answered, closing his large saurian eyelids.

"I'm just plagued by one question, my dear Pablo," the president said after a little while, draining his glass.

"What's that, Salvador?"

Cayetano listened with attentive silence.

"How am I to keep a man as my ambassador when he incites his colleagues throughout the world to murder the head of the empire, even if only with poems?"

For Neruda, that question was already resolved.

"Don't worry," he replied, resting his palms on the last page of the open manuscript. "Right this moment, face-to-face with you, I'm stepping down from my post in Paris. It's time to defend the revolution in Chile. I can't be absent from this battle. As an ambassador, I can't say everything I want to say as a poet. Your hands are free, Salvador."

Allende stood, and the poet did the same. Then Cayetano saw them melt into a wordless embrace in front of the window, the bay shining behind them under a clear sky, ringed with faraway mountains. As he dried glasses he'd already washed several times, he sensed that it was a good-bye, that they would never see each other again.

The president began to slowly climb the steps toward the roof. The poet followed him. Cayetano came behind them, in his waiter's disguise. They paused in the studio, where the president examined the old Underwood and the shelf brimming with crime novels. Allende picked up *The Mask of Dimitrios*, by Eric Ambler, and asked the poet if he could borrow it, as his defense secretary, Orlando Letelier, had just recommended it. Then they went out to the breezy roof, where Sergio was chatting with the pilot.

Cayetano watched them say good-bye with one last embrace as the blades began to turn with a deafening whir. The president boarded the helicopter, closed the hatch, and sat down beside the pilot. He had returned to his bubble.

With his hands in his pockets, the poet smiled at the president as the wind disheveled the little hair he had left. The helicopter rose from the terrace and began to fly, swinging over the roofs of Florida Hill as Allende waved and gesticulated at the world below. From Collado Way, Alemania Avenue, and plazas lined with palm trees, from windows and wooden balconies, neighbors responded by waving flags and chanting his name. It was as though Valparaíso had burst into a carnival. Pablo Neruda and Cayetano Brulé kept their arms high in the air until the helicopter became as a minuscule golden dragonfly and disappeared with a remote whistle into the ponchos of snow draped over the Andes.

They went back inside, silent, gazes lowered, and after some time Cayetano felt compelled to reopen their conversation. Not to break the tension, but out of loyalty to the matter still at hand.

"We've got to investigate in Bolivia, Don Pablo."

Don Pablo didn't answer, nor did he look up. He seemed to be turning it over and over in his mind.

After a while, he said, with difficulty breathing, "I see that the readings I've recommended have been effective, young man. To that end, I've got another novel for you, *Twenty-three Instants of a Spring*, by Konstantin Simonov. You should read it. Soviet espionage in Nazi Berlin."

Cayetano followed his drift. The visit must have left him too excited to immediately discuss action. "Is it better than Simenon?" he asked.

"As a disciplined activist, I should say yes. But between us: Nobody beats the French in matters of food or culture. You've got to read that novel. I have no patience for people who read only good books. It's a sign they don't know the world."

"What about the trip to Bolivia, Don Pablo?"

Again Neruda was slow to respond. And his words were a surprise. "No, young man, never mind that. The case is over."

Now it was he, Cayetano, who was left speechless. But his inner detective rose up bravely, to do the talking.

"What do you mean, it's over?"

Don Pablo paced the room slowly, hands behind his back.

"I made a mistake," he replied without looking at him. "I've been wrong many times in my life, but this time Salvador's visit really opened my eyes. I have no right to spend my energies on a personal obsession, a ghost of my own past, when the destiny of Chile, of socialism, of all the things I believe in and have defended all my life are in jeopardy. When I was young, I lived like a sleepwalker, immersed in my own dreams and speculations, far away from real people, and if I woke up, it was thanks to communism and the Spanish Civil War. 'No, the time has come, so flee, / shadows of blood, / stars of ice, retreat to the path of human steps / and take the black shadow from my feet!' " he recited, as though seeking the strength he needed in those verses he'd written years before. "Now history is repeat-

ing itself, it's the same, the same. There's too much to do here
for me to gaze at my navel and hunt ghosts, Cayetano."

He stopped but did not look up. Cayetano, however, didn't
take his eyes off Neruda.

"That ghost is made of flesh and blood, Don Pablo. And
you've already let it escape once before."

The poet changed his tone. "You're not the first detective
I've hired, Cayetano. This situation has been eating at me for a
long time. I've spent several thousand dollars on professional
investigators who didn't find anything, and some of them even
tried to trick me. With photographs and everything. At the
end of the day, Matilde was right to chase them off. It
wasn't only jealousy. It wasn't only me she didn't trust." Now
he looked at Cayetano, but his eyes had changed. Something
cold and distant gleamed in them. "That's why I came to you in
secret, Cayetano. I needed someone I could trust, and your
youth made me trust you. But you yourself are another of my
fictions."

He felt the need to defend himself. "I'm not a fiction anymore, Don Pablo. I've found some answers and convincing
proofs."

"Answers to what? And proof of what?" He frowned at Cayetano, standing in the center of the living room. "Here Chile is
suffering through the worst abyss imaginable, and we're lost in
conjectures over my resemblance to a German actress. I send
you out to investigate something that happened thirty years
ago, when we should both have our five senses in the here
and now!"

Don Pablo was fleeing, as he had so many times before.
Perhaps he was fooling himself, but despite the undeniable
urgency of the political situation, he wasn't fooling Cayetano.

Like Galileo Galilei, the poet feared pain; and the deepest pain, the one for which he was least prepared, didn't threaten him from current circumstances, but from the past, from the heart, from the depths of his own memory.

"Thirty years ago you renounced your daughter. You've just renounced your post, and now you want to renounce more things. It's the easy way out. Anyone can live like that."

The former ambassador took no offense. As a recidivist fugitive, he'd likely heard such reproaches more than once in his life.

"You don't understand me, Cayetano," he said, as if surfacing in a lake after a long dive. "Didn't you hear what I said to Salvador? If being an ambassador means censoring what I say as a poet, then I need to stop being an ambassador. My poems are what will survive when I am gone!"

"That's not what you said before you sent me to Cuba, Don Pablo."

The poet remembered perfectly. He didn't deny it, but could no longer stand by his own words. "I was caught up in my hopes, Cayetano. I needed them to keep on living. Now that whole undertaking seems like another facet of my egoism. What need could that young woman have for me, if as you say she's an actress with the Berliner Ensemble, living in the best neighborhood of East Berlin, known and admired? You have your whole life ahead of you, Cayetano. Keep being a detective if you wish, you've proven that you have the nose and persistence of a bloodhound." The poet couldn't hide the irritation in his voice, though he maintained his sad nasal tone. "But it's time for me to drop the nonsense and false hopes and to face reality. If my destiny is not to leave any descendants other than my books, then I should accept it with dignity and without protest."

In addition to being a poet, he was still a diplomat. Under the surface, he'd offered a pact: he would leave Cayetano with the identity he'd created for him if, in return, Cayetano would leave him in peace. In that case, they should make a pact, but the agreement should be different.

"Don Pablo, you're Chilean. I'm Cuban. You've given your word to Chile. I'm here because I followed a woman who has since left me. Let me go to Bolivia. That way each person can remain in his place: you as a poet, and I as a detective. It's the best thing for each of us."

He felt that he'd never been so eloquent in his life. He must have learned something about diplomacy from the poet, and from the books he'd recommended. After a silence, the poet resumed his pacing, making the floorboards creak, and said, "Go to La Paz first thing tomorrow. I know a comrade there who may be able to help you. And now, my Maigret del Caribe, I think it's best if you leave me alone. There are times when I simply tire of being human."

51

The first night Cayetano Brulé suffered through the altitude of La Paz, Bolivia, he wondered whether he'd survive the agony. As soon as he got off the two-engine aircraft at Lloyd Aéreo Boliviano and tried to rush to the terminal, a steely weight pressed into his chest and kept the thin mountain air, cold as spring water, from reaching his lungs. He sat on a bench to recover his breath.

"Altitude sickness. This will make it pass, sir," a toothless old Indian promised as he showed him a cup of coca leaf tea. "But for God's sake, don't even think about getting involved with a woman from La Paz, you'll go directly to hell," he added seriously, wrapped in his poncho, palm outstretched.

Cayetano felt better by the time he entered the lobby of his hotel, where the poet's friend waited to meet him. Emir Lazcano had studied literature in Santiago, at the University of Chile, during the legendary period of reform. That was in the sixties, when the nation brimmed with a rebellion propelled by long-haired youths addicted to marijuana, free love, flowered shirts, and bell-bottom pants. They admired Janis Joplin and Joe Cocker, were pacifists, and didn't trust anyone over thirty. Cayetano appreciated this man's kindness, as well as his slow and deliberate way of speaking and pronouncing the letter *s*. They dined on a succulent lamb-and-pea stew at a cramped, narrow dive with exposed beams along the ceiling, near the Palacio Quemado.

"I advise you to keep drinking coca tea while you're here," Lazcano suggested, nursing his beer. "Altitude sickness is no laughing matter. It takes many tourists over to the other side. They arrive in La Paz happy, then eat, drink, and fornicate too much. The altitude gets the best of them, and they leave La Paz lying horizontal in the belly of a plane."

The academic had met the poet in the sixties, during a Communist Party event at the Caupolicán Theater in Santiago. For a while, Neruda had helped him finance his stay in the Chilean capital. Lazcano had heard rumors about his poor health but had not imagined that he could be dying. He had preferred not to broach the subject when the poet called and requested that he help his emissary with a task so secret that not even the Bolivian Party could get wind of it.

Cayetano showed him the photo of Beatriz posing with a man in front of the social club, and asked if he knew her.

"I've never seen her," Lazcano said after examining the photo.

"And her companion?"

"No, never. They're standing in front of the most exclusive club in Santa Cruz, which lets in only the very rich."

"And you're sure you don't know the man?"

"Who are you looking for? The woman or the man?"

"The woman."

"If you're looking for information about a foreigner, there's no problem," he clarified curtly. "But if you're looking for an influential Bolivian, you should be very careful. Things aren't all rosy here. If they catch you, as a Cuban coming from Chile, it could end badly."

"I need to find that woman, or at least the man. Don Pablo assured me I could count on your help. There's nothing political about this mission."

"I still suggest you tread lightly."

"Perhaps one of your comrades could locate this man, or help us find the woman."

People were still entering the restaurant, massaging their hands, numb with cold, wrapped in coats and parkas. They were silent people, mild-mannered, the opposite of Cubans, with their constant, boisterous self-expression, Brulé thought, remembering that outside, the night's blade could cut one's cheek.

"I repeat: things are complicated," Lazcano insisted. "We're facing a difficult situation: on one side, the miners' union could go on strike at any moment, and on the other side we're threatened with a possible military coup. The infernal circle of this country."

"Listen to me, Emir. I'm going to make you an offer in the name of our common friend."

Lazcano lit a Viceroy and waited, slouched, gazing down at the table, unsettled by the conversation.

"If you help me find these people"—Brulé lowered his

voice—"I'll give you a first edition of *Canto General*, signed by the bard himself. Do you realize what I'm saying? A first edition, autographed by the most important living poet in the Spanish language. So will you or won't you help me with this little matter?"

TRINIDAD

52

Simón Adelman was a Jewish lawyer of German origin, who had made his fortune by representing Bolivian mining companies. But his heart still veered to the left, and now he devoted all his time to fighting labor abuses and uncovering Nazi war criminals who masqueraded as innocent settlers in the remote regions of Beni. Seven of his relatives had perished in the Holocaust at the concentration camp in Buchenwald, on Ettersberg Mountain, near Weimar, Goethe and Schiller's beautiful city; and this spurred Adelman to study all aging German hermits in Bolivia with a magnifying glass.

When Lazcano introduced him to the lawyer, Brulé was struck by two things. The first, that his attire made him resemble a rural schoolteacher, which was unprecedented in La Paz, where the rich made their social standing crystal clear through cars and clothing. His shiny pants, wrinkled jacket, and lack of a tie didn't give the impression of a successful attorney at all. The second thing was that, although he belonged to the upper class, which was predominantly Catholic and conservative, he was a leftist.

According to Lazcano, the lawyer could be trusted, although the party didn't look on Adelman kindly because he was a Trotskyite. Nevertheless, he was known throughout the country as a man of discretion, who knew how to rub elbows with the crème de la crème of influential circles and frequented their clubs. His only unpardonable sin was his admiration for Leon Trotsky, whose house in Coyoacán he visited regularly, always leaving a wreath of flowers and a pebble at his tomb.

"Do you know this woman?" Cayetano showed him the photo without preamble.

"Certainly. I also know that club," Adelman said impassively. "It recalls another era, with its crystal chandeliers, beveled mirrors, and smooth floors. Dinners and sumptuous soirees take place there, and during them the fate of many Bolivians is sealed. It's also the headquarters for proponents of separatism for Santa Cruz."

They were at a table in Café Strudel, which was decorated with latticed walls and posters of Bavaria, a region belonging to Mennonites. The door was slightly ajar and let the cold glide in. Through the windows, they saw the chipped buildings that lined the street.

"I'm interested in the woman," Cayetano clarified. "Her name is Beatriz, widow of Bracamonte. Though I'm not sure that she goes by that name here. How can I find her?"

"I saw her a couple of times at receptions." Simón had blue eyes, gray hair, and a gaunt face. He was probably about seventy years old. "But her name is not what you say it is."

"What?"

"Her name isn't Beatriz."

"What is it, then?"

"Tamara. Tamara Sunkel."

"Are you sure you're talking about the woman in this photograph?"

"Absolutely. She's German, from Frankfurt am Main. I spoke with her about some of her real estate plans."

"Does she have any children?"

"I don't know. La Paz is small, but it's not some tiny village, either."

A waiter served them coffee in large, cracked cups. Cayetano looked around him. There were many office workers, in suits and ties, smoking or reading the paper, lost in thought or conversing calmly. In the Andes, as in Havana, there seemed to be plenty of time.

"Do you also know the man in the photo?"

Adelman turned to Lazcano. "Can he really be trusted?"

Lazcano nodded with little conviction and averted his gaze to the street, where indigenous women in traditional dress were passing by, impervious to the drizzle that tinged the afternoon with sadness.

"Let's say that in Bolivia, he isn't a well-known face," Adelman continued, choosing his words carefully for his mustachioed Caribbean visitor. "That is to say, only certain people know who he is."

"Why is that?"

"You're sure he's trustworthy?" Adelman asked Lazcano.

"Even though he's coming from Chile, yes, he is," asserted Lazcano, his head sinking between his shoulders.

"That man is Colonel Rodolfo Sacher, Mr. Brulé. In 1967 he headed a top-secret Bolivian intelligence squad."

"I don't understand." Cayetano placed the photo on the

table and sipped his coffee. The brew tasted worse than he thought it would.

"Sacher was the CIA contact for the Palacio Quemado, our presidential headquarters."

"For what?"

"You know the story of Che Guevara, right?"

"Of course. He died here in Bolivia, in 1967, ambushed by rangers."

"Actually, they killed him at the little school in La Higuera, where they took him once he was wounded. Not that they transported him out of consideration. One official even had his picture taken with Che. They put him on a stretcher and had no idea what to do with this man who was too much of a man for them. The order arrived from Washington, though they said it came from the Palacio Quemado."

"So what role did Colonel Sacher play in all this?"

"He was the one who infiltrated the guerrillas' support network in the city. Without knowing it, Tamara Bunke, Che Guevara's lover, led him to Che and his men. She had earned the trust of the Bolivian military and oligarchy, and was under express orders from Havana not to contact Che. But she disobeyed them. Do you know why?"

"Revolutionary enthusiasm," Cayetano said, thinking of his wife in her olive-green uniform in the Cuban jungle.

"Out of love for Che," Adelman corrected him. He fell silent, nodding his head, as if he weren't entirely convinced of what he was saying. "For Sacher, it was enough to follow Tamara to find the Argentinean's troops. And he didn't only arrest the commander, but also gave the execution order at La Higuera . . ."

"Are you sure he had the power to make such a decision?"

"At least enough to impose order among the little soldiers shitting themselves with fear of their prisoner. Barrientos, the president at the time, had no idea what was going on. In the end, he held a funeral with honors for Tamara Bunke, who had become a Bolivian citizen and made contributions to scholarship on our national folklore while she was an undercover agent. The Cubans blame Régis Debray for betraying the guerrilla, but the fact is that Che was lost by the German revolutionary who loved him."

Cayetano pushed his cup aside and examined the photo again. Sacher had the features of a fox: a sharp face, elongated eyes under bushy eyebrows, and sparse hair neatly combed back. He wondered why Beatriz kept changing her name and appearing in such contradictory places. Perhaps Beatriz was not Tamara Sunkel, whose first and last name sounded suspiciously close to that of Che's German lover in the guerrilla movement. Someone, either Adelman or the poet, had mistaken the woman in the photo for someone she was not.

He scanned the street through wet windows. "How can I find Tamara Sunkel?"

"I'm afraid it won't be easy to get in touch with her."

"Didn't you say you knew where she was?"

"I used to know. She disappeared from La Paz some time ago. She sold her properties and left."

"Where to?"

Adelman snorted. "Germany, perhaps."

"When?"

"Around five years ago. Though I could be mistaken."

"So what happened to Colonel Sacher?"

"He died."

"He wasn't old enough to die," he heard himself say. He was

immediately struck by the stupidity of his own comment. One was always old enough to die, from the moment of conception.

"He died when his vehicle drove off a cliff on the way to El Alto Airport."

"Before or after Che's death?"

"A little while after."

"Before or after the disappearance of Tamara Sunkel?"

"Before," the lawyer said laconically.

❧ 53 ❧

He put his coca tea down on the nightstand and gazed out at the dense veil of the Milky Way through the misted windows of his room. The night was a black block of granite encrusted with diamonds. He preened his mustache and thought that he was coming to see the world as the poet did. He couldn't sleep. Air, thin as a strand of the cotton candy sold near school during his childhood, barely entered his throat.

If the poet's lover's last name was Bracamonte in Mexico, Lederer in Cuba, Schall in East Germany, and Sunkel in Bolivia, then there were two possibilities: The first was that there were two different women involved, and he'd been thrown off track early in his search, because detective work was much more complicated than what Simenon described and what the poet imagined. In that case, the woman with whom Neruda had fallen in love had disappeared without a trace and had nothing to do with the women in Havana, East Berlin, and La Paz. But it was also feasible that those women were the very one he was looking for: the unfaithful young wife of a Cuban doctor, a twenty-year-old beauty, seduced by the artist's verses while he was living with sixty-year-old Delia del Carril. Of course, that possibility did not necessarily mean that Beatriz's daughter was also a child of Neruda's. The second possibility also had a disturbing side, he thought, dizzy from lack of air, reaching for the coca tea on the nightstand. The woman of many names was turning out to be an extraordinarily enigmatic person: in the forties, she'd been the lover of a communist poet, then appeared briefly in revolutionary Havana, and in the sixties she'd settled down in the German Democratic Republic, on the other side of the Wall, working in an ideological indoctrination school for Third World youth. And then, suddenly, she showed up in Bolivia as a businesswoman and companion to a colonel involved in the death of Che Guevara.

He sat up and dialed Adelman's number. "Simón?"

"Speaking."

"This is Cayetano." He exhaled cigarette smoke and put on his glasses, as though they could help him speak better. "I need to talk to you again. Could we do it now?"

"Now?"

"It's just that I'm leaving Bolivia tomorrow."

Outside, the night lay curled in wait; cold air and the low moan of trucks slid through the poorly sealed windows.

"Ask the taxi driver to take you to the French Club," Adelman told him. "He'll know it. I'll meet you there."

When Cayetano arrived in front of the well-lit establishment, Simón was not yet there. He waited in the lamplight, out in the cold, his hands plunged into the pockets of the sheepskin-lined jacket Ángela had bought him in Mendoza. At that hour, his wife—or ex-wife, he no longer knew for certain—would be camping among palms and ceiba trees, listening to the frogs croaking and the gentle murmur of tropical foliage, with her sleeves rolled up to establish socialism in Chile. Poor Allende, he thought. He was caught between a rock and a hard place: on one side, the right wing and the United States denounced him as a radical revolutionary trying to build another Cuba, and, on the other side, the far left of his own nation called him a mere reformist of the Chilean capitalist system. While he worked around the clock in his house on Tomás Moro Street to strengthen his peaceful revolution, behind his back in Havana others were plotting a people's war drawn from manuals as distant from the reality of Chile as the streets, bars, and bistros of Georges Simenon's novels.

Adelman arrived moments later, walking quickly, wrapped in a long coat. A waiter's flashlight led them through a dark and noisy room to a table with a small red lamp. People chatted, drank, and laughed heartily at tables arranged around a thrust stage, where a man in a suit and tie sang a bolero, accompanied by two guitarists. They ordered pisco with Coca-Cola.

"What's going on?" Adelman asked gravely. He was wearing the same suit jacket as he had that afternoon, and the collar of his shirt was unbuttoned.

"It's about Tamara Sunkel. You haven't told me everything you know."

"You're wrong. I told you all of it. I have no reason to hide anything."

"In that case, you wouldn't have agreed to meet me here."

Lethargic applause swirled through the shadows. The bolero singer began to croon "Nosotros" with the melancholy of an exile.

"Are you a detective?" Adelman asked.

Cayetano thought of the novel he was reading. An older

Maigret, with gray hair and a few extra pounds, went on vacation, but ended up entangled in a case making headlines in Paris. He felt like that European detective, dragged against his will into a matter that, strictly speaking, was none of his business.

"I'm not a detective, but I sense that you know more about Tamara," he said, lighting a cigarette. The small flame of his match danced in the lawyer's pupils. "She must have been part of the German community, and that couldn't have escaped your notice."

"I've already told you everything I know."

"You must have found out more. You frequented the German Club, you must have met Tamara Sunkel and the colonel. They're exactly the kind of people who awaken your interest as an investigator."

"I told you all of that this afternoon."

"All of that, but not something that surely must have caught your attention: the sudden disappearance of Tamara Sunkel after the colonel's death."

"That's a matter for the police."

"Adelman, I need your help," said Cayetano. "I came to Bolivia because I need help. It's a humanitarian issue."

The bolero players left the stage, and the indifference of the audience upset Cayetano, since those men probably had wives and children, rented modest homes at the outskirts of La Paz, bought their outfits on installment, and had once dreamed of capturing that slippery creature called fame. But the room burst into loud applause when a blonde in a tight dress and high heels appeared onstage, swinging her hips to the rhythm of "The Pink Panther Theme" as her painted lips smiled into empty space.

"I've already told you what I know." Adelman followed the stripper's steps with hungry eyes.

Cayetano paused a moment for the woman to remove her blouse and expose her breasts, which were scarcely covered by a skimpy black bra, but when he realized the whole procedure would take a while, he said, "I don't need to know what Tamara was involved in. I only need to see her on behalf of someone she was very close to a long time ago."

"Who is that person?"

"I can't reveal his identity, except to say that he's terminally ill and wants to speak to her. That's why I came to La Paz, Simón. I mean it: this person is dying."

"I've already said I don't know where she is, or how to get in touch with her." Adelman drank his pisco and Coke, his eyes glued to the blonde. Now she was dancing in nothing but a bra and panties.

"I don't believe you. If you know of a way of getting in touch with her, you wouldn't have asked me who was trying to reach her."

Adelman kept silent, watching the dancer, stroking his glass with the back of his hand. The blonde shook her hips furiously, proving the firmness of her flesh and stirring murmurs and whistles of approval in the audience.

"They just need to see each other briefly," Cayetano insisted. "Tamara will be grateful. She probably thinks my client died years ago, taking their shared secret to his grave."

The blonde circled the stage and turned her back to the spectators as her hands slowly unclasped the bra. She let it fall and faced the audience again, her arms over her breasts, moving to the rhythm of a sad cumbia, until she finally bared her fruits, which were remarkable and slightly drooped, and took off her panties. It was a kind of magic trick that made the whole place go silent. She stood completely naked, center stage, smiling, arms high, legs crossed, as the spotlight caressed her perfect body. The public gave her a long ovation, peppered with shouts and whistles. She wasn't a real blonde, Cayetano observed as he put out his cigarette and sipped his drink.

"Nobody will find out that you told me her whereabouts," he said when the applause had abated.

"I have no idea where she lives."

"If Tamara was a businesswoman, I can believe that she disappeared from Bolivia overnight, but not that she could liquidate her assets with the same speed."

"What does that have to do with me?"

Cayetano crossed his arms on the table, adjusted his glasses, and looked solemnly at the lawyer. "You must know who kept her books."

When the false blonde disappeared behind the curtain, a bald, scrawny old man emerged and reluctantly gathered her clothes from the floor.

"They say that's her father," Adelman said, watching the guy skeptically. "I don't buy that nonsense."

"Don't change the subject on me, Simón. Tamara Sunkel's accountant has got to know where she is," Cayetano replied, a new cigarette between his lips, though he couldn't light it because the club's stuffy air barely filled his lungs. "And don't even try telling me you don't know how to get in touch with that accountant."

≈ 54 ≈

"Thank goodness you called!" the poet exclaimed with impatience. "The curiosity is making me restless. I'm headed for another sleepless night. It happens to us when we're old. It must be so we can better say good-bye to the realm of the living. Matilde is in Isla Negra, so we can talk freely. How's it going in La Paz?"

Though it was late, Cayetano had called La Sebastiana because he sensed the poet needed to hear from him. He didn't expect to find him in such a good mood. All the better: he hurried to catch him up.

"I've got good news: the woman we're looking for lived here."

"So where is she now?"

Fortunately, Neruda seemed to have recovered his optimism. Cayetano explained what he'd found in a day's work, though he didn't mention the new change to Beatriz's identity. Now the poet almost seemed to enjoy hearing about his adventures, as though he were reading a crime novel with Cayetano as the protagonist.

"The East German embassy sent me a brochure for the Berliner Ensemble," he said. "It includes photos of the actors in *Galileo*, with Tina playing Virginia, but she isn't clearly visible. And what a stage name she picked for herself! Well, those grandiloquent ways ease up with time. Did you know that in my youth I once named a book *The Attempt of the Infinite Man*?"

It pleased him to find the poet in better spirits, but his frivolous humor also shocked him. Saddened, he let Neruda talk without listening to him. He tried not to think. Then, as he bent to untie his shoes, he felt blood suddenly rush to his head and his chest tighten terribly, while an immense fatigue swept over him, as though he'd aged from one moment to the next. He lay down on the bed, still holding the receiver. A buzzing sound bore into his brain.

"Are you listening, young man?"

"Yes, I'm listening, Don Pablo." He closed his eyes. His ears felt clogged, as though he were diving deep inside the warm waters of Havana's Malecón.

"In any case, we needed to talk, because this afternoon, as the sun was setting over Playa Ancha and making pearly sparkles in the water, I fell asleep like one of those shitty old people who start snoring the minute they hit an armchair. And do you know what I dreamed?"

"No, Don Pablo."

The room spun around him like a mad carousel. He felt chills and nausea. He opened his eyes and counted the water stains that hovered on the ceiling like dirty clouds. Beyond them he saw faded curtains and a frameless mirror over the

chest of drawers that reflected the crucified Christ above Cayetano's head. Everything spun without cease.

"Of course, I'm such an idiot. How would you know? I've
been lost in the clouds lately."

After the intense confidence he'd just exhibited, this new
conciliatory tone impelled Cayetano to speak. "It's normal,
Don Pablo. Don't worry. There's been so much going on, and
it's taken a toll on your nerves, and mine. How's the treatment
going?"

But Don Pablo, deep down, had to be doing very badly.

"Don't treat me like a child." He took a deep breath, clearly
annoyed, and added, "You know very well this can't be fixed.
So there's no use in your coming at me with dumb-ass questions or white lies. We're lucky to be mortal."

He said it with an anger that seemed to suggest the opposite,
but Cayetano replied that he was right; in any case, he could
barely hear him. He turned off the light. The room now spun
like the carousel in a Hitchcock film he'd seen at the Mauri
Theater. His throat was dry, and he was shaken by chills. Altitude sickness, for fuck's sake, that damn altitude sickness was
getting the best of him. He recalled the warnings of the Que-
chua man at the airport. Now not even coca tea could save him!

"So I dreamed that I was on a theater stage, that I was an
actor, like Tina, only I was playing Aeneas," the poet continued, with the same desperate arrogance. "Do you remember
Aeneas, Cayetano?"

"More or less, Don Pablo." He thought of Tina. He had
seen her only once, but as he recalled her, she seemed marked
by a definitive, irreparable solitude.

"You can't just read Simenon, young man. Aeneas was the

Trojan who left his homeland because Jupiter ordered him to go to Italy and founded Rome. On the journey, he passed through Carthage, where he fell in love with Queen Dido, a woman who risked everything to be his lover. When he left, she killed herself. That's in the *Aeneid*, Cayetano. As soon as you finish Simenon, at least read Virgil and Homer."

"As soon as this passes, I will."

"Are you all right?"

"Yes, Don Pablo." His bones hurt, his teeth chattered, and his body was bathed in cold and sticky sweat. Neruda was no detective, he thought; he made no attempt to find out more.

"So I was Aeneas, walking through the world of the dead, and I saw the ghost of my former lover, Dido. Without knowing why, I started reciting Aeneas's words from memory, words I just found in the *Aeneid*: 'Oh, tragic Dido: was it true, what the messenger said, when he came to tell me you were dead and gone from us? And was I—such pain!—the cause of your death? I swear on the stars and the gods, I swear on faith itself, if faith exists here in the depths of the earth, that I was forced to leave your shores, oh Queen.' Are you listening, Cayetano, do you realize what was happening in my dream?"

"Of course, Don Pablo. Go on."

"'With their ineluctable laws, the commandments of the gods impelled me, as they impel me now, to travel through these shadows, through these places covered in mold and through this deep night: nor could I ever have believed that my departure would have caused you such fierce pain. Wait, don't go, don't leave my sight. Where are you fleeing to? What I am telling you is final, it's the will of fate . . .'"

He heard his own glasses crash to the floor, and the sound returned him to his hotel room in La Paz, to this exhausting conversation with the poet, and to the complicated text being read or recited to him from La Sebastiana.

"Do you see?" asked Neruda. "Aeneas is me, and Dido is Beatriz. This means that my story was already told by Virgil two thousand years ago. But there's more: if I was Aeneas, then I took advantage of Dido, when she was young and happy with a decent man. I arrived in her country, seduced her with my cosmopolitan air and a whirlwind of words, and I turned her into an unfaithful wife, only to leave her to face her destiny alone. Beatriz may no longer be alive, Cayetano, and I have to get used to the idea of dying with the horrible feeling that I used her and that I'll never be able to know the truth."

At last the mask was falling, though the voice, as had occurred at other times, remained dramatic, playing its part in *The Tragedy of Pablo Neruda*, with its unmistakable sole protagonist. But by now Cayetano had learned to see behind the curtain.

"Don Pablo, it's nighttime, and you're tired. Try to sleep, if you can. You'll see that tomorrow, when the sun rises over the Andes, everything will have a different color."

"I now see myself as that person Sor Juana Inés de la Cruz talked about: a being who 'is a corpse, is dust, is shadow, is nothing . . .'"

It was too much, almost pathetic. He had never heard him in such a state, not at such an extreme. Nor did he want to hear it. "Don Pablo. Stop."

"Beatriz isn't my only Dido, Cayetano. Josie Bliss was one, too, the malignant one with her visceral jealousies and gleaming dagger. And so was María Antonieta Hagenaar Vogelzang, the mother of the daughter I renounced."

There were no more boundaries. Impossible to tell confessions from recital of text.

"Don Pablo, whom are you trying to scare?"

He didn't listen. "And then I was Aeneas with Delia, whom I dispensed with when she was old, too old to start a new life with another man. I betrayed her while she was secretly carrying my manuscripts from one place to another, risking her life for my sake. And I repaid her by leaving her for a woman thirty years younger, with whom she couldn't compete in age or beauty. I've been an Aeneas, Cayetano, an unscrupulous bastard. I've been a master of the art of escape, and I've just now come to understand it in my hour of twilight. I'm condemned to die remembering all the suffering I caused in my pursuit of happiness. There's no one more thoughtless than the man who seeks only his own contentment. Are you listening, Cayetano? Cayetano?"

∽ 55 ∽

"Are you referring to Mrs. Tamara Sunkel, of Santa Cruz, Dr. Adelman?" the accountant asked. He was an older man, with brown eyes besieged by deep wrinkles.

"Precisely. The one who acquired the Antofagasta."

The office of Elmer Soto Ebensberger, CPA, was on the mezzanine of a downtown building, not far from the Palacio Quemado. The neighborhood teemed with food stalls and street vendors, most of them indigenous, who displayed their wares on blankets spread over the sidewalk.

The most sought-after accountant in the German community of La Paz stood up from his desk, which was cluttered with files, and went to an adjacent room, where his employees processed invoices. Cayetano and Adelman waited in silence, staring out at the buildings across the street, which were still under construction but already inhabited on the first floor.

The accountant returned to his office with an array of black notebooks. "You're referring to Tamara Sunkel Bauer, the German woman, right?" he asked, leafing through pages.

"I'm talking about the wife of Colonel Sacher."

"May he rest in peace. In that case, we're referring to the same woman."

"Mr. Brulé wishes to find her on behalf of an old friend of hers."

"She was my client for a while, Dr. Adelman. But I don't know that I'll be of much use to you now," Soto Ebensberger murmured as his index finger roved the notebook. "A charming woman, of course, refined and reserved. Extraordinarily punctual with her payments."

"We're speaking of this woman, right?" Cayetano showed him the photo of Beatriz in Santa Cruz.

The accountant studied it for a moment, then said, with a pompous air, "That's certainly her. And there she is with the colonel."

"Her husband."

"Not by law," Soto Ebensberger corrected. He interlaced his hands. A bleeding Bakelite Christ hung on the wall behind him. "They weren't married in the manner God intended. I know, because I prepared her tax returns, and hers alone."

Cayetano returned the photo to his jacket pocket. "She left the country a while ago, didn't she?"

"That's right."

"In a surprising, mysterious way . . ."

"From one day to the next, really. But I wouldn't say it was illegal." He unfurled a condescending smile. "She was doing very well here. High income, low profile, rubbing elbows with the elite. The death of the colonel must have devastated her."

"That's why she left?"

"I imagine so. And since she was a foreigner, she preferred to go abroad."

"So the accident led to the disappearance of Mrs. Sunkel?"

"I suppose so, because it was a strange accident. The officer's Dodge Dart ran off a cliff in El Alto. The steering failed. We're talking about a brand-new car, the latest model. Several rumors circulated afterward."

"For example?"

"That it was an act of political revenge." He stared hard at Cayetano.

"Revenge for what?"

"Well, the rumors held the colonel responsible for catching Che. He specialized in collecting information. Understand?"

"Yes, I know a little about Sacher. So where is Mrs. Sunkel now?"

"That's the million-dollar question, Mr. Brulé."

Cayetano stroked the tips of his mustache. "But if she owned property, she couldn't have disappeared from Bolivia overnight."

"You've missed a detail: like a good German, she prepared her affairs very calmly and in detail." Soto Ebensberger became solemn. "She liquidated all her properties before she left."

Cayetano lit a cigarette, inhaled deeply, and exhaled the smoke toward the window. "Didn't she leave you an address before she left? If you were her accountant, then she must have. There are always follow-up details in tax matters."

"A professional owes discretion to his clients."

"Don Elmer, it's a matter of life or death," intervened Adelman.

"You wouldn't like revealing anything, either, Doctor."

"Mr. Brulé's client is dying, Don Elmer."

He stood and walked back to the adjacent office. He returned with a red notebook.

"Really, Doctor, only because it's for you. . . . When she left, Mrs. Sunkel left her information for a last-minute bank transfer from the sale of a parcel of land. I don't think it will help Mr. Brulé, since it's a temporary address. We made the transfer and sent her a copy of the records, but we got back a proof of receipt."

"What address did she give you?" asked Cayetano.

"She left a care-of in the name of a Maia Herzen."

"Maia Herzen," he muttered. "Where?"

"In Santiago de Chile. But it's been five years, Mr. Brulé. I doubt you'll be able to find Tamara Sunkel Bauer there now."

$\approx$ *56* $\approx$

The LAN airplane stirred up dust as it hit the landing strip at Santiago de Chile Airport on September 10, 1973. After retrieving his baggage, Cayetano called the poet's house in Valparaíso from a booth at the terminal, but received no answer. He then tried to reach him at La Chascona, in the capital's Bellavista neighborhood, but the staff there said he was at his Isla Negra home, on the Pacific Coast.

He tried calling there. No luck. A man's voice informed him that the poet was sleeping, and to try again later. Out of sheer curiosity, Cayetano asked for Alicia, but the man responded that he knew no one of that name. He took a taxi into Santiago to investigate the address the Bolivian accountant had given him in La Paz. Excavations for a future subway system on the Alameda had become trenches and quarries for the Allende government's sympathizers and adversaries, who fought in the Santiago streets with sticks and fists.

"This can't go on much longer," the taxi driver said as they passed the Palacio de la Moneda, which was protected by squads of riot police, with their cars and buses. The flag raised high over La Moneda conveyed that Allende was still in his office. "As a tourist, you have no idea what it's like, sir. This country is going to shit."

Outside the window of the Ford Zodiac, Santiago was an anarchic city, empty of supplies, besieged by an invisible enemy. Interminable lines stretched at grocery stores, at supermarkets, and at the stops of bus lines that no longer ran. Cloth banners hung from buildings, supporting Allende or demanding he step down. In the streets, piles of burning tires emitted whirls of pestilent black smoke, leftist and right-wing groups battled heatedly as ululating police sirens mixed with the sound of shouting, and tear gas poisoned the city's air. On the corners, riot-police cars and mobile-unit buses stood ready to enter the fray, despite the fact that some of them already had broken windows and punctured tires. Farther on, rows of young people with helmets, sticks, and flags demanded the expropriation of *El Mercurio* and of all the nation's land. The taxi driver veered away from the chaos downtown and took Vitacura to its intersection with elegant Luis Carrera Street.

Cayetano asked the driver to wait a few minutes for him. He was in front of the very house that Tamara Sunkel had given the La Paz accountant as her temporary Chilean address five years before. In 1968, it supposedly belonged to Maia Herzen, a person whom Tamara trusted, according to Soto Ebensberger. It was a one-story house, white and sturdy, with a tile roof; its long shape extended back into trees and bushes, while Manquehue Hill rose up behind it.

He rang the bell at the gate and waited, gazing at a large

palm tree in the backyard. He saw two parked cars: a white Fiat 125S, and a sober beige Opel. Someone must be home, he thought. Hopefully this was still the residence of Maia Herzen. Through a window, he spied wicker furniture, a ceramic floor, rubber plants with large polished leaves, oil paintings, and pottery near the fireplace. Then he saw the letters poking out of the mail slot. He took them out surreptitiously.

The first letter, from the gas company, was addressed to Maia Herzen. So was the second, from the phone company. And the third as well. He smiled with satisfaction and ran his fingertips down his lilac tie with the small green guanacos. He was definitely in luck. Maia Herzen still lived here and surely she would know how to find Tamara Sunkel. Later he'd call the poet to give him the fantastic news. He felt that he was truly turning into a Caribbean Maigret. He didn't care whether or not anyone opened the door, because the matter was resolved, he thought, taking a pack of Bolivian cigarettes from his pocket. Or, at least, resolved to a point: he'd found the woman the poet was looking for. The rest of the matter lay in Don Pablo's hands. He lit a cigarette and inhaled the smoke, satisfied, proud of himself. This would make Neruda happy. Perhaps it would give him the energy to write more poems. What should he do next? Go to Isla Negra to relay the news?

The sound of a car engine returned him to Santiago. Someone was coming home. He felt excited. Waters always flow back to their riverbed, he thought as he returned the letters to the mail slot. He walked toward the street with the cigarette hanging from a corner of his lips, feeling, for the first time, like a true detective. That was when he realized the sound had come from the taxi that had brought him here. It was speeding down Luis Carrera, leaving nothing but a trail of smoke. He cursed the taxi driver a thousand times and said a silent good-bye to his luggage and the indigenous doll he'd bought for Laura Aréstegui in the La Paz airport.

~ *57* ~

He wasted the whole morning in a Barrio Alto police station, filing a police report on his luggage. The officers didn't have time for cases like his, busy as they were combating the black market, managing the lines outside grocery stores, and preventing people from throwing stones at the few trucks and buses that still ran. The national transportation and commerce strike was well under way, and would extend, as its organizers put it, "until the final consequences," a euphemism for the toppling of Allende. The country was fatally paralyzed and divided.

He wasn't able to reach the poet, nor could he find a bus to take him to Isla Negra, nor could he book tickets to Valparaíso on the Andesmar Bus, Tur Bus, or Condor Bus. The last train to the port city had already left Mapocho Station. He had no choice but to check into a hotel.

With the money he had left, he got a room at the Gala Hotel, near the Palacio de la Moneda. It was after nine p.m. on

September 10 when he went out to eat. Plaza de Armas was deserted. He found an empty soda fountain, where the waiter prepared him a hot dog without mayonnaise or sauerkraut, and a weak coffee. He ate quickly, feeling like one of those miserable characters who wandered station platforms in the film *Doctor Zhivago*. He returned to his hotel. In the distance, he heard gunshots and explosions. The radio brought alarming news. Opposition leaders were demanding that the president resign, all power be turned over to the leader of the Senate, and new elections be called. Meanwhile, government transmissions warned that civil war could be at hand. There was no way he could sleep, so he went back out for a walk.

A thick, cold mist filled the streets, redolent with gunpowder. He wandered despondently through downtown Santiago until, all of a sudden, as he turned a corner, La Moneda appeared in front of him, illumined like a ghostly sailboat surging out of dense fog. He crossed Plaza de la Constitución, passing the presidential palace, which glided majestically in a sea of surreal calm, and entered the Carrera Hotel. He wanted a strong drink. The bar was full of foreign correspondents, diplomats, spies, and gentlemen in suits and ties who insisted that only a military government could save the nation. In the midst of the conversations swirling around the tables—some whispered, some shouted—he downed two double rums in a row and paid for them with the last of the poet's dollars. Then he watched the news on the opposition's television channel, which was playing above the bar.

Things had clearly worsened since he had been away. General Augusto Pinochet now headed up the army, a man who in the past would have stood out for his apolitical stance and loyalty to government and constitution, but who wasn't half the man that General Carlos Prats had been, and didn't have a drop of his charisma. The air force was facing internal unrest. A similar situation seemed to plague the navy, which planned to initiate an operation along the Chilean coast the following day, in conjunction with a fleet from the United States. The news cameras covered the widespread food shortage, the long queues, chaos on the streets, terrorist attacks from the right, factories taken over by workers and land taken over by peasants, and die-hard protests on the left and right. Almost all the buses and trucks in the entire country were parked in a coastal area north of Valparaíso. There they slumbered, deprived of essential parts by the strikers so that no one would be able to drive them. The opposition's strike, backed by opposition parties and business-men, and financed by Washington, had vowed to cease only if Allende resigned. While the Unidad Popular Party urged the president to respond to the coup attempt with a firm hand, the opposition was refusing further dialogue with the head of state. The country, Cayetano thought with another rum in his hands, was advancing irrevocably toward a precipice, and would never be the same again.

He left the bar, filled with a deep bitterness, and headed to the lobby, hoping to get some fresh air and clear his mind. He looked through the windows and glimpsed La Moneda again. It was essentially a large silver ship, its candles swollen in the night breeze. There was even a light in the president's office, on the second floor, to the left of the main entrance. So Allende was still working.

"Allende clearly doesn't want to leave La Moneda," a bar patron had said, a bald, bearded man in suit and tie.

"Let's put an end to them before they put an end to us," another had said, garnering applause.

"The only good communist is a dead communist," a third man had added, emboldened, drawing an ovation.

Cayetano decided to return to the bar's heated atmosphere, and sat down on a leather armchair, some distance from the throng. Strange, he thought as he recalled the current chaos in the nation: in this hotel, a refuge for the foreign press, businessmen, diplomats, and right-wing politicians, there was no shortage. Not of rum, nor of whiskey, nor of chicken or beef sandwiches, nor of sausage or cheese. It was as though the place belonged to another era, and another country.

A waiter suddenly placed a glass in his hand, brimming with what seemed to be a respectable amber rum; a first-class amber rum, to be exact.

"What's this?" he asked, startled.

"A Bacardi, seven years old," the waiter said, putting on airs.

"Compliments of the house?"

"Compliments of someone waiting for you outside."

Cayetano took a long gulp with his eyes closed, an elated, voluptuous gulp during which he briefly thought of Kurt Plenzdorf in his little office in Berlin, and then he stood and followed the waiter, glass in hand, curiosity pricking the soles of his feet to move faster. Outside the windows, beyond the trees of Plaza de la Constitución, the flag still glowed over La Moneda, against the September night.

"If you would be so kind," the waiter said, and gestured toward the woman seated in front of the window.

"Cayetano Brulé?" The woman rose. She was tall, white, with light-colored hair. "A pleasure to meet you," she added with a measured smile. "I'm Beatriz. Beatriz, widow of Bracamonte."

Cayetano stood, astounded, amid the marble floors, crystal lamps, lush drapes, and beveled mirrors of the lobby. The waiter returned to the bar, where outburts from the customers continued to fill the air.

She was, without a doubt, Beatriz, the widow of Bracamonte, the woman he was looking for, the woman the poet had fallen in love with decades earlier in Mexico City. He felt his chest seize up with emotion. This was the same face that appeared in the photo taken outside the Social Club in Santa Cruz, the one he had stolen from the apartment in Berlin. He had studied those features so many times that they were deeply imprinted in his mind. Slender and well groomed, with a determined gaze, Beatriz was still a striking woman.

"The pleasure is mine," he mumbled, managing to hide his surprise. He extended his hand.

"Will you tell me why you're looking for me?" she asked. Her eyes searched him; he felt daunted.

"How do you know I'm looking for you?"

"I've been hearing about it for some time. Today, for example, you were at my house. I assume you weren't there to speak to my husband."

HERE WAS PROOF OF WHAT he'd guessed all along, he thought with relief. Years ago, in 1969, Tamara Sunkel of La Paz had gone to Santiago de Chile and become Maia Herzen. There was no Maia Herzen. Maia Herzen was Tamara Sunkel, who was the same as Beatriz, the widow of Bracamonte.

"That's right. It was me."

"Why are you looking for me?" she insisted, in a serious tone.

"Because I have a message for you," he replied, smoothing his patterned tie with satisfaction. Now he would be the one to ask questions. Not her. That much he'd learned from Maigret's conversations with suspects, those slow exchanges in which he drew out details like so many crumbs from the whole loaf of truth. Yes, now it was his turn. Now he would ask about what he really wanted to know: whether her daughter was, in fact, what the poet longed for her to be with all the strength he still possessed—namely, the extension of his own life into future space and time.

"Could you be clearer, please?"

"Maybe if I tell you that you're still remembered at the school on the shores of Lake Bogensee, you'll understand me better."

"I don't know what you're talking about."

"And that in La Paz, an accountant is still waiting for confirmation that a money transfer has been received . . ."

"Why don't we go for a ride?" she suggested, keeping her poise. "My car is parked nearby."

They walked down the steps, and the doorman in marshal's uniform held the door open for them with a deep bow. Cayetano had the distinct impression that Beatriz was a slippery fish who'd escaped his hands only to appear farther away, in clearer, stiller waters, willing to be caught there and to receive his questions. They got into the Opel parked in front of the hotel. It was a little after midnight. A deceptive calm had fallen over Santiago, the calm before the storm, Cayetano thought. The woman drove past La Moneda and turned on the Alameda, heading east.

"Have you been to Leipziger Allee in East Berlin?" he asked.

She kept driving as though she hadn't heard him, then asked, "Whom do you work for, Cayetano?"

The fact that she knew his name sent a chill down his spine, as it meant that she must be a powerful woman. "You can already imagine the answer, or else you wouldn't have sought me out. First, tell me this: who are you really?"

"You already know that. I've been in Chile for several years."

"But before that you lived in La Paz, where you were a real estate investor, and the companion of a Bolivian officer. Before that, you worked at Bogensee, and before that in Havana. And in the beginning you lived in Mexico City . . ."

"You see?" She sounded sarcastic. "If you know everything, why ask?"

"Because I see too many discrepancies. What do you actually do for a living?"

The car kept driving east. They drove past the stately building of La Unión Club, and the central headquarters of the University of Chile, where a painted wall called on the people to face down sedition. The road was full of military jeeps. On the grounds of the United Beer Company, a group of workers stoked a bonfire. Their banners proclaimed that the business was in the hands of its workers. As they advanced into the tree-lined neighborhood of Barrio Alto, with its lush gardens, the Chilean capital began to appear less gloomy and desolate.

"I've searched for you all over the world, Beatriz. But in the end it was you who found me. It's an urgent matter: Don Pablo needs to speak with you."

"Don Pablo?"

"Don't pretend you don't know who I'm talking about. I know you do."

"I'm not pretending. I haven't seen him in over thirty years. I know he's ill."

"Gravely ill."

"Why does he need to see me?" Her voice sounded indifferent.

"He only hired me to find you, Beatriz. The rest is not my concern."

"I still don't understand."

"I imagine he wants to talk about what happened between you in the forties, in Mexico City . . ."

"And why would his love for me suddenly rear its head after all this time?"

"You know why."

"No. I don't know anything, Cayetano."

"Because of Tina. Tina Bracamonte."

"Hold on a moment. Just a moment." She sounded tense.

They were waiting at a red light on Eliodoro Yañez Street. "Don't come at me now with strange stories. What could he want with Tina?"

"You can imagine what. It's not for me to comment on this matter."

She shifted into first gear, and accelerated. She seemed to be losing control over herself, and the car. She turned onto a side street and drove at full throttle; the tires screeched. After a few minutes, they reached the Catholic University, where anti-government banners hung on the walls and students stood guard with helmets and slingshots.

"They're about to topple the government, and Pablo's hung up on concerns like these," she said. "Do you see those right-wing youth who took the university in defense of democracy, claiming Allende is a threat to it? Well, tomorrow, when the military governs with an iron fist, they'll rush to offer themselves as collaborators. Take a look at them and don't forget. Today they're in their walking shoes, country pants and parkas, crucifixes at their throats, nunchucks in hand. Tomorrow they'll be in suits and ties to defend the indefensible."

She sped down the deserted avenue. After passing Plaza Italia, where people waited in line beside bonfires to enter the supermarket when it opened the following day, they arrived at the headquarters of Patria y Libertad, an ochre fortress with boarded windows and doors. On the wall facing the Alameda, an enormous painted black spider menaced the Santiago night.

"The nationalists," Beatriz said with disdain. A banner hanging nearby proclaimed: "YAKARTA IS COMING!" "Today they call themselves patriots, tomorrow they'll applaud the murder and imprisonment of Chileans. Then they'll wash their

328 · Roberto Ampuero

hands like Pontius Pilate. The very worst is about to happen,
Cayetano, and Pablo's expending this much energy to find out
about something that happened decades ago?"

He listened to her indignant diatribe: Pablo was clearly the
same egotist as ever, and it was far too late to rectify history. At
this stage, she said, it didn't matter what he imagined about
their affair. There was nothing left to be done, the die had long
been cast, and no one could change the past or what had sprung
from it.

Twenty minutes later, they reached the neighborhood of
Macul, with its gated Pedagogical Institute, now taken over by
leftist students. Bonfires burned on patios, and helmeted night
watchmen took shelter on the roofs. A green-and-red MAPU
banner hung from a cornice, urging Allende to hold his ground.
A red-and-black MIR banner called on the people to rise up
and form militias.

"You see those youngsters?" she asked. "All daddy's boys.
Until 1968 they sided with the Frei Montalva government, and
at the last minute, when they saw Allende was going to win in
1970, they switched to Unidad Popular. Today they're ambassadors, ministers, or investors, and they're more revolutionary
than anyone else, as if they'd always been that way. If things
fall apart they'll be the first to save their own necks, renege
everything, and adjust to new times. They're bourgeois kids
playing at revolution to calm their own conscience. It comforts
them to know that later their relatives in the church, the military, the justice system, or big business will save them from the
mess they got themselves into."

They headed back toward downtown on bleak, dark streets
fraught with potholes and puddles. On one corner, they saw
beggars sleeping under cardboard, accompanied by stray dogs.

Beatriz had not answered Cayetano's question. And the more he pressed his case, the more she avoided the issue and instead kept holding forth on the national drama and the poet's irresponsible egotism.

"He was always that way," she said again. "He fled Mexico when the time came to clear matters up. He appears again now, when clarification is superfluous, of no use. That's no way to act, Cayetano."

"I understand what you're saying, Beatriz, but you still haven't told me whether Tina is the daughter of Ángel or the poet," Cayetano finally said with new resolve. This time, he thought, the fish wouldn't be able to slip through his hands. The city passed outside the car window as in a black-and-white film. "Do you want to answer, or should I?"

∽ 59 ∽

In the Opel's headlights, the highway to Valparaíso pushed into the darkness like a saber down the night's great throat. Beatriz had offered to take him all the way home. They traveled in silence. The drone of the engine provided a backdrop to political commentaries from the airwaves. The crisis had become utterly polarized, extreme, and untenable, with socialist leader Carlos Altamirano proclaiming that if a coup should take place, the left would infiltrate the marines and turn the nation into another Vietnam. Every once in a while they glimpsed blazes stoked by country dwellers demanding ownership of the land they worked on. The news grew even worse: military squads threatened workers at the factories they'd overtaken, the opposition's statements were becoming more and more seditious, and the response from the left, with the exception of the communists and the president, was becoming increasingly radical in tone.

At that instant, Cayetano's gaze fell on the Army of Chile badge on the windshield.

"Whose side are you on, Beatriz?" he asked. In the darkness ahead, he saw a soldier positioned at the edge of the highway, and caught the furtive shine of his gun. It made him think of that night many years before when the poet had glimpsed the murderous wink of Josie Bliss's dagger through a diaphanous mosquito net.

"Whose side do you think I'm on?"

"Judging by your time in Havana and East Berlin, you should be sympathetic to the Allende government. But if I look at your life in La Paz and Santiago, I see you as committed to the right. You're a walking contradiction."

"Things are more complex than you realize, and aren't always what they seem. You're young and full of feeling, idealistic to a fault. That's why you're helping Pablo find the daughter he wishes he'd had. But life is an iceberg, Cayetano. We can't see the most essential parts."

"That sounds nice, but you're not answering my question."

"A good listener requires few words."

"What work are you doing here in socialist Chile?" he pressed. "Construction is at a standstill. Nobody's building so much as a shack, or making investments. How do you make your living here?"

They watched a caravan of jeeps and trucks full of marine troops pass by. They were headed in the opposite direction: away from Valparaíso, toward the capital. Who was ruling the country now? Cayetano wondered. Was it really Allende, with his Chilean flag raised high over La Moneda, or was power already in someone else's hands?

"Luckily I have some means available to me," she said. "I don't need to work. Does that satisfy you?"

"Your daughter lives in East Berlin under a surname different from any of yours. In Bolivia, you had connections with a military officer involved in Che's assassination. I don't think you would have been able to be Colonel Sacher's friend if he had known your daughter lived in an East German neighborhood reserved for the political elite."

She kept driving in silence, to Curacaví, where she pulled up in front of an empty restaurant. The night was a cold cup of coffee.

"Listen, Cayetano. There's nothing left to do here," she said as she turned off the engine. "The government exists only on paper. The military holds all the power. It's just a matter of time before the coup."

"How do you know? And why don't you do something to stop it if you're so sure?"

"Don't you understand that history has its own logic, and nobody can violate it without getting burned? What's been taking place here for the past three years should never have happened. In today's global situation, this socialist experiment of Allende's, with its red wine and empanada flavor, can't prosper. Who will support Chile? Moscow is far away, Cuba's too poor, Nixon has crossed over and gone on the offensive. I know things from the inside. Understand? Also, for you, as a Cuban, things are only going to get worse. Listen to me. You have to leave Chile."

"I'm struck by your certainty. Where does it come from? And who told you I was looking for you? Was it the Bolivian military, or the Chilean? Who?"

They got out of the car and entered the restaurant's pale atmosphere. A fire burned in the corner, and from a radio, the voice of Víctor Jara sang "Plegaria a un Labrador." They sat down at a table and ordered coffee.

"Be happy with what I'm able to tell you, Cayetano," she warned. The flames from the fireplace glimmered on her cheeks. "It should be enough to know there's nobody who can attempt to forge a peaceful road to socialism."

"Let's not be apocalyptic. Instead, why don't you tell me whether Don Pablo's suspicions are well founded."

Beatriz paused as the waiter poured hot water over the powdered coffee in their cups, and walked away. Then, with a light smile and uncertain tone, she said, "Knowing that won't change history. What can Pablo get out of learning the truth after all this time? A peaceful death? So how would that affect Tina?" She fingered her spoon for a few moments. "It would turn her life upside down. For what? And what would it change for me? What would be different?"

She fell into a deep silence, and nothing he did could pull her out of it. They finished their coffee, left the restaurant, and started driving again. The hot drink had comforted Cayetano and brought him back to earth. Being in the car with Beatriz immersed him in a vague, surreal realm that flowed slowly before his eyes and felt like a dream or, more precisely, like a nightmare. When they entered Valparaíso through Santos Ossa, she took Colón, heading south, driving along Francia Avenue until, a few minutes later, they were on Alemania Avenue, winding through shadows.

"Pablo's house is here, right?" She stopped the car in front of the Mauri Theater. Alí Babá was closed, and Collado Way stretched out desolately, its yellow flagstones lit gently under a single streetlamp. Beneath the theater marquee, a dog was scratching his fleas.

"When he comes to Valparaíso, he stays at La Sebastiana," Cayetano said. "Today he's in Isla Negra, due to his health . . ."

"Let's walk."

They got out and went up Collado Way; before them, the bay city unfolded like an immense accordion of lights. In the distance, the ships of the Chilean navy glided out to meet the United States Marines. It was the month of Unitas, an annual joint naval operation. Cayetano and Beatriz gazed at Valparaíso in silence. At their backs, behind the garden, Neruda's house rose up, ghostly and robust.

"There's one more thing I don't understand," Cayetano said after a while.

"What's bothering you now, detective?" She scrutinized him harshly, though without aggression.

"How did you, the naive wife of Dr. Bracamonte, become . . . well . . . what you seem to be?"

The woman sat down on the steps that descended into lower Valparaíso, let out a sigh of what seemed like annoyance, and said, "As it turns out, Pablo's political causes won me over. I was very young. I needed to believe in something that transcended me, in a utopia."

"And he gave you that."

"In a way, you could say he created me."

"After everything that . . . well, he did?"

"That's not what I mean," she said, and lowered her gaze with a smile. "But to a certain extent, he created me because he shared his political beliefs with me when I was young and inexperienced, and above all because his poems encouraged me in times of fear, uncertainty, exhaustion, and despair. Also, in a way, we're all born from our own loves. The fulfilled ones, and the ones that fail."

Cayetano stroked his mustache, absorbed. So she, like himself, was simply a character born and molded out of the poet's fantasies, he thought, his gaze still on that splendid, mysterious woman, who stared out at the bay as though it held a hidden message in its waters. And so the poet created not just verses, but also flesh-and-blood people, even though he erroneously believed that he could be a father only to himself and his poems. Perhaps this woman, and he himself, and the bay and everything happening in this divided, hate-filled country as well as his investigations in Mexico City, Havana, East Berlin, and La Paz were nothing more than verses in Neruda's sweeping final poem, he thought with a chill.

After a while, Beatriz stood up. "I have to go back to Santiago."

They returned to Alemania Avenue. Cayetano told her he preferred to walk home. Beatriz got into her Opel.

"You still haven't told me who you work for," Cayetano insisted, smoothing his mustache again, leaning toward the driver's side window.

"I do it for a good cause, Cayetano," she answered solemnly. "I believe in something, I'm committed to it, and that's what I fight for. I've always fought for the same cause. My work is like my daughter's work: I act, I put on disguises, I pretend to be something I'm not. I'm not what I seem to be, Cayetano, I'm always something else. Have I made myself clear? I believe that now you should understand my migrations, my names, and why I navigate contradictory worlds."

"So, you're a . . . ?"

"I can't tell you what I am, because I'm always something else. I can only tell you that I'm not what I seem. Is that enough?"

"Who told you I was looking for you? Adelman, the lawyer?" He recalled Neruda's words about life being a parade of disguises.

Beatriz placed her hands on the steering wheel and smiled. Then she answered, in a low voice, "A man in a white raincoat told me." She looked at him conspiratorially. "When you talk to Pablo, tell him I'm sorry, but we can't see each other now. Tell him that my daughter was named Tina after a woman he and I both admired greatly, a beautiful Italian photographer."

"Tina Modotti?"

"That's right, the companion of Julio Antonio Mella."

"I'll tell him."

"And give him this." She handed him a small black-and-white photograph. "That's Tina in front of the Berliner Ensemble, the first day she rehearsed on that stage."

He took it with deep emotion. "He'll thank you for it."

"And one more thing. Something even more important," she added as she started the car.

"I'm all ears."

"Please tell him that Tina's middle name is Trinidad."

"Trinidad?"

"Yes, like his beloved grandmother. That should give him some peace."

The Opel slowly pulled away, and Cayetano walked down the middle of the avenue, photo in hand, free of luggage, alone in the Valparaíso night, knowing that nobody awaited him at home and that he was, at last, his own man. He felt overcome by excitement and sheer joy. The fact that Tina Feuerbach bore Neruda's grandmother's name could mean only one thing, he thought with a shudder that clouded his vision for a moment. He hurried down the pavement and, for an instant, as his eyes grazed the Pacific, he had the brief impression that the fleet of warships was returning at full speed to Valparaíso, lights off, in the middle of the night.

≈ 60 ≈

The first thing he did the next morning was turn on the radio on his nightstand for the news. The night before, he'd failed to get in touch with the poet, as his phone went unanswered, and it was too late at night for him to show up in person without raising Matilde's suspicions. Radio Magallanes announced that it was raining torrentially throughout the central zone and on Easter Island. How anomalous, that it should rain in September. He opened his eyes, and as he looked out the window he caught the high, limpid sky of the Pacific coast as it usually appeared only in early spring, when the city's façades shone in the clear air as though someone had just polished them with Brasso. He got up, disconcerted. Something wasn't right about what the speaker on the left-wing station kept saying with such insistence.

The phone rang. He answered. It was Laura Aréstegui, the Ph.D. student, in Playa Ancha.

"Have you seen what's happening?"

"I just woke up. What's going on?"

"There's been a coup—"

"What are you saying?"

"The armed forces rebelled," she exclaimed in agitation. "A military junta has formed in the capital."

Now he understood why, the night before, the squadron had returned with its lights off instead of heading out to meet the U.S. fleet. He looked out between the blinds. Chilean warships were stationed throughout the bay. They looked like toys. He was about to tell Laura that he'd witnessed their secret return, but she wasn't on the line anymore.

He tried her number several times, with no luck. Then he waited, in case she was trying to get through to him. In vain. He tried the number Beatriz had given him in case of emergency, but his effort was fruitless. The telephone system seemed to have collapsed. He tried to contact Pete Castillo, and the same thing happened. Strangely, a woman answered his call to La Sebastiana. He asked for the poet. She told him what he'd already suspected: he wasn't there.

"Where can I find him? This is urgent."

"I have no idea."

"I'm Cayetano Brulé, a friend of Don Pablo's. I need to talk to him."

"Don Pablo isn't here, or in Santiago."

"Perhaps he's in Isla Negra?"

"Probably."

As he was dialing the number for Isla Negra, his phone went dead again. He nervously turned on the radio in the kitchen. Radio Magallanes was saying that the members of the military junta—Generals Pinochet, Merino, Leigh, and

Mendoza—had threatened President Allende and ordered him to turn over power, but that he had dug in his heels at the Palacio de la Moneda and refused to comply.

Cayetano dressed hastily, thinking about what balls the president had. Any other Latin American president would have run off to the airport long before to save his own neck and his bank accounts full of U.S. dollars. What now? he thought, gripped with panic. His wife was a contact for the Unidad Popular Party, in case of emergencies like this one. But now, Ángela Undurraga Cox was probably crawling like an alligator through the swamps of Punto Cero, under the blistering Caribbean sun, rehearsing for a war she would never fight. When they saw each other again, if they ever did, she would say she'd been right to urge the people to take up arms and prepare to fight against sedition. Revolutions without weapons? Only in fairy tales, she'd scoff. He heard the rattle of helicopter blades flying over the city, which brought to mind the day the president had said good-bye to the poet at La Sebastiana. Their embrace. A thought paralyzed him, like a stab wound: that Neruda could fall into the military's hands. They wouldn't let him write or go to his radiology sessions; they'd burn his manuscripts; the poet would die of sadness. Somehow he had to get to Isla Negra before the military did, so he could tell Neruda the news about Tina. Perhaps that would help him better survive the end of the popular government, and whatever else he would come to face.

He looked for his checkered jacket until he remembered that he'd lost it to the taxi driver in Santiago. Magallanes was calling on citizens not to be intimidated, and to show up to their workplaces prepared to defend Allende. But how could they defend him without arms? From their workplaces? With what? He looked out onto the street. A Marine truck climbed up steep Bartolomé Ortiz, full of troops. Their helmets shone under the morning sun. Guns echoed in the distance, and in the south, over Playa Ancha, a helicopter traced a great circle in the sky.

He ran down Diego Rivera, through the warm Pacific air. If it weren't for the disaster taking place, he thought, this would have been a gorgeous day. He reached a small plaza called Ecuador, where the news had already interrupted daily routines. People were walking back home, quickly, their faces full of terror and amazement, while pairs of soldiers stood on every corner. Cayetano continued on to Errázuriz Avenue, hoping he could find a ride to Isla Negra. It wouldn't be easy, but he had to try. Perhaps this September 11 would only be another June 29, he thought, and Allende would crush the coup attempt and call the people into the nation's streets and plazas that very night to celebrate their victory.

Much later, a Sol del Pacífico bus pulled up half a block away to let out passengers, and he managed to board. It was headed to Quinteros, which suited him, as Isla Negra would be close by. The passengers traveled in silence, tense and overwhelmed, as the vehicle drove along the shores of an unkempt ocean. In the south, in Valparaíso Bay, he could still see the precise outlines of the navy warships.

As soon as he turned into Quinteros, the bus driver stopped and would go no further, because he lived there. The people disembarked in resignation, without a word. Cayetano found an open soda fountain beside a dense old grapevine. He ordered coffee and waited for someone to pass down the highway. The soda fountain's radio announced that Hawker Hunters from the armed forces would bomb La Moneda if the president didn't surrender. He felt his mouth go dry. He couldn't believe what he was hearing. It wasn't possible that, while he was struggling to get to the poet's house, Chilean warplanes were about to bomb the government's headquarters with the president still inside it. This was no new June 29, he realized; it was a tragedy of horrendous proportions. But Allende wouldn't surrender. A Chilean president never surrenders.

Once again he recalled Allende and Neruda's parting embrace beside the helicopter, and the way people had leaned out of windows and flooded streets and alleys to celebrate the aircraft's takeoff. Now the radio crackled with agitated voices, bursts of shots and shrapnel, the wail of bombs, police and ambulance sirens, and the roar of low-flying jets. It was war.

He asked for a beer, or whatever alcoholic drink they had on hand. He would have liked to have done something, something brave and heroic, but circumstances once again condemned him to passivity. The waitress brought him a glass of pisco, which he drank straight up, with trembling hands and a sense of unreality as he looked out at the sparkling Pacific Ocean. A flock of pelicans pressed elegantly through the sky; meanwhile, bombs were raining down on the capital. Now the radio called on leaders of Unidad Popular to report to their closest police stations. He listened to a long list of names: ministers, governors, senators, local leaders, and officials who must surrender or else be annihilated without mercy. His fear grew when he heard that subversive foreigners should also report to police stations or military barracks. What was he? he wondered. A mere innocent foreigner, or a subversive one?

He paid and left. Now more than ever, he urgently needed a ride to Isla Negra. He couldn't stay on the street, out in the open. As he walked, he heard chilling news through the open windows of country houses scattered along the highway: tanks and troops had surrounded La Moneda, the president's police officers were leaving Allende alone with a handful of bodyguards, an unequal gun battle was intensifying between soldiers and civil defenders of the government, and Hawker Hunters flew over Santiago carrying deadly explosives. A nightmare.

Just the night before, he'd seen La Moneda brandishing its flag against the night. Now Allende and his allies battled for survival behind its old walls. He sat down in the shade of a hawthorn tree. He felt shattered. An hour later, a battered pickup truck pulled up beside him, crammed with pots, pans, and enormous copper plates that shone like suns.

"Where are you headed, my friend?" said the driver, an old Gypsy, traveling alone in the cab.

≈ *61* ≈

Before he parted ways with the Gypsy, he felt obligated to buy a copper frying pan with black rivets. Then he disembarked in front of a green kiosk where bread, drinks, and vegetables were sold. He'd lost track of events because the pickup truck had no radio. At the kiosk, he exchanged the gleaming pan for two bottles of Bilz soda and sat down to wait by the road. Military marches poured out of the store's radio, tuned to the junta's station.

After a while, the woman working at the kiosk quickly turned the radio dial. Cayetano recognized the calm, grave voice of Salvador Allende, shrapnel sounding in the background. Allende was alive! Had the bombings stopped? Could this be another June 29, after all—could he be announcing a return to normalcy? All too soon he realized his mistake. Allende was resisting from inside the presidential palace. It gave him chills just to imagine him there, in La Moneda, besieged by tanks and planes. He was speaking to the country. He promised to stay loyal to his constitutional duties, declared the rebel generals traitors, and called police chief César Mendoza despicable. But there was something disturbing in his words: he urged the people not to make sacrifices, and said he'd pay for his loyalty to them with his life, that "the seed we've planted in the worthy conscience of thousands and thousands of Chileans cannot be entirely destroyed." It seemed like a message of hope, the hopes for the future of a defeated man.

From Quinteros came the echo of isolated gunshots and machine gun bursts, and then a devastating silence as the voice of Salvador Allende—after affirming that sooner or later the great avenues would reopen and a new man would travel down them again to build a better society, and after he finally shouted, "Long live Chile, long live the workers!"—vanished into thin air. The woman at the kiosk turned the radio's knobs in desperation, trying to recover the president's voice, but found only a shrill, sharp whistle, followed by a military march. She didn't give up. She kept searching the dial insistently, coming across more and more stations playing edicts and marches. The woman began to sob, huddled close to the radio, wiping her tears with a handkerchief.

Cayetano watched it all from the other side of the highway, mechanically drinking his soda, at a loss for words, sitting under the hot morning sun. Suddenly the woman at the kiosk fixed her gaze on him, and he pretended to be looking at the sky, the same sky in which, at that moment, seventy kilometers to the east, jets were flying in their attack of La Moneda. Now the highway gleamed in silence, interrupted only by occasional gunshots and the rattle of a distant helicopter. He thought that the Pacific seemed inflamed.

"Mister, you'd better go home," the woman shouted. She started to close down her kiosk. "The curfew is about to start. They'll shoot you if they catch you on the road."

Cayetano looked at his watch, and then at the empty highway. He drank the last sip of his second bottle. There was no way for him to go anywhere. It wasn't feasible for him to carry out her advice. "Is there any kind of lodging in Quinteros?" he asked.

"Only in the summer. Not in this season."

He remembered Margaretchen. She'd answered similarly weeks earlier when he'd asked about hotels in Bernau. He couldn't ask this woman for a place to stay. Under the new circumstances, she wouldn't dare open her home to a stranger.

He crossed the street, bought a bottle of Cachatún, and started walking, hoping someone would take him to Isla Negra before he ran into soldiers. Who the hell had made him come live in this far-flung corner of the earth? Didn't Cubans have enough problems at home and abroad? How could he have gotten embroiled in another country's mess?

As he walked, he thought of Ángela, and pictured her listening to news from Chile with incredulous frustration. She'll certainly come to the confrontation well prepared, he thought sardonically. He also thought of Laura Aréstegui, the Ph.D. student who worked at DIRINCO and dreamed of publishing a book about Neruda. And he thought of the poet, who must be at his Isla Negra house, listening to events, overwhelmed and impotent; waiting hungrily for the news he needed to die in peace.

He was still walking on the highway when he heard a vehicle in the distance. His face lit up with enthusiasm. At last! It had to be the last Sol del Pacífico bus before the curfew, he thought, turning happily toward a stretch of road that curved away into the hills. Surely it was that bus, the final one to travel that arid, rocky land studded with cacti, hawthorns, and boldo plants; flanked on the west by a coast that shuddered with waves.

But when the vehicle approached, a chill ran down his back and petrified him. It was a military truck. Cayetano pressed his hands against the water bottle, helpless to do anything else. The truck pulled up beside him, shaking the very earth. It was full of prisoners with their hands tied behind their backs. He knew what awaited him.

A couple of soldiers with Mausers ordered him to climb into the back. He threw down the bottle, which shattered against a rock, and raised his hands into the air. As he climbed in, he saw that the top of the truck was crammed with men, women, and children. No one spoke to him. The kiosk had long been closed, and the truck sounded a death rattle as it started up its engine and began to speed down the highway. On their left, hills rose and glittered, while on their right, it now seemed to him, the Pacific Ocean was definitely writhing with fury.

≈ *62* ≈

They set him free about two weeks later, exhausted, bruised, and hungry. But he considered himself lucky, because others had had a far worse time. He suspected that they were releasing him by mistake. It was September 23, a warm Sunday morning, when he left the Puchuncaví camp. Dante, the young official who'd played the role of good cop during interrogations, during which he'd been accused of colluding with the Cuban embassy, advised him to leave the country as soon as possible.

"We're building a new Chile here," the captain said as he escorted him to the gate of the camp. He had brown hair and large hands. "This nation will no longer be a sanctuary for extremists, either native or foreign."

He never found out why he'd been arrested, or why he was released. Some prisoners murmured that the military had lists of names provided by infiltrators, informers, and the tortured. For a while, he thought Ángela's father, the powerful businessman, must have helped him. It was safe to assume that he'd supported the coup. He also guessed that help could have come from the United States embassy, since he, as a Cuban exile, had a North American passport. Nor did he rule out the possibility that he owed his freedom to Maia Herzen, who, through her military ties, could have anonymously given him a hand. By the time he was back out on the highway—the sun stung brutally, stones dazzled, and hawthorns undulated in the distance—he already knew that Allende had died in La Moneda, that Pinochet had headed up the dictatorship, and that the dead, exiled, and imprisoned numbered in the thousands.

The driver of a Sol del Pacífico finally took him to Isla Negra without charge. Once there, he hurried to the poet's house, feverishly hoping to find him safe and sound.

"They took him to the capital half an hour ago," the housekeeper said when she opened the door, scared to death. Waves shook the nearby crags and sprayed white mist over the motorboat and old steam engine in the front garden. "He's in a very bad state, he won't even get up anymore. The coup destroyed him."

"I have to see him. I have an urgent message to give him."

"I don't think he'll recognize you." She dried her hands on her apron. She invited him in for some scrambled eggs and tea, and to see the havoc caused by the military raid. They walked past walls covered with oil paintings and carved prows; past oak furniture, cabinets displaying sailboats and fine glassware, shelves crammed with first editions and collected shells, stones, and colored bottles, until they reached a hall, where broken pottery, piled books, and wall hangings lay strewn on the floor, as though someone had been in too much of a hurry to take them before leaving. "Don Pablo is in an ambulance to Santiago," the woman said.

"To which hospital?"

"I don't know. Doña Matilde took him. It was an emergency, they left very fast. There wasn't time for anything."

"And Sergio, his driver?"

"The soldiers took him the day of the coup. And my husband, too," she said, weeping. "We haven't heard a thing about them."

Cayetano returned to the highway with the feeling that everything was lost and that he'd never be able to give the poet his news. He boarded another bus and paid with money the housekeeper had given him. Somehow, he thought, he'd have to find the poet in the capital, in whatever hospital he was in. He hadn't traveled half the world and solved the mystery only to surrender now, when he was so close to his goal. Though he was fatally ill, Neruda had to be waiting for his news.

What hospital was he in? Santiago had several. And how could he possibly ask around for such a famous man without drawing the attention of the police? Neruda was the needle, Santiago the haystack, he thought, momentarily pleased with his own choice of metaphor. But later, as the bus was driving down a stretch of highway lined with poplars and sweet acacias, and with the Andes rising straight ahead, he thought the poet would have deemed it a tired metaphor.

A truck of prisoners passed them, and he felt a chill of fear and empathy, remembering his days at Puchuncaví. He knew what awaited those men and women. It was rumored that Allende's sympathizers were being shot in summary proceedings and that many of them, though this was hard to believe, were being thrown from helicopters into the Pacific, tied to chunks of iron so that they'd never resurface.

An hour later, the bus stopped in front of a military checkpoint. A line of vehicles waited to have their trunks and ID cards inspected. It would take a long time, as the soldiers were being painstakingly thorough in their duties. No one on the bus dared say a thing. At that moment, Cayetano glimpsed an ambulance at the front of the line. It had to be the poet, he thought, full of hope. He got off the bus and ran past the waiting cars. From a distance, he thought he recognized Matilde's thick hair. She was speaking to an officer while soldiers looked into the ambulance through the open back. They were interrogating the poet as he lay in the ambulance, the bastards! he thought angrily. He sped up and ran with fresh energy because now, at last, he would see Don Pablo again.

"Stop! Stop!" voices shouted at him, but he kept running, deaf to orders. He was meters from the ambulance when a soldier pushed him and made him fall facedown on the pavement. His glasses flew from his face.

"Where are you going, you asshole?" someone shouted. He felt a kick to his kidneys and a rifle butt hitting his right shoulder.

He raised his head and met with the black mouth of a Mauser. He couldn't make out the soldier's face. He reached for his glasses, but a boot crushed his hand. He had to stay down with one cheek stuck to the hot asphalt while the soldier kicked him and demanded to know why he was running.

"I want to talk to the sick man in the ambulance," he explained, sore and bruised.

The boot's pressure eased slowly, until his fingers could grope the ground and find his glasses. They were intact. Thank God for that, he thought, spitting out pebbles. He put them on clumsily and was able to make out the outline of the ambulance, the faces of the soldiers who surrounded it, and the green shoots of spring in central Chile. Another round of kicks re-

minded him of the treatment he'd received in the camp at Puchuncaví.

"Wait your turn, asshole. Order rules here now," an officer
shouted, a pistol in his belt. "Why are you so interested in the
old man in the ambulance?"

"Because he's a friend."

"Do you write a bunch of crap, too?"

"I want to say good-bye. He's about to die."

"Well, there's no running allowed," the officer replied, looking at the vehicle, which was starting up again. "Anyway, he's
gone. Where's your luggage?"

"I have no luggage, my captain," he replied, imitating the
Chilean twang. If they found out he was Cuban, he'd be behind
bars again. A prisoner at Puchuncaví, an actor at the Theater
Institute at the University of Chile, had taught him how to hide
his Cuban accent. He had also told him he should shave his
mustache, something Cayetano could never do, as he considered it a non-negotiable part of his identity. "I'm traveling on
the bus at the end of this line, my captain."

"Well, get back there and wait your turn like you're supposed to, you faggot. You can look for the poet in Santiago."

"The capital is very big, my captain. If I lose him now, I'll
never find him again."

"I thought the poet was oh so famous! If that's true, how
hard can it be to find him? Go on, get back to your bus, you
worthless son of a bitch!"

$\backsim 63 \backsim$

He arrived in Santiago thirty minutes before curfew, and found a room in a hotel for romantic trysts near Mapocho Station. At a nearby soda fountain he had a Barros Luco with a lot of avocado, and two beers. Then he walked out, concealing his burp from the prostitutes sitting outside. They were offering to spend the entire curfew period with one man for a sale price. Business seemed bad for them, as people were going home early and very few could afford the cost of a whole night.

The shop windows were packed with merchandise again, thanks to the free-market pricing decreed by the new regime. There was no more black market. Everything was back, but at astronomical prices: bread, butter, rice, flour, oil, noodles, chicken, even meat. Whoever could pay the new prices was able to eat, and for this reason the city now wore a worn face, as though its will to live had been scraped away. As the afternoon waned, military troops began to fill the corners, plazas, and alleys, taking cover behind sacks of flour piled up like walls. As soon as darkness overtook the capital, he heard machine-gun bursts, the whir of helicopters, and occasional gunshots.

They're shooting people point-blank, the housekeeper at the poet's house had told him. They prefer to do it at night so that the sound will intimidate the populace. He walked a few blocks, wanting to return to his hotel without encountering military posts, until he reached Veintiuno de Mayo, a street that stretched out gray and desolate, as though painted with coal by a dejected artist. All of a sudden, a military jeep turned a corner. It was headed his way. He shuddered at the thought of being arrested again, this time without identification. He pressed against a wall, ears pricked, with no idea how he would escape.

Someone tapped a window behind him. He turned on his heels, tense with terror. The jeep was closer now. They'd see him in a matter of seconds. He let out a sigh of relief. The noise had been made by a mechanical monkey in peasant garb, the size of a real chimp. It struck its wooden baton rhythmically against the window of the shop where Cayetano had sought momentary refuge. It was a hat and turban factory with a curiously Bolivarian name: Sombrerías Americanas Unidas. The jeep had almost arrived. Cayetano kneeled on the ground, crouched against the factory door. The vehicle passed, its motor hoarse, its soldiers distracted by the monkey, who struck the window sadly with his baton.

He arrived back at his second-floor hotel room bathed in sweat. He'd had to run those final blocks because the curfew was beginning. He peered through the lace curtains at the window. The street was calm, its cobbles damp, its houses shrouded in darkness. A helicopter flew low over the roofs. Cayetano glimpsed the face of the soldier manning the machine gun at the aircraft door. He was scanning the city with his arms around his weapon, frowning, austere. One thing was sure: Simenon's novels never said a word or knew a thing about circumstances like these, he thought as he lay down in bed with his clothes on, trembling from cold or fear, he no longer knew which, and turned off the small lamp on the nightstand. The Belgian's plots, however well wrought, belonged to a terrain alien to him; they were literature, fictitious worlds tacked together through the skill and imagination of a famous writer. But he currently faced the cruel, implacable, chaotic reality of Latin America, a world whose plot had no known author or preestablished script that could make all things possible.

As the night unfolded, its sounds increased: gunshots, shouts of warning on the street, and the screech of tires as cars took off with kidnapped citizens. He couldn't sleep. He was too scared that the police would come to his room. Suddenly he felt the building shudder. He got up and went to the window. Trucks drove by, packed with prisoners, escorted by military jeeps. He turned on the battery-operated radio he'd borrowed from the reception desk, but all he could find on the stations was the song "Lili Marleen."

He went back to bed. The mattress creaked beneath his weight. He covered himself with a stained, smelly blanket. But this was a thousand times better than the cement floor of Puchuncaví. He thought about the prisoners being transported like cattle to the slaughter, about their relatives, about the likelihood that they'd be tortured and killed, about the fact that none of this could possibly be true. In the uncertainty of that night, he longed for three things: for the hotel to be free of raids, for dawn to come quickly, and for his own arrival at the poet's side.

A few heavy vehicles pulled up outside his room, making the building groan. Cayetano broke into a sweat. He thought his heart might leap out of his mouth. He crept to the window. Across the street, in front of a house, he saw a truck full of prisoners and two military jeeps. A searchlight suddenly illuminated the house as soldiers started kicking the door, until it was opened by an old woman in her petticoat. They pushed her aside roughly and entered the home. A few minutes later, they reemerged, dragging two youths in undershirts and underpants. They pushed them into the truck with their rifle butts, turned off the searchlight, and drove off. The woman remained on the street, lying on the ground outside the door of her house, moaning with grief. A neighbor came out after a while to guide her back inside. After that, a graveyard silence cloaked the neighborhood.

The next morning, Cayetano rose, feeling helpless and uneasy. He washed his face, dried it with an old newspaper he found under the bed, and went down to the first floor, where the receptionist was drinking a cup of tea, wrapped in a blanket. The cramped entryway was dim, the shutters still drawn.

"They took the kids across the street," the man said. "That poor old lady went out this morning to look for them. She doesn't know if she'll ever see them again."

Cayetano called Laura Aréstegui, who answered immediately. He asked her how she was doing. She said not bad, though she feared they might come for her at any moment.

"Why don't you go somewhere else?"

"And do what there? Look, why don't you just tell me what you need from me."

"I have to find the poet."

"You've really gone crazy. Forget about that for now. You've got to be very careful."

"I need to talk to him."

"They say they buried Salvador Allende in an unmarked tomb in Viña del Mar. They guard the cemetery to prevent protests."

"I heard that on the news. But I have to see the poet . . ."

"It seems they checked him into Santa María Clinic, in Santiago. Be very careful: they interrogate everyone who visits him."

Soldiers with machine guns guarded the clinic door. A spring breeze scented with eucalyptus blew down from nearby hills, and the sun shone with determination. At the information desk, he discreetly asked for the poet's room.

"Third floor," the receptionist said as she wrote the number down on a piece of paper.

He went up to the third floor and walked down the hall, looking for the room. A short-haired man in a dark suit and sunglasses asked him what he was looking for. Cayetano feared he might be police, and gave him a different room number.

"Keep going as you are. You'll find it on the right."

He pretended to follow the man's instructions, but returned as soon as he thought no one was looking. He found the poet's room and stopped. Should he knock or go right in? He knocked and stood waiting to hear an "Enter," but heard nothing from inside. The poet must be alone, he thought, which would be ideal. That way he could immediately tell him, in private, everything he'd learned about Beatriz and her daughter. When he heard Tina's middle name, he'd deduce the truth, become happy, and perhaps even gather some strength with which to weather these painful weeks.

He knocked again. The hall was still deserted. Perhaps the poet was sleeping. He pressed the door gently, and it ceded smoothly. The bed was empty, the sheets tangled, and no one was in the room. But he smelled the poet's French lotion. He entered and closed the door at his back. Perhaps he was in the bathroom. But the door to it was open, and it was dark inside. He thought it best to wait; they might have taken him for radiation.

A nurse entered the room. "Who are you looking for?" she asked, her face unfriendly.

"The poet."

"He's on the first floor now."

"Which room?"

"You'd better ask in the hall," she answered as she unhooked a bottle of serum from the metal rod beside the bed.

He went downstairs and came to a hall where several patients in hospital gowns waited in silence in front of a door. They looked at him as though he were an intruder.

"Where can I find Mr. Neruda?" he asked a nurse. From the city, he heard gunshots and police sirens.

She pointed toward the end of the hall. "They've got him one floor down."

The underground floor smelled of moisture, and shadows floated down the hall. The signs on the doors were illegible. He tried to open a few, but they were locked. He breathed the rancid air, struggling to contain his frustration. It occurred to him that the closed doors, icy shadows, and chilling echo of his heels on the concrete were a metaphor for what Chile had become. He walked on. The poet couldn't be far away. Radio-therapy was conducted on this floor. After a few more paces, he stumbled onto a bed against the wall. Someone was lying in it. Once again, distant bangs tore at the morning. Then silence.

"Excuse me," he whispered to the prone patient. "Do you know where I can find Don Pablo Neruda?"

The patient didn't respond. He was sleeping. He slept on his back, placidly, not caring about where he'd been placed. Cayetano decided to keep looking—but then he caught the scent of the poet's lotion.

"Don Pablo! But . . . what the devil are you doing here?"

The poet went on sleeping.

"Don Pablo, why have they put you here? It's me, Cayetano. I've come back. I've got news for you. The best news you can imagine. Are you awake, Don Pablo?"

The poet slept. It seemed that he'd just finished radiotherapy. It always happened the same way, he recalled. After a treatment, he'd be exhausted, and would sleep for hours, so deeply that nothing could wake him. The poet himself used to say it: Don't disturb me after my sessions. This time, he'd have to bear the interruption, because Cayetano was eager to give him the news immediately. But when he touched the back of the poet's hand, fear gripped him. Like an electric shock. He touched the hand again. It was cold. Completely cold. Like marble. He searched for a pulse. In vain. He found nothing. He looked at Neruda's ashen face, his inert chest.

Cayetano wept; he wept disconsolately beside the poet's body. He'd arrived too late, and Neruda had left without learning the results of the mission he'd launched. He brought his own trembling face close to Neruda's, felt a horrible tightness in his heart, and told himself he could be mistaking another man for the poet. He wiped his tears with his guanaco tie, and studied the corpse's face again through the shadows. His large, closed eyelids; broad, smooth forehead; cheeks with their moles and sideburns; a grimace of relief at the corners of his lips; hands clasped over his belly; that beloved checkered jacket; those thick-soled shoes. It was him.

"Don Pablo, Don Pablo, what the hell—why didn't you wait for me? Because, see, you were right. Your poet's intuition didn't trick you. Why didn't you wait? Can you imagine how things would have gone if you'd waited just a little longer? Damn it, Don Pablo, why the hell did you go?"

Suddenly, between his own sobs, he heard steps echoing down a staircase. Soldiers, he thought with fear.

"It's this way," a man's voice said.

He placed both his palms over the poet's hands, kissed his forehead, and tucked the photograph of Tina Trinidad, the one Beatriz had given him in Valparaíso, into the upper pocket of his jacket. Then he rushed down the corridor in the dark, tears streaming down his cheeks.

～ *65* ～

The next morning, when he arrived in Bellavista, where the poet had his Santiago home, Cayetano Brulé immediately saw crowds on the winding streets and soldiers in combat gear on every corner. So it was true, then, what Pete Castillo—who was still in Valparaíso, beardless, short-haired, and wearing a suit and tie—had told him the night before: the funeral would take place that very Monday.

It hadn't been easy to catch an Andesmar bus back into Santiago. The day before, after leaving the clinic, he'd tried to talk to Maia Herzen, but her telephone went unanswered. He decided to return to Valparaíso. The city breathed tensely, quietly, and shots rang out through the night. Laura Aréstegui had become impossible to find, the blinds of Hadad's soda fountain were closed, and warships hovered close to the breakwater.

He'd run into Pete by chance in a small café in La Pérgola de las Flores. He was pale and frightened, barely recognizable. As they drank coffee, he told Cayetano that he planned to seek asylum at the Finnish embassy, and he'd given him the information on Neruda's burial. Then they'd parted ways. The next day, Cayetano Brulé left his house early and headed to the city center. He stopped for a bite at Bosanka, where he perused the permitted newspapers—the leftist ones had been closed down—and then he boarded a bus by the greenish-yellow walls of the Pacific Steam Navigation Company. He wore his best suit, a white shirt, and the violet tie covered in small green guanacos.

As soon as he disembarked at Mapocho Station, he crossed the river at the law school and entered the neighborhood of Bellavista. It was a cool Santiago morning, the sky tinged with gray. A few youths were whitewashing the revolutionary walls of the Ramona Parra Brigade under the keen gaze of soldiers. They were erasing the city's memory, Cayetano thought, embarrassed to find that he was speaking like Neruda, and wondering if poetry might be contagious, after all. From the inner patio of Quimantú, the publisher, a black cloud of smoke ascended toward the sky. They were burning books published under the Unidad Popular government that had been popular. The flames weren't devouring only Trotsky's *History of the Russian Revolution*, Marx and Engels's *Communist Manifesto*, and Ostrovsky's *How the Steel Was Tempered*, but also novels by Julio Cortázar, Juan Rulfo, and Jack London.

If the city's gray restlessness had intimidated him that morning, in Bellavista a moderate optimism cheered his soul. The neighborhood's melancholy tipped toward a mad, barely concealed solidarity among those who'd come to say their last good-byes to the poet. He was moved by the presence of men and women, workers and students, who, despite the fear and insomnia etched on their faces, held carnations and books by Neruda in their hands. A helicopter flew low over their heads.

When he turned onto Fernando Márquez de la Plata, he realized that he wouldn't be able to reach the poet's residence because a dense throng already filled the street. People gazed toward the cement house, smoking and murmuring, scanning their surroundings and the sky. Murky, viscous water poured over the paving. Someone behind him said the army had diverted a canal to flood Neruda's house. They hadn't looted the houses only in Santiago and Isla Negra, but in La Sebastiana too, another said. And a third murmured that soldiers had entered the residence of President Allende, on Tomás Moro Street, and had been vile enough to show footage on television of the closet where he kept his suits and the small cellar where he stored his wine. Cayetano put his hands in his jacket, feeling that something serious, vague, and bloody could take place that morning. There seemed to be more and more soldiers and police officers appearing at the demonstration, which was the largest since the coup.

And suddenly, as though obeying some secret order, applause erupted. At first hesitant and inaudible, then strong and determined, and finally thunderous. Cayetano looked at the poet's house and felt his skin prickle. A group emerged from the door carrying a brown coffin. Behind them walked Matilde, her eyes lowered. The people began to clap and chant the poet's name, as though attending one of his readings. "Comrade Pablo Nerudaaa!" a tremulous voice shouted from somewhere. "Present! Now and always!" the crowd replied in unison, their faces transfigured with emotion, tears flowing, voices hoarse. "Comrade Pablo Nerudaaa!" someone else repeated, farther

away, and the prodigious tide now flooding the streets of Bellavista answered, "Present!" Again Neruda's name, interspersed
with Allende's, was shouted, and each time it was followed by a
reply and applause en masse, and each time someone else, again,
would call out, "Comrade Pablo Neruda . . ." and Cayetano, unable to contain himself, responded with all the strength his
lungs could muster: "Present! Now and always!"

Shouting, applauding, sobbing, pushing his way through
the multitude, he approached the coffin. The cheers for Neruda,
Allende, and Unidad Popular continued, defying the bewil-
dered soldiers. No one was cowed by their guns or uniforms
anymore. Now it was the soldiers' turn to be afraid. The an-
gered mob shouted and clapped under the spring sky. The helicopter reappeared like a desperate buzzing fly over roofs and
chimneys, but headed swiftly away toward Santa Lucía Hill.
The chants grew bolder and louder, as though taking place at a
political demonstration in the glory days of a democracy now
lost.

Cayetano brushed his fingertips against the poet's bur-
nished coffin just as it entered the funeral car. Before the crowd
resumed its chants, he looked over at Matilde, and could have
sworn she held his gaze for a few endless seconds; her look was
both kind and sad, as though expressing a final conspiratorial
nod toward his detective mission. Did she really know who he
was and why her husband had hired him, or was he just imagining that her eyes had locked with his? he wondered, unsure,
as he watched her walk unsteadily, absently, surrounded by
friends, toward a diplomatic vehicle that waited with open
doors. At that moment, suddenly, without a single warning, the
human tide parted for the widow and closed behind her like the

waters of a biblical sea, making Matilde vanish, and leaving him no choice but to join the procession as it began to pour down streets that no longer held soldiers or police officers, only civilian men, women, and youths whose songs and slogans brimmed with hope.

66

The radio at the Café del Poeta now played the strong, unmistakable voice of Juanes singing "La Camisa Negra," and Cayetano Brulé quickly polished off his coffee with a dash of milk. His coffee had long gone cold because his memories had plunged him into a devastating, melancholy loneliness.

The poet's remains had rested beside Matilde's since the 1990s, in the garden of their home in Isla Negra, overlooking the Pacific Ocean. He never heard from Margaretchen again, even though the Berlin Wall had fallen seventeen years before, and technically he could have gone to visit. Nor had he ever received news of Tina Trinidad. He'd also lost track of Beatriz, who, according to some rumors, had ended her days in a narrow prefabricated apartment in a working-class neighborhood of Zwickau, alone, retired from an institution that had been dissolved in 1989 with the disappearance of East Germany. He occasionally received a little information on Markus, who lived in East Berlin and traveled widely, giving lectures on his extensive experience as a spy. Regarding Ángela Undurraga, his ex-wife, he knew she now resided in Manhattan, was married to a Wall Street magnate, and devoted all her energies to promoting animal rights and vegetarianism. And to think that it had all begun in Valparaíso, he thought, on that cloudy winter morning when his knuckles had knocked on the aged door of La Sebastiana.

Now the city unfolded before him, rife with honking cars, the shouts of street vendors, the songs of beggars, and raucous buses passing by. In today's Valparaíso, boutique hotels, sophisticated restaurants, and attractive cafés abounded, ready for tourists. The streets featured clean, painted buildings, menus printed in several languages, and a mix of agitated bohemians who danced hip-hop and rap but also nostalgically listened to the Beatles, Gitano Rodríguez, and the Blue Splendor, as well as Inti Illimani, Los Jaivas, and Congreso. And Neruda's house was now a beautiful museum enjoyed by visitors from all over the world. Hope seemed to newly infuse the people of Valparaíso, as their city revived and reinvented itself on the rubble of failed strategies and political corruption. He left a tip on the table for the goth girl, and left the Café del Poeta for Errázuriz Avenue, anxious about how late he was now for his appointment.

Luckily, a taxi driver with suicidal tendencies got him to his destination in fifteen minutes, dropping him off in front of the imposing office building at 8 North Avenue, in Viña del Mar. It was 1:20 p.m. The subsidiary of Almagro, Ruggiero & Associates was on the eighteenth floor. He took the elevator up, opened a heavy larch door, and entered a spacious, well-lit room decorated with oil paintings by Matta and Cienfuegos. Through the windows, he glimpsed the Pacific, the casino, and beaches filled with vacationers from Reñaca.

"I'm here to see Mr. Almagro and Mr. Ruggiero," he said. "I'm Cayetano Brulé, they were expecting me at noon."

"Of course." The secretary swiftly picked up the phone. "Don Pedro Pablo? Mr. Brulé has just arrived."

She escorted him through a bronze-handled door into an air-conditioned office with minimalist flair: parquet flooring made with *mañio* wood, a table flanked with erect chairs, a desk with a flat-screen computer, and leather armchairs. Next to the table stood two smiling men in their sixties, in white shirts and silk ties. From the elegance of their office and attire, Cayetano surmised that they led a highly privileged life, and no doubt downstairs a uniformed chauffeur was waiting for them in their Mercedes-Benzes or BMWs. The secretary left, closing the door.

The bearded man seemed vaguely familiar.

"You've made no mistake, Cayetano," the man said, shaking his hand effusively. "I'm Pedro Diego Almagro. We met one night, a long time ago, in the days of Unidad Popular, at the Hucke factory, when you were guarding it. Remember?"

He recalled the trembling old machines at the factory, the sweep of an army jeep's searchlights over the cold, damp paving, the echo of faraway gunshots, a hammer he was supposed to bang on the floor in case of alarm. But this man, Pedro Diego, who was he?

"I was studying architecture," Almagro went on. He stroked his beard, giving Cayetano the chance to admire the impeccable white face of his Patek Phillippe. "You were looking for someone who knew about Pablo Neruda. I suggested you speak to a cousin of mine."

"With Laura Aréstegui?"

"That's right."

"So you're Prendes? Comandante Camilo Prendes?" he exclaimed, unable to hide his amazement.

"One and the same, in the flesh, Cayetano! You have no idea how glad I am to see you again. You look good, with a few pounds more and less hair, of course, but you're the same man. Those were crazy years!" Almagro said, fingering his gold cuff links. "Back then I was Prendes, fancying myself a guerrilla fighter, overseeing the takeover of a factory. Of course, then the coup came and we went into exile. You know how it goes. Please, sit down. I went back to the Sorbonne, naturally, where I'd studied in the sixties. Remember?"

"So what happened to Laura?" Cayetano did not sit down. Instead, he gazed at the oil painting of Old Havana, by René Portocarrero, that hung on a white wall. "I never heard any more news of her."

"Well, she's doing quite well, with a little restaurant in a neighborhood of Warsaw. She ended up exiled in Poland, poor thing. After the fall of Jaruzelski, she stayed on. She's not doing badly for herself at all, though she never returned to literature. That's how life is. But how wonderful to see you, Cayetano!" Almagro insisted, stroking his beard again.

"You and I also know each other," the second man stated in a serious tone. His long hair was tied back in a ponytail, and his damask tie was held in place with a gold pin. He seemed to be playing up his undeniable resemblance to Richard Branson, the blond owner of Virgin Airlines. "I'm Anselmo Ruggiero Manfredi. I remember you perfectly, because it was the first time in my life I ever spoke to a Cuban. I've been following your professional career in the local paper." He revealed his impeccably white teeth. "It's a pleasure to shake the hand of such a distinguished sleuth. Do you remember me?"

"I'd be lying if I said yes." Ruggiero was shaking his hand again, this time with the zeal of a weight lifter. "No matter how long I look at you, I still can't associate you with anyone I know."

"A few years ago it would have been most inconvenient to remember the circumstances in which we met, but things have changed a great deal . . . and just as well."

"I still don't recognize you. Please give me a hint."

"September 1973. The highway between Valparaíso and Isla Negra. Does that ring a bell?"

Cayetano could see the highway oscillating into the distance, under the sun, the roadside kiosk, the woman listening to the bombing of La Moneda on her radio. Then he recalled the truck crammed with prisoners, coming toward him. He bit his lips, still unable to place Ruggiero, who now pressed his index finger against Cayetano's green-and-purple guanaco tie, and smiled.

"A friend of mine pushed you into that truck," he said. "They took you to Puchuncaví. You stayed there, under my orders, in a cool room, with a window through which you could see boldo plants, flowering blackwoods, and the clean, clear September sky."

"Dante?" Cayetano whispered in astonishment. Now he began to connect this man with the young official who had interrogated him at Puchuncaví. He had played the part of the understanding interrogator. He hadn't mistreated him, unlike the soldier called Salinas, who had beaten him to make him confess where he was hiding weapons. He recalled, out loud, the quotation from *Inferno* written on gray cardboard that had hung at his office door. LASCIATE OGNI SPERANZA . . .

". . . *'voi ch'entrate* . . .' But who among us wasn't a poet in his youth, Cayetano?" Ruggiero exclaimed, laughing loudly, eyes wide, face red with emotion. "Anyone who wasn't a poet in his youth simply has no soul."

"Of course, now I know who you are, damn it! Dante! The twists and turns of life, for God's sake. We meet again, and once again in your office. But this time, in your office, under democracy, Dante," Cayetano added thoughtfully. "Damn it, how things change in this country."

"In the end, you were only with us for a few days," Ruggiero added, glancing sidelong at Almagro. "It was for your own good. The highway was dangerous. People were getting killed at the drop of a hat. And you see, our intervention gave you something. Today you're here, in a renovated, reconciled nation, modern and prosperous, transformed into a peerless, irreplaceable private investigator."

"Don't flatter me, Dante."

"Of course, back then you had an enviable godfather . . ."

"What do you mean?"

"After a few days, we received an order to release you. The order came from Santiago. We weren't the only ones who were lucky, Cayetano," Ruggiero said, letting out another booming laugh.

"Who gave that order?"

"We never found out. But it came from high up. Very high up. You're a sharp one, Cayetano, a sharp one."

Almagro and Ruggiero smiled, hands in their pockets, ties flashing, teeth brilliantly white.

"Now I recall you both perfectly," Cayetano said uncomfortably, wondering bitterly who might have interceded on his behalf all that time ago. "I hadn't forgotten anything that happened, only your faces. We've all changed quite a bit in thirty-three years."

"Well, I think it's fantastic that we can keep working together after, let's say, this long parenthesis, Cayetano," Almagro said, to summarize. "It's a sign the nation has reconciled. With my associate here, who's long retired from the military, I co-founded this international consulting firm some time ago. And we're doing splendidly. We say with pride"—he placed a hand on his chest—"that we're almost as old as the democracy itself, and enjoy the very best connections with government and business, with ministries and the opposition party. We represent our clients in a loyal and responsible way. You understand. And we can't complain. Anyone who wants something from the government, no matter their professed political beliefs, knows to come first to AR and A. We have the keys they're looking for . . ."

"Forgive me, but I still don't see what I have to do with all this."

"I'll explain immediately," Almagro said. "Listen, we recently started a new company. We've begun negotiations with your island, and we're about to do the same with the rest of the former communist world. In that regard, we also can't complain."

"But tell him in clear terms why we've invited him here," Ruggiero put in with impatience.

"In that case, let's get down to details," Almagro said, crossing his arms. "We'd like to contract you for a top-secret mission. Don't worry about the fees: we're extremely generous with our people. AR and A is always loyal to its central motto: 'For a world without exclusions.' Sit down, please—make yourself comfortable, relax, and listen. But Cayetano, before we start, how about a good Chivas Regal on the rocks?"

New York / Iowa City
June 6, 2008

❧ Author's Note ❧

Don Pablo, my neighbor

Every day of my childhood, when I woke up for school, I'd glimpse Pablo Neruda's house through my bedroom window, high up on one of Valparaíso's fifty hills. Today, that house has become a museum, named after the poet, that attracts tourists from all over the world. When I was growing up near his home, it was mysterious and solitary, and no one was ever seen to exit. It has five narrow floors of different sizes, each one smaller the higher it is, which make it resemble a tower as it ascends toward the sky. The first two floors—occupied by a married couple, artists befriended by Neruda—are made of concrete, while the rest is constructed from wood and large picture windows, contributing to its ethereal feel and to its stylistic echo of the other houses that riddle those hillsides, battling for the best angle from which to gaze out over the Pacific. I must confess that on those childhood mornings, when I looked out (I am speaking of the 1960s), Don Pablo's house seemed to me like a white boat with its sails unfurled to the wind, on the brink of gliding off through the translucent air of Valparaíso.

I'd admire that fanciful edifice from afar and imagine its owner, the most important living poet of the Spanish language. Although his presence was sporadic and invisible, just the thought of his proximity delighted and intimidated me. The truth is, we almost never saw him. The reason? Although Don Pablo was a disciplined member of Chile's Communist Party, he lived like a true bourgeois: he owned two more houses. One stood on San Cristóbal Hill, in the heart of Santiago, the capital city, and its dining room featured a hidden door through which the poet liked to surprise his dinner guests, disguised in one of the exotic costumes he liked to collect; the other house was on the sea in Isla Negra, on the coast of central Chile, where he kept his collections of shells, bottles, and antique iron, and where his remains now rest beside those of Matilde, his last wife. But La Sebastiana—as he'd named his Valparaíso house, in honor of its first owner, the Spaniard Sebastián Collado—was unique because it had been built out of air and blended into the city's crazed architecture. In Valparaíso, that house was like a fish in water, or a star in the sky. On three separate occasions, I went to La Sebastiana, in my school uniform and carrying my briefcase full of notebooks, and stood at the door to the poet's garden, which held a papaya tree, bushes, roses, medicinal herbs, and birdsong. All I wanted to do was talk to the poet. But all three times, I was petrified, my fist raised just centimeters from the door, not daring to knock and ask to enter the realm where Neruda dwelt with his secrets. Half a century after these frustrated attempts, which I'll regret for the rest of my life, my detective Cayetano Brulé has dared to enter, in this novel, the space that boyhood shyness kept closed to me.

On two occasions, I saw the Nobel laureate on the curves of Alemania Avenue. Chile was a stable, democratic nation then, neither rich nor poor (though with deep social inequalities), peaceful, safe, where few people could imagine that we would soon have a socialist government under President Salvador Allende (1970–1973), which would be ended by the bloody coup d'état and repressive dictatorship (1973–1990) of General Augusto Pinochet. When he went out for a walk through Valparaíso, the poet was invariably surrounded by a swarm of admirers who seemed to buzz like bees around their queen. He walked with the air of a cardinal, emitting words with a nasal tone and melancholy gestures. Sometimes he wore a blue peaked cap at an angle, and a finely woven wool poncho on his shoulders. He enjoyed the stir he caused whenever he passed. Another time, at dusk on a windy Sunday, as I was walking through the neighborhood with my father, we saw him sitting in the backseat of a car driven by a woman. Beside her sat a man wearing glasses with thick black frames. "Don't forget those gentlemen," my father said. "One of them will receive the Nobel Prize one day, and the other will be president of Chile." And he was right. The man riding in front was Allende.

But in those days—as I strolled the heights of Alemania Avenue with my father, gazing out over roofs and belfries, the city's steep streets and twisted stairs, and the vastness of the Pacific Ocean—Chile was a calm country, and even, to a certain extent, a happy one, or so it seemed to me, a middle-class boy attending private school. Years later, on September 4, 1970, Allende took power in free elections, and began implementing a popular socialist agenda that became a symbol of Latin American people's demands for a more just world. That agenda included the nationalization of businesses, radical agrarian re-

form, and international policies that broke from those of the
United States. I was politically initiated at the university, where
I supported Allende's revolutionary agenda. The dream ended
abruptly on September 11, 1973, when Pinochet led a coup and
Allende killed himself in the presidential palace, La Moneda.
The Chile I had known in my childhood as an oasis of peace
and stability sank like the *Titanic* amid the polarizing forces of
Allende's supporters and adversaries, and amid an enormous
economic crisis. The military coup established a dictatorship
that lasted seventeen years, and left thousands dead, disappeared, or exiled; it propelled me to leave my parents and my
nation on December 30, 1973, to join a diaspora that continues
to this day.

President Allende fought tirelessly for social justice. He was
idealistic, and at the same time full of contradictions, impossible to categorize: he believed it was possible to build socialism
while respecting a parliamentary democracy. He died defend-
ing that democracy, amid the bombs of a seditious military, the
unyielding opposition of the right, and the subversive actions of
Richard Nixon's government, which backed the overthrow
with the CIA. In his last days at the helm, Allende was caught
between two fires: that of Chile's right wing and the United
States, on the one hand, who labeled him a communist and an
ally of Fidel Castro and the Soviet Union; and the influential
ultra-left, on the other, who considered him a reformist with
revolutionary rhetoric. I believe Allende was a social reformer
with radical discourse, someone who believed Chile could overcome social backwardness and inequality through an economy
with strong state involvement. He placed too much hope in the
construction of a socialist Chile, and didn't realize that the So-

viet Union and its allies no longer had the funds or enthusiasm to finance another revolutionary project in the West after Castro's Cuba.

I wrote this novel about Neruda, staying true to the actual history of Chile between 1970 and 1973, because I admire him as a poet, because I was curious about him as a neighbor, and because his personal life intersected with crucial moments of twentieth-century history. Neruda was a Chilean diplomat in remote countries, and a privileged witness to the Spanish Civil War (1936–1939). He became a communist in 1946, and during his exile (1948–1952) he sought refuge in Eastern Europe and in Italy. During the Cold War, he aligned himself with the Soviet Union, although he preferred Paris and Rome to Moscow and Bucharest; he criticized the United States for the wars in Korea and Vietnam; and he collaborated faithfully with his friend President Allende.

But I had another, powerful reason for writing this novel: Sheltered by the license of fiction, I strove to portray the Neruda of flesh and blood, the real human being with his grandeur and meanness, loyalties and betrayals, certainties and doubts, the poet who could love passionately and at the same time leave everything to embark on a new affair, a more feverish and impassioned one, that would allow him to write better poetry. Neruda was a towering poet, a sharp politician, a human being who searched tirelessly for love, and a man who enjoyed the pleasures of bourgeois life. He contradicted himself. It isn't easy to write a novel that captures the real human being, as Neruda's fame is so solid and universal that written works about him tend toward the apologetic and adulatory, keeping him on a pedestal. I believe that both his genius as an artist and his authentic side as a man spring from his complex spirit, his light and shadow, and the passion of his human condition.

Three sources contribute to this novel. First, the inspiring image that Neruda imprinted on my childhood; second, the narrative that his three houses conferred on me; and perhaps most important, the judgment placed on the poet by the women who knew him. With respect to the first source, in my childhood, I discovered that the great poets are not necessarily dead, that one of them, a giant, was even my neighbor. Thanks to this, poetry escaped from dull scholastic texts and came out to stroll along my street, winked at me and sang to me with an everyday substance that was unsuspected by my classmates. Also, thanks to the careful restoration of his houses, and their transformation into museums open to the public, Neruda's homes still harbor the poet. Anyone who enters them with keen senses and an alert imagination can feel him walking through those rooms. Especially in the Valparaíso house. One day, as I was sketching out the first notes for this novel in the ample living room of La Sebastiana, with its blue fireplace, adjacent dining room, and large picture window overlooking corrugated metal roofs, twisted outdoor staircases, steep streets, and the vast Pacific Ocean beyond, I suddenly felt Neruda begin to tell me unknown aspects of his life. I recall the precise instant that it happened: I was lost in thought, gazing out at a boat gliding into the bay, when I felt a curious call at my back. I turned. I saw a Chinese wardrobe with glass doors; Pablo and Matilde's robes hung inside, and the poet's slippers rested on the floor. I sensed that the parts of Neruda's private life that I was drawn to tell began with that revealing, ordinary detail. Those slippers, with their fuzzy wool and their heels worn unevenly by the poet's thick, tired feet, allowed me to discern the world I searched for.

I am convinced that the women in Neruda's life are the ones who hold his secret. The ultimate keys to his personality, and to his work, cannot be found in the academic treatises on him, but in the voices of the women who mattered in his personal life— what they said, and what they kept silent. I believe that only these relationships convey the flesh-and-blood poet, that profoundly contradictory being, so full of light and shadow, that I sought and found in order to write this novel that blends fiction with actual history. The rest is a matter of interpreting the words—both poetic and everyday—that Neruda used throughout his life to protect himself, to hide, and to project the image of himself that has become so legendary. The first woman to play a decisive role in his life was his beloved stepmother, who took him in, loved him, and raised him after his mother's early death. When he was a university student, his first loves were either platonic or simple passions lacking in fantasies or stunning feats; they were sad loves in cold rooms and dark Santiago winters; it was in remote regions of Asia, where he arrived as a very young Chilean consul, that he discovered the pleasures of passion and learned the skills of an experienced lover. The person who taught him these techniques was Josie Bliss, that mysterious woman lost in Asian landscapes, whose voice we never hear directly. We only glimpse, in Neruda's poetry, his amazement at her slim, agile body and her mastery of the erotic arts. The Dutchwoman María Antonieta Hagenaar Vogelzang gives him everything, trusts him, marries him, and bears him a hydrocephalic child; he leaves them both when he falls in love with Delia del Carril, an aristocratic Argentine twenty years his senior who converts him to communism and persuades him to abandon the hermetic poetry he was composing, and to write in a manner everyone could understand. And then comes Matilde Urrutia, a young dancer who dazzled the poet when he was in his fifties, and who would be at his bedside when he died in 1973. But there are many more women in Neruda's life. So many that, among his friends, he was known as a "serial monogamist." There were romances, both loves and flings, that remain shrouded in secrecy, buried in the untold annals of the past. His love affair with Beatriz could be one of those lost romances. As I said, I didn't find the most thorough explorations of Neruda's relationships with women in academic books, but in the memoirs and recollections of the women who knew him, and who describe him and reflect on who he was. From them, from their portrayals and evocations, but also from their omissions, emerge the fictional characters of Beatriz and her daughter, Tina, as well as the monologues of Neruda's memories and troubled conscience as he waits in the solitude of his Valparaíso home, in the twilight of his own life and of his friend Allende's government.

Neruda died on September 27, 1973, when Pinochet's dictatorship was sixteen days into its seventeen-year duration. He died of cancer, but also from the pain of watching the tragic end of his political dream. He couldn't bear the bombing of La Moneda, or the death of Allende, or the murder and imprisonment of thousands of people, or the echoing shots of nocturnal firing squads or the chilling sound of armored helicopters as they patrolled the city. In 1990, Chile returned to democracy and freedom. Pablo Neruda's poems, many of them born in his Valparaíso home, were a source of inspiration for many people as they fought the dictatorship and strove to create a more just society. As his Valparaíso neighbor, I owed Don Pablo a novel that portrayed his full being.

Iowa City
August 2011

ABOUT THE AUTHOR

Roberto Ampuero is an internationally bestselling, award-winning author. He has published twelve novels in Spanish, and his works have been translated around the world. *The Neruda Case* is his first novel published in English. Born in Chile, Ampuero is a professor of creative writing at the University of Iowa and currently serves as Chile's ambassador to Mexico. He lives in Mexico City and Iowa City.

ABOUT THE TRANSLATOR

Carolina De Robertis is the translator of *Bonsai*, by Alejandro Zambra, and other works published in *Granta*, *Zoetrope : All-Story*, and *Two Lines*. She is the author of the novels *Perla* and the international bestseller *The Invisible Mountain*, which was translated into fifteen languages and received Italy's Rhegium Julii Prize. It was also awarded an *O*, as *The Oprah Magazine* Terrific Read of 2009, and named the *San Francisco Chronicle* Best Book of the Year. Robertis grew up in a Uruguayan family that emigrated to England, Switzerland, and California. She is the recipient of a 2012 Fellowship from the National Endowment for the Arts.